PRAISE FOR *THREE DAYS MISSING*

"A skillfully twisting plot that flings you headlong
into a riveting conclusion that you'll never see coming."
—CHEVY STEVENS,
author of *Never Let You Go*

"Buckle up and turn the pages as fast as you can.
This one's a winner!"
—DAVID BELL,
author of *Somebody's Daughter*

"A highly entertaining thriller with crisp writing,
believable characters, and a plot that delivers...
I almost swallowed this book in one sitting."
—JULIA HEABERLIN,
author of *Black-Eyed Susans*

"A chilling, twisty tale pitting two moms against each other
in a desperate search for a boy and the truth. Gripping."
—KAIRA ROUDA,
author of *Best Day Ever*

"Enough twists and turns to keep you guessing—
Three Days Missing has all the right stuff
for an engaging, suspenseful read."
—WENDY WALKER,
author of *All Is Not Forgotten*

"Exactly what you want in a thriller—riveting,
edge-of-your-seat storytelling.... Absolutely unputdownable.
I couldn't let go of this book until I'd devoured the last page."
—MINDY MEJIA,
author of *Everything You Want Me to Be*

"Taut, intelligent, heart-pounding...a spellbinding tale
of suspense and family drama that twists and turns
until the final pages. I couldn't put it down!"
—KAREN KATCHUR,
author of *The Secrets of Lake Road*

"GRIPPING...A FIRST-CLASS READ." —B. A. PARIS, *Behind Closed Doors*

Praise for the novels of Kimberly Belle

"You need to check out *The Marriage Lie*. This domestic thriller will keep you reading into the wee hours of the night to find out how it all ends."

—*Redbook*

"This delicious, serpentine thriller starts from a simple premise: what if your husband was not who you thought he was…. A good, old-fashioned page-turner, with a poisonous sting in the tail."

—*Daily Mail*

"Fans of *Gone Girl* and *The Girl on the Train* will eat up Belle's latest novel. The pace is relentless, and the plot never runs in a straight line…. This one is a true brain twister!"

—*Bookreporter.com*

"With plot twists around every corner, Belle isn't afraid to keep her readers guessing until the very last page of this heart-pounding story of one woman's desperate search for answers."

—*Booklist*

"[A] compelling domestic thriller."

—*BuzzFeed*

"The suspense builds rapidly…. A compelling adventure."

—*Kirkus Reviews*

"Belle's *Three Days Missing* is her best book yet. And that's saying a lot. This one is vividly written, emotional, and engaging, with real, three-dimensional characters who will always keep you guessing…. This one's a winner!"

—David Bell, *New York Times* bestselling author of *Somebody's Daughter* and *Bring Her Home*

"A missing child, a desperate mother, and enough twists and turns to keep you guessing—*Three Days Missing* has all the right stuff for an engaging, suspenseful read."

—Wendy Walker, author of *Emma in the Night* and *All Is Not Forgotten*

KIMBERLY BELLE

PARK
ROW
BOOKS

PARK
ROW
BOOKS

Recycling programs
for this product may
not exist in your area.

ISBN-13: 978-0-7783-0771-6

Three Days Missing

Copyright © 2018 by Kimberle S. Belle Books, LLC

For questions and comments about the quality of this book, please contact us at CustomerService@Harlequin.com.

ParkRowBooks.com
BookClubbish.com

Printed in U.S.A.

For my parents, who always believed.

Also by Kimberly Belle

The Last Breath
The Ones We Trust
The Marriage Lie

THREE

DAYS

MISSING

KAT

MY PHONE IS ALREADY BUZZING WITH WORK email as I rush Ethan through his morning routine. Get up. Get dressed. For the love of God, brush your teeth and hair. In none of his eight short years has my son ever been a morning person, and I've never been the most patient of mothers, not even when I didn't have a boss clocking the second I step off the elevator.

Not that stay-at-home moms don't have plenty of stress, but at least then Ethan and I were united in it, members of the same team tiptoeing around the eggshells Andrew left lying all over the house. But this is the habit we've fallen into these past six months, ever since the separation. Ethan dallies and I nag.

"Come on, baby, we gotta go."

His hair is still sticking up where it was pressed against his pillow. His T-shirt is stained and wrinkled, which means he probably plucked it from the dirty pile on the floor. My son is an unapologetic slob. He's uncoordinated and more than a little awkward looking. His ears are too big and his curls are too fickle and his glasses, constantly clouded with fingerprints, never seem to sit straight on his nose.

But I love him with everything inside of me—not despite all his quirks but because of them. If there's one thing Andrew taught me, it's that you can't love only pieces of a person. You have to love *all* of them, even the ugly parts.

I hustle Ethan down the stairs, down the cramped hallway and out the back door. Our tiny ranch is not much, but divorce is expensive, and every time my attorney thinks we're getting close, Andrew comes back with another ridiculous ultimatum. The antique side table we bought on our honeymoon. A pair of crystal candlesticks he broke ages ago. The negatives for Ethan's baby pictures. As long as it's not Ethan he wants, I give in to his every demand.

Ethan stops in front of the car, still half-asleep. "What are you waiting for? Get in."

He doesn't move. I check the time on my cell—six-twenty-seven.

"Ethan." When there's no response, I give his shoulder a little jiggle. "Come on, sweetie. Get in the car. Otherwise you'll miss the bus."

Which leaves in exactly thirty-three minutes, from a parking lot across town. Today's destination: Dahlonega, an early gold rush town an hour north of Atlanta. Ethan's class will be traipsing through mines two hundred feet under the ground, panning for gold and semiprecious stones, sleeping in a cabin under the stars. When he brought the permission form home from school last month, I thought it was an April Fools' joke. What kind of teacher takes a busload of second graders on an overnight trip on *purpose*?

"But we do it every year," Miss Emma assured me when I questioned her. "We stay at a YMCA summer camp facility so it's perfectly safe. One teacher or chaperone for every five students. The kids look forward to it all semester."

It was the speech I heard her give every second grade helicopter mom, but in doing so with me, she missed the point. It wasn't Ethan's physical safety I was worried about, but his emotional. Ethan has an IQ of 158, a level of giftedness that comes with a particular set of challenges. This is a kid who's brilliant but socially awkward. An analytical thinker who needs constant stimulation. An insatiable learner with a never-ending stream of questions. His speech, his interests, the way he thinks—his world is so different from his peers that there's practically no point of contact. He's been at Cambridge for two years now and hasn't brought home a single friend. No playdates, no sleepovers. Nothing.

But his class has been learning about the mines all spring, and Miss Emma has filled his bottomless brain with tales of hydraulic sluices and a network of underground tunnels. Lode mining, my son informed me, and up until this morning, he was desperate to see it for himself—despite having never slept in a bed that wasn't under the same roof as me or Andrew. He begged long enough that I caved. I swallowed down my worries and signed the damn form

He climbs onto the backseat, and I toss him a peanut-free breakfast bar, which he ignores.

"What's wrong, baby? Are you sick?"

"No." He looks at the wrapper and makes a face. "Just not hungry."

"Well, eat it anyway. You'll need the fuel to climb all those steps to get in and out of the mines." The last bit is a deliberate reminder, meant to drum up some of his previous excitement.

But my son is onto me, and the look he gives me is textbook Ethan. Dipped chin. Arched brow. Eyes on the verge of rolling. He heaves a sigh so forceful that it lifts his little body from the seat.

"You're always starving in the morning. Why not today?"

"I don't know." His glasses slip down his face, and he wriggles his nose to push them back up. They're too loose, the fake tortoiseshell too heavy for his head. Ethan is eight, but he's small enough to be six, yet another disadvantage he faces. "I'm just not."

You need to stop coddling him. I hear Andrew's voice as clearly as if he were sitting here, in the passenger's seat beside me. *Otherwise that kid will never toughen up.*

You need to. *He'll* never. This is one of Andrew's more impressive accomplishments: he's an expert at assigning blame. He's only been practicing it for years.

But Andrew's not here, and I need to get to work. I can barely afford my half of Cambridge Classical Academy's tuition, not with the clock still ticking on this divorce and the stack of bills by the toaster, as terrifying to me as Ethan's fear of the monsters that live under his bed. My boss doesn't have kids. She doesn't understand that Ethan's little Einstein brain needs longer than others to weigh the pros and cons. I need this job, which means I need to get him on that bus. I start the car and back out of the driveway.

All the way to school, I watch Ethan's expression in the rearview mirror. Not for the first time, I wish the uncoupling between his father and I wasn't so explosive. That our conversations didn't have to happen in writing and from a minimum physical distance of two hundred feet. The restraining order sure makes coparenting hard, especially when your Dahlonega-bound son sits staring out the window like he's on the way to a root canal.

I hit the button for the radio, silencing the morning-show prattle. "Sweetie, please tell me. What is it? What's wrong?"

His gaze flicks to mine, sticks for a second, then slides away. He bounces his shoulders, even though he knows the answer. Ethan *always* knows the answer.

"Are you worried about the other kids?"

He frowns, and I know I've hit a nerve.

"Is someone bothering you again?"

I purposefully don't say *bully*, the *B*-word that his teacher has been avoiding, along with the name of the little shit—though both of us knew who she was talking about. Miss Emma tried to blow off whatever happened as a silly squabble, one she promised she had under control. But that's part of the problem. She dismisses all the bullying as petty, silly squabbles, even when things turn bloody.

"If you tell me what happened, I can help you fix it. I'll talk to Miss Emma and make sure she's aware of the problem. Miss Emma and I are on your team here, you know. We want to help."

"It's nothing, okay? Nobody's bothering me."

"Are you worried about being away from home?"

Ethan frowns into the rearview mirror.

"Because you shouldn't, you know. Miss Emma will take good care of you."

No answer. He slumps in his seat, his palms cupping his elbows, his fingertips tapping out a nervous rhythm on his skin—a tic he's picked up when he doesn't want to talk about something.

We drive the rest of the way in silence.

By the time I race up the tree-lined drive that leads to Cambridge Classical Academy's parking lot, I don't have to check the dashboard clock to know it's well past seven. The yoga-toned mothers milling about on the lawn, the squealing kids swirling in circles around their legs, a pacing Miss Emma with her phone pressed to her ear. Their pinched faces say it all.

Late.

I pull into the first spot I see, hit the brakes with a screech and clamber out.

"Sorry," I call out over the roof of my car. "We're here, we're here. Sorry."

Ethan steps from the backseat, pausing to watch the kids race around the lawn. His face betrays his thoughts, his longing so obvious it's almost written in the air. It hits me right in the stomach where his body used to, back when I was nine months pregnant and he kicked so hard his tiny foot would almost punch through my skin. My beautiful, brilliant son wants nothing more than to belong, and I don't know how to help him.

With a sigh, he reaches inside the car, hoists his backpack onto a shoulder.

I poke him on the other. "Hey, I got you a surprise."

The look he gives me is dubious. Ethan knows money is tight, and surprises are reserved for special occasions. "What kind of surprise?"

I pop the trunk. He tips his head around the side, taking a peek, and when he returns his gaze to mine, his eyes have blown wide. "You got me the mummy bag?"

I grin. "I got you the mummy bag." The sleeping bag that had made him desperate with want when he'd spotted it at Walmart. Not because it comes with a flip-over hoodie and a built-in pillow, but because of the hidden pocket for the raggedy strip of baby blanket he doesn't want any of his classmates to know he can't sleep without. "Your you-know-what is already in there, zippered into the inside pocket."

The smile that creeps up his face is worth every hard-earned penny.

"Do you like it?"

He reaches in, clutches the roll with both arms to his chest. It dwarfs his tiny body, looking like it might topple him over. "It's totally *awesome*."

"Excellent. Then maybe you won't even need the other thing I brought you."

His eyes narrow into slits. "What other thing?"

I reach in the car, into my bag on the middle console, and pull out a worn, brown leather pouch.

Ethan recognizes it, and his face alights with excitement. "Your great-grandpa's compass?"

Or more accurately, his surveyor's compass. This one is from the mid-1800s, with a pair of brass flip-up sights on opposite ends, which my great-grandfather used to measure the wooded land along the border of Tennessee and Kentucky. It's probably not worth much, thanks to the web of scratches and the star-crack in the northeast corner, but since it's the last thing my mother gave me before she died, to me it means the world.

He grabs it from me now and presses it with both hands to the mummy bag. "I'll take real good care of it, Mom. I promise."

"For the record, I am not giving it to you—not yet. But you can borrow it for a couple of days if you think it might make being away from home a little easier." I bend down, looking him in the eye. "And to be honest, it makes me feel better knowing you have it. If you get lost, you can use that thing to find your way back home."

He gives me a happy grin. "I'm not gonna get lost."

"I know. But take it anyway."

Behind us, the bus starts up with a loud rumble, a sleek black machine more suited for a rock star and his entourage than a couple dozen screaming eight-year-olds. Most of them are already inside, bleating their excitement from behind the tinted windows, telling us it's beyond time to go. Miss Emma turns, looks our way. Her gaze catches Ethan's, and she smiles and raises both hands in question. *Are you coming or not?*

We gather his stuff and hustle across the lawn.

At the edge of the lot, I squat, putting me face-to-face with Ethan. This farewell will be quick. Clean and clinical, as much for him as for me. "Be good. Listen to Miss Emma and the chaperones." I straighten his glasses, fix his rumpled collar. "And have the very best time."

He gives me a close-lipped smile. "I'm pretty sure I can do that."

I think back to the first time I held him, in the hospital delivery room. He was so tiny, so pink and sticky and fragile. I remember how he looked up at me, his tiny mouth opening and closing against my arm like a fish, how that first swell of motherly love took my breath away. The hopes and intentions and fears—they're nothing compared to what I feel now.

"God, I'm going to miss you." I pull him into a hug, one that's quick and fierce and strong enough he can't wriggle away. I inhale his familiar smell—shampoo and detergent and the tiniest whiff of stinky puppy.

"You ready, Ethan?" Miss Emma, holding out a hand to him. She looks at me and smiles. "We'll take good care of him, I promise."

I nod and hand him off, telling myself he'll be fine. Ethan will be cared for and looked after. Maybe outside of schoolyard and classroom constraints, he'll even make a friend.

Please, God, let him make a friend.

With one last wave, Miss Emma nudges Ethan toward the rumbling bus. Hours from now, it will be this very moment I keep returning to, replaying the images over and over and over in my mind, not the part where my son disappears behind the smoky glass, but the part where an icy chill creeping up my spine almost makes me stop him.

KAT

3 hours, 13 minutes missing

I'M AWAKENED BEFORE DAWN BY A COMMOTION outside my front door, and my first thought is of Andrew. Not the sweet, charming Andrew who used to hook his pinkie around mine in the grocery store or wash my car every Saturday, but the drunken, domineering version who'd appeared more and more often the further we got into our marriage. The stack of self-help books on my nightstand would call my thinking of him now a textbook example of conditioning, a learned response to a repeated stimuli, like ducking from an oncoming backhand. I don't need a book or a psychologist to tell me it's Andrew's fist downstairs now, beating on my front door.

I drag a pillow over my head and wait for the sound of his wails to worm their way through my wooden bedroom door. *Kat, I can fix this. Why won't you let me fix this?*

But Andrew's voice doesn't come. Only a steady rain drumming the roof and the old, rickety house holding its breath.

I toss the pillow aside and check the alarm pad on the far wall, an electronic line of defense I installed after things in my house kept getting moved around. My framed photographs crooked on the walls. A pile of papers, shuffled and shifted. The woven throw rug, pulled out from the easy chair's legs. It was Andrew's way of fucking with me, of letting me know that even though he didn't have a key, he was still the one in control. It stopped six months ago, on the day a DeKalb County judge signed a paper ordering him to stay two hundred feet away. Just in case, I stabbed an alarm company sign into the dirt by the front steps. *This place is secured by ADT, asshole. Don't even try it.*

A glowing red light tells me the system is armed, but another thumping from downstairs tells me Andrew is as determined as ever to haul me out of bed. The restraining order is great in theory, but so far mine has proved to be useless. I know from experience that by the time the police arrive, Andrew will be long gone. I reach for my phone, then remember I left it downstairs in the kitchen.

From downstairs comes another pounding, five sharp thuds on the door with a fist.

Normally, this would be the moment when Ethan comes stumbling into my room, his curls sticking up every which way from his pillow, his fingers scrubbing the sleep from his eyes. I've tried to protect him from his father's and my histrionics, but there have been enough moments like this one to make me wonder if our constant fighting hasn't left permanent scars. Divorce is a cesspool of soul-sucking sorrow, especially for the innocent child stuck in the middle.

As I push back the covers and step out of bed, I worry that Andrew's ruckus will wake the neighbors. I worry he'll take his frustration out on my rosebushes or punch a fist through the glass. That this might be something else has yet to cross my mind.

And then I open my bedroom door.

The upstairs hallway, normally lit up with the muted yellow glow of a streetlight, is a blaze of red and blue. The colors crawl up the walls and slash across the ceiling and send me hurling across the carpet. I trip over an overflowing laundry hamper and a pair of Ethan's ratty sneakers, catching myself just in time to fly down the stairs. I take them by twos and threes, my legs suddenly wobbly with terror. It's the middle of the night, my son is who-knows-how-many miles away and there's a police car in my driveway.

God forgive me, I'm praying this is somehow about Andrew. He had an accident. He was arrested.

Just please, God. Don't let it be about Ethan.

At the bottom of the stairs, a man fills the vertical window next to the door. He's huge, six feet and then some, with wide shoulders and the kind of bulk that comes from kickboxing and barbells, not doughnuts. His blue eyes lock onto mine, and the hairs rise, one at a time, on the back of my neck.

He presses a badge to the window. "Brent Macintosh, Atlanta Police Department. I'm looking for Kathryn Jenkins."

Everything inside me turns to stone. If I open this door, if I verify that yes, I'm Kat Jenkins, he's going to tell me something I don't want to hear. For the longest moment, there's no sound except for my breathing, too hard and too harsh.

He's not in uniform but his clothes are dark. Dark shirt, dark pants, the fabric inky as the sky behind him. "Ma'am, are you Kathryn Jenkins?"

I clear my throat. Nod. "It's Kat."

He slips his badge into his pocket, stepping back to reveal his car on my driveway behind him. The siren lights turn the falling raindrops red and blue, dots of color swirling through the sky like a kaleidoscope. "Could you please open the door?"

I turn on the foyer light, flip the locks and tug on the handle, and a siren splits the air. *Oh shit*, I think in that half second before my body snaps into action, lurching to the pad to punch in the code. My shaking fingers won't cooperate. It takes me three fumbling tries to get the sequence right.

The house plunges into a silence so intense it's like a whole other sound ringing in my ears.

His expression is carefully blank, but his body language makes me brace for what he says next: "Is your son, Ethan Maddox, with you?"

"No." My heart gives an ominous thud. "He's away, on a school trip."

"Then I'm sorry to have to tell you this, but Ethan has been reported missing from Camp Crosby."

Static hisses in my ears. My mind has shoved aside all of his words but one—the most important.

"Ethan is missing?" I need this man to explain it to me. I need him to be exact and specific.

He does so without consulting his notes. "Ethan's teacher conducted a head count sometime around 2:30 a.m. and found Ethan missing. She and another chaperone searched the surrounding area, and when they couldn't find any sign of your son, they alerted the authorities at 3:07. The Lumpkin County Sheriff's Office arrived at the scene shortly thereafter and has initiated an organized search of the camp. So far they've been unable to locate him."

"I'm sure he… He probably just…went to the bathroom or something and couldn't find his way back."

"It's one of the scenarios they're looking at. A city kid in the woods could get turned around easily, especially in the dark."

"What… What are the other scenarios?"

"At this point, they're not ruling anything out."

I picture my son out there in woods darker than a nightmare, and there's a teetering in my balance, a slow unraveling in my chest. Ethan still sleeps with a night-light. He still insists on leaving his bedroom door cracked and the hallway sconces on, so the light can creep across the carpet to the foot of his bed. I think of him out there in the cold, dark woods, and I feel his panic, as tangible as electricity in the air.

Every mother lives with this secret terror. The kind we let creep into our consciousness in our darker moments. It wheezes with hot, sour breath in our ears our most primal fear—that some sort of harm will come to our babies. We console ourselves by dismissing it as an impossibility. Not us, we tell ourselves. Not our children. It's how we survive the danger that the worst could happen, by shoving our terrors to the dustiest, most forgotten corners of our mind.

But sometimes, when the house is quiet and everyone is asleep, we allow ourselves to wonder. What would I do? How would I respond?

I respond with legs of jelly and lungs of concrete, no air moving in or out. My skin goes hot and my blood goes cold and my vision goes blurry with tears or lack of oxygen or both. Something sharp and biting tears into my stomach, doubling me over at the waist.

Ethan is *missing*.

The words play over and over in my mind, along with images of him in the pitch-black woods, a pack of wild animals nipping at his toes or dragging him by the skin of his neck through the underbrush. Is he hurt? Is he conscious? Is he alive?

I lurch upright, my breath returning with a series of choked sobs.

The policeman steps inside, shutting the door with a soft click and reaches for my elbow. "Let's find you a place to sit down."

I swat his hand away. "How long have they been searching?" My voice is too high and too shrill. The hysteria has thickened into a spiky knot in the center of my chest. I can barely talk around it. "How long?"

He checks his watch. "Somebody's been looking for just under three hours now. We've been trying to reach you for most of that."

"Three hours! Three… How many people?"

"I don't know the exact number, ma'am, but a missing child is about as high priority as you can get. If they don't have the staff on hand, they'll be calling in nearby precincts and recruiting volunteers. It takes a little longer to pull a search party together in the middle of the night, but the sheriff knows what he's doing, and his guys know those woods like the backs of their hands."

If that were true, if the sheriff and his guys knew every moss-covered stone, every cave and fallen tree trunk Ethan could be hiding in or under or behind, wouldn't they have found him by now?

"I'm very sorry, ma'am, but I have to ask. What time did you arrive home last night?"

Maybe it's the lack of sleep or the shock or the terror, but my brain can't process his question. "What?"

"Last night." His gaze wanders over my shoulder to peer down the dark hall. "What time did you get home, and is there anyone who can verify your whereabouts?"

My throat funnels shut, because that's when it occurs to me: he's asking me for an alibi. My child is lost in a forest hours from here, and this man has been sent to accuse me of taking him.

"I was at work until almost nine," I say through gritted teeth. "After that I came straight home. I haven't left since.

You can check with the alarm company if you don't believe me. I'm sure they have a record of when I turned it off and back on."

And then I realize something else, something that buzzes under my skin like an electric current. "Oh my God. Do you think someone *took* him?"

"Not necessarily, but when we couldn't reach you... Like I said, I had to ask." His tone is almost apologetic, but there's a relaxed alertness to him that tightens my gut. "The sheriff would like you up in Dahlonega as soon as possible. Do you know where you're going, or do you need me to write down the address for you?"

I spin on my heel and sprint down the hallway, the robe flapping at my ankles. In the kitchen, I fumble in the junk on the counter for my phone, wake it up to find twenty-seven missed calls. Twenty-seven.

A good mother would have slept with her cell phone next to her bed while her son was away. She wouldn't have been oblivious the very moment he vanished into the night. She would have *known*.

"Do you have someone you can call? A friend or family member who can give you a ride?" The cop looms in my kitchen, his gaze taking in the shadowy debris of a working mom and a messy eight-year-old. A sink overflowing with dirty mugs and crumb-strewn plates, a mini mountain of school notes and papers and mail, the pair of cereal bowls on the table, crudded with the remains of our breakfasts.

I shake my head, then nod, then shake my head again. I am an only child, an orphan, and the people I have left to call are not even remotely local. High school friends from back home, a tiny town at the top end of Tennessee. Lucas, my brother in every way but blood. Izzy—the only Atlanta friend I kept from my life Before Divorce—sailing the British Virgin Islands with her latest lover, Tristan or Tanner or some other pompous *T*-name. The only one left is Andrew.

Not going to happen.

I drop my cell onto the counter with a clatter and bolt to the back door. The key hook next to the alarm pad is empty. I swipe a hand across it just to be sure. No keys. I flip on the lights and search the floor, kicking away Ethan's schoolbags, the jacket he can never remember to hang up, a pair of fuzzy pink slippers. Not there, either.

Where *are* they?

Another wave of panic rolls in, flickering under my scalp like a swarm of angry mosquitoes. I need to be in Dahlonega. I need to be out there in the woods, screaming Ethan's name until my throat is raw. I need to help them find my son. No—I need to somehow figure out a way to travel back in time to yesterday morning, so I could floor the gas and whiz right past the turnoff for school and none of this would have ever happened. Ethan would be safe and snoring upstairs in his bed. I would be on the other side of the wall, lurching from my mattress with a gasp, tangled in sweaty sheets, limp with relief that it was only an awful, terrifying nightmare.

I whirl around, knocking into the cop's massive body, solid as a brick wall. He edges back to let me pass, saying something that hits my frenzied thoughts like elevator Muzak—background noise where not a single note registers.

I need to find my keys. *Think*, dammit.

Back in the kitchen, I fumble through my purse, flinging the contents on the counter. My wallet, a ridiculous amount of crumpled-up receipts, a handful of mints, but no keys.

The cop is still talking, something about slowing down, sitting down, calming down, and I can't think with him here. I shove my hands in my hair and squeeze my eyes closed, trying to block out his voice, trying to remember where I left the damn things. I came in last night, dropped my purse and phone on the counter, poured a glass of wine and—I shove past the cop and yank on the refrigerator handle and hallelujah, the jumble of silver metal, glinting under a golden Whirlpool light.

I grab for my keys, but I'm not fast enough. A long arm reaches around me, a giant fist closing around them before mine can get there.

I slam the door and pivot around, and suddenly it's all too much. The fear, the shock, the worry, combined with my exhaustion and the key-snatching cop, the fact that there's nobody here but me. The tears come in a well of frustration and helplessness and maybe a tiny bit of self-pity.

The cop's shoulders soften, and he drops my keys into his pants pocket. "Go get dressed. Make sure whatever you put on is comfortable, and wear sneakers. Pack an overnight bag with the basics—change of clothes, your toothbrush, any toiletries you need. Pack one for Ethan, too, and toss in any toys or stuffed animals he might want for when we find him." He plucks my cell phone off the counter, waves it in the air by his ear. "Where's the charger for this thing?"

I'm too shocked to answer with anything but, "Upstairs, I think."

"Pack it, too. We'll leave as soon as you're ready."

KAT

3 hours, 23 minutes missing

MY EAST-ATLANTA NEIGHBORHOOD, A RAM-shackle development on the wrong end of Tucker, is the kind of neighborhood that's used to seeing cop cars roll by in the middle of the night. The people who live on my street are rough—chain-smoking women waving their fists at strangers from the stoop, potbellied men with gold teeth and sleeves of faded tattoos, teens with saggy pants lounging on the curbs with kids too young to be smoking. The houses aren't much better—run-down and raggedy, with drooping gutters, peeling and patchy paint jobs, overgrown yards choked by weeds. I watch them pass by on the other side of the cop's rain-soaked passenger-side window, taking in their sad state under the dingy glow of the streetlamps and the occasional front porch light. I thought marrying Andrew would save me from a neighborhood like this one, yet thanks to the countless sneaky smoke screens Andrew erected to hide his company's money and assets, here I am all over again.

"How you holding up?" the cop asks, and I startle. "Sorry, didn't mean to scare you."

"How come you're not in uniform?" The question comes out unsteady and without rhythm. I am surprised I am able to speak at all; my throat is desert-dry, and my tongue feels like a deadweight, swollen to twice its size.

"Because I'm not a patrol officer. I'm a detective working the night shift."

"Isn't this a little above your pay grade?"

"What, a missing child?"

"No. Carting me all the way to Dahlonega. What is it, fifty miles?"

Without taking his eyes from the road, he says, "More like sixty-five."

The number makes me more than a little uncomfortable. I know this man has sworn to protect and serve, but it's the middle of the night and I'm a stranger—one he initially suspected of having a hand in her own son's disappearance. Does he still see me as a suspect? Did he offer to drive me in order to stay close, to watch for signs? I try to push my suspicions away, but I can't. Ever since Andrew, my once-sharp instincts have gone haywire. Who knows why anybody does anything?

And speaking of Andrew, has someone called him? Did an officer bang on his door and haul him out of bed, too? The thought of seeing him again, of having our first face-to-face in months at the camp, makes my skin itchy with nerves.

I dig through the bag by my feet, fumbling for my cell phone. "I need to call Lucas."

The detective reaches for the volume knob and silences his car speakers, which up until now have been bleating copspeak in intermittent spurts.

The first three tries shoot me to voice mail, just as I knew they would. Finally, on the fourth attempt, Lucas's deep and dusty voice creeps down the line. "What's wrong? Is it Andrew?"

"No, it's Ethan." I say his name, and my voice cracks. "He's missing."

"What do you mean he's missing?" It was pretty much my first question, too. There's a reason why I called Lucas first. "Missing from where?"

"From the cabin where he was staying with his class. He was on that field trip to Dahlonega, remember? His teacher did a head count and he wasn't there." A fresh wave of terror surges, hitting me like an anvil right between the ribs. "He's been gone for over three hours now, Lucas."

There's a rustling, a squeaking of mattress springs, and I picture him sitting on the edge of his bed on the south side of Knoxville, in a house only slightly bigger than mine but minus the leak spots on the ceilings and the mold climbing the walls of the cellar. Lucas works in construction, which, ever since the housing crash, means he'll do whatever it takes to make a buck. He's a welder, a bricklayer, a craftsman, a roofer, a painter, an electrician, a landscaper, a plumber, a handyman and a jack-of-all-trades.

He's also an ex-marine trained in search and rescue. He can track any animal through any forest. If he leaves now, he can be there in just over three hours.

A sleepy female voice floats up from the background, and he shushes her. Lucas is a good-looking guy with a tool belt and a Harley. There's always a woman in his bed, though it's rarely the same one. More rustling, the click of a door. "Okay. Tell me what happened. Start at the beginning."

"That's all I know. He was there—now he's not. The cops are looking for him now."

"How many?"

"I don't know."

"Have they called in the dogs? The volunteers and helicopters?"

"I don't know, I don't know, I don't *know*." The panic is building inside me like a scream, a tightening noose.

"Shit. Okay, I'm on my way. Where are you?"

I look for a road sign, trying to get my bearings. By now we've merged onto the highway, citywide and busy, filled with big, lumbering trucks that cling to the right lanes. Up ahead, a green sign points us north to Cumming.

"We're about to get on 400, so that's what, another hour or so?" The detective dips his chin. "Yeah, he says another hour."

"Who's 'he'?"

"The detective who came to my house. He's driving me." I know he showed me his badge, said his name and credentials through my front door window, but none of it stuck. The panic and shock of finding a strange man on my doorstep washed it all away. I pull the phone away from my ear. "I'm so sorry, but I've forgotten your name."

He glances over. "Detective Brent Macintosh, Atlanta PD."

I repeat the words to Lucas, who says, "I'm walking out now."

Relief hits me square in the chest, followed by a spark of something sharper. "Do you think he just… I don't know, went to the bathroom or something and lost his way back?" This is the version I keep telling myself, that Ethan's disappearance is as simple as an accidental turn, a mistaken path. I want so badly to believe that it's only a matter of time before someone finds him hunkered down behind a tree. The alternative is too awful to contemplate.

"He's too smart for that," Lucas says, and I wince, even though I know he's right. "Look, wherever he is, he couldn't have gotten far."

On the other side of the windshield, the wipers slap out a frenetic beat, but they can't clear the glass fast enough. I think about the dangers that could come from a downpour in the mountains—freezing pools of swirling water and leaves; saturated ground, boggy as quicksand; mudslides, fast and heavy, taking down everything in their path.

"It's still dark out, Lucas."

"I know."

"And it's pouring. He'll be drenched."

"I'll be there as soon as I can."

"Okay." I tell myself to breathe, trying to dampen down the panic. Lucas is a fixer, as evidenced by his choice of careers. He'll fix this for me. He has to.

"Who else have you talked to?"

"Nobody. You're the first."

I know he's really asking if I've called Andrew. The man who Lucas assumed was the reason for this call. Lucas has never been a fan.

I sigh. "I'll call him in the morning, if they still haven't—"

"They'll find him," Lucas says, cutting off that depressing sentiment with a voice that's sure and determined. "And if they don't, I will."

My breath comes out in a whoosh, a hot sigh fueled by relief. They're the words I've been waiting to hear, the reason, if I'm being completely honest, why I called. Lucas is on his way. He won't rest until he finds Ethan.

A not-so-tiny voice inside of me prays Lucas is not too late.

I knew Ethan was special three days after his ten-month birthday, when he handed me his bottle of milk and said, "No, I want juice." Four little words and not very special ones at that, but a full sentence. Subject, verb, direct object. Unheard of for a baby his age.

Andrew insisted we have him tested as soon as the psychologist said it was possible, when Ethan was two. I'll never forget Andrew's face when that woman, a straitlaced type in a pencil skirt and pearls, told us that Ethan's score fell in genius territory. All of a sudden, Andrew didn't care that his toddler was obsessed with the mating rituals of penguins, or that the only way to quieten a terrible-two meltdown was to dial the radio to Bach. Ethan's weird quirks had an explanation—one worth showing off to the world.

"My son is brilliant," Andrew would say to our friends, his tennis teammates, the strangers behind him at the checkout counter, and in a voice meant to carry. He's always been loud, but he likes to notch things up a few decibels when he's bragging. "No, like, *seriously* brilliant. Equivalent to an IQ of 158, which is only two points lower than Einstein's. The psychologist says it's genetic."

Of course Andrew meant him. His son's intelligence had come from *him*.

"Ethan is a genius," I say to Detective Macintosh now, cringing at how it makes me sound just like Andrew. "My son is not an outdoorsy type, but Lucas was right—he's smart enough to figure out how to get to the bathroom and ba— the compass!"

The detective glances over. "What compass?"

"I gave him one, just this morning. Well, it's an old surveyor's compass, but it's operational, and he knows how to use it." Hope expands in my chest, soft and light like cotton candy. "If he's lost, he can use it to find his way back."

"Or find his way out."

"Out of the woods?" I shake my head. "You don't know

my son, but he wouldn't go deeper into the forest on purpose. He's scared of the dark, and even if he had a flashlight, he's too much of a rule follower. I just don't see him doing it."

"Make sure you tell the sheriff all these things when we get there. He's going to want to get into Ethan's head, to better understand what he's thinking."

By now it's close to six, and the sky has gone from pitch-black to gunmetal gray, swollen clouds blocking out the first of the morning light. Most of the 18-wheelers and rush hour travelers are headed in the opposite direction—toward the city—leaving the northbound lanes largely clear. Mountains rise up like behemoths on either side of us, dark rolling ridges disappearing into a thick layer of haze.

Ethan will be okay, I tell myself, repeating the words over and over like a mantra. *He's just lost. Someone will find him soon.*

But other words—heart-pounding, breath-stealing words—are louder, firmer, fiercer, tattooed like angry graffiti across my vision. Hungry animals. Bottomless ravines. Toppling trees. For an eight-year-old on his own, the mountains are a perilous place.

"How much longer?"

The detective checks the GPS. "Another forty minutes or so."

In the dim light of the car, he looks young, almost boyish, but his face carries the weathered look of someone who's seen it all. As a detective in a city like Atlanta, one that consistently ranks in the top twenty most dangerous places in America, I guess he would have.

A burst of noise erupts from the radio, then falls into silence. It's been doing this since we left Atlanta, intermittent squawks and disembodied voices speaking in codes and numbers, a secret language of emergency that sends me spiraling into panicky shakes each time I hear them.

"What did they say?"

"Dogs haven't caught his scent yet. Or at least not his most recent one."

"What kind of dogs?"

"Air scenters, trackers, trailers. Probably all three, I'd imagine. I don't know where these ones came from, but a well-trained search-and-rescue dog can find somebody a heck of a lot faster than a human can, and they don't need daylight to do it."

"But Ethan disappeared almost four hours ago. What's taking them so long?"

The detective glances over. "Scent contamination would be the biggest hurdle they'll have to face. The dogs are trained to discriminate, which means they'll be able to pick your son's out of all the other kids' scents, but it'll take them a minute to find the right trail, and the most recent one." He gestures over the dash, to the wipers sloshing rain across the windshield and beyond. "Rain's not helping, either."

And it's the kind of rain that goes on for hours and hours. No sun. No strips of blue sky. Just dark clouds dumping water in blinding, never-ending sheets.

"Because it makes things harder to see?"

"No, because it makes things harder to *smell*. Search-and-rescue dogs are highly effective, but they can't scent something that's washed away, which is what happens after about three inches of rainfall. Wind isn't good news, either, and neither is cooler air, which creates an updraft when it hits the wet ground. The dog trainers'll know how to combat weather, and they'll take all this into account when positioning the dogs, but honestly, these conditions don't make their job any easier."

My eyes sting, struck by his less-than-optimistic update. As hard as it is to hear, I appreciate his honesty all the same.

The car radio crackles to life, and I hold my breath and lean in, electric with equal parts hope and dread. I strain to make out the words over the noise of the wipers and rain, but the message emerges slushy with interference. I look to the detective's expression for guidance. His eyes crinkle into a squint and he rolls his neck before he looks over.

"They're requesting a description of Ethan's backpack."

My heart freezes, and I grip the seat on either side of my legs. "Why, did they find it?"

"Sounds like they're trying to locate it and need confirmation of the description. As many identifying details as you can give would be helpful."

"It's light blue and black, with an Angry Bird on the front. His first and last name is written in Sharpie on the inside flap."

He relays my answer to the person on the other end of the radio, along with what I just told him about the compass. The voice sputters something back, and he presses the device to his thigh. "Is there anything else that might be used to track him? A cell phone, an iPod touch, gaming electronics, things like that?"

"No. He doesn't own a cell phone, and I don't like him playing video games. He's allowed to use my old iPad, but it's at home."

Because I was worried about him losing it. Because I was worried about the cost. A stupid hunk of metal and glass, irrelevant and immaterial until now, when it might have been used to find him.

He repeats my answer into the radio, and there's a long, static-filled pause. "Copy that," the voice says, and then is gone.

Macintosh hangs the headset on the hook. "We're going

to want access to your home in order to get to that iPad, see if he's made any contact with anyone online. They'll want to take a good look at his bedroom, too."

"What for?"

"Same reason they'll have a long list of questions for you—to get in your son's head. To see if there was anything going on in his life that might be relevant to his disappearance. And before your mind starts going to dark places, the fact he took his backpack is a good thing. It means he was prepared."

I shake my head, certain of exactly the opposite. "I just don't see Ethan wandering off in the middle of the night. He wouldn't have left that cabin, not without explicit permission from his teacher. What about Miss Emma and the chaperones? What about the kids? Somebody must have seen something."

"If I were standing in your shoes, those are pretty much the first questions I'd ask of the Lumpkin County police. How Ethan disappeared when he was surrounded by all those people."

And right here, my mind goes to all those dark places the detective told me to avoid. Why didn't Ethan scream, alert the chaperones? Did he go kicking and screaming or willingly, at the barrel of a gun? How did none of the other kids hear? How come no one saw it happen?

By now Detective Macintosh has veered off the main drag and is following 19's fat, looping curves that lead into Dahlonega. The lanes are narrower here, the asphalt pitted and half-buried in places, deep, dark puddles that catch the tires and send us fishtailing toward the guardrails. I hold tight to the door handle as we lean into another curve, which he handles with the skill of a NASCAR driver.

"And the second question?" I say, once we're back on solid ground.

He keeps his gaze superglued to the road, his words slow and careful. "The second is to start asking yourself who might want more time with Ethan. Because the longer your son is gone, the longer nobody can find him, the higher the odds climb that he's not lost."

STEF

3 hours, 33 minutes missing

I BLINK INTO THE DARKNESS OF OUR ATLANTA bedroom, and I don't have to flip on a light to know that I'm in bed alone. No sounds of Sam, brushing his teeth or banging around in his closet for his running gear, which can only mean he's already downstairs. My husband is a good man and a terrific mayor, but in his own house he lives on Planet Sam, where morning rituals are not performed with regards to those of us still sleeping. If he was still in here, I'd for sure hear him.

I roll toward my nightstand and check the time—six-oh-three. Twelve minutes before my alarm would normally send me shuffling down the hall to Sammy's room to get him ready for school. Unlike his father, Sammy sleeps like the dead. Rousing him from underneath his blankets often feels like trying to tug an elephant through a bottle neck: impossible.

But this morning, Sammy's bed is empty, and Sam and I are taking a rare day off. No endless, snaking car pool lines for me. No donor meetings or campaign rallies or schmoozing city council members for him. And best of all, no Josh, Sam's ever-available chief of staff, to call or text or interrupt at the worst possible moment like he tends to do. Nothing but me and Sam and a long stretch of empty hours.

Heaven.

I swipe a hand over Sam's side of the mattress, running my fingers along sheets that have long gone cool. Once upon a time, Sam and I stayed tangled in the sheets until noon. Granted, that time was pre-Sammy, pre–Sam throwing his hat in the ring for mayor, which he won in a surprise landslide, but still. I sure do miss those days.

I'm about to hit the switch for the blackout shades when the bedroom door opens and Sam steps in. He's cradling something in a hand, his former-football-player silhouette lit up from behind with the hallway's golden glow. He sneaks into the room in pajama pants and bare feet, the distinct sound of porcelain clunking in a hand. Sam curses under his breath.

"It's fine. I'm awake."

I flip on a lamp, and the shadows in the bedroom take shape. The sandalwood dresser on the far wall. The tufted chaise by the floor-to-ceiling window. Sam, approaching the bed with two steaming mugs of coffee in one hand. The scent hits me and so does his smile—warm, wholehearted, seductive.

He shifts one of the mugs to his free hand and hands it to me. "Extra strong, with the tiniest splash of coconut milk."

As perfect an example as any of why Sam was elected mayor—his ability to give you exactly what you want before you even know you want it. The first sip provides a welcome and instant zing, like a tuning fork to the bloodstream.

"I'll admit to being annoyed when I woke up alone, but you are officially forgiven. This is perfect, thank you."

"So I've been thinking…" he says, sinking on the bed by my feet. He drapes a palm over my foot. "Why don't we rent some bikes and ride the BeltLine? We could grab lunch at Ponce

City Market and cupcakes at Saint-Germain, then spend the rest of the afternoon doing a pub crawl. It's supposed to be a gorgeous day, not too hot. What do you say?"

"I thought today was supposed to be just you and me."

It's the only thing I asked for. A day without obligations. Without appointments and voter polls and mile-long to-do lists. After four years of craziness—and with the next four looming—I don't think it's too much to ask for. All I want is a day—a whole, glorious day—just us two.

"You, me, sunshine and cocktails," Sam says. "What's not to love?"

"The thousands of constituents who will recognize you, all of whom will want to slap you on the back and take a selfie to post to their social media, alerting everybody in the entire state of Georgia where to find us. *That's* what's not to love. And I know you. You'd never tell anyone to take a hike, not when it might cost you a vote. Our day won't belong to us at all."

Sam concedes the point with a shrug. "Okay, then. What would you like do?"

"What's wrong with what we're doing now?"

"Not a thing." He pauses, feigning confusion. "What exactly *are* we doing?"

"Absolutely nothing."

Sam's brow folds in a frown. My husband lives life by the two-birds, one-stone concept. Doing nothing is something he has a hard time wrapping his head around—which is exactly why he needs it so badly.

"What about the cupcakes?" he says.

"That's what DoorDash is for."

"So you're suggesting we just...do what exactly?"

"Lie around the house in our pajamas all day. Read the paper and eat crackers in bed. Do nothing and not get dressed, except to maybe float around the pool on a blow-up. Ignore everyone and everything except each other. Come on, tell the truth. Doesn't that sound delicious?"

"I'm intrigued." He swipes the coffee cup from my hand and settles it onto the nightstand next to his, then plants both hands on either side of my knees. "Tell me more about this not getting dressed business."

It's times like these that remind me how much I love my husband, why I gave up everything to move here and live this life. Samuel Joseph Huntington IV is smart and funny and handsome and charmed and charming. If he didn't have this bone-deep need to serve, if he didn't work day and night to prove to millions of Atlantans he's never met that he's worthy of their vote, he'd be damn near perfect.

Sam leans in for a kiss, right as his phone buzzes from the pocket of his pajama pants. I know before I see the screen who it is. Sam's chief of staff is like a jealous mistress, intruding into our lives at the worst possible time and tempting my husband with the longings of needy constituents.

However, it's not Josh on the phone but Brittany, his communications director. Sam hits Ignore, then tosses the phone on the bed. Almost immediately, it buzzes from between the sheets. This time when he reaches for it, he powers it down and drops it in the nightstand drawer.

"See?" he says with a proud grin. "I can tell people to take a hike when I want to."

"Pushing an employee to voice mail is not exactly telling her to take a hike, but you do get points for trying."

He crawls over me, moving up the soft, messy sheets. "How many points?" he whispers, his breath hot on my neck. "What do I win?"

"Me." My arms wind around his waist, my body pressing

into his, long and lean, my mouth craning up for his. "You win me."

I wrap my legs around him and we are instantly coiled, our bodies fitting together like two pieces of the same puzzle.

He kisses me, and the house line rings.

Sam's lips freeze on mine.

"If you answer it, I will kill you."

Sam looks at the phone, then back to me. I shake my head.

The phone rings again, shrill and insistent.

All around us, the love spell settles like faded confetti.

Sam rolls off me with a groan. He swipes the handset from the holder, stalks to the sliding glass doors, heaves one of them open and hurls the handset into the backyard. A few seconds later, I hear it hit the water with a plunk—the brand-new Bang & Olufsen sinking to the bottom of the pool.

He turns back, victorious. This is the Sam I fell in love with—unpredictable, surprising, just the right side of naughty. Slayer of my dragons, even if only for a day.

"Now. Where were we?" He puts a knee on the bed.

I hold out my hand for his.

And that, dammit all to hell, is when the doorbell rings.

KAT

4 hours, 56 minutes missing

WHEN DETECTIVE MACINTOSH TOLD ME TO start thinking about who would want some more time with Ethan, is it conditioning or dread that my mind goes straight to Andrew? I think about what the repeated stimulus might have been, all those times he brought our son back late on his given weekends. First five minutes, then ten, then a half hour or more, though he never said a word. Never asked for an extra day, or if next time he could keep Ethan for one more night. Just handed Ethan over with a wave and a casual "See you in two weeks, buddy," even though we all knew it was more than an hour past Ethan's bedtime.

And honestly, Andrew is not that subtle. If he had wanted more time with Ethan, he would have bitched about the schedule ages ago. He would have had his lawyer bury mine under an avalanche of letters and memos, all of which demanded a hasty—and expensive—response. Death by a million cuts seems to be his divorce strategy, and my bank account is proof that it's working. Why change course now?

And of *course* Andrew wants more time with his child. Any

father would. If I were faced with visitation rights of every other weekend, holidays and school breaks at his discretion, it wouldn't be enough for me, either.

But none of that means he'd steal Ethan from his cabin. Does it?

The last six miles take an eternity.

The road becomes a twisting, turning thing lined on both sides with thick walls of trees and steep ditches. Detective Macintosh steers us up the wet asphalt as fast as he dares, but the rain is still unrelenting, falling from the sky in steady, blinding sheets, and the speedometer rarely tops forty. By the time he slows at the turnoff and a steady beeping from the GPS signals we've arrived at our destination, I'm wound tight and my knee won't stop bouncing.

He pulls into a narrow dirt road next to a small hand-painted sign. The letters are faded, most of them hidden behind a two-foot stump and thick tufts of weeds. Were it not for the incessant beeping and the Lumpkin County police car parked on the grass, I would have missed it entirely.

Camp Crosby.

The car door swings open, and a police officer steps out, pulls his collar up against the weather and hustles across the grass. The detective waits until he's close, then hits the button for the window. Rain and cooler air blow in, along with the scent of pine needles and wet dirt.

He flashes his badge. "Detective Macintosh, Atlanta PD. I've got the boy's mother."

The cop leans down, peering at us through the window. His glasses are dotted with water, which does little to conceal his squinty eyes, or the pillows of fatty skin sagging underneath. He dips his wattled chin in a show of respect. "Ma'am.

Very sorry about your son." His accent is thick and syrupy, the words sticky with a mountain twang.

"Any news?" the detective says, beating me to the question.

"Alpha Team's out there with their dogs, but the kids have been in the forest all afternoon. The trainers are dealing with some contamination, but right now we're more concerned about the rain."

"Any changes to the forecast?" Detective Macintosh asks. After our conversation earlier, I'd pulled it up on my iPhone. The downpour is supposed to ease to a light drizzle around ten, then blow off before noon. But this is mountain country, where weather can change on a dime.

"Not as far as I know. But if this rain doesn't stop soon, we're gonna have a problem. I reckon we've had a good couple of inches at least, and most of it's fallen in the past couple hours. Haven't heard yet if the scent's holding."

My gaze flips to Detective Macintosh's profile, his ominous warning of a three-inch limit filling my mind, but his face gives nothing away. He just thanks the man, puts the car back in gear and points the nose up the drive.

Four feet in and the woods swallow us up, the forest narrowing into a leafy tunnel. The overhanging branches form a solid arch, pressing around us on all sides. I grip the vinyl seat and lean into the dash, my gaze sweeping the tree line for Ethan, which I know is far from logical. He's not going to just wander out and reveal himself now that I'm here, as if everything up to now was an elaborate game of hide-and-seek. But I'm seduced by hope, by despair, and I peer into the swaying brush as we pass, praying for movement, a flash of skin, anything. But all I see are wet, slick trees.

The detective steers us across a rickety bridge, then skids around the bank of a small pond, the surface a dark spot

of shivering glass. The wheels slip and spin in the mud before catching on a patch of gravel, and we hurtle up the hill.
We swerve around potholes and switchbacks until finally we
emerge in a clearing, a wide expanse of sloping lawn with
wooden cabins clinging to the hillside. More than a dozen
police cars line the bottom perimeter, their noses pointed up
the hill at the cabins and beyond, to the tree line that rises up
like a thick, dark wall.

"Which cabin?" I say, meaning Ethan's, the one where he
disappeared.

Detective Macintosh shakes his head. "Definitely not one
of these. Wherever it is, they'll have it cordoned off. Look for
the one with the yellow police tape."

He squeezes us into a spot at the edge of the grass, and I
scramble out. Rain and cool air slap my cheeks, pushing a
million tiny chill bumps through my skin. I stand there for
a long moment, watching people race back and forth across
the rain-soaked ground, uniformed police officers and plain-
clothed folks, people dressed like aliens in head-to-toe rain
gear. They call to each other from cabin porches, huddle in
clumps under trees, hurry across the churned-up grass. So
these are the people in charge of finding my son.

A noise pushes through their moving bodies and chatter—
the sound of dogs barking in the distance, followed by far-off
shouts of my son's name. *Ethan! Where are you, Ethan?*

My head whips in that direction, my gaze bumping up
against the woods. I picture the rain-soaked people trudg-
ing through them, searching in places I'm scared that they
search, looking for something I'm terrified they'll find, and
my chest screws tight. I want to help them as much as I want
to run and hide.

The detective steps up beside me. He hands me my phone,

positions an umbrella over both our heads and tugs me up the hill. "Let's go."

I follow him without question.

A man calls down the hill. "Ms. Jenkins?"

"Yes. That's me."

"Thomas Childers, Lumpkin County Sheriff. I sure am glad you're here. We've been trying to reach you for hours."

He's not exactly what you'd expect from a small, mountain-town sheriff. No potbelly. No handlebar mustache. A round, boyish face, tan and unlined despite his fifty or so years. A generous mop of dirty blond hair is plastered to his head by the rain and a broad-brimmed hat over a parka hanging open from his shoulders. Judging from the drenched uniform underneath, it's more for form than function.

"I know. I'm sorry. I fell asleep with my phone downstairs."

The detective introduces himself, followed by a long string of qualifications that sound like he's reading from his APD website bio. Three little words pop like firecrackers: missing persons investigations. The sheriff looks more than a little relieved.

"Seeing as I'm spectacularly shorthanded, I'm not going to say no to an extra pair. Come on." He hitches his head to the long, squat cabin behind him, the largest of the buildings surrounding the clearing. "I'll fill you in on everything as soon as we get inside. And watch your step. The rain's turned this lawn into one hell of a slippery slope, and I don't mean that metaphorically. Wet Georgia clay is like black ice, and the patches tend to sneak up on you."

The climb is slow and treacherous, the ground saturated and slick. The hill is littered with rocks and roots, bulging up like those Halloween decorations Ethan loves to scatter all over our front lawn. My sneaker catches in one of them, pitching me forward, and Detective Macintosh yanks me upright before I can brace for the fall. By the time we reach the top, I'm panting and soaked, the wetness creeping up my pants legs like a rising flood, turning the denim heavy as ankle weights.

The sheriff waves us across a stretch of churned-up lawn to a set of stone steps. "Let's keep walking, shall we? I don't know about you, but I'd sure like to get out of this weather."

My sneakers sink into the soggy ground. Rain beats against the umbrella with a loud patter, but it can't drown out the sound of my teeth chattering. I'm shaking from the cold, my whole body rattling, bone against bone. "Please. Just t-tell me." Until he does, I refuse to take another step.

Sheriff Childers stands there, the rain running down his skin and uniform like a river. "I've got thirty-seven men out there in the woods, and there's more on the way. Choppers should be here shortly, too. Between all that and the dogs, air scenters and ground trailers plus all their handlers, somebody's bound to find something soon."

Something could mean anything. A footprint. A broken branch. A body. I press a palm to my stomach, nauseous. "How soon?"

"As soon as humanly possible. We're getting held up by the weather, and that's putting it mildly. It's almost impossible to see out there. The dogs are only doing marginally better."

Logically, I know I am in no way prepared to join the search. This camp is pressed up against the Blue Ridge Mountains, and I have no rain gear, no dry clothes, no clue where I'm going or the ground they've already covered. Only a flimsy umbrella and the map on my iPhone, which last time I looked was operating on 38 percent battery.

But maybe Ethan is still within hearing distance. Maybe

he'd come crashing out of his hiding place if he heard it was me, calling his name.

"Ms. Jenkins."

The sheriff's expression says he knows I'm about to take off running, and his stance, the way he's bouncing on his toes says he's ready to stop me. He shakes his head. "You'll only get in the way."

I picture Ethan, scared and freezing in the woods somewhere. His pajamas will be soaked to the skin. His feet will be bare and muddy. "He's eight." My voice cracks, my throat burning like acid. "And he's out there all alone."

"The sheriff's right," the detective says. "Search and rescue works much faster if they don't have to worry about you getting in their way."

Sheriff Childers dips his head, and pooled rainwater spills over the brim of his hat. "The best way you can help right now is by coming inside and answering some questions."

The detective steers me to the staircase, and I let him. A helicopter swoops over the camp, the thudding of its blades vibrating all the way into my bones, and it's too much. The rain and the noise and the people running everywhere. The world tilts and it feels like a nightmare—a sick, feverish nightmare.

Somebody drapes a blanket, warm and dry, over my shoulders.

"There are heat sensors on the choppers," the detective says as soon as the chopper has moved on. "If Ethan's out there, he'll be glowing."

"The infrared will pick up his body heat," the sheriff explains. "The bodies glow on the screen."

Much like the way I find Ethan most nights, reading a book under his covers, the gleam of his flashlight lighting up the room through the fabric. *Glowing.*

"What about everybody else? All the other bodies." I don't remember exactly how many the sheriff said were out there, but it was somewhere in the high thirties.

His lips curl down on one side. "That's an issue, I'm not gonna lie. The pilot will be looking for a body set apart from the rest. It could be moving, or if Ethan's hurt, if he's fallen and unable to get himself some help, he'll be stationary. If the pilot's not sure of what he's seeing, he'll make contact with the head of S&R."

"Search and rescue," the detective explains before I can ask.

I watch the rain splatter the leaves for a moment, trying to take some calming breaths, but the panic won't settle. Ethan will be so cold. So scared.

The sheriff steps to the door. "There's coffee and a long list of questions inside. Now, if you don't mind—"

"You have to find him. You *have* to. My life doesn't work without him." My son's life is in the hands of complete strangers, and I need these two to hear me. To understand the importance of what is at stake.

But they don't respond, and their silence ignites my panic, a stockpile of flammable fuel.

"Please. I'm begging you. Ethan is my everything." For a moment I can't speak, but my next words are too big, too important to leave out. "Please find him."

"Then come on." The sheriff pulls open the door with a creak. "Let's get to work."

KAT

5 hours, 7 minutes missing

I STARE ACROSS THE CAVERNOUS DINING HALL at a whiteboard someone has set up in a corner, my son's name in big red caps across the top. Underneath, a list of descriptors is scrawled in blue and green marker. Words like *brown curls* and *slight build* and *red and black pajamas* and my skin goes cold. Rain beats against the corrugated metal roof above our heads, echoing through the space with a deafening, tinny ring, but all I can hear is the sound of my own terror churning in my ears.

I should have never let him come. Yesterday at school, I should have hauled Ethan off that bus, called in sick to work and spent the day with him at home. I remember watching him scramble up the bus steps and disappear behind the smoky glass, the sudden catch in my chest, that tiny tug of panic I tried to ignore. By the time I swallowed it down, the bus was pulling away. Ethan was already gone.

"Ms. Jenkins?"

My gaze lingers on Ethan's latest school picture, which someone has scrounged up from God knows where and taped to the dark window. I remember not loving it when he brought it home—too stiff and posed and expensive, the studio prices far beyond my budget. But now I pick up every detail: the corkscrew curls a confused whirlwind around his face; the kink in the collar of his shirt because I didn't have time to iron it; the dark smudge of a dent, an almost dimple on his smiling left cheek. I want to rip the picture off the wall and press it to my chest. I want to call up the studio and order every single copy.

"Ms. Jenkins, we're in a time cr—"

I pivot around, the fury that's been growing in me like a tumor erupting in a voice that is not my own. "Where's Miss Emma?"

The sheriff and detective raise matching brows at my tone, but neither of them answer. Their clothes drip matching puddles onto the rickety floorboards.

"His teacher. Where is she?"

My hatred for that woman is a hot, pulsing thing inside my chest, shocking me with its sudden intensity. I want to slap her, to tear at her shiny hair, to scream at her until this rickety building shakes on its cinder block foundation. I want her to look me in the eye and tell me how she let this happen to my son.

The sheriff moves to one of the picnic tables, grabs a towel from a pile, tosses it to the detective and takes another for himself. "I know you want to cast blame," he says, his face disappearing behind the scratchy material, "and believe me, so do we. But first things first. Let's focus on finding your son. We can sort out all the finger-pointing later."

"I deserve answers."

He whips the towel over a shoulder. "And you'll get them, but right now we're wasting daylight. Sun's been up for over an hour." He drops onto a bench and hollers into the empty room, "Dawn, you in here?"

A ponytailed woman in a Lumpkin County Sheriff's Office T-shirt leans her torso around the corner of the industrial kitchen that runs along the entire back side of the building, separated from the rest by a low wall and a metal prep table. "Just making a fresh pot of coffee, sir, and then I'll be right in." Her gaze catches mine, and she gives me a warm smile, then disappears back behind the wall.

Detective Macintosh nudges me toward the table, and we sit.

"Now," the sheriff says once we're settled. "We've moved the kids and chaperones over to the Days Inn on Chestatee for questioning. The last thing we need at this camp is a bunch of scared and hyped-up eight-year-olds. The woods are already a ragbag of scents from when they were out there earlier. Some kind of scavenger hunt, apparently, which is part of what's holding up the dogs."

"Is the scent holding?" I say.

"Let's just put it this way. I'd do cartwheels down the center of this room if someone told me the rain stopped an hour ago." He points a finger up at the metal roof, still being hammered by a loud and determined downpour. My heart sinks at the sound.

The sheriff searches through the pile of papers on the table, maps and printouts and scribbled notes scattered across the wooden surface like a tornado dropped them there. They're held down with a couple of soggy towels and a handful of foam cups, the rims chewed and stained with what smells like burned coffee. Nobody seems bothered by the chaos, but I am. What kind of operation is this?

Finally, he locates a yellow legal pad, then flips to a fresh page. "All righty. Let's start with any personal identification marks Ethan might have. Birthmarks or scars. Something that's unique to your son."

I touch a finger to my right temple, just under the hairline. "He has a scar on his forehead, right about here, and a birthmark on his left thigh. It looks like two overlapping nickels."

"What about medical conditions?"

"He's allergic to peanuts. He carries an EpiPen."

The sheriff's pen freezes on the notepad, and he and the detective exchange a look. "How allergic?"

"That depends on how much he eats. Trace amounts typically only result in hives and wheezing, but a spoonful of peanut butter could kill him. He's had the allergy all his life. He's well aware of what he can and can't eat, and he knows how to use his EpiPen."

Sheriff Childers curses under his breath. "Dawn," he barks so sharply that I startle. "Get his teacher on the line. I want to know why this is the first time we've heard of this allergy. And reconfirm there were no pens found among the kids' stuff. I want to be one hundred percent certain that Ethan's is still in his backpack."

Her voice calls out from the kitchen. "On it."

The sheriff makes a scribble on his notepad, then turns back to me. "Does Ethan know how to swim?"

A new terror seizes my heart, squeezing it to a standstill. Ethan can swim, but he doesn't like to go where he can't touch the bottom, and he has the tendency to panic. I think about the pond we passed on the drive up, the way the raindrops shimmered on the smooth, dark surface, and I feel sick.

Sheriff Childers must read the answer on my face, because he writes NOT A SWIMMER in big block letters across the top of the page. "What about sleepwalking? Does he ever get confused in the middle of the night, start wandering around the house?"

"No. Never." My gaze bounces between the sheriff and Detective Macintosh seated on the bench beside me, and I remember his advice in the car. To share every detail I can think of about my son. To question every fact presented to me. "How did Ethan get out of the cabin? Wouldn't somebody have heard him? Wouldn't the chaperones have been guarding the door?"

Suddenly, it occurs to me that these are the kinds of questions a good mother would have asked prior to signing the permission form. *Who's manning the exits? What are the safety precautions? How do you know—absolutely know with 100 percent certainty—that my child won't disappear in the middle of the night?*

"There was a fire," the sheriff announces, and my heart gives a hard kick. I have so many questions I don't know where to start. I open my mouth, but the sheriff waves me off with both hands. "I know, I know, but let me just get through this, and then I'll answer every question you've got. Like I was saying, there was a fire just outside the cabin. Not a big one, but big enough to wake up some of the kids. The father chaperone—" the sheriff checks his notes, flipping back a few pages for the name "—Avery Fischer ran back to the offices for assistance while Ms. Quinn rounded up the kids. She conducted an initial head count at that time, and the numbers checked out. Every child was accounted for. Once Mr. Fischer returned and the fire was put out, she did another one, and this time she came up one child short. Ethan was gone."

The only thing I know about Avery is that he runs the school's capital campaign, one he's called me for a number of times, even though my answer is always the same. If he's as dogged with his chaperone duties as he is with funding the

front office renovations and Promethean boards in every classroom, I have no idea. What kind of mother doesn't know the
people responsible for watching her child?

The detective is the first to jump in. "Was the fire inten-
tional?"

"Yes. Whoever set it used an accelerant. An arson investiga-
tor is already on the way, but she's coming from Chattanooga
so we've got another hour before she gets here."

"And the teacher remembers seeing Ethan at the first head
count?"

"Negative," the sheriff says, and I force myself to focus on
his words, and not the way his eyes are tight and strained.
"She remembers counting eighteen bodies, but according to
her last statement, she can't one hundred percent guarantee
that one of those belonged to Ethan."

I shake my head, trying to clear the cobwebs, but I still don't
understand. "Who else could it have belonged to? Surely she
wouldn't have counted another kid twice. And what about the
other kids? Doesn't anybody remember seeing him?"

"Some do, some don't. It was dark and the kids were in a
tizzy. The chaperones, too. We're still in the process of questioning everybody, but most of our witnesses are children operating on a few hours' sleep. That all goes to say this is taking
more time than I'd like it to."

"What about tracks?" the detective asks. "Any indication
which way they went?"

The sheriff grimaces. "The rain started coming down
shortly after the fire, which is part of what helped put it out.
Any tracks were washed out."

"But he has a compass." I slap my palms to the table and lean
in. "If he has his backpack, it'll be in it and he knows how to
use it. He'll be able to navigate his way to safety."

For the longest time, no one speaks. No one quite looks at me, either.

The sheriff shifts on the bench, restless and uncomfortable. "Ms. Jenkins, I know it's not what you want to hear, but in all likelihood, the compass is not going to help your son. Now, it's still possible that Ethan wandered off in the confusion of the fire, but it's not looking that way. Every indication points to his having some help."

The sheriff's words fall into the room like a bomb, and the ugly fear that's been creeping through my veins grows and pulses with heat, clawing at my consciousness. I think about the helicopters swooping over the trees, searching between the branches for one, maybe two glowing bodies, and I feel unsettled, panicky.

"Has somebody called Andrew?"

This gets everybody's attention. The sheriff cocks a brow, and he grows an inch or two on the bench. "I assume you're referring to your husband."

"Ex-husband. Has somebody talked to him?"

The sheriff shakes his head. "So far, we've been unable to reach him."

"Well, send somebody by," I yell. "Tell them to pound on his door until he opens it."

"We've done that, just like we did with you. So far, nobody's answered."

I flip through the logical explanations in my mind. It's still early. Andrew is not a morning person. He'll have his phone ringers off and his noise machine on. There's no waking him once he's out.

But still. The suspicions sneak in like smoke, silent and deadly.

"But why?" The question is as much for me as for anyone here. "Andrew *loves* Ethan."

The sheriff hikes a shoulder. "When people are desperate enough, they'll do all sorts of things they wouldn't do otherwise."

"How is Andrew desperate? He's paying me bare-bones alimony and stretching out the divorce just long enough to hide all his assets." I turn to the detective. "You saw where I live. If anybody is desperate here, it's me. And before you start accusing me of having something to do with Ethan's disappearance again, I was at home asleep."

"I wasn't accusing you. I was questioning you, and I'm not going to apologize for it. Like I told you in the car, we're looking at every possible scenario. That includes close family, starting with the parents."

Of course, they are looking at Andrew. If I'm a scenario, then so is a soon-to-be ex-husband with an arrest record.

I shake my head, speechless. No matter what Andrew thinks of me, he adores his son. He'd never do anything to hurt him... Would he?

The sheriff reads my expression. "Parental kidnappings aren't all that uncommon, unfortunately, especially when the parents are estranged, which I understand you and Andrew are."

"We're estranged, but he and Ethan aren't. Andrew can see Ethan anytime he wants."

"According to a court order filed with the DeKalb County clerk, Andrew's visitation is every other weekend."

"Yes, but that was what the judge decided. Not me. When I told him I wanted a divorce, I promised Andrew we would share custody fifty-fifty. This arrangement is only temporary. And why go to all the trouble to kidnap him here? Why wouldn't he just… I don't know, not bring Ethan home one Sunday night? I mean, it's not like he doesn't have plenty of other opportunity."

"I don't know, but like the detective said, we're looking at every scenario. Including the possibility your son might be lost out there in the woods, or that he's with someone unrelated. We also have to consider that it might have been a stranger."

"What kind of stranger kidnaps an eight-year-old little boy?"

The sheriff doesn't respond, but I hear the answer in his silence.

A predator.

A psychopath.

A monster.

I dig my phone from my pocket with shaking hands, pull up Andrew's number on the screen. Screw the restraining order. No, screw *him* if he's done what I think he has. The phone rings once, twice, three times. It flips me to a recording, Andrew's slightly nasal voice asking me to leave a message. I call him four more times, each time with no response. The same happens with his home line.

The sheriff reads the answer on my face. "Keep trying. We will, too. In the meantime—"

The walkie-talkie on the sheriff's hip crackles to life, a deep voice spouting something in fits and starts. I squeeze my eyes and strain to make out the words, but I don't catch them all. The dogs caught a trail. They tracked it a mile and a half to the northwest. Something about a mountain.

"God*dammit*." The sheriff slams a fist to the table, rattling my frayed nerves and toppling one of the cups. A brown liquid, the remnants of someone's forgotten coffee, creeps across the papers like sludge.

He heaves himself to his full height and hustles off.

"What?" I call out, but he doesn't slow. Two seconds later, he's out the door.

"The dogs are confused," the detective says. "They're all over the place. Running around the woods then back to the camp, basically heading in opposite directions. One of them caught a scent, but it dried up at a place called Black Mountain." He shuffles through the papers until he finds a map, then spreads it across the table. His fingertips fly over a sea of green to the north of Dahlonega, decorated with swaths of black squiggles—the Chattahoochee National Forest.

I clamp on to the edge of the bench, my knuckles going white with fear, with hope. If the dogs caught his trail once, if they tracked him up a hill, then surely they can track him down the other side.

Dawn rushes back in the room, and her expression punches a bright red panic button in my chest. She heard the update, too. "Black Mountain's not a place," she says, and she looks sick. Physically ill, and now, so am I. "It's a road."

Detective Macintosh's hands freeze on the paper, and he looks at me with a compassion that clamps around my heart like a vise.

The realization, one I've been battling since the detective showed up at my door, dawns in brilliant, horrifying color.

Ethan is not out there, wandering the woods or huddled from the rain under a tree. He's in somebody's *car*.

But with whom? Going where? I think about all those movies and TV shows featuring children shoved into a trunk or the back of a van, then push the images away. Those stories never end well, the real-life statistics too grim. What is it all those advocacy groups say in their warnings? Scream, kick, fight, but whatever you do, do not get in that car. Because the minute that door is slammed with you on the inside, it's too late. Statistics say you're already dead.

A vibration starts up somewhere in the very core of me, somewhere deep and primitive. It rattles my bones and throbs in my veins, pushing outward in quakes as violent as a seizure. My mouth fills with bile and a scream, but my frozen lungs can't push it out. It echoes, loud and horror-movie wild, through my head.

Dawn sinks onto the bench beside me, wrapping a hand around mine. "I know it's scary, but this development changes things."

I look at her. Shake my head.

She nods hers. "We will be doubling down now, expanding the roadblocks and the canvassing area. We were already going door-to-door at every home within a five-mile radius of the camp property line, but now we'll concentrate on the homes and trailers on Black Mountain Road. Hopefully, one of them saw something and can give us a description of the car."

Her words electrocute my heart, sending it into a panicked dance. "Oh my God. Oh my *God*." I press my free hand to my mouth and try not to throw up.

"I need you to start thinking of the people you know both a little and a lot, okay? People you run into during a normal day. People who might be looking for more time with Ethan. The vast majority of children are taken by someone who knows them somehow." She pauses, and I know from her expression, from the way her mouth straightens out and tightens, what's coming next. "I need you to tell me about Andrew."

Her words make me dizzy. My soon-to-be ex-husband. The man who once told me he would love me forever. Who brought me lunch at work and flowers just because. Who even in our worst moments could always make me laugh.

And now these people are suggesting he might be behind this? I'm as repulsed by the idea as I am tempted to believe it. At least if Ethan were with Andrew, he'd be safe. Andrew wouldn't hurt him.

But pushing up through all the chatter are two questions I can't escape, no matter how hard I try to smother them.

Where is Andrew?

Why isn't he answering his door?

STEF

5 hours, 13 minutes missing

I PAUSE ON THE TOP STEP, LISTENING TO THE voices drifting across the foyer downstairs, trying to identify them. My husband's, deep and powerful. A male voice I don't recognize. A softer, higher tone that can only belong to a female.

I turn around and head back up.

People who don't know me, those who see me trailing Sam around town to openings and fancy fund-raisers, assume that Sam chose me because I'm arm candy. A pretty little wife selected for her sample-sized figure and red-carpet smile, curated with the sole purpose of elevating the mayor's standing. I'm supposed to cheer him on, champion his causes, boost his popularity, hike up his poll numbers.

Yes, I look good on his arm, but most people don't know I once had dreams and plans that had nothing to do with Sam. A master's in Art History from Columbia, a love of all things French, a holy grail goal of one day working at the Louvre. People don't know this about me because they don't ask, and sometimes, I get so caught up in this life as the mayor's wife that I forget it myself. Dreams don't die as much as they fade into the background.

Sam and I met at the tail end of grad school, when I was here for a monthlong internship at the High Museum. My mother had just moved to town, and I was staying with her, sleeping on her pullout couch and pounding away at my thesis, the visual hagiography of St. Margaret of Antioch in thirteenth-century stained glass. I was biding my time here, a quick pit stop on my road to Paris.

And then I met Sam.

It happened at a Falcons game, where my father had dragged me to a VIP suite high above the field. Dad was a busy, busy man. If he could knock out a business deal while also celebrating his daughter's thirtieth year on the planet, the night was a win-win for everybody—except me.

Just after halftime, I felt someone sink into the seat behind me.

"It'd sure be nice if the D could get some stops during garbage time instead of letting the other team run their asses ragged." He leaned forward in the plush chair, pointing over my shoulder with his long arm. "We thought we had a blowout on our hands, see, so the Falcons sent in the second-string team. But being too cocky is never a good thing. Makes you sloppy. The defense is paying for it now."

My answer was an uninterested hum. I'm not a football fan, have never understood the appeal of grown men fighting over a piece of leather and air.

He didn't take the hint. He reached his arm around to offer a hand. "Sam Huntington."

I hadn't been in Atlanta long, but even I knew who Sam Huntington was. Old Atlanta royalty and rising political star, the youngest deputy attorney general ever appointed in Atlanta, a city that bore his last name on more than one street sign. Sam's great-great-grandfather thought Atlanta might be a good spot for a railway terminus, and the long line of Huntingtons have been profiting from his vision ever since.

But there was his hand and I had no other choice but to shake it. He had a warm, firm grip. A politician's grip. The grip of a guy who would go far.

"Stefanie Lawrence."

"Nice to meet you, Stefanie Lawrence. I take it you're not a fan."

"I couldn't care less about football," I said, turning back to the field.

"I meant of me." I looked at him in surprise, and he grinned. "Reading people is my superpower. A necessary one in my line of work, but still. People tell me I'm pretty good at it. Right now, it's telling me you wish I'd go away so you can finish pretending to watch the game." He reclined in his chair, sweeping an arm over the back of the empty seat next to him. "So? How'd I do?"

I couldn't help but smile. "Who's cocky now?"

Sam laughed.

"And for the record, I'm not *not* a fan. I'm just…I don't know, trying to make it through the game, I guess."

"Still. I'd prefer you were a fan."

"Surely you don't need another." My tone was teasing but firm. Looks and money and the Huntington name—of course I could see the appeal. But the combination was too heady, too dangerous for someone on her way out of town. With a polite smile, I turned back to the game.

"All right, fine. I can take a hint. I'll leave you alone, but only if you tell me something about you." He leaned far forward, his head coming flush to mine. "I don't care what."

I gave him a sidelong look. "One thing?"

He lifted a single finger. "Just one. And then I'll clear out, I promise."

I could have told him about the discovery I'd uncovered in my research, that the depictions of Margaret in the cathedral of Chartres were tailored to each window's location in the church and the surrounding imagery. I could have told him I missed my friends, my Manhattan apartment, that sidewalk café on Columbus Avenue where they make the most perfect macchiato. What came out surprised even me: "Today's my birthday."

Sam looked disappointed. "I guess I should have qualified that with the word *truth*. Tell me something about you that's true."

"It is true." His frown didn't clear, so I added, "Do you want to see my driver's license?"

"Why would you spend your birthday watching a sport you just told me you hated?"

"I do hate it. My father, however " I pointed over his shoulder, to where my father was talking to a man so tall he could only have been a basketball player "—does not."

Sam smiled, but the gesture looked a little sad. "Well, now, that is a goddamn shame." He unfolded his long body from the chair, leaning in to whisper in my ear, "Happy birthday, Steffi. I hope you get everything you could ever wish for."

The tears were pretty much instant, though I didn't let Sam see. At the time, I blamed them on homesickness and hormones and hearing the sound of my nickname in a strange city, rolling off a stranger's tongue, but the truth was, it had been a shitty birthday. My best friends were thousands of miles away. My mother was pissed I was spending the day with my father, whom I rarely saw and who had flown in for the occasion. My father had brought me to the last place on earth I wanted to be, and was now too busy schmoozing the bigwigs to pay me much attention. So far that day, neither of my parents had wished me a happy birthday. Sam's words hit me like an unexpected gift.

He surprised me again two days later, when he showed up at the High with a slice of cake and two forks. He lit the birthday candle with a silver lighter that looked like it belonged in the case of antiquities on the museum's bottom floor. Our first kiss tasted of sugar and vanilla.

Sam was easy to fall in love with. I did it that very day.

Muffled voices make their way up the stairs, prodding me across the bedroom to the closet, where I peel off my T-shirt and slip into a silky tank. I pull a pair of hot-pink pumps from the shelf, step into them one by one. At the bathroom mirror, I take down my ponytail, run my fingers through my hair, dab on some under-eye concealer and lip gloss. When measuring yourself against anyone, even if it's only your former self, high heels and makeup always help.

I find Sam seated behind the Italian desk in his study downstairs, a masterpiece of walnut and smoky glass. This room is Sam's domain, with modern furniture and leather wall paneling and burgundy velvet curtains that pool like blood on the black oak floor. All dark and sleek and masculine like him, all but the silver bowl on the corner of his desk, which I filled with gardenias from the backyard. They scent the air with a sweet perfume that sticks out like an escort in a boardroom.

Across from Sam, in one of the matching blue swivel chairs, sits Brittany, his director of communications. A police officer stands to her left.

None of them look happy.

"What's wrong?" I say from the doorway.

Brittany twists in her chair, giving me a perfunctory smile. "Good morning, Mrs. Huntington. Sorry to disturb so early on a Saturday."

For some reason I can't quite explain, her formal greeting makes me hate her just a little. Maybe it's because she's still clinging to her twenties, and the further I get from that decade, the more I resent girls as pretty and smart as Brittany. The entire world is her oyster—what is she thinking, wasting her youth here in Atlanta?

Sam gestures across the desk to the empty chair next to Brittany. "Come sit down."

Something about the way he says it makes my heart beat faster, and not in a good way. I glance at the cop, then Brittany, whose all-business expression doesn't match her outfit. Salmon-colored shirt; purple running shorts; long, bare legs with just the right amount of muscle. This was supposed to be her day off, too, and she looks like she came straight from the gym.

I move to the chair, but I don't sink into it. "Just tell me. What's going on?"

"One of the kids from Sammy's class went missing last night," Sam says. "A little boy named Ethan Maddox. The police are working on the assumption he was taken."

My eyes go wide, and I press a hand to my stomach. Poor Ethan. Poor Ethan's *parents*. "Taken as in kidnapped?"

Sam defers to the police officer, who nods.

My legs give out, and I fall into the chair. "Oh my God. Do they have any idea who?"

I have an idea who: Ethan's wife-beater felon father. I've heard the schoolyard rumors about their divorce, have watched the video some eyewitness uploaded to YouTube. Any man capable of assaulting his wife in a CVS parking lot in broad daylight, with dozens of iPhones pointed at his face capturing every blow in full-color, high-definition, is capable of kidnapping his own child.

"The Lumpkin County Sheriff's team is looking at a number of possibilities," the officer says carefully. "Folks connected to the school, to the child's family, as well as any locals listed on the offender registries."

My gaze zips to Sam, whose expression turns to stone. He's thinking the same thing I am: a sexual predator lurking at the edge of the camp, surveying the kids like a starving man at a farmer's market, selecting the ripest fruit. It could have been any kid. It could have been Sammy.

I am suddenly thinking about where I left my car keys. Thinking about navigating morning traffic to hightail it to Dahlonega. I am desperate to see my child.

"Call Josh," Sam says to Brittany. "I know he's visiting his sister but haul his ass back up to the city. I need his input on how we can best respond to this. The school hasn't finished alerting the parents yet, and we've got to be careful how we approach things. We don't want to incite panic or step on the sheriff's toes, but I want to have a statement ready as soon as he gives us the go."

Brittany swivels back and forth in her chair. "I've left Josh like a hundred messages already. Apparently, they don't have reception wherever his sister lives."

Probably not far from the truth. I don't remember the name of the town, but Josh's sister lives in the backwoods of southern Georgia, a tiny blip on a bright red map. No streetlights, no Walmart, just a couple of neighbors sitting on lawn chairs, waving Confederate flags.

"Keep trying, will you?" Sam says. "In the meantime, let's you and I put our heads together and come up with a plan."

She slides a laptop from the bag at her feet and begins clacking away. The police officer stands pressed against the bookshelves, his hat clutched in his hands, awaiting orders.

Sam turns to me with a pained look, and I stop him with a shake of my head. An Atlanta child is missing. There's no need to apologize.

I turn to the police officer and Brittany. "How do you two take your coffee?"

The last thing Sam needs to worry about is me.

KAT

5 hours, 24 minutes missing

EVER SINCE THE DOGS SCREECHED TO A STOP at Black Mountain Road, the game plan has changed, something that becomes clear when the dining hall fills with rain-soaked bodies, shouting orders with a new sense of urgency. They see me and avert their eyes, a sign of respect that hits me like a cold, hard slap. Dawn notices and hauls me out of there, guiding me outside to a cabin across the clearing. She parks me on a tiny two-seater couch.

"Why don't I make us some tea?" she says. "I don't know about you, but I could use a little warming up."

It's then I notice that my teeth are chattering. I bite down hard until the noise stops. "Tea would be great, thank you."

The cabin is dark and tiny, a square space with a round table, a musty-smelling couch and the most basic of kitchenettes lining the back wall. The glass of the lone window is filthy, coated with cobwebs and crud and framed with two strips of faded floral fabric. The air in here is just as cold as outside, just as damp, and I shiver.

Dawn flicks on the electric teapot, then settles on the couch next to me. Her eyes are kind.

"We've told you why we are taking a good, close look at Andrew. Why don't you start by telling me why you think we're mistaken."

Her question surprises me more than a little. From the second the detective showed up at my door, I've been trying to talk myself out of the possibility Andrew would have anything to do with this, and my denial hasn't gone unnoticed. Do I think they're mistaken? Maybe, but I also never thought Andrew would hurt me like he did, either.

"I suppose you know what he did." I can barely push out the words. My mouth is a desert, my tongue sandpaper against my teeth.

"I've read the police reports, yes." The kettle turns off with a sharp click, the water bubbling into a rolling boil. Dawn pushes up from the couch. "But I'd really like to hear it from you."

I hesitate, trying to summon the strength to rehash all that ugly drama. The thing is, I've spent a good part of the past half year trying to *not* think of Andrew, and I still cringe whenever his name tunnels unintentionally across my consciousness. The way we broke apart was messy and painful, and I'm still fighting to find forgiveness—for him and for myself, for the way Ethan has unwittingly ended up in the middle.

"Things had been bad between us for a while," I begin, my breaths coming fast and hard, like I just jogged up three flights of stairs. "At least a year, maybe more. He was drinking too much. He was under all sorts of stress at work, and he took it out on me and Ethan. When Andrew attacked me at the CVS, I had just filed for divorce."

I don't bother cataloging my injuries—a black eye, two

broken fingers, a bloody scalp from where he ripped out big chunks of hair—or the way Good Samaritans pulled him off me, a couple of tourists in town for a Falcons game. They told the cops he'd threatened to kill me. As a police officer, Dawn would know all this, as well as the way he took off before the police could get there. They arrested him the next day at work, marching him in handcuffs past his staff, the office security guards and dozens of wide-eyed witnesses.

"Sounds like a pretty ballsy guy." She hands me one of the mugs and sinks with hers back onto the couch, watching me with clear blue eyes.

"No, just the opposite, actually. I saw his face when those men pulled him off me, and Andrew was just as surprised as I was. Surprised and humiliated. I'm sure he regretted it immediately."

Actually, I'm positive Andrew regrets the aftermath the most. Gossip has a way of dancing around, and Andrew lost clients and friends because of what he did. He tarnished his precious reputation. He lost every last bargaining chip he could have cashed in for the divorce. Proof in point: when the judge heard about the attack, when he saw all but the tips of my right-hand fingers confined to a hot-pink cast, he granted me temporary full custody without question.

Dawn reaches for a legal pad on the table and digs a pen out of her bag on the floor. "Still. Andrew lost control."

"With me. Only ever with me. Never with Ethan."

"Prior to the attack at CVS, had Andrew ever hurt you physically?"

A familiar sick rises in my throat, because what do I say? Yes, but never enough to leave a mark? That I slapped and shoved him right back? There was that time when he grabbed my arm too hard or when he shoved me into the fireplace or when he held me down on the bathroom floor, but none of his outbursts hurt me *that* much, and they always ended in a more loving, considerate Andrew. They call it a cycle for a reason.

"Yes. Never at that level, but yes. I knew it was abuse."

"Did you ever threaten or attempt to leave?"

Even now, six months later, the question still hits me as judgment, and it reminds me of some of my former girlfriends, loose-tongued women who cloaked their questions about the attack under a mask of compassion. Dawn might as well have said *if you knew it was abuse, why didn't you just leave?* My former friends certainly did. Everyone but Lucas and Izzy.

"It's not that easy. We had a child together, one I gave up my job to stay home and care for. I didn't have any money, no family to depend on or move in with. I knew exactly how difficult leaving would be, and that Andrew would never let me walk out of there with half of anything, especially Ethan. I'm not looking for sympathy. I'm only trying to explain why I didn't bring it up, not even once."

"Not until he attacked you in broad daylight."

I lift a shoulder. "As awful as that was, at least it put me in a position of power. Everybody, including the judge, knew what he did."

"So far I haven't heard any reason to think he wouldn't be capable of taking Ethan."

She says it with a soft smile, which does nothing to soften her words. No woman wants to think the man she once loved—the father of her only child—capable of such evil.

"Okay, then how about this—because he loves Ethan."

"Maybe Andrew wants more time with his son than a few hours every other weekend."

I throw up a hand in frustration. "Then why not just keep him one Sunday night? Why come all the way here to do it?"

I've already had this conversation today, and the more I have it, the harder it is to talk myself out of my suspicions.

Dawn's answer gets cut off by the unmistakable *thud-thud-thud* of helicopters—more than one—swooping over the camp, shaking the air and rattling the cabin's wooden walls.

"Why are you trying to talk me into this?" I say once the sound fades. I feel jittery, keyed up, like I have to restrain myself from jumping off this couch and running out there to join them in the search for my son. Every second we sit here, yammering on about Andrew, is another second Ethan is not found. "Andrew would not try to steal his own son."

"Have you considered the possibility that Ethan's disappearance could have nothing do with your son..." She pauses, and that ever-pleasant half smile she'd been wearing disappears. "And everything to do with you?"

My skin goes cold, a chill snaking down my spine. "With me, how?"

"Let me put it this way. If Andrew were angry and hurt and looking for revenge, what do you think he would do? What would he see as your one biggest weakness?"

And just like that, I'm a believer. My one biggest weakness is Ethan.

KAT

5 hours, 57 minutes missing

OUTSIDE THE CABIN, A BIG BODY IN WORK boots comes clomping up the stairs with a gait I'd recognize anywhere. Dawn looks up expectantly, but I pop off the couch, lurch to the door and yank it open, right as Lucas raises a fist.

He looks like hell. His skin is pale. His shirt is untucked. He needs a haircut and a shave. Under the frayed orange rim of his ancient University of Tennessee baseball cap, his hazel eyes are crinkled with strain.

But he's here and I fall into him, even though Lucas is the kind of guy who'd sooner put me in a headlock than a hug, and I'd sooner punch him in his stomach than throw my arms around his waist. As unaccustomed as I am to this embrace, I'm awfully glad for it. I press my face into his chest and fall apart.

"You gotta stay strong, Kitty Kat." A nickname I haven't heard from him since my high school days. He drapes a big palm on the back of my head. "For Ethan. You have to stay strong for him."

I tip my head back, look up at Lucas through my tears. His face may have a few more wrinkles, his once-thick hair thinned out on top, but for me he'll always be that solemn-faced man-boy who lived across the street, the one who took me in after my mother's death made me an orphan at sixteen. "You would get eaten alive by foster care," he said to me then, and Lucas would know. He spent more than a decade in the system, and to this day, the only thing he'll tell me about it is that it was no place for a girl like me.

"I am. I will be. I'm just so glad you're here."

"Yeah, well, those two cops down at the turnoff didn't make it easy on me. It would have saved me some trouble if you'd told them I was coming."

I don't ask how he got by, mostly because I don't care. All that matters is he's here.

He untangles us, heaves a battered duffel from the porch floor and walks me backward until we're both inside the cabin. Behind him, the rain has stopped. A hazy mist rises up from the woods, smoky puffs that hang suspended in the air like ghosts.

While I mop up my face with a paper towel, Lucas introduces himself to Dawn. Like pretty much every other red-blooded female on the planet, she eyes him with interest. "Dawn Whittaker," she says, shaking his hand.

I toss the towel in the trash and point to the duffel in Lucas's fist. "What's that?"

That is no overnight bag. It's a bag big enough to carry every pair of jeans, T-shirt and sweater in Lucas's very meager wardrobe, but a clinking of metal on metal sounds from inside the canvas. He drops it on the floor, where it lands like a chunk of concrete.

"My tracking gear. GPS. Night goggles. That kind of stuff." Lucas pulls out a chair, flips it around and sits on it backward, his big body facing me. "What's the word? You never texted."

I fall onto the couch while Dawn spouts off acronyms I only vaguely recognize and will never be able to remember: NCIC and BOLO and GBI. She gives him a quick rundown of everything we've learned until now, which is frustratingly little. That there was a fire just outside the cabin while everyone was sleeping. That Ethan disappeared somewhere between the rush outside and the chaperone putting out the fire. That the dogs had some trouble catching his scent at first, until one of them led searchers a mile and a half through the woods, where it dried up at a road. Lucas's reaction to the last one makes me grip the table tighter.

"Sounds like a trap," he says, and Dawn doesn't argue. She thinks it sounds like a trap, too, and honestly, who wouldn't?

I turn back to Lucas. "They think it might have been Andrew."

He frowns, but he doesn't look particularly surprised. "Of course they suspect Andrew. Don't you ever watch *Law & Order?* It's always the parent." He turns to Dawn. "Did you call him? Did you send somebody to bust down his door?"

"Yes to the first, but we can't do the second without a warrant, which the Atlanta PD is working on. By now they've knocked on his door often and loud enough to wake the neighbors on either side. It looks like nobody's at home."

He curses.

Dawn examines him carefully, her pen stilled. "It doesn't seem like I need to ask whether or not you think Andrew would be capable of kidnapping his own son."

"Hell yeah, I think he would. He's smart, he's sneaky and don't even get me started on that man's mental state."

That Man. The Wife Beater. Captain Douchebag. Just a few of the nicknames Lucas has coined for my soon-to-be ex so he would never have to say Andrew's name again.

But Lucas is right about one thing: don't get him started on Andrew. Lucas is the kind of man who makes a decent living off sweat and elbow grease. Who values pulling your own weight, making an honest buck and taking care of your own. God. Country. Family. Maybe he could have respected Andrew if he'd built his company from the ground up instead of using a significant chunk of his parents' life insurance settlement. The other half he sank into our six-bedroom home on a half-acre lot in Dunwoody, where he now lives alone. Lucas has never been shy with his opinions, and he's always had a long list of reasons I should have never married Andrew: too self-important, too focused on the material, too headstrong and controlling. Later, after his drinking had become a problem, he was too quick-tempered and unpredictable. By the time I saw what Lucas did in Andrew, it was too late. We already had Ethan.

But the last thing I need right now is to rehash yet another *I told you so.* "So now what?"

Dawn pushes up from the couch. "Now I need to do a quick check-in with Sheriff and the team over at the dining hall. In the meantime, I want you to start making those lists we talked about. Places Ethan goes on a regular basis, people he knows and interacts with, websites he visits and people he talks to. I want the names of every adult Ethan has come into contact with in the past year. People he knows well. People he knows not so well. We want to take a look at anyone he might have formed an attachment to."

I know what she means.

She means anyone who might have formed an attachment to *him.*

She points to the legal pad balanced on the arm of the couch, where she scribbled a phone number across a fresh page. "That's my cell. If you need me, I can be back here in less than five minutes."

Lucas watches her shrug into her coat and collect her things, jaw clenched. Muscles and tendons twitch under the cotton of his T-shirt.

Dawn slips out the door, and he turns to me. "What do you need me to do?"

I don't hesitate. This is the reason I called him here, to bulldoze the woods and search for clues, to follow my baby's footsteps through the terrain. As much as I want him to stay here and comfort me, I *need* him to find Ethan. Never have I needed anything more.

"Find him, Lucas." I hold his gaze, and his eyes glisten with marching orders. "Go out there and find Ethan for me."

Lucas jumps up, swipes his duffel from the floor and disappears out the door.

As soon as Lucas is gone and I'm alone in the cabin, I try Andrew's numbers but get flipped to voice mail again. The sound of his voice after all these months scrapes across my nerves like a patch of stinging nettle.

At the beep, I take a deep breath.

"Andrew, this is Kat… I've been trying to reach you for hours now. Ethan's missing. If you had anything to do with it, if he's there with you right now, I'll do anything you want. I'll give you anything. I'll cancel the restraining order. I'll beg the judge to give you fifty percent custody. I'll take out a full-page ad in the *AJC* and tell everybody you never laid a hand on me if you want me to…" My throat threatens to funnel shut, but I force myself to shove the words over my tongue. "Just please. Don't take Ethan from me. I'm begging you. Please don't take my baby away."

I hang up just in time, right before a sob pushes up my throat and steals my voice. I toss the phone on the table, cover my face with my hands and let the tears come, the images flitting through my mind like a horror show. Ethan on the backseat of Andrew's Mercedes, wondering where they're going. Andrew laughing every time he sees my name pop up on his cell phone screen. Are the police tracking it? Are they watching the blips move farther and farther away on some computer screen? It's almost nine. They could be halfway to Mexico by now.

I jump out of my chair and begin pacing.

I think about what it would be like to never see Ethan's face again, to live the rest of my life not knowing, never finding answers. I think about Ethan, blindfolded and bawling, in the back of some unmarked van. His little body, mangled beyond recognition. My thoughts are wild things, chasing me around the tiny room.

"No." My voice is thin and reedy in the cabin, and I try it again, this time louder. *"No."* I can't do this to myself. I swipe the legal pad and pen from the couch and force myself to sit still long enough to make a list of names.

The first dozen or so come without much effort. Lucas. Izzy and two—no, three of her ex-boyfriends, none of them lasting more than a few months but long enough that Ethan remembers their names. Our old neighbor, Mrs. T, who still drops by on Christmas with hand-knit socks nobody ever wears. Andrew and our old friends, most of them people I haven't seen since the afternoon outside the CVS. Are they still in his life? Are there new friends I don't know about? I have no idea.

And what about my neighbors? I don't know their names, but I know I don't trust them. Ethan is not allowed to play in his own front yard without me there, a lioness watching her cub. Though why would any of them drive all the way here to steal the kid who lives across the street?

I make a list of places we go—school, the Publix down the street, the deli on the corner where Ethan once asked me why a homeless man was rummaging through the Dumpster. "Because he's hungry, I guess." Ethan gave the man his sandwich. Fresh tears prick my eyes, because that's the kind of child I have, one who is constantly reminding me there are people in the world who have it worse.

I think back to what Dawn told me earlier, about roadblocks and neighborhood canvasses and all those strings of letters that sounded straight out of a crime show. One pops miraculously in my mind: *BOLO*. Be on the lookout for. But did she mention where they were looking? Which direction? I wish I'd thought to take notes.

The questions beat an insistent drill in my skull. Where else are they looking? How many police officers are on the case? Has the media been alerted? What about an AMBER Alert? Are there other state and national alert systems for missing children? Are there others working to spread the word, too?

I flip to a clean page, start jotting down the questions before they can flit away. I've barely recorded one before the next one thrums its way into my consciousness. Before long, the paper is covered in blue ink and scribbles. I flip to the next sheet and keep going.

What about the teachers and chaperones? How certain are the police that they were where they said they were? Have they all been questioned, accounted for? What about the camp staff, the other kids? Surely somebody heard or saw something. Who's talking to them?

And then there are the more sweeping questions about missing children, morbid generalizations I can't help but consider. What are the statistics on the first few hours, the first few days? If we don't find him soon, what does that mean for the likelihood of finding him at all? At what point will Dawn sit me down and tell me to start preparing for the worst? After two days? After three days missing?

Before I know it, I'm crying again. I think about Ethan climbing onto the bus at school, my mind already flitting to my endless to-do list at work, and my stomach aches. I see myself standing on the sidewalk, waving up at the dark smudges behind the bus's tinted glass. I couldn't even tell if he was waving back, or for that matter, if it was even Ethan. I just picked out one shadowy lump and waved and waved and waved, because the sooner that bus left, the sooner I could race off to work.

The last time I saw Ethan, I didn't see him at all.

STEF

MY MOTHER ARRIVES AS I'M WORKING MY WAY
through the Cambridge staff directory, so far with zero success.
She barrels into the foyer, dumps her stuff, clasps my face in
both hands and kisses me on each cheek despite the cell phone
pressed to my ear. She smells of incense and Chanel perfume—
the scent of complicated nostalgia. Screaming and door slam-
ming, that's what I remember most from my childhood.

"Hi, Mom." I point to my cell, which has been bleating
an old Norah Jones song on repeat for the past six and a half
minutes. "I'm on hold with the school. I can't get anybody
on the line."

It's been almost two hours since Sam told me the news—
hours I've spent pacing the floor and waiting for the school
to call. I realize they're dealing with a crisis, but honestly, so
am I. My need to see Sammy, to know he's okay, sizzles like
electricity in my chest.

"You go right ahead, dear." Mom plucks a canvas shop-
ping bag off the floor and shoves it in my free arm. "I baked."

The scent hits me, nuts and butter and cinnamon, as does

the bigger picture. "You came all the way from Woodstock to bring me some banana bread?"

"You say that like Woodstock is halfway across the country or something."

Twenty-six point three miles, to be exact. Fifty-two minutes door-to-door. A distance you'd think would be too far for unexpected drop-ins, but you'd be wrong.

I take in the other bags behind her—a beat-up Michael Kors bag I gave her six Christmases ago and a black pleather duffel that looks suspiciously like an overnight bag. I want to ask what she's doing here, but I'm afraid I already know the answer.

The music stops, and I hold up a finger as a female voice comes down the line. "You've reached the voice mail of Nicolien Eckelboom, Lead Early Learning Teacher at Cambridge Classical Academy. I'm sorry I missed your call. Please—"

I hang up and hit Redial on the school's main number, waving Mom deeper into the house. The lights flip on as we pass, a combination of motion sensor and magic. Villa Eco is Sam's baby, a sleek and sustainable work of art constructed of 100 percent repurposed materials, with photovoltaic panels on the roof, solar tubes that light up the interior rooms, geothermal heat pumps and rainwater-collecting cisterns. Sam likes to think it was part of the reason he got elected—this living off the grid, practicing what he preaches when it comes to saving our planet—but he's kidding himself. Samuel Joseph Huntington IV has ridden the coattails of his baronial name his entire life.

"I've been getting a lot of conflicting information this morning," Mom says as we come into the kitchen, "and it all involves you."

A line plenty of people would pay good money to hear. Dr.

Melody King—Dr. Mel to her fans, a list that includes every last one of my girlfriends—normally charges $425 an hour for her party tricks. Now Mom's giving it unsolicited and for free.

I check the school directory, running my finger down the list for the next name. "I swear, it's like they ordered every staff member to not answer their phones or something." My finger lands on the extension for the head nurse. I punch in the number, but it goes straight to voice mail. I hit End and drop my cell on the counter with a clatter. "I think I should drive over there."

"To the school?"

I nod. "It's Friday. Every class but Ethan's will be in session."

"What for?" Mom shakes her head. "Nobody there has the answers you're looking for."

"So, what, you think I should go up to the camp? Sam told me not to, that I'd only be in the way. He said to wait for the school's call."

Mom empties a pocketful of rocks onto the marble counter. "Carnelian, agate, smoky quartz. These are all for physical protection, and this one." She taps a murky purple stone streaked with white. "This is a particularly strong amethyst. It's for protection during travel, though I'm also getting some information that feels like that boy is fixed to one spot."

"Did you bring some rocks that will tell you where he is?" I don't bother muzzling the sarcasm in my tone. Whatever window my mother thinks she has into the supernatural, I've never bought it.

Mom gives me one of her ever-patient smiles. "That's not the way it works, darling—you know this. I can't change what has happened or what is to come, only transmit the wisdom of what I receive. But the angels' chatter is confusing. The energy is conflicting. The spirits are telling me he's safe and in danger at the same time. It doesn't make any sense."

"Can you at least see where his energy is coming from?"

"Sweetheart, have I taught you nothing? I don't *see* his energy, I *feel* it. More specifically, I feel the distortions in his energy systems, and though I can do some healing of them from afar, I can't actually see his physical location. I'm getting only a vague sense of his thoughts and emotions, though they might provide clues."

"Such as?"

She closes her eyes, tilts her face up to the ceiling and the heavens beyond. "I'm sensing fear, of course, that's to be expected, and I think he might be cold because look." She shoves up her sleeves to reveal skin covered in chill bumps. "But I'm also getting boredom. Why would a kidnapped child be bored? Maybe the mix-up is coming from electromagnetic pollution. It can distort the energy sometimes, you know, if the sender is surrounded by things like antennas or wireless devices."

"So what you're saying is, the kidnapper is hiding out at a place with Wi-Fi. A Starbucks, maybe?"

She raises a brow. "You were always such a skeptic."

As was my father. As is my sister, Amelia. As is Sam. The only true believer in the family is Sammy. My mother would say it's because he is a natural empath, too, but I pray it's because he's eight and my mother is the only grandparent he has left. Mom's spiritual mumbo jumbo may have sold a shit-ton of books, but it doesn't exactly make for the most practical of role models.

Like now, for example. Mom pushes plates away and closes her eyes, balancing a crystal in the center of each skyward-facing palm. Her breaths come long and loud through her nose, hissing like waves washing onto shore. Her lips are moving, but her mouth isn't making a sound. A marching band could come through the kitchen and she wouldn't notice.

My gaze moves past her to the kitchen's plate glass window. After three days of rain and gloom, the sun is finally out. A ray hits on the vines looping up the trellis, and they explode into a sea of yellow and purple blooms like a Van Gogh painting, so bright it hurts my eyes. I close them against the color and picture Ethan, standing under the flowers. Same messy curls as Sammy, same scrawny build that barely makes it onto the doctor's growth chart. I'm not the only one who says the two could be brothers.

On the other side of the house, a door opens and a burst of voices tumbles into the hall. Sam and Brittany talking over each other, both of them on their phones. I spring off my chair and race through the dining room, heels clacking on the floor, hurrying to head them off in the foyer. I get there just in time. Brittany files past with a brisk nod, still talking, but Sam stops at the door. "Give me two minutes and I'll call you right back," he says into the phone, then hits End without waiting for a response.

Sometime in the past hour, he's gone upstairs to shower and change into his best navy suit. His shirt is crisp and white, hung with a red silk tie. He smells of coffee and aftershave, power and professionalism.

"What's the news?"

Sam slips the phone into his pocket. "Looks like whoever's responsible took him out of there in a car, which is basically the worst news possible." He winces, reconsidering. "Make that *second* worst news. Police are taking a good, hard look at the father."

"That's the first person I thought of, too. He has a history of violence."

"He's also not answering his phone or his door."

"What about the kids?" I say. "Are they on their way back?"

"Not until tonight, probably. The sheriff's team is taking them through another round of questioning. The school's working on a coherent message to the parents, and as soon as they have it, you'll be getting a call from them with pickup instructions." Sam glances out the open front door, to where Brittany is still on her phone, watching him from the circular driveway. She lifts a subtle brow, and he turns back to me. "I've got to go. Chief Phillips and I are making a joint statement as soon as I get down to the station."

"Go. Do what you need to do." I press up onto my toes and give him a kiss.

His steps are crisp and measured down the stone staircase to Brittany's waiting Lexus. She's already behind the wheel, the engine purring on the pavement, her face hidden behind the smoky glass. A man's muffled voice blares on the car speakers.

Sam stops halfway to the passenger's door. "If Josh shows up here, point him my way, will you? I still haven't gotten a hold of him."

I nod, then think of one more thing. "Oh, and Sam?"

He stops walking, but he's shifting on his feet, eager to get going.

"Call me as soon as there's news."

KAT

7 hours, 7 minutes missing

A BIRD'S DISTRESS CALL SLICES THROUGH THE silence, hauling me upright with a full-body jolt. I blink into the room, trying to get my bearings. The cabin. The camp. Ethan. Reality in crisp, excruciating focus.

I scramble for my phone and check the time. Nine-thirty-seven, which means I've been asleep for less than an hour. Shit. Almost the entire time Lucas has been in the woods. No calls or texts from him, and my heart leapfrogs into my throat, as much from terror as from hope. What does his silence mean? I try calling him, but the call won't go through.

I hit Redial and try again, looking around the cabin. Now that the sun is good and up, the place looks even worse. Rundown and grungy. Dirt creeps up the plain, unadorned walls. The mugs are chipped and stained with more than just tea. The chairs are ragged, the metal legs bloody with rust. Last night's rain has seeped through the cabin's cracks, cooling the air and making everything sticky and damp— my clothes and my hair and my lungs. I shiver and think of Ethan.

I check my phone, and it's then I notice that I have no bars, and my phone battery is at 5 percent. I think of the charger I left in my overnight bag in Detective Macintosh's car. I haven't seen him since I left the dining hall, hours ago. Is he still here?

Watching the screen for a signal, I carry my phone outside and down the fern-lined dirt path that leads back to the clearing. Murky sunlight filters through the trees, marbling the path. The sky beyond them is poisonous—a deep slate gray with low, racing clouds of purple and black. The death throes of last night's weather.

And just as eerie is the empty clearing before me. There's nobody here. No police officers barking orders, no searchers trampling in and out of the woods. I stop at the edge, my phone suddenly bleeping with an influx of work emails, and try not to throw up. What does this mean? Where did everybody go?

The hill before me is a horror show, a churned-up mess of trampled grass and mud. At the bottom, rain-filled trenches and footprints are all that remain of the police cars—gone all but one, an Atlanta Police Department cruiser covered in dew. Relief warms some of the dread from my bones. The detective is still here, which means my charger is, too.

I pull up the number for Lucas and try again.

"Yo." He answers, his voice a little out of breath and distracted. "Over here," he says, and then to me, "how you holding up?"

"Where is everybody?"

"What do you mean?" His voice crackles, the words cutting in and out.

"I fell asleep at the cabin after you left. When I woke up, everybody was gone. The cars. The people. Everything." I gaze across the clearing to the dining hall. The inside lights beat out a golden glow, but the morning sunlight winks fire where it hits the glass, and I can't see inside. I hurry along the edges of the clearing, following the driest path. "Did they call off the search or something?"

"Hang on. Let me see what's going on." A muted conversation with at least two separate male voices comes in fits and starts, and I strain to hear it over the morning birdsong and the bad reception. A few seconds later, Lucas is back, but so is the static. "…just told me the sheriff sent the volunteers and dogs home. Forensics are still hanging around, but they're moving…"

His explanation sets my nerves on fire, and I stop halfway up the hill. "What does that mean, that they're moving?"

He says something indecipherable, then his voice cuts back in. "…left the area. And before you start freaking out, that doesn't mean they're giving up on the search. The—"

The silence is so abrupt, I pull the phone from my ear and check the screen. One bar, but the call is still connected. "Lucas, start over. The what?"

Silence.

"Lucas, the what?"

A beeping, then nothing. The call went dead, and then, so does my phone. The screen goes black, the battery depleted.

I slip it into my back pocket and hurry as fast as I can across the dirt and slime to the detective's car, which I'm relieved to find unlocked. I dig my charger out of the side pocket of my overnight bag, leave the rest on the floor and shut the door.

I'm trying to decide the least treacherous path up the clearing to the dining hall, where I'm hoping to find the sheriff and Dawn, when a man bangs out the door. He sees me and stops at the edge of the porch, pausing in a shaft of sunlight that lights up his red hair like a fireball. "Oh. Hey. You looking for Dawn? Last I heard, she was still at the cabin."

I gesture across the mud to the cabin I just came from. "I was there, but Dawn wasn't."

The man shakes his head, pointing in the opposite direction, deeper into the woods. "Not that cabin. The kids' cabin. Forensics is just finishing up."

My heart gives a hard kick. The last place Ethan was seen, the place where he was until he wasn't. I desperately want to see it, if for no other reason than to breathe the same air.

He clomps across the porch and down the steps, hooking a hand through the air for me to follow. "Come on. I'll take you. We wanted to get you over there anyway to confirm what's his and what's not."

I hurry up the hill. "But he took his backpack with him, right? His backpack and compass."

"We believe so. The kids left behind a mountain of stuff, and we're pretty sure some of it's his, though we've not yet identified the backpack. And then there's his sleeping bag, which I'm sure you know we used as scent for the dogs. We've already got a positive ID on that from his teacher, so this is really just a formality. Still, best to hear it from the mom." He sticks out a hand. "Bill Mabry, Lumpkin County Search and Rescue."

"Kat Jenkins."

I follow him deeper into the thicket of woods, where the shadows are inky and the air a good ten degrees cooler than in the sunshine of the clearing. I pull my sweater tighter around my chest and hustle after him. His legs aren't that long but his stride is quick, and I take two steps to every one of his. The entire way, Bill doesn't stop talking.

"So I don't know if you heard, but the sheriff's moved HQ back to the station. It's not all that far from here, only five miles or so, but it's a real office, one with Wi-Fi and cell reception."

"Oh." I realize this is the message Lucas was trying to tell me over the phone, and it hits me like a punch to the gut. Leaving the camp without Ethan feels like a bad thing. No, like a *very* bad thing. Like giving up, admitting defeat. I am not in any way prepared to leave him behind. "What about the search?"

"Oh, the search is still very much on, it's just the tactics that have changed. The choppers have moved farther out, which is why we can't hear them. The police moved from the woods to the roads hours ago, setting up roadblocks and going door to door. The sheriff moving HQ is not a bad thing, I promise. Cops are better equipped to run an operation from an office, where it's warm and there's plenty of doughnuts."

I know he's trying to lighten things up, but I can't choke up a smile. A frantic swarm of hornets is eating away at my chest.

He's still chattering away as the path snakes us through the forest to another clearing, smaller this time. We stop at the edge of the tree line, and Bill points to a cabin, one of the six pressed against the woods, half tucked behind the brush. "That's it. Well…obviously."

The cabin is roped off with police tape, just like Detective Macintosh said it would be, long strands of yellow streamers rippling in the wind. Bright, kid-sized shoes are neatly lined along the edge of the porch. My heart wrenches at Ethan's navy Converse knockoffs at the far end, along with what looks like a filthy sock. A University of Georgia sweatshirt is tossed across the railing, bright red and adult-sized, and I wonder who it belongs to. One of the chaperones? One of the searchers? There are a good half dozen of them here, milling in and out of the cabin in mud-streaked jeans and matching navy jackets.

Dawn stands just inside the door with a cell phone pressed to her ear, beside a balding man in cargo pants and a sweatshirt. Her gaze flicks to me, and her chin lifts. She holds up a finger.

While she finishes up her call, I turn back to the stone fire pit in the center of the clearing, surrounded by Adirondack chairs. The wind shifts, and I catch a whiff of wet ash, spot a strip of charring on the wood that looks fresh. "Is this where the fire was?"

"No. Well, yes and no. The chaperones had a campfire going here, first with the kids and then after the kids went to bed, just the two of them until close to midnight." Bill points to two chairs, set closer to the fire than the rest. "Both had a clear view of the front door. Even if they weren't looking directly at it, it's what—fifteen feet at best? There's no way they could have missed anyone going in or out."

I picture Miss Emma and the kids out here in the dark, roasting marshmallows and talking, watching the sparks dance into the nighttime sky like fireflies. Was the kidnapper already watching from the woods?

Once again, my mind goes straight to Andrew. I think of the first weekend Ethan spent there after the divorce, when he came home looking like a kid after Christmas, full of stories about train sets and video games and a bed the shape of a race car—all those things Andrew labeled as too indulgent when we were married. As I listened to Ethan describe his new bedroom, I tried not to let on that I was simmering inside. Of *course* Andrew would try to buy his son's love, just like he'd once tried to manipulate mine. And clearly, his strategy worked. Ethan soon stopped telling me things—he's a sensitive child, and he saw how it upset me—but he still skipped out of the house every other weekend, eager to return to his shiny new toys.

But even if Ethan went willingly with Andrew, one of the chaperones would have noticed.

And then I realize something else: Bill said both chaperones had a good view of the door. Both as in two.

"Where were the others?" Bill's forehead rumples, and I add, "Miss Emma assured me there would be one adult for every five kids. How many children were sleeping in the cabin?"

"Eighteen, including your son."

"So there should have been at least one more adult. Where was she?"

Bill shakes his head. "I'll double-check, but as far as I know, it was just those two."

My skin heats with a flash of fury that's as much directed at Miss Emma as it is at myself.

"But the other fire," Bill says, gesturing for me to follow, "the one you were referring to, happened out back."

He leads me around the side of the cabin, pushing through weeds and underbrush that's virtually impenetrable, handing me branches that would otherwise snap back and smack me in the face. There's no path here, no easy way to move through the heavy growth tickling at my damp pants like great daddy longlegs. It creeps all the way up to the building, climbs with sticky vines up the wooden siding.

He points to a charred piece of wall on the far corner, amid a wide swath of forest cordoned off with police tape. "There. Obviously."

The sheriff wasn't kidding when he says it wasn't big. Even before the rain started falling, the ground would have been too damp, the trees and ferns too fat with spring showers to have caught fire without some help. Accelerant, the sheriff said, and just enough to engulf a square yard of brush in flames. They cleared the ground and licked up the wall, blackening the wood but as far as I can tell, the cabin didn't catch fire. But the point is, whoever set it created a fine distraction.

Bill points to a warped, wooden door in the center of the wall, adorned with a rusty knob and a shiny sliding latch, the kind you see on public bathroom doors. The lock looks brand-new and sturdy enough, but I don't know why anyone bothered. One good kick and the wood all around it would crumble.

"The kids went out the front door," Bill says, "moving away from the fire. Not that they could have done anything else, because as you can see, that door locks from the outside. And there were no prints, in case you were wondering. If someone touched that latch, they either wiped it clean or used a sleeve."

"Do we know for sure that Ethan ran out the front door with the other kids? Maybe he was taken out the back."

"At this point, it's still unclear. What we do know for sure is that my guys tracked him that way." Bill turns and points into the forest behind us, a sea of green with an occasional squiggle of red. I look closer, see that they're strips of yarn tied to a bush, on a broken twig on the ground, dangling from a hanging branch. Markers. "Well, my guys and Lucas. The sheriff went ballistic when he heard a civilian was contaminating his crime scene, until I told him Lucas was faster and better. I suppose he learned his skills from the Marines."

I shake my head. "From the Cumberland Gap National Historic Park. The Marine Corps is just where he perfected them."

Lucas lives in woods just like these, a forest thick as a fairy tale stretching from the backyard of his house. He knows every hill and tree, can follow their countless paths with his eyes closed, his fingers skimming the tree trunks like braille signposts. Whenever anybody loses their way, whenever a hiker or camper takes a wrong turn and can't find their way out of the brush, the park rangers call Lucas. These woods may be different, but give him five minutes, and he'll know every creature out there.

Dawn is waiting on the front porch by the time we make our way back around. She points me inside the cabin, where a trio of rubber-gloved investigators are sorting through what looks to be the aftermath of a punch-drunk slumber party. The wooden floorboards are papered with clothing and shoes and dirty socks and tattered comic books. Colorful backpacks are piled in heaps among rumpled sleeping bags, arranged every which way, and I do a sweep of them for Ethan's, just in case. I point out his sweatshirt, wadded and tossed in the corner, and his jacket hanging by the tag from a hook by the front door. I scan the room again, then one more time just in case. Nothing. The rest of his stuff must be with Ethan, in his backpack.

"Did you find the compass?"

Dawn shakes her head, but she doesn't say anything. I know what she's thinking—that there's no logic behind my constant harping about the thing, and maybe she's right. My desperation for Ethan to have the compass is more emotional than anything. Ethan knows its history, has watched me clean the hinges with a Q-tip and hold it to my chest while I cried. Even if he can't use it to lead himself out of the woods, at the very least, maybe it will bring him some comfort.

One of the men by the door steps closer. "Ms. Jenkins, would you mind confirming your son's sleeping bag for me?"

I turn, my gaze settling on a spot in the very center of the room, where the camouflage mummy bag I bought for Ethan is laid out, wedged in tight among a sea of black and navy nylon. I picture him there, whispering with the kids on either side long after he should have been asleep, and a tiny ray of joy lightens my heart.

"That one," I say, pointing. "The camouflage mummy bag."

Bill and Dawn exchange a confused look.

"Are you sure?" Dawn steps carefully over the bags, careful not to contaminate any of them with her shoes, then stops at an unzipped puffy bag stretched out by the far wall. It's black and expensive looking and utterly unfamiliar. "It's not this one?"

"No." I point to the bag I gave him just yesterday morning, smack in the middle of the chaos. "*That's* his sleeping bag. I bought it for him specifically for this trip. The receipt is still in my wallet. There's a strip of his baby blanket tucked in the inside pocket." The one he didn't want any of his classmates to know he still slept with.

Dawn snaps at a man in rubber gloves, and he hurries over, squats beside it and pulls out a well-loved chunk of yellow fabric. The sight of Ethan's blanket makes me dizzy, and it's everything I can do not to snatch it out of his hand.

"Yes." I give him a stiff nod. "It's Ethan's."

"Then whose is this?" Dawn says, stabbing a finger at the black sleeping bag by the door.

"I have no idea."

A long, pregnant pause, followed by an uproar of angry chatter. Dawn pulls out her cell phone and begins screaming at the poor sucker on the other end. A furious Bill turns to the rubber-gloved men, admonishing them for something I don't understand. The men bicker among themselves, animated accusations of who's to blame. I try to sort through the words, but they fly through the air like knives, sharp and deadly, and I can't pick out more than a few.

"What?"

My question gets lost in the commotion in the room. Nobody answers me. Nobody even looks my way. They just keep doing what they're doing. Screaming. Arguing. Cussing.

I grab on to Bill's arm, give it a shake, raise my voice until it rises above the clatter. "Tell me. What's going on?"

"We were working under the assumption that Ethan's was the black sleeping bag, the one by the wall," Bill says with a wince. "That's what the teacher told us, and at least three of the kids confirmed it." He pauses, and he looks like he might throw up. "It's why we used it for the dogs."

It takes a few seconds for my sleep-deprived brain to catch up, for it to process what he just said. They let the dogs smell the wrong sleeping bag, sent them out into the woods chasing the wrong scent. "So whose scent did the dogs chase to the road?"

"That's just it. We thought it was Ethan, but now... Now we're not sure."

KAT

7 hours, 28 minutes missing

WE END UP BACK IN THE DINING HALL WITH A skeleton staff—Dawn and Bill and an exhausted-looking sheriff. A mud-smeared man named Keith, who's been in the woods with Detective Macintosh and Lucas, barreling toward Black Mountain Road on Lord-knows-whose trail. A couple of the rubber-gloved men whose names I've already forgotten. The rest of the searchers have packed up and gone, relocated to the police office across town. Somebody made a fresh pot of coffee, and it sits untouched at the far end of the table, next to a pile of crumpled sugar packets and a stack of foam cups. The bitter smell churns like acid in my stomach.

"This explains why the dogs have been running in circles," the sheriff says, "and why half of them kept coming back to the camp. If the kids were swapping sleeping bags, the dogs are confused. There are too many scents in those woods. They don't know which one to chase."

Hope alights in my chest. "So Ethan might not be in a car?"

"Whatever trail they caught led them to the road, and since Ethan's the only one missing, I'm going to assume it's his. Best way to know for sure is to ask the humans who are tracking it. In the meantime, we're calling the dogs back in. I want them to start over with a scent that belongs only to your son. They should be here within an hour."

"Do you have something we could use?" Dawn says. "A shirt. Some pajamas. Something you know for sure hasn't been contaminated."

She scrubs at her face with both hands, and her tone tells me that she's still royally pissed but doing her best to hold it together. I notice the tight lines around her mouth, the dark puddles under her eyes, the way her hair has gone limp and lifeless. Dawn is working on less sleep than I am, and I'm sure she wants nothing more than to go home, shower off the mud, fall into bed and sleep until next week.

"I brought some of his clothes from home, but they're clean. He hasn't worn them since they came out of the washer. Oh! I threw in one of his stuffed animals. He normally sleeps with it, but he didn't want his classmates to know so he didn't bring it."

"Perfect. Where is it?"

"In my bag, on the floorboard of Detective Macintosh's car."

"Somebody go get it," the sheriff says to no one in particular. His eyes are glassy and so bloodshot they're practically glowing.

One of the rubber-gloved men rises from the table and hustles off.

"And *you*." Sheriff Childers stabs a finger across the table at Bill. "Go over to the hotel and fetch that teacher. If she fucked up something as fundamental as the sleeping bags, I need to know what else we got wrong."

My stomach stirs into a sick stew at the idea there could be more bad news.

Sheriff Childers digs a map from the tornado of papers on the table, spreads it across the top of the pile. "All right, Keith, tell us what you got."

Keith rises up on an elbow and leans over the map. He points a finger to a sea of green, a forested area wedged between the outskirts of Dahlonega and US 19. "When I left Lucas and the detective, they were here, following the trail to the northwest. Assuming they're maintaining the same pace, I'd put them somewhere around here by now." He slides his finger a half inch to the left, taps it twice. "They've got, oh, about another forty minutes before they come up on the road."

"And we're sure they're tracking a human?" Dawn asks.

"Lucas for sure knows the difference between human and animal tracks," I say. "He'll know everything down to the size and weight of any other human tracks he comes across. He'll be able to distinguish if it's Ethan or someone else."

"Call over there and find out," the sheriff says, waving at somebody to pour him a cup of coffee. "I want details on the trail they're following, and tell them for now to ignore wherever the dogs are pointing them. I need them to go at warp speed and to let us know the second they have something Kat might be able to identify. No more mistakes."

Dawn nods, handing the sheriff a cup of coffee and two sugar packets.

He thanks her by barking out his next order. "Call the feds. Find out what's taking the CARD team so long." He shakes the sugar packets against his wrist, aiming his gaze across the table at Keith. "And hit the pause button on that AMBER Alert—"

My heart stutters. "What? Why?"

"Because we don't have a description of the abductor or vehicle, which is one of AMBER's main requirements, or which

direction he's headed. That's the whole goddamn problem—
we don't know diddly, and we may have wasted precious hours
chasing the wrong damn trail. We'll order the choppers to
head back over the woods with the heat sensors. Essentially,
though, we're back to square one."

"No, we're not. Ask Lucas. He'll know if this is the right
trail or not. He'll know who he's following."

The sheriff ignores me. "Back to work, people. There's a
little boy out there who needs finding, and he could be anywhere."

Anywhere could mean in the back of a van. At the bottom
of a still, murky pond. Chained to the pipes in somebody's
basement. Hurtling toward the Mexican border on the backseat of Andrew's Mercedes.

"Dawn," the sheriff says. "Call the volunteers back in, and
then start working your way down the sex offender list."

Those two words—sex offender—are like coming upon a
bear in the forest. I suck in a gasp, loud and strangled, but if
the sheriff hears, it doesn't slow him down.

"I want eyes on every pervert within a fifty-mile radius.
Every period Single period Goddamn one exclamation point.
Keith, you gather up everybody who's still here and start the
search again from scratch. Now that it's light and dry, I'm
expecting things to move a hell of a lot quicker than the last
time around. One of you call Atlanta PD and see where they
are with the warrant for the father's house. And both of you,
I want progress reports every half hour, on the half hour, and
that's nonnegotiable. Now go."

Everybody scatters but the sheriff and me.

He holds my gaze across the table, and I couldn't look away
if I tried. His awful words still thrum between us, angry

drumbeats that rumble through my mind and turn me inside out.

Sex offender.

The sheriff's brows crumple into a frown. "Aw, hell," he mumbles, and despite the profanity, it's the kindest I've ever heard his voice.

I open my mouth, but I can't respond. My chest has completely locked up. I gulp at air, telling my lungs to breathe, but they don't obey. No oxygen moves in or out. It's like the air in the cabin has suddenly turned solid, like someone wrapped my face in Saran wrap while I wasn't watching. I claw at my throat with both hands, my lungs screaming, burning, on fire. Across from me, the sheriff's face blurs and the edges of my vision darken.

"Listen to me, Kat. I need you to puff up your cheeks and blow, okay? I know you feel like your lungs are gonna explode, but blow anyway. Blow like you're blowing up a balloon. Blow like you're blowing out a million birthday candles. I want to feel your breath on my skin, all the way over here." He reaches across the paper chaos, gives my arm a squeeze, then a jiggle. "Come on, now. Blow as hard as you can."

The body is an amazing thing. Just when I think I'm going to pass out, the concrete in my chest dissolves and my lungs release. Air rushes out of me in a great gasp. My needy body sucks more in too quickly, and the concrete starts to harden all over again.

"Again," the sheriff commands. "Keep going, keep going, keep going. Good. One more time." He coaches me through another round, and then another, until my breathing calms to a light wheeze. And then he plunks his elbows on the table and leans in. "Listen, Kat, you can't lose it on me now. You and I are partners in this thing, okay? I need you, and you need me, and together we are going to find your son. No matter what."

I want to weep at his words. They're the ones I've been so desperate to hear, and from the person I was so desperate to hear them. I give him a shaky nod.

"Now. As much as I need us to get along, I can't be holding your hand the whole time. My priority is to your son, and I won't have time to explain every single decision I make as I'm making them. That's what Dawn's for, so anytime you have questions or concerns about my approach, you take them to her. You have her number, don't you?"

I nod, even though the paper she wrote it on is in a cabin across the clearing, and my cell phone is dead at the bottom of my pocket.

"Great. But since she's not here and I am, is there anything you'd like to ask me now? Anything at all. Now's your chance."

I think back to the long list of questions I made back in the tiny cabin, the way they flipped through my mind almost too fast for me to record. A new one floats to the top like a rotten egg.

"Did anybody find Andrew?"

"Yes and no. According to the TSA, he left the country on Saturday headed to St. Martin and has not reentered by plane or sea. I've got someone working their way down the island's hotels and resorts, but so far, no hits. For now, it looks like if your ex-husband had anything to do with Ethan's disappearance, it's by proxy."

"Oh." I don't know whether to be relieved or dismayed. When it comes to choosing between Andrew versus a sexual deviant, I'd pick Andrew any day. Even though it means Ethan would still be gone, at least then I know he'd be with someone who loves him, someone who wouldn't harm him. "So now what? What are the next steps?"

"Now I really need you to rack your brain for who else might have taken him. It's not gonna be pleasant, because I'm asking you to think about people you know. Neighbors. Family and friends. Teachers or somebody at school. People who've got some access to your son but might be looking for some more. The more names you can give me, the better."

"I already started a list. It's in the other cabin."

"Good, keep going with that. And just because we put a hold on the AMBER Alert doesn't mean we are clamping down on the others. We've got every police department in the vicinity keeping an eye out for your son, and we've already distributed Ethan's description to the media. He'll be the lead item on every news station in a hundred-mile radius. And like I said before, CARD's on the way."

"CARD?"

"Child Abduction Rapid Deployment teams. They're FBI agents experienced in child abductions in multijurisdictional settings, like this one. These guys are the big guns, okay? They should be arriving any moment."

"Okay." I tell myself this is good, that the sheriff is committed and capable, but fear still trickles up my neck.

"In the meantime, what are your thoughts on making an official statement?"

His question confuses me, as does his hopeful tone. "A statement?"

"I'd like to get you in front of the news cameras and have you make an appeal to whoever took Ethan. We'll write it, you read it word for word. Do you think you can do that?"

I think about standing at a podium before a sea of journalists, bathed in the glare of their camera lights and bursts of flashing bulbs like a movie star. The idea makes me want to throw up. "Yes."

"You're going to have to be calm and clear and say things you don't mean. Things like if he lets Ethan go, if he returns him to you safely, then you promise the police won't hunt his ass down and kick it straight to prison."

"You're asking me to lie?"

"No, I'm telling you to lie your ever-loving ass off and be convincing about it. This guy needs to not just feel sorry for taking a little boy away from his mother, but to believe every promise coming out of your mouth. He has to believe you mean it when you say that we won't come after him. Now I'm going to ask you again. Do you think you can do that?"

I swallow, then swallow again. "I can do anything if it will bring back my son."

For the first time since we met, the sheriff smiles. "Good girl. I'll have Dawn set it up."

The sheriff's walkie-talkie crackles, then erupts in a burst of dialogue. Two, maybe three voices, talking in fits and spurts. I don't catch all of their words, but I understand enough of them. I'm off the bench and bolting for the door.

Outside, three men and two women—fresh faces in clean clothes—are working their way up the muddy hill. I fly out the door and slip on the muddy stairs, landing tail-first in the dirt. "Are you okay?" one of them calls out. I hoist myself up and take off into the woods without replying, sprinting down the winding path to the kids' cabin.

Where Bill has arrived with Miss Emma.

I don't slow down long enough to think about what I will say to her. My body is on autopilot, my brain buzzing on high-octane anger and base instinct. All I know is that I have to confront her. I run until I come out in the tiny clearing.

Bill steps out onto the porch, followed closely by Emma. She sees me and lets the screened door of the cabin slam behind her. The sound echoes like a tinny cymbal through the forest.

Her skin is pasty, her eyes swollen from crying or lack of sleep or both. The pretty makeup she was wearing the last time I saw her is gone, scrubbed or cried off. Her hair, usually a glorious mane of blond curls, is shoved in a messy ponytail that hangs tangled and listless over one shoulder. She's breathing fast, her chest heaving with effort and emotion.

Bill takes a step in my direction, then halts at the top of the stairs. "Ms. Quinn verified that Ethan was in the black sleeping bag. The one by the far wall."

Emma's gaze creeps to mine, and she confirms it with a nod.

The cool morning air stretches tight between us. I stand in the clearing and wonder if the woods will tear in half.

"This is our fault, Kat. We should have asked you to identify Ethan's things earlier. As soon as you got here. And Sammy's name was on his. We just missed it somehow, and then the dogs were—"

"Why?" The word shoots out of me like a bullet, abrupt and deadly.

Bill glances between us, looking uneasy. He frowns like he doesn't know what to do first, comfort Emma or pacify me. "Why what?"

"Why was Ethan in a sleeping bag that wasn't his? You know his was the camouflage one. I gave it to him for this trip as a surprise. You took it from his arms when you helped him onto the bus."

Emma shakes her head, a jerky back and forth. "I have eighteen students. I can't keep track of all their things."

"No, I guess not. How could you, when you can't even keep track of *them*?"

The sarcasm is a technique I gleaned from Andrew. As much as I detested it when he aimed it at me, it sure hits its target now. Two pink spots bloom high on Emma's cheeks.

"You *know* how much I love my students. I love those kids like they're my own." She presses both hands into her chest, but it doesn't stop her hands from shaking. "I am traumatized about Ethan, Kat. I am *devastated*."

I hate this woman. I hate her with such an intensity that I have to hold myself back from slapping the distressed look off her face. I know Emma is not the one who sprayed kerosene at the back corner of the cabin and lit the match, but I don't believe her I'm-just-so-devastated attitude, either. What she should be feeling is guilt. This is *her* fault. *She* let this happen. If she really loved my son, she'd have been paying better attention.

"My son disappeared on your watch."

"I counted the kids, Kat. Twice! I counted them and there were eighteen, but it was so dark and Avery couldn't put out the fire. They were frantic, and so was I. We all were."

"You looked me in the eye and told me you'd watch out for him. You *promised*."

"I know. Oh my God, of course I *know*." The last word dissolves into a wail, and her face collapses. "And I *did*. He was there when we ran outside, I'm almost positive of it. You have to believe me, Kat. This isn't my fault."

Her defensive attitude only infuriates me more, as does Bill's not-so-subtle calm-down look.

"When the kids make fun of him at school, when they call him names or shove him on the playground, you pretend not to notice. My son comes home at least once a week in tears because his bullies are torturing him, and they get away with it because you do nothing. You say nothing. So of *course* I blame you. What happened here is *all* your fault."

Her mouth drops open, and whatever she was about to say is sucked into the clamor of a helicopter circling overhead. Her face crumples, and she cries into her hands.

I grip my hands into fists, grit my teeth against Emma's tears and Bill's stare and my fury that rushes like ice through my veins. "Maybe you are telling the truth. Maybe you were right there, guarding those kids the whole time. Maybe whoever took Ethan would have taken him regardless. But every night for the rest of your life, I hope you think of my son, shivering and alone in somebody else's sleeping bag. I hope you see his tearstained face and remember that that's on you. *You* let that happen."

I don't wait around for her apology, partly because we both know I don't forgive her.

But also, so she won't get the satisfaction of seeing me cry.

STEF

"STEFANIE HUNTINGTON! WHAT A LOVELY SUR-prise."

Alexis Fischer greets everyone by their first and last names, and with a sugarcoated enthusiasm that matches the head-to-toe Lilly Pulitzer dress I know she's wearing. Not that I can see her tropical-print outfit through the phone, but I've never seen her in anything else—not even in the dead of winter.

Alexis and I are not what I'd call friends, though she's never been unpleasant or unkind. She's never said a bad word about me, not to my face or behind my back. She saves me a seat at school concerts and lets me cut in front of her in the car pool line, and she never complains when I neglect to return the favor. She tries so hard to be likable, yet no matter how hard I try, I can't seem to make myself like her.

But Alexis has a son in Sammy's class, and she's married to Avery, who somehow snagged the hot-ticket role as field trip chaperone. Despite whatever opinions I might have of her, I will suck it up now and play nice.

I slip out the back door and onto the patio, the pad of paper

I've been scribbling notes on all morning tucked under an arm. "Hi, Alexis. So sorry to disturb, but—"

"Oh, you're not disturbing anything. I'm just enjoying these last few hours of peace and quiet before the kids get back. I don't know about you, but I'd vote for another day or two of this. I haven't missed Timmy for a second." She laughs and lowers her voice. "Don't tell anybody I said that."

I force myself to slow down long enough to be friendly. "Your secret's safe with me, I promise. But the reason I'm calling is to ask for the number of Avery's cell. It wasn't listed in the school directory."

Her friendly tone dips a full octave. "I suppose you haven't heard."

My mind whips through the possibilities. Ethan was found. He's in the hospital. The morgue.

I sink onto the couch, dizzy with dread. "Heard what?"

"That for the past two and a half years, Avery has been getting hot and heavy with his secretary. Now, I know what you're thinking—his *secretary*. I mean, how cliché can you get, right? But don't you worry. I've got Gina Winters on the case. She's going to take him to the cleaners."

My heart settles in my chest—for Ethan, not for Avery. Gina Winters is a name both revered and feared in moneyed Atlanta. A powerhouse divorce attorney who takes *all* her clients' cheating husbands to the cleaners. I hope for Avery's sake he's not too attached to his homes and bank accounts, because Gina Winters never loses.

I toss the notebook onto the coffee table and curl my feet up onto the cushions, settling in. Any conversation that includes the words *husband* and *cleaners* is not going to be a short one. "I'm so very sorry to hear that. Divorce is never fun, no matter which side you land on."

She makes a throaty sound. "Yeah, well, save your sympathy for Avery. He's the one who's going to be sorry. Anyway, I'd love to give you his number, but I've removed every trace of him from my life, and that includes his number from my phone."

I roll my eyes. Alexis has been married to Avery for how long now? Surely she remembers his number. "Alexis, I really—"

"I learned that from your mother, you know. Dr. Mel says the only way to truly let go of the past is to do just that— let go of it. And to do that I had to completely expunge him from my being. She said to think of it like a reset. A control-alt-delete of my heart and soul, and boy, was she right. I feel so much better now that I've gotten all that negative energy out of my life."

There are so many things I could say here. That I'll never understand why my mother's fans act like cult members. That even with a full-time nanny to run interference, it's pretty much impossible to expunge anyone from anything when you share ten-plus years and two children. That if Alexis expects me to believe she doesn't remember Avery's number, she's as ridiculous as her wardrobe.

"I appreciate what you're going through, Alexis, but this is an emergency. I really need to talk to someone up at the camp, and Emma isn't answering her cell. I don't know who else to call."

"Did you call the school?"

"Of course I called the school. I left messages on at least a dozen people's voice mails. So far, nobody's called me back, and no matter how many times I hit Redial, I can't get a human on the line. It's like nobody's there."

"Why?"

I frown. "Why is nobody at the school?"

"No. Why do you need to talk to Avery?"

I fall silent, thinking. On the one hand, I don't want to incite panic among the parents, which telling Alexis will for sure do. She's never been the close-lipped type, and she has an obvious penchant for gossip over facts, which in this case are far too sparse to be the least bit sensational. If she doesn't know about Ethan—and it seems clear that she doesn't—no way am I going to be the one to tell her.

On the other, Brittany showed up at our front door hours ago with the news, and there's still no word from the school. No sorrowful statements, no updates, nothing. The longer this radio silence stretches, the twitchier I become. Call it mother's intuition, call it a premonition, but my body won't relax. Not until I know for certain that Sammy is okay.

I decide on a careful version of the truth. "It's not Avery I need to talk to, but Sammy."

"Well, why didn't you just say so? My boys both have cell phones—one of the few perks of being a child of divorce. Give Timmy a call. Wait, don't call him. He responds better to WhatsApp or FaceTime. Actually, do you have Snapchat?"

I reach for the pad and a pen. Thank God for parents like Alexis, who think the school's no-cell-phone policy doesn't apply to them or their children. "What's Timmy's number?"

She rattles off a string of digits, then launches into her ideas for the fall fund-raiser she's in charge of planning. A long, drawn-out account that I know from experience will end in an ask: for my money, my time, my assistance. I'm waiting for a pause in her monologue when my cell phone beeps with an incoming call.

"Sorry, Alexis, but I really need to take this. Thanks again!" She's still talking when I hang up.

The call pops up on my screen, but not with a number.

With a single, solitary word. *Unknown.* A call that on any other day, any other situation, I would decline.

I press the phone to my ear. "Hello?"

KAT

8 hours, 34 minutes missing

BACK IN THE TINY CABIN ON THE OTHER SIDE of the clearing, I plug my phone into the socket by the sink and flip the switch on the kettle. I'm not so much thirsty as I am freezing, my bones and teeth rattling from both my still-damp clothes and the terror gripping my insides. I rummage through the cabinet for a tea bag and drop it into a mug marked with stains I'm too exhausted to think about.

"Clean yourself up." That's what the sheriff said when I walked back into the dining hall, his gaze raking over my stringy hair, my muddy skin, my jeans dark with dirt and dew. "Press conference is in an hour. Be ready in a half. You're gonna need some practice rounds."

While the water rouses itself into a boil, I lean into a rusty mirror above the couch and wince. Wild hair, skin splotchy and sallow, pale everywhere but the two half-moons of purple and green that sit under my eyes like bruised fruit. My nose, normally small and straight, is puffy from five hours straight of crying, the skin around it mottled and peeling. I dig a tube of hand cream from my bag and rub some into my face and hands, then instantly regret it. The smell, citrus and jasmine, churns my empty stomach.

The kettle flips off with a sharp click, at the same time my phone springs to life with a series of incoming messages. I drop the tube in my bag and rush across the floor to my phone. Work has already begun, and most of the emails and text messages are from the office. As the newest personal claims agent in the department, I'm the lowest on the employee totem pole. My inbox collects the claims no one else wants. Lost dentures. iPhones dropped in toilets. Cockroaches floating in soup. My workdays are spent wading through everyone else's shitty leftovers, but not today. Today I can't contemplate any of it.

I pull up my boss's contact card and fire off a quick email—Won't be in today. Family emergency.—but the message won't send. The emails must have come through in a rare burst of reception, and now I'm back to no bars.

I flip over to a handful of voice mails, and my heart stutters and misfires. There are five, and they're all from Andrew.

With shaking hands, I tap the screen to listen to the first one, checking the time on the clock. He left it only twenty minutes ago, about the time I was hyperventilating with the sheriff in the dining hall.

"Kat, it's me. What is going on? My phone has been blowing up with messages from the police about Ethan. Have they found him yet? Call me back as soon as you hear this. I've got my ringer on and I'm not putting my phone down until I hear back."

Hearing his voice again ungrounds me. Six months limited to no contact means my body's reaction now is knee-jerk. My muscles go tight and tense, bracing for impact even though he's I-don't-know-how-many miles away. The distance doesn't stop his words from stirring up first hysteria, then confusion.

He sounds worried. Normal. Human. If Andrew is behind Ethan's disappearance, then his performance on this voice mail deserves an Oscar.

I click to the next one and press the phone to my ear.

"Me again. I heard your voice mail and now I'm pissed. I can't believe you think I have something to do with this. In fact, why don't we talk about your culpability instead? *You're* the one who let an eight-year-old go on a camping trip without one of us there as chaperone, not me. You do realize how irresponsible and careless that is, right? How utterly stupid. I sincerely hope the reason you haven't called me back is that you're out there in the woods searching for my son, because I will tell you this—I am going to spend the rest of my life and every last goddamn penny of my money fighting you for custody. I'm not fucking around, Kat. Call me back."

The recording ends, and I look behind me. Actually twist my body around to check for Andrew in the empty air at my back. Even though I know he's not there. Even though I feel ridiculous. But everything about my body's reaction—pounding heart, clenched muscles, limbs braced for fight or flight—tells me he's standing right behind me.

Pull it together, Kat. Ethan's disappearance is not my fault, and the abrupt swing from concerned to hostile is quintessential Andrew, as is his tone: loud, arrogant and demanding. I tell myself this is the Andrew I've come to know, the one that comes in guns swinging. Andrew was always the vinegar, I was the honey. He agitates, I smooth over. He's the master at manipulating a situation to suit his version of reality, and as awful as his words are to hear, at least now we're back in familiar territory.

I listen to the rest of the messages, which only go downhill from there. Obscenity laden and filled with threats and hateful names. By the last one, I'm shaking with both fright and fury, the weight of his words crushing my chest. Once this nightmare is over, once the police find Ethan and hand him back to me, I'll be swept into the next nightmare—a custody battle I can't afford, with a man who has already proven that he doesn't play fair.

But the more pressing point is, Andrew has surfaced. Dawn and the sheriff will want to know.

I'm turning for the door when Lucas's voice booms from somewhere outside the cabin, disturbing the silence that is everywhere except in my head. "Kat, you in here?"

I drop the phone on the counter with a clatter and rush to the door, flinging it open. "Did you find him?"

He clomps up the steps, panting like he ran all the way here. "No, but I found everything he put there. Ethan left a trail from the back door of the cabin all the way to the road."

"Are you sure it was his?"

Lucas gives me a don't-be-stupid look. Sometime since the last time I saw him, he's draped his body in head-to-toe camouflage, from the canvas hat pulled low on his forehead down to the pants that tuck into his muddy brown hiking boots. The fabric is darker than it should be in wet patches on his chest, under his arms, on elbows and knees caked in mud and dirt and sweat. It drips in dirty lines down his face and neck, disappearing into the pink skin around his collar.

He steps inside, and I shut the door behind him. "Snapped twigs. A dropped pencil or candy wrapper. A stone pressed into the bark. He left us something every twenty feet."

"What good is a trail when Ethan is long gone? He's in a car, Lucas. A *car*."

"Because studying the trail will tell us things the dogs can't. He left all sorts of litter behind, and his pace was shorter than it should have been for a kid his size. That means he was deliberately walking slow, trying to delay his escape. He wasn't running, that's for sure. The second trail belonged to someone more than twice his size. An adult."

"Male or female?"

"Height and weight could be either, and so could the size of the boots. Unfortunately, the rain made it difficult to get a good print, but they're still trying."

"So basically, you learned nothing." I return to my bag, burying a fresh bout of tears and rummaging around for my brush. "Ethan's maybe with Andrew, maybe with someone else, a man or a woman, but by the time you were following his tracks through the woods, he was long gone."

"I know it seems like nothing," Lucas says, stepping closer, "but—"

I turn around, pointing at Lucas with my brush. "But what? The dogs took forever to catch the scent because they were using a sleeping bag that didn't belong to Ethan. His teacher confirmed it. There were too many scents in it for them to be sure, so the sheriff is calling the dogs back in to start over from scratch. They're using Sweetie Honey this time so there's no contamination."

I don't have to explain Sweetie Honey, Ethan's stuffed rabbit, to Lucas. He's the one who gave it to Ethan one year for Easter, the same Sweetie Honey that's now squished into a giant ziplock in the dining hall, infusing the air inside the bag with Ethan's one-of-a-kind scent.

I step to the sink, run my brush under the tap and start dragging it through my hair. I have less than a half hour until the sheriff plunks me in front of a room filled with television cameras, where I am supposed to beg some nameless, faceless person, who may or may not be Andrew, to give me back my son.

Lucas leans a hip against the counter and watches me. "I'm telling you, another run of the dogs is only going to slow us down again. That was definitely Ethan's trail I was on. No question because those wrappers I just told you about? They were from those disgusting dollar store treats you try to pass off as candy. Look."

He pulls a clear plastic bag from his jacket pocket, and my stomach twists. If I was holding out any hope the dogs chased the wrong human scent to the road, it just died with the muddy strips of orange and yellow paper in Lucas's hand. The kind of snacks I buy in bulk because they're cheap and peanut-free. The kind I toss in Ethan's backpack every morning.

"I also found this."

Lucas hands me a brown leather bag, and I don't have to turn it over to know the leather's cracked on the bottom, or that there's a long, ragged scratch that runs diagonally across the back. It's my great-grandfather's old pouch, the one he used to hang from his belt while surveying the wilderness of southern Kentucky. I fling open the flap and it's empty.

"I double- and triple-checked a hundred-mile radius around that thing," Lucas says, his voice low and steady, "but I didn't find the compass. Ethan must still have it on him."

A huge silent sob racks my body, and I turn back to the mirror, my image going blurry with tears.

Lucas steps up behind me, draping both hands on my shoulders. "Kat, I know it's hard, but this is good news."

"How? How is any of this good news?"

"It means we're on the right trail. It means we know which way he went. Stay positive, because we are going to find him.

I'm not leaving here until we do, and neither is Mac. He swore he'd stay until Ethan is brought home."

I frown. "Who's Mac?"

"Your detective."

It takes me a couple of seconds to realize Lucas is referring to Detective Macintosh. "He's not my detective, and I thought his name was Brent."

Lucas bobs his big shoulders. "I dunno. He told me to call him Mac. Anyway, you can fix your hair later. Mac and I wanted to—"

He stops when, suddenly, the air vibrates with the roar of an engine. One of the helicopters, I think at first, buzzing back over the camp, until I realize this sound is different. Not a chopper but a big car—a truck maybe—its motor gunning. It's like the soundtrack from *The Fast and the Furious*, playing on giant speakers right outside the cabin.

Lucas's reaction time is much faster than mine. I'm still looking toward the window, trying to decide whether to run or brace for impact, and Lucas has already leaped to the door, flung it open and charged outside.

"Holy shit." His startled voice comes from the porch, right before a crash shakes the floorboards, the sneakers under my feet, the very pit of my stomach. I race after him out the door.

STEF

8 hours, 54 minutes missing

MY CAR SKIDS TO A STOP ON THE MUDDY HILL, and I shove at the door. I ram my shoulder into it, pushing with all my weight into the middle console, but it's no use. The door won't budge. Stuck from when I slid out of the last curve and into a patrol car, punting the thing downfield like an amusement park ride. I crawl over the center console and tumble out the passenger's side door.

The brand-new hot-pink pumps I slipped my feet into this morning sink into mud thick as tar. I lurch out of them with two wet plops, then hurry on bare feet farther into the clearing. The sloping lawn before me is treacherous, as slick as an ice rink. My feet slide around before catching hold, my toes digging in for purchase. I scan the cabins clinging to either side of the hill, searching for someone.

Anyone.

"Hello?"

My desperation to see Sammy is a primal thing, clawing at my chest with the need to touch him, to hold him, even worse than when they pulled his little blue lump from my belly and whisked him away for the longest sixteen minutes of my life. I need to know that he's okay. That he's safe. That he's not the little boy some monster stole from the cabin.

When the blocked number had sprung up on my screen, I was thinking of Sam's promise to call with news, of all those voice mails I'd left. I was thinking it might be someone from school, whatever poor sucker they'd appointed to deliver the bad news about Ethan. Then I heard his words—staggering, heart-stopping words—and I thought it was a mistake.

The memory of his voice hits me like a nightmare. *Listen carefully, Stef. I have Sammy.*

Not Sammy, I kept saying over and over. *Ethan.*

I've spent the seventy-two minutes since in agony, covering sixty country miles in half the time it should have taken me while hovering between disbelief and full-blown terror, and with no one to talk me off the ledge. Sam is in meetings or parked before television cameras, unreachable by anyone in his office. Josh's and Brittany's and Jimmy's numbers kept sending me straight to voice mail. Emma's, Sammy's teacher, rings and rings and rings. Even Dr. Abernathy, Cambridge's head of school, wasn't picking up, and she *always* picks up when I call.

Call the police, the voice said, *and your son dies.*

I sense movement to my left. A man dressed in head-to-toe camouflage at the top of the hill, taking in the wreckage behind me.

"Who's in charge here?" I yell in his direction. "I need to speak to whoever's in charge."

"Get back," he says, not to me but to the woman rushing down the path behind him. There's something familiar about her—pale skin stretched thin over wide cheekbones, dirty blond hair with darker roots, willowy frame draped in clothes that were fashionable five years ago. Ethan's mom. I can't remember her name. She tries to push past the man, but he's too big, too strong. He holds her back easily with an arm, stepping in front of her in a protective move.

I start up the hill to them, but I don't make it very far. I slip and my body pitches forward, landing on my knees and hands in the mud. "Have either of you seen Sammy?" I push myself to a stand, swiping my filthy palms down the front of my jeans. "I need to see my son right away. Where are the kids?"

There's commotion on the other side of the hill, cops streaming out of a long and squat cabin. They're all holding guns, dark things aimed down the clearing at me, as if I'm the enemy. I hold up my mud-streaked hands, right as one of them, a large guy in dark clothes, tells them to stand down. Three little words float down the hill, ones I've never been so happy to hear until now: "The mayor's wife."

I'm not the type of person to name-drop. I don't use my status to get out of speeding tickets, to scoot to the front of the line, to book tables at the city's hottest new restaurants. Up until this very moment, I've never pulled that card—*don't you know who I am?*—but I'm glad as hell somebody did it for me now.

My hands drop to my sides. "I need to see my son, Sammy, right this instant. He's here on a field trip with his second grade class."

For the longest moment, no one speaks. No one moves. Except for the steady *ding ding ding* coming out the open door of my car, the camp is silent, a communal holding of breath. I can't take the silence, the lack of response another second.

"Somebody take me to Sammy—*now.*"

My words echo around the clearing, a feverish call and response, and I know how it sounds. It sounds like an overwrought mother losing her shit, like an addict frantic for her next hit. I can tell by their expressions that my hysteria is not doing me any favors. They think I'm crazy. Out of control. Exactly the way that I feel.

A man steps forward. He's a kid, barely out of college, but he's in uniform and I latch onto it. Finally, a person in charge.

"Where's my son?" I'm scrambling up the hill in his direction, but for every two steps I take forward, I slide one back down.

He braces on the railing with both fists, leaning over it to holler down the hill. "Mrs. Huntington, you can't be here. This is an active crime scene."

By now I'm twenty feet away, close enough to see the trio of deep lines slicing across his forehead, the guns in the other men's hands, their twitchy fingers. They're worried I'll do something rash. "You don't understand. I spoke to someone this morning who said—"

"Ma'am, stop right there."

"Just tell me. Is he okay? Where is he?"

"Stefanie," a woman's voice calls from right behind me. My name on her tongue is angry and sharp.

My head turns to see Ethan's mother step into the clearing, the wet ground squishing around her sneakers. A breeze flutters the hair around her face, and her eyes latch onto mine. They're not kind.

Now that I've seen her, seen the dark circles bleeding out under her sunken eyes, I think it can't be Sammy who was taken. This woman looks like the mother of a missing child, not me. Not Sammy.

"For fuck's sake, Kat," the man behind her mutters. He's not old enough to be her father, but he's protective like one. Her brother? A lover? He takes up her rear, scowling at me over her shoulder.

I ignore him, focusing everything I have on her.

"Please, Kat," I say, and my voice breaks. "Please help me find Sammy."

She watches me with envy, with hatred. As if my worst nightmare is somehow stealing the thunder from hers. This woman doesn't want to help me, that much is clear. She'd sooner scratch my eyes out than give me an ounce of relief. She stares at me, and I feel myself turn to stone.

And then something in her expression breaks.

"He's fine," she chokes out. "*Your* son is perfectly fucking fine."

And then suddenly, both of us are crying.

KAT

9 hours, 6 minutes missing

"MRS. HUNTINGTON," THE SHERIFF SAYS, "I'M trying really hard to understand why you're here."

The cabin is claustrophobic, jammed with bodies that reek of rain and woods and earth. The sheriff is huddled around the table with Dawn, Detective Macintosh—Mac—and Stefanie, while Lucas and I are notched into the cranny on the other side, shoulder to shoulder and pressed against the metal kitchenette counter. The air is alive with energy, with electricity.

Stefanie has tidied up some at the sink, but she's still a mess. Her face is smeared with leftover makeup, light brown and sparkly. Her hair is in shambles, blow-out curls that have long since lost their bounce. But God, she's beautiful, like every movement of her perfect body is choreographed. Even now, with mascara track marks on her cheeks and clothes caked with mud, she's stunning.

She stares across the table at the sheriff with eyes swollen from crying. "When can I see Sammy?"

"I assure you, ma'am, your son is fine. I'll have one of our officers bring you to him as soon as we're done here. In the meantime, if you would just answer the question, please. Why did you come all the way up here? The school was supposed to make very clear to parents that the children would be returning sometime later today. They were to be explicit in that parents were not to come up here to fetch anyone themselves."

The sheriff has pushed his chair so far back from the table that he's practically up against the wall. His long legs are stretched away from the table, his boots crossed at the ankle.

Stefanie slaps her hands to the table and leans across it, and her voice spirals into the high hysteria she used out on the lawn. "I haven't spoken to anyone at the school. No one was picking up the phone, and they haven't returned my messages."

"Then why are you here?"

"Because of the other phone call. He told me not to call the police, and I didn't know what else to do. I had to see for myself that Sammy's safe."

I'm trying really, really hard to give Stefanie the benefit of the doubt. If she thought it was her son who went missing, then she's probably still in shock. If I were in her designer pumps, which someone fished from the mud and rinsed under the tap before handing back to her, I wouldn't relax until I saw my son, either.

But I also need her to stop playing around and eating up precious time. It's nearing noon, which means Ethan has been missing for more than nine hours. I want to climb over the table, shake Stefanie by the shoulders and tell her to go the hell home.

And then I notice Mac's face. The way his skin has tightened, how without moving any other muscle in his body, he shifts his head toward Stefanie. His poker expression is perfect except for his eyes. They glitter with new interest, with eagerness. I flash a glance at Lucas, and his do, too.

"What other phone call?" the sheriff says, losing patience just like the rest of us.

"The one I received this morning." Stefanie seems a little calmer now, even though she's still not very forthcoming. Her gaze scans the faces around the table. "The person on the other end told me they had Sammy. *That's* why I came up here, to see if it was true."

The room goes still. Stefanie has just stunned us silent.

The sheriff clears his throat. "You're saying that you received a phone call this morning from a person who claimed to have kidnapped your son, Sammy?"

Sammy, the kid who, on more than one occasion, called Ethan a "crybaby loser." The one who earlier this semester invited every boy in the class to his birthday party but Ethan.

"Yes," she says. "He said he had Sammy, and I didn't know what else to do. My husband's not answering his phone and neither was anybody else, and I couldn't just do nothing. I drove here as fast as I could."

"Did you call the police?"

"No. He told me not to. He told me he'd kill Sammy if I did."

My heart backfires, then takes off at a steady sprint. I can't think about her words just yet, can't think about what that means for *my* son, so I steer my mind away from it. I grab Lucas's elbow instead. "I don't understand. They took Sammy, too?"

"No!" Stefanie twists around in her chair, her lithe body strung tight, ready to pounce. She juts a thumb over her shoulder, to the sheriff. "*He* just said Sammy was fine. I demand to see my son right this second."

The sheriff glares across the table at Dawn. "Call over to the hotel, talk to whoever's got eyes on the boy. I want verbal and visual confirmation."

Dawn pulls up a number on her cell and moves to the edge of the room. I can barely breathe because my heart is exploding with a new, desperate hope. Maybe it's not Sammy across town in the Days Inn but Ethan. Maybe this whole ordeal has been one huge, horrible mistake.

While Dawn repeats the sheriff's orders into her phone, he returns his attention to Stefanie. "Start at the beginning. From the second your phone rang—which was when, exactly?—until now. As much detail as you can remember."

"Well, I was at home, on the phone to another class mother when—"

"What time?"

"Sometime just after ten. Five minutes maybe? Certainly not much more."

The sheriff gives her a *go-on* bob of his head.

"Anyway, I was on the patio when my phone rang. I figured it was the school since Sam told me to watch for their call. I picked up even though I didn't know who it was."

"Who was it?" at least three people say at once. I am one of them.

Stefanie shrugs. "The caller's name was blocked. The screen said Unknown."

Mac reaches across the table, palm up. "Can I see your cell?"

She slides an iPhone from her jeans pocket, ticks in her passcode and passes it to Mac.

"Keep going," the sheriff orders. "What did the caller say?"

"So first I heard this weird beeping, like something electronic, and then the voice. He said *I have Sammy.*"

"That's it? Just *I have Sammy*?"

"Well, first the beeping and then he asked if he was speaking to me—"

"You're certain the voice belonged to a male?"

"Yes." She pauses, then frowns. "Well, maybe. It was distorted, like one of those apps that make your voice unrecognizable, so I can't be one hundred percent certain. But the voice was really deep, so I just assumed it was male."

"And he called you by name?"

"Yes. He said, *Is this Stef Huntington?*, and when I said that it was, he said, *Listen carefully. I have Sammy.*"

"Call came in at 10:02," Mac announces, "and lasted for six minutes and forty-three seconds." He waves the phone at the sheriff. "Do you have someone who can trace the call?"

"Probably a burner, but worth a try. If we're lucky, we'll get a location. Give it to Dawn when she's done, and she'll run it over to the tech lab."

Stefanie bristles. "You're going to take my phone?"

"Ma'am, your phone is evidence in a child kidnapping case."

"But what if he calls back?"

And just then, the phone does the unthinkable. It comes alive in Mac's hand, buzzing and lighting up, and a familiar tune drifts through the air. Marvin Gaye's "Let's Get it On."

Matching pink spots bloom on Stefanie's cheeks, and she lunges for the phone. "That's my husband. I've left him like a hundred messages. I'm sure he's frantic." Her hands are shaking as she answers. "It wasn't him. It wasn't Sammy. It was another kid."

The last two words—*another kid*—are as physical as a slap. My entire body jerks. From the very first day that I met this woman, on Ethan's first day of kindergarten, this has been my problem with her; she's just so goddamn entitled.

"His name is Ethan," I say through gritted teeth.

Her glance my way takes two tries before it sticks, and then her brows rise in alarm. "No, I haven't seen him yet," she says into the phone, "but someone from the sheriff's office is contacting the teacher now. I'll text you as soon as she confirms it's him." A pause, and then she holds out the phone to the sheriff. "He wants to talk to you."

"Tell him I'll call him later. For now—"

"You do realize this is the Mayor of Atlanta on the phone."

A dark flush rises up the sheriff's neck, but he keeps his voice in check. "I don't care if it's my dear departed grand-mama calling from the great beyond. A little boy is missing, and you are sitting on information that could lead us right to him. Now hang up the phone so we can get back to it."

She stares at him, her eyes wide with insult, then mumbles to her husband that she'll call him back later.

The sheriff doesn't even wait for her to hang up. "After the caller confirmed it was you and told you he had Sammy, then what did he say?"

She ends the call and slips the phone back into her pocket. "Well, it went back and forth for a while. I was in shock, as you can imagine, and it took a bit before I realized what was going on. I mean, his words were just so unexpected. I couldn't believe them at first. I thought it was some kind of sick prank."

"And when you understood his message?" The sheriff leans in, pushing aside a notepad with his fist. His gaze is latched onto hers like a laser, never once budging from the outlines of her face. The rest of us are breathless. This is the sheriff's show, and we are all spectators.

"Then I jumped in my car and drove like a madwoman all the way here."

"I meant, what did you say?"

"Oh, well, I screamed a lot, I remember that much. I was trying to figure out who it was, who would do such a thing. I begged him, told him I'd do anything he wanted, give him anything he wanted, just please don't hurt my son."

"Did he ask for money?"

"No. In fact, he specifically said it *wasn't* about money."

"Then what were his demands?"

"He kept circling back to Sam, something about preserving the Bell Building downtown. He wouldn't be more specific than that, but he said Sam would understand."

"Your husband. Sammy's father."

"Yes, but obviously, this was about Sam in his role as mayor."

"Did he say anything else?"

"Not that I remember."

"Were there any other voices? Any background noise?"

She scans the people in the room, flustered, studying each face as if for backup. None of us give her any; we are on the sheriff's side here. We want her to answer the damn questions.

"I...I don't think so," she says defensively. She looks at the sheriff, and her face screws into a frown. "Like I said, I was frantic. I was trying to figure out who it was. I made all sorts of wild accusations, told them I would give them anything, *anything* to get Sammy back."

"Who did you think it was?"

"The owner of the Bell Building, whoever that is, or maybe one of the neighbors, some preservationist kook who's angry about the developers taking over downtown. Sam's opponent, or someone working for him. Lord only knows. The crazies came out as soon as Sam announced his bid for mayor, and my cell number isn't exactly top secret. Anybody could get their hands on it. There are a million people it could have been."

The sheriff grunts. "Ethan has been missing now for nine hours. I'm gonna need you to think really, really hard."

She squints, and her eyes glint with self-righteous anger. "For the past ninety minutes, Sheriff, I thought this was *my* son we were talking about, so you can stop with that tone, and you can definitely stop with all the lectures. I understand the importance of this situation. I am doing my very best to answer all your questions. But I was panicked and flustered and your pushing me now isn't making it any easier for me to remember, so I suggest you just back off and give me a minute." She spits out that last bit like a threat, which it clearly is. It hangs over the table like a black cloud, electric and oppressive.

"Got it," Dawn says from the corner, then pulls up a video on her cell phone. She drops it in the middle of the table, and everybody leans in. Lucas and I move closer so we can see.

The first image on the screen is of a woman wearing a Days Inn uniform. She looks into the camera, states her name and the date, May 21, then the camera pans to the little boy seated beside her.

His dark curls are wild and a tad frustrated, just like Ethan's. His ears poke out from the messy locks like fleshy handles, just like Ethan's. Even his glasses, crooked and milky, look just like Ethan's.

But the little boy is not Ethan.

It's Sammy.

He smiles and waves at the camera. "Hi, Mom."

Stefanie bursts into tears, and so do I. Her son is safe, her terror a false alarm, and I hate her for both.

Lucas curls an arm around my shoulders, pulling me against him in a steely grip, and the tears burn down my cheeks like acid. I don't want to be bitter. I try not to be. But I can't help myself. Mac's gaze catches mine over Stefanie's head, and his poker face is gone, twisted into one of such naked pity that it makes the tears flow harder.

The sheriff asks Mac to take Stefanie to the hotel so she can be reunited with her son, and Lucas pulls me tight.

Mac nods, but he doesn't push to a stand. He shifts on his chair, restless. Impatient. "One more question," he says to Stefanie. "What was it this guy said that made you believe?"

She looks up, as if the question surprised her. "I'm sorry. What?"

"What convinced you that the caller had Sammy?"

"Oh. It was his voice."

"Whose, the caller's?"

"No. The little boy's." She pauses, gives me a pained glance, then focuses her attention on Mac. "Well, I guess it was a little boy's. The voice was still distorted, but definitely different than the first. Higher. More faint."

"What did he say?" The question comes from me, but they're the words on everyone's tongue. I just got there first.

Stefanie's gaze creeps to mine, and I know by the way her head is ducked that the answer is not good. The hairs on the back of my neck rise, one by one. Her eyes fill, and then, so do mine.

She winces and looks away. "He said, *Mommy, help.*"

STEF

9 hours, 28 minutes missing

THE REPORTERS HAVE GOTTEN WIND OF THE situation by the time I screech into the Days Inn parking lot in my banged-up SUV. Multiple clusters of them stand huddled under the overhang by the entrance, the only dry spot in a shower that came out of nowhere. I clamber out of the passenger's door and take off running through the rain.

A man in a raincoat sees me coming and steps into my path, a physical barrier between me and the door. I give him a don't-try-it look, and he smiles like this is a game. As soon as I'm close enough, he thrusts his microphone in my face.

"Mrs. Huntington, can you tell us anything about the Atlanta child who went missing during a school field trip?"

I veer to the right, and he matches me step for step. "No comment."

"According to your husband's statement, police suspect foul play. Any thoughts as to the kidnapper?"

I try not to glare at the man operating the television camera, but I'm covered in mud and I just found a spider in my hair, so right now I hate him just as much as every other ass-hole standing between me and my son. "I said, no comment."

I step to the left, and he follows.

The reporter tries again. "I understand your son, Sammy, was one of the students. Did he tell you if he heard or saw anything out of the ordinary?"

"You're shitting me, right?" The reporter grins, both at my answer and my testy tone. He wasn't expecting an answer from me, and honestly, I wasn't expecting to give one to him, but after the past few hours my nerves are shot, and now, so is my patience. "It's pretty goddamn obvious to anyone with eye-balls that I haven't seen Sammy yet, thanks to you and your linebacker cameraman. So either you move out of my way, *now*, or I will have you arrested for harassment."

They don't move, but they don't try to stop me, either, when I push past. The glass doors open with a whoosh of air, and I rush inside.

The middle-aged man behind the counter takes me in with interest. His gaze rakes down my body, lingering not on my curvier spots but on the Georgia clay. The streak on a sleeve, the caked and flaking chunks on my jeans, my brand-new suede Manolos, soaked and ruined. I look like a designer-clad mud wrestler.

"I'm looking for the Atlanta kids," I tell him, and his gaze snaps to mine. "Ms. Quinn is expecting me."

He hikes his chin to the corridor behind me. "Down the hall to the left. The door'll say Employees Only but go on in. There's no way they'll hear you if you knock."

No kidding. I can hear the pandemonium from here, high-pitched squeals and laughter that can only come from excited kids, interspersed with the occasional yelp of an adult. I thank him and hustle down the hall.

The employee break room is teeming with bodies—kids coloring on the white-topped table, clambering across the leather three-seater couch by the wall, running circles around the war-weary adults who've given up trying to corral them. Three boxes of Dunkin' Donuts lie demolished on the far countertop, next to a half-empty gallon of sweetened iced tea.

My gaze seeks out the curly-haired boy by the window. His back is to me, his attention laser-focused on Juliette, a precocious blonde with emerald eyes. They're arguing about how many steps they climbed in the gold mine. She's schooling him, a kind of mini-mansplaining in reverse, but I'm not really listening to her words. I'm thinking that from this angle, Sammy looks exactly like Ethan.

The entire world shrinks down to that one thought, cloaking the ruckus in the room around an absolute eye of silence. It could have been Sammy. It was *supposed* to be him. For seventy terrifying minutes, I didn't know if it was Sammy or Ethan who vanished into the night.

I'm not the type of mother to lose control, have never been the type for public meltdowns. But when he turns to face me and I see my son's face, the relief is just too great. My knees buckle and I collapse, my legs folding up underneath me on the shabby linoleum. Animal sounds of grief pierce the eye of silence, and I realize with a shock they're coming from me.

One by one, every head in the room turns. Sammy pushes through the bodies, his expression hovering somewhere between confused and embarrassed. He's only seen me fall apart like this once, four years ago, when my father died of a heart attack, dead before he'd hit the green of the seventeenth hole. I tell myself Sammy is fine—he's *fine*—but I can't seem to stop crying.

"What are you doing here?" he says. "How come you're so dirty?"

I snatch him to my chest, the loops and tangles of his hair getting caught between my fingers as I rock his body back and forth. I know I'm causing a scene. I know I'm confusing and scaring the kids. They are gathered around us, watching the scene with open mouths and uncomfortable giggles. Their unabashed stares bring me slowly back to reality.

Suddenly, I can only think of one thing.

"Come on," I say, pushing to a shaky stand.

Sammy looks at me in confusion. "Where are we going?"

"Home," I say, to him and the room at large, to the kids and Miss Emma, who can't quite meet my eyes, and in a tone that dares anyone to try and stop me. "I'm taking my son home."

Rather than push through the sea of reporters still camped out under the canopy, Sammy and I sneak through the back and call a taxi, an old four-door Nissan with tattered upholstery and rubber mats on the floorboards. The tough-skinned man behind the wheel couldn't believe his luck when I told him where we were headed, and he even apologized before he asked me for $350. A ludicrous fare for a sixty-mile ride, but I fell onto his backseat without so much as a counteroffer. After seeing the wall of reporters between me and my car, I would have paid him twice as much.

My cell lies faceup on the backseat between us, still and dark. In the end, the police let me keep it, but only if I swore to keep it charged and on at all times. There's something strange about knowing they're monitoring all my calls, listening in on every call that comes in from Sam, my girlfriends, my hairdresser calling to remind me about Thursday's appointment. A necessary measure, they said, for when the kidnapper makes contact again. *When*, not *if*, though I don't know what's fueling their certainty—experience or hope. Either way, waiting for the thing to go off is like living on a *Big Brother* set—you don't know what's going to happen other than it's going to be bad. Every time it chirps or buzzes, my body fills with dread.

Sammy sits strapped to the seat on the other side, kicking his feet and watching the scenery fly by outside the window, his shoulders relaxed like this is a joyride. I know he needs an explanation, but the problem is I'm still trying to decide how much to tell him. I heard the chatter at the camp, read all their grim expressions. The police don't think they'll find Ethan alive, either.

The driver takes a sudden left, steering us down a two-lane ribbon of country road.

"I guess you're wondering why I showed up at the hotel, frantic and covered in mud," I say, turning to Sammy.

He bounces his shoulders. "I don't know. I guess."

Sammy-speak for *yes, but I'm too weirded out to ask.*

My gaze travels to the back of the driver's head, and he catches my eye in the rearview mirror. He looks away quickly, strumming his thumb to the beat of the pop song coming through the radio speakers, but what's the chance I'll read a gross exaggeration of my words in tomorrow's newspaper? High, probably. I lower my voice and choose my words carefully.

"This morning I got a phone call from a man who said he had you. A bad man, probably the one who has Ethan." I tell my nerves to calm, but they don't listen. My hands are still as sweaty as my feet feel inside my sodden shoes, and I wipe them on the seat. "I couldn't reach your father or anyone from the school, and I didn't know what else to do. I drove to the camp to see for myself."

Now, finally, Sammy turns his face to mine. His eyes are magnified by the lenses of his glasses, making him look perpetually wide-eyed. Under the messy hair of his bangs, his forehead is crumpled.

"Sweetheart, do you understand what I'm telling you? I thought it was you, not Ethan, who went missing." I press my palm to the back of his head to flatten a maverick curl. "That's why I'm here. That's why I'm such a mess."

"Oh." His voice is tentative. "But the bad man didn't take me."

I blink back fresh tears. "No, and thank God he didn't. But it was the most scared I've ever been in my whole entire life. Even worse than when the doctor told me you had to come out of my belly a whole seven weeks early."

It's a story Sammy knows well, how I went in for a routine checkup and didn't leave the hospital for days, how the doctors pulled him, blue and silent, from my belly. It's a story with a happy ending, much like the one today. I want to tell him Ethan's will end well, too, but I also don't want to lie. The truth is, I'm already bracing for the worst.

"But why *did* he take Ethan?"

I shake my head. "I don't know. The police don't know. We think it's because he wants something."

"Does he want money? Because Ethan's parents don't have any. He doesn't even own an iPhone." A statement, not reproach.

To myself, I think: *if an iPhone is your point of reference, then maybe we've given you too much.*

But technically, Sammy is not wrong. I've seen how Ethan comes to school, in a rolling rotation of Kmart specials that are too short, too tight, too small—with the glaring exception of those Mondays after a weekend at his father's. Then his jeans are designer, his trendy polos still sporting fold marks from the packaging. Even so, I don't have the idea that Andrew is rolling in cash. Nine times out of ten, people who are that flashy and loud have a lot less money than they'd like you to think, which makes me doubly worried for Ethan. What happens if this guy calls back with a ransom?

"Sweetheart, do you understand how serious this is? A bad man took Ethan, and the police think he meant to take you instead. I'm not telling you this to make you worry, though, or be scared for your own safety. Your father and I will keep you safe until the police find whoever did this."

A short silence while Sammy takes this in. "Will they find Ethan?"

"I hope so. They're working very, very hard. They're doing everything they possibly can."

He nods like he already knows this. "Yeah. They asked us a lot of questions. Like who was at the mines earlier. If we saw anybody at the camp. Things like that."

I fiddle with a lock of his hair. Sammy isn't always a big talker, but once he gets going, there's often no stopping him. I've learned to savor these moments. "And what did you tell them?"

"Well, there was this dude with a million tattoos panning for gold. One of them was a red-and-black snake that looked like it was crawling up his neck. He was pretty weird." A rare and unfettered stream of information.

"Did you tell the police about him?"

"Yeah. They thought his tattoo was pretty weird, too. Oh, and nobody liked the bus driver. He smelled like dirty socks."

I don't put too much stock in Sammy's finger-pointing.

Decorating your neck with permanent pigment doesn't say anything about a person other than that they have a high pain threshold and questionable decision-making skills, but a snake tattoo would certainly get a man noticed by a group of sheltered eight-year-olds.

"What about at the cabin? Did anybody see or hear anything?"

He looks at me with eyes that are wide and dry. "There was a fire, Mom. Mia Davis woke up first, and then she screamed so hard she almost busted my eardrum. Miss Emma told us to run outside and meet by the chairs, so we did. Mr. Fischer went around back to kick some dirt on it, but the fire was too big. We could see the flames coming over the roof."

"That must have been scary."

Another shrug, a one-shouldered bounce, an unenthusiastic *I guess*. "It was mostly boring. We stood around forever while Mr. Fischer ran for help. By the time he came back, the fire was a lot smaller. He put it out with a fire extinguisher."

"And where was Miss Emma while all this was happening? What was she doing?"

"The girls were pretty freaked out. She was trying to calm everybody down."

"And where was Ethan?"

"He was the last to come out because he wanted his backpack even though Miss Emma said to leave them. And then he started crying and wailing like all the girls."

"He was there the whole time?"

"I guess. When Miss Emma couldn't find him, everybody just figured he'd gone off to look at rocks or something." Sammy's mouth curls down at both ends, like it often does when he speaks of Ethan. "He's *so* weird."

A weirdo. A crybaby and a tattletale. These are just some

of the words I've heard Sammy throw around when referring to Ethan. Is it possible to be allergic to another person? Because that's the only way I know to describe it, how exposure to Ethan seems to alter something at Sammy's cellular level. A flushing of skin, a rushing of poisons through the blood, much like when Ethan's lips touch a peanut. One tiny whiff of Ethan, and Sammy seethes with venom and vitriol.

"Sweetheart, someone took Ethan. Doesn't that make you feel scared for him?"

"It's probably just his dad. Miss Emma said so."

A flash of irritation heats my chest. What was Miss Emma thinking? What kind of teacher says such a thing to children?

"But whoever took Ethan meant to take you, remember?" I give Sammy time to do the math, and I see when he realizes his mistake. His eyes go wide with awareness, with new interest. "Ethan is in real, serious danger."

"Oh."

"I know the two of you have never been the best of friends, but I'd really like it if you could try to say only nice things about Ethan from now on. Do you think you can do that?"

Sammy presses his lips together and plucks at a loose thread in the seat cushion. My son owning his power to be silent.

I will myself to stay still instead of reprimanding him, to keep my finger from wagging and my tongue firmly planted in my mouth. What is it my mother used to say? If you can't say something nice, better to say nothing at all. I tell myself that's Sammy's strategy now, that his silence stems from manners, not spite, and yet I know that's a lie.

"Mom?"

I turn to him with a smile. "Yes, sweetie."

"When we get home, can we go to Chick-fil-A for lunch?"

STEF

11 hours, 28 minutes

IT'S NEARING TWO BY THE TIME WE PULL INTO
our Tuxedo Park neighborhood, quiet, leafy streets in the shadows of the Governor's mansion. The driver steers us past stacked stone mailboxes and sprawling lawns, each with a multimillion-dollar home rising up like a colossus from the center of the grass. For me, luxury is a penthouse overlooking Central Park, not these monstrosities of brick and stucco, but Atlantans do love their square footage.

"Who are all those people?" Sammy says, leaning forward on his seat.

"Reporters."

A good two dozen of them with film cameras and zoom lenses, lining the street by the gate. Their vans are parked at the curb behind them, satellite dishes swirling like sunflowers tipped to the sun. They see us coming and rush the taxi like paparazzi, shouting questions and pressing their cameras against the glass as we pass through the gate. Sammy gives them a timid wave, but I duck my head, refusing to give them a clear shot. Over the past four years, I've gotten used to occasional media attention, but this feels claustrophobic, a kind of scrutiny I didn't sign up for. My lungs lock up until we're safely on the other side.

Mom comes rushing outside as I'm paying the driver.

"Darling," she says, opening Sammy's door and dragging him into a hug. He all but disappears into her arms. "Heavens, am I glad to see you. Are you okay? Are you all right? I've been working on your energy from afar—could you feel it?"

Whatever he says gets swallowed up in her torso. I thank the taxi driver and climb out of the car.

Two men I don't recognize wait by the front door, and it's a good thing Sam just texted me about the pair of security guards he hired for our protection, because our house has a remote-controlled gate. A ten-foot perimeter fence. Security cameras aimed at every corner of the property. People don't just show up at our door, and the ones that do are generally not here to borrow a cup of sugar.

"Welcome home, Mrs. Huntington," the tall black man says. The other is shorter and stockier. They are dressed in matching uniforms, midnight fabric stretched across bulky bodies, with identical logos on the upper chest. "I'm Gary, and this is Diego. We're going to have to ask you to get yourself and Sammy inside the house as quickly as possible."

I don't ask questions, and I don't argue. I hustle Mom and Sammy through the front door, lock it and activate the alarm. By the time I turn back around, Sammy is already racing up the stairs, the hunger he'd been complaining about for the past half hour forgotten. I debate calling him back down for a sandwich, then decide to let it go. His grumbling stomach will send him down soon enough.

"How are you?" Mom asks, her face twisted in concern even though I texted her twice. Once from the camp, a brief message that took a half-dozen tries to go through, then a longer update from the taxi on the way home. "Where's your car?"

"At a garage in Dahlonega, getting fixed. I had a little fender bender, but I'm fine. Well, not fine, but better. Thank you." I push up a shaky smile to let her know I mean it. Standing in my own foyer, knowing there are two guards patrolling the perimeter, has me practically weeping with relief. Now all I need is Sam, who promised me he'd be home for dinner.

"I've been watching for updates on TV," Mom says, "but they're not saying much. A child went missing, search parties were dispatched, stay tuned for more updates. That's about it. They don't even mention the little boy's name."

"They're being vague on purpose. The sheriff canceled his press conference, and he ordered me not to talk to anybody other than Sam and the police. He's worried what the kidnapper will do when he discovers he's got the wrong child. But what if he already knows? What if that's the reason he still hasn't called me back?" I check the time on my cell—no new calls. "It's been four hours already."

"Somebody on the internet is claiming it was an inside job," Mom says. "That the teacher was in on it from the beginning, and that she handed him over to a band of gypsies."

"That's ridiculous. There are no bands of gypsies roaming through the North Georgia forests."

"I believe the PC term these days is Irish Travelers, darling, and if you ask me, those folks have gotten a bad rap. The ones I've met have been lovely. Anyway, I didn't say it was true, only that I heard it."

A sudden rumbling drifts down the stairs like an approaching locomotive, vibrating the hairs on my skin and rattling the door in the jamb. Mom glances up at the ceiling. "What on earth?"

I was once that mother who swore the dreaded video game would never cross her threshold. Boys should run and swim and play outside, not sit in a dark room with a television screen and a joystick. And then three years ago, Sammy broke his foot during a particularly brutal soccer game, and he was confined to a wheelchair until the swelling went down. By the end of day two, a slightly unhinged version of me was forking over my credit card to a bearded hipster at Best Buy, who slid a slew of electronics into my trunk with a little too much glee. The Xbox quickly became Sammy's favorite.

"*Gears of War*, by the sounds of things." By now I'm well versed in his video game sounds.

I kick off my ruined shoes and wiggle my toes, leaving a dusting of dried clay on the floor.

"Well, I suppose he does need a distraction. He feels so badly about what happened, you know."

I ponder all the things I don't want to say. That I *don't* know, and there's no way she can, either. That I'm in no mood for her passive-aggressive parenting advice. If Sammy feels bad, he's doing an awfully good job of hiding it.

"The spirits are telling me Sammy feels somehow responsible." Mom is still in her psychic bubble, her expression as serious as I've ever seen it. "What's blocking his energy paths is guilt."

"Well, of course he feels guilty. The kidnapper meant to take him instead of Ethan."

She sighs, a heavy breath that reeks of disappointment. "Sweetheart, you're not paying attention."

I roll my eyes, thinking *this* is why my baby sister moved her family halfway across the United States, because of our mother's new-age nonsense. The spirits are telling her. She's been working on his energy. Why can't she just be a normal grandparent, the type who knits tea cozies and tells bedtime stories under the covers? Honestly, I don't know how my father put up with her as long as he did.

"Just spit it out, Mom."

"Sammy knows more than what he's willing to say. He knows more than what he's telling you."

My exasperation mixes with the day's leftover terror into a bitter brew. I mumble something about a shower, then turn and head up the stairs, but as I'm passing by the video game thunder rumbling behind Sammy's door, it occurs to me why suddenly I'm so angry.

Not because I don't believe her, but because I do.

That night, it's not Sam who shows up at dinnertime, but Josh. Sam's chief of staff, who went AWOL at exactly the wrong time, a man who also happens to be a distant cousin. His face, rounder and more wrinkled than Sam's, is pressed to the window when I come down the stairs. Looming behind him are the two stone-faced guards.

I open the door and wave Josh inside.

Depending on which branch of the family you ask, Josh's grandpa Ned was either a genius, a scoundrel, a saint, a con man or a fool. The one thing every Huntington can agree upon is that Ned married the wrong woman—not Josh's grandmother but Ned's second wife, Maureen, an ex-administrative assistant with questionable typing skills and the figure of a Playboy bunny. When exactly Ned took up with her, while his first wife was withering away of cancer or after her casket was rolled into the family crypt at Oakland Cemetery, is still a point of contention at Christmases and family get-togethers.

Regardless, Ned fell hard and fast, and Maureen was sleeping in his bed before his wedding band had tarnished in the drawer.

Like any good Southern family, the Huntingtons weren't exactly subtle about their disapproval, and their censure drove a wedge between Ned and his three siblings, including Sam's grandfather. Ned sold his shares in the family business, a portfolio of real estate investments up and down the East coast, for more money than he and Maureen could ever spend. Then they proceeded to spend it. They bought vacation homes, racehorses, yachts and cars and airplanes. But the shiny new toys attracted the wrong kinds of people, and Ned got suckered into a string of sketchy investments. His and Maureen's days of living large were over in less than a decade. Maureen moved on. Ned died soon after, and his daughter—Josh's mother, an only child who'd just flunked out of Barnard—was left destitute.

All this goes to say, Josh and Sam may be cousins, but they grew up worlds apart. Sam sailed through life with the Huntington name and trust fund, while Josh weathered a one-bedroom apartment on the wrong side of town. He went to public school and took public transportation and, later, worked his way through public university and then business school. Sam has always admired the way Josh is the first Murrill in three generations to pull himself up by the bootstraps. When Sam decided to run for mayor, Josh was his first hire.

"You look like shit," I say to him now. In the natural light of the foyer, his face is puffy, his skin paler than usual everywhere but under his eyes, twin dark smudges that bleed into his cheeks. "What happened to you?"

Josh gives a sarcastic snort. "What happened is an Atlanta child went missing while I was visiting my sister in the boondocks. If it weren't for some trucker with a transistor radio at the Denny's, I'd still be sitting on my sister's front-porch couch right now, watching the grass grow."

Josh's sister, however, is much less of a self-starter. Her

straight-D squeak through high school was followed by a series of dead-end jobs waiting tables or scrubbing floors, all of which she managed to get fired from before the first paycheck had cleared. As far as I can tell, she lives off unemployment, food stamps and the few hundred bucks Josh presses into her palm whenever he drives to South Georgia to visit, which is often.

"Anyway, I'm on my way downtown, but I wanted to stop by and check on you and Sammy. How are y'all?"

As much as Josh loves my husband and me, he adores Sammy. The two are often disappearing together to go rock climbing or laser tagging or go-cart racing around the track in Alpharetta. Josh claims the dates with Sammy keep him young, but Sam says Josh has always had a taste for adrenaline. I sometimes worry that he's teaching my son the same, but then Sammy comes home so full of excitement that I can't bear to tame their time together. And besides, Josh would never let any harm come to Sammy.

"We're fine, thanks." Are we fine? I say it again, more for my sake than his. "Sammy and I are fine. Or we will be, as soon as they catch whoever did this. Have you talked to Sam?"

Josh shakes his head. "He's been tied up in meetings with the police all afternoon. Still no news on who's behind this, which means the police have no clue where to look for that boy." He moves closer, his rubber-soled shoes silent on the foyer floor. "I know it's the last thing you want to be talking about, but can you give me a quick rundown of that phone call?"

I pause, summoning my strength to recount the drama for what feels like the hundredth time. I go through the phone conversation word for word, telling Josh everything I can remember, and it takes me right there, back in the thick of it. To the sound of that man's voice coming through the phone and the feverish drive to Dahlonega. To my hysterical blab-

bering into Sam's voice mail when I didn't know where our
son was or if he was alive or dead. To the panic rising in my
chest all over again, choking me until I can't breathe.

"And you're certain the caller was male?"

"The voice was distorted, so no. I can't know for sure, but
it seemed awful low. Too low to be coming from a woman,
I think. And there was a long stretch when I was trying to
understand what he was telling me. I was talking in panicked
circles, but his voice never went screechy or high, not even
when he told me to shut up and listen. It stayed low and calm
the whole time."

Josh shakes his head. "Did he say when he'd call back?"

"No. Just that ultimately, what happened next was up to
Sam. He said not to demolish the Bell Building, and that Sam
would know why."

Josh's forehead crumples, and his eyes narrow into slits.
"Why?"

"I don't know. I don't know anything about the Bell Building."

"It's part of the Marietta redevelopment downtown. A real
eyesore. I can't imagine why anyone would want to keep it.
Did you talk to Sam?"

Marietta is a street near the aquarium, one that's been all
over the news since Sam's office started fielding bids from
developers to repurpose an entire city block. Sam is behind
a LEED-certified mixed-use development, one that includes
mass transit, retail, green space, and above, apartments and
condos. It's a cornerstone of his reelection campaign.

And now, apparently, cause for a kidnapping.

I nod. "Only briefly, but he was in a room full of people.
The only thing he really said was that we'd talk tonight."
I glance behind me and then up the stairwell, making sure

Mom and Sammy haven't sneaked into the foyer, eavesdropping on the conversation. By the sound of the video game rumbling, they're still upstairs, but I lower my voice anyway. "Josh, what's going on here? Is Sam's administration in some kind of trouble?"

"I don't know."

I stare at him in disbelief, his uncertainty only heightening my panic. Josh is the self-proclaimed wizard behind the mayoral curtains, the reason many people, Sam included, say he got elected. "What do you mean you don't know?"

"Has Sam mentioned anything to you about the leaks?"

"No." I shake my head, stepping back. "What leaks?"

"Somebody's been feeding Nick Clemmons information. His media plan, his community outreach, even his campaign poster looks like the one we were about to unveil. He knows everything we're about to do, right before we do it, every goddamn time."

Nick is Sam's opponent, the candidate who came out of nowhere and whose platform is built on the sole selling point that he's not a tree hugger like Sam.

"Who's telling him?"

"That's what we're trying to figure out, and before it completely sabotages our campaign. As of this morning, we were only up by a four-and-a-half-point split."

This is interesting enough to dampen some of my worry. When Sam ran the first time, he jostled for attention in a crowded field of eight candidates, and he won by a surprise margin that for those first few months, grew his head by a good two sizes. This time around it's just him and Nick, and whatever hopes Sam and Josh may have had for another landslide are long gone. Nick has surprised them, and not in a good way.

And then I think of something that prickles my arms with gooseflesh. "Do you think the leaks are connected to the kidnapping somehow?"

"It's possible. I don't know. I need to talk to Sam before jumping to any conclusions." Josh checks his watch, reaching in his pocket for his keys. "Jesus, what a nightmare. We've got a fund-raising event at the Fox on Thursday, a donor lunch every day this week, a hundred and eighty days left in the campaign, and Chief Phillips calling for a total media blackout, which is the very last thing we need to be doing. If we don't get out in front of this mess, Nick Clemmons is going to crucify us."

"Do you want something to eat? I could make you a sandwich or something."

"Thanks, but Sam's waiting, and I hit a drive-through on the way here." Josh pats his paunch, which has spread since Sam took office—a combination of not enough gym time and too many fast-food dinners at his desk. "Hey listen, when all this is over, what do you think of me and Sammy disappearing up to Asheville for a couple of days? I've been promising to take him white-water rafting forever now, and you and Sam could use a break."

I smile. "Sammy will be thrilled, and so would I."

"Give him a hug for me, will you? Glad y'all are all right." He drops a kiss on my cheek and disappears out the door.

KAT

ONE WEEKEND, WHEN ETHAN WAS STILL IN diapers and Andrew was away on a business trip, Izzy came over to keep me company.

Andrew and I were in the midst of yet another spat, and my skin was still stinging at the angry words we hurled back and forth before he wheeled his suitcase out of the house. This was back before our relationship had reached the tipping point, before either of us had said words that couldn't be snatched back, when the inevitable still felt evitable. Izzy was there to help me dissect our relationship like a high school biology earthworm and study it from every angle. I wanted her to point to a spot with her scalpel and say *here*. Here is where this can be fixed.

I lamented over a bottle of wine while Ethan played on the carpet at our feet, a slice of late-afternoon sun lighting up his curls like spirals of fire. Izzy had come equipped with a gift, a set of old-school alphabet blocks to keep him busy, and Ethan was stacking them into a tall, teetering tower. As he was putting the last block onto the pile, Izzy poked the tower with a toe, and the blocks came tumbling down. Ethan's brow puckered, but he didn't cry. When she tried to rectify her clumsiness, he pushed her hands away, his little face determined.

But it wasn't another tower that he built. It was a long, snaking line of blocks across the carpet, and he'd arranged them in perfect alphabetical order. Not one block out of sequence. Not one letter turned upside down. Izzy was stunned that a thirteen-month-old could do such a thing, but I remember only feeling weepy, because that's when it hit me: I would never understand what was going on in my own son's head. Ethan may have come from my body, he may have my DNA coursing through his veins, but his brain was a beautiful, brilliant fluke. There were thoughts inside there I would never know, ones I could never come close to comprehending. I may have been his flesh-and-blood mother, but never have I felt so far removed from my own child as I did in that moment.

Never, that is, until now.

Now I'm standing on the front porch of the tiny cabin at Camp Crosby, hugging the plastic bag filled with clothes I'd brought for Ethan to my chest. The forest rustles all around me, changing colors with my tears—chartreuse to emerald to a deep olive green. Except for a few stragglers, the camp is empty, the sounds of dogs and choppers and shouts long since faded into birdsong. Everyone is gone except us.

"Are you ready?"

I startle at Mac's voice, coming from just a few feet away on the porch.

I shake my head. "I need a minute."

He nods and leans a hip onto the railing, settling in like he has all day.

Earlier, when the sheriff's team packed up their equipment and took their operation across town, to an office with walls and cubicles and Wi-Fi, it felt wrong. Even after Stefanie showed up, throwing the camp into a tailspin with that mysterious six-minute phone call, I can't contemplate leaving. Leaving now—without Ethan, without answers—feels too much like saying goodbye.

"There have to be more clues. There must be something we missed." I read once everybody has a sixth sense; we just don't all know how to tap into it. My gaze searches the woods like they hold the answer. There's a gravitational pull between me and my son. He's out there somewhere, I'm sure of it.

Mac leans down to brush some brambles from a pants leg. His once-nice slacks are ruined, snagged in spots and covered in streaks of orange clay. There's a stick caught in his hair, but I don't know him well enough to tug it out.

"Just because we're leaving doesn't mean we're giving up, or even that all of us are leaving." He juts a finger over my shoulder, past the cabin to the trees and the forest beyond. "The feds are staying, and they're out there right now following the same tracks that we did. If we missed anything, they'll find it."

I nod, wanting to believe him. The wind stirs, whisking a chunk of hair across my face and crawling up my spine, covering it with goose bumps despite the sunshine. Like somebody walked over my grave, Lucas would say, and I cringe. *My* grave. Mine. Not Ethan's.

"What if he comes back?" I say. "What if somebody finds him and I'm sixty miles away in Atlanta?"

I've already been through this line of questioning, first with the sheriff then with Mac and Lucas, all of them multiple times. The sheriff is already gone, and so are most of his team. Only the FBI team is left, sweeping up whatever we've missed. Even Lucas thinks it's time to go, though he's coming home with me instead of turning north for Tennessee, following behind us on his bike.

Mac gives me the same answer as before. "Then Lucas or I will bring you back."

Across the clearing, Lucas comes banging out of the dining hall in the same clothes he had on when he first arrived, jeans and boots and his faded orange ball cap. His leather coat is clutched in a fist. He stops at the edge of the porch and slides on his sunglasses before stepping into the bright sunshine. Sometime in the past few hours, the sky has cleared into a brilliant blue.

Time to go. Mac pushes off the railing. "Do you have everything?"

I stare down at the bag in my hand. "Everything" is all I have left of my son, the empty compass pouch and the stuff Mac instructed me to pack from home. A change of clothes, Ethan's toothbrush, a spare pair of glasses. The only thing missing is his stuffed rabbit. The sheriff wanted to keep it for the dogs. As soon as he told me, I ran outside and threw up in the bushes because I knew he meant cadaver dogs.

Mac takes the lead down the stairs, and I'm following behind when my phone buzzes in my back pocket. That rare spot of service on the pathway to the clearing. I stop and pull out my phone, sucking a noisy breath at the word popped up on the screen.

Unknown.

Every hair on my body soldiers to attention. When the kidnapper called Stefanie, his name was blocked. Her screen said "Unknown," too.

Mac sees I'm not following and doubles back. "What's wrong?"

I turn the screen so he can see.

Blood roars in my ears, loud enough I barely hear the phone's second ring.

"Put it on Speaker." He steps close, so close we're practically chest to chest. My phone is wedged between us in a palm, screen to the sky. "I want to hear it, too."

I nod, then with shaking hands, answer the call. "Hello?"

There are no weird clicking sounds like Stefanie described. No voice distorted beyond recognition. Just a deep, male voice that feels somehow familiar. "Hi, is this Kat Jenkins?"

I look at Mac, who as far as I can tell is not breathing. He dips his chin in a nod.

My voice is high and squeaky. "Yes, speaking."

"Kat, this is Sam Huntington. Sammy's father."

The breath whooshes out of me in a rush, chased by... What? Relief? Disappointment? My whole body is shaking, panting like I just sprinted up to the edge of a cliff.

Sam Huntington and I have never spoken. We've never run into each other at school. I know nothing about the man beyond what I see on TV, but now I know where I've heard this voice.

My name is Sam Huntington, and I approved this message.

"Mayor Huntington," I somehow manage.

Mac takes a step back, then swipes a hand through his hair. He turns to Lucas, motioning to wait at the bottom of the hill.

"Please, call me Sam. After everything that happened today, you and I are on the same team. We should be on a first name basis. May I call you Kat?"

"Of course."

"Excellent. You know, Kat, I spent a good chunk of time trying to come up with what to say to you right now. I mean, there's not really a protocol for this situation. Whoever took your son meant to take mine instead. Ethan has been put in harm's way because of something involving me and my family. The only words I could come up with are I'm sorry. Truly. I'm so sorry this is happening to Ethan."

His words touch me in a way I can't quite explain. Maybe because I wasn't expecting them, or because he sounds so sincere. Either way, it's a hell of a lot more than his wife said to me, only a few hours ago.

"Thank you. That means a lot."

"This isn't some empty campaign promise. Whoever did this came after my son. My family. This is personal now, and I'm going to go after your son as if he were my own. I am going to hunt this monster down and make him pay. I won't rest until he's behind bars."

And suddenly, I know why this man was elected mayor. Why people trust him with their well-being, their lives and their livelihoods. I don't follow politics and I've never trusted politicians, and yet I don't for a second doubt he means every word.

"Are you on your way back to Atlanta?"

"Yes. Well, almost…" I sigh, my eyes burning at the thought of quitting this place. "It just doesn't feel right, leaving him here."

"You are not leaving him, and no one is giving up. No one. If anything, we are doubling down on the search for your son. I've already allocated more funds and manpower to the investigation, and I will call in the National Guard if I need to. This is my cell we're on. If you have questions, if you need anything at all, even if it's just a middle-of-the-night pep talk, you call me, okay? I'll text you the number as soon as we hang up."

I nod, because I suddenly can't speak. Stefanie's antics, Sam's sincerity, the stealthy woods and my empty arms. It's all too much. I look helplessly up at Mac, who takes the phone from my hand and says all the words I wish I could say. That I'm grateful for Sam's support. That I appreciate the effort and this call. That I look forward to his updates.

And then Mac hits End and hands me back my phone, and there's nothing left to do.

Time to go.

STEF

28 hours, 37 minutes missing

I WAKE UP ON SATURDAY MORNING ALONE.

Sam is already up, which wouldn't normally be a surprise, if he didn't slide into bed at well past three. He didn't say a word, either, didn't offer up explanation or apology for coming home eight hours late for dinner, but I could tell the day had been brutal by the way we made love. Raw. Urgent. Desperate.

Despite the morning's quiet, my mind is noisy. I check the time on my cell and do the math. Just past seven, which means Ethan's been missing for more than twenty-eight hours. An eternity for a missing child. I know because I spent most of last night researching the statistics, reading every horror story the internet could cough up. A six-month-old baby vanished from her crib. A toddler from his stroller at a theme park. A second grader walking home from school. All gone without a trace. One of the 800,000 children that go missing each year. Most missing children aren't found weeks or months or years later—not unless they're a corpse.

I roll toward my nightstand and hit the button for the black-out shades, thick swathes of material that turn daytime into the darkest night, and they whir up to reveal a brilliant spring morning. Sunshine streams through the windows, painting the walls a golden yellow that's far too cheery for the second day in the search for a missing boy. I push back the covers and slide out of bed.

On my way to the bathroom, I spot motion in the backyard. Sam, his cell phone pressed against an ear, pacing the length of the pool. Nobody, not even Josh, calls the mayor at seven o'clock on a Saturday morning unless it's bad news.

I slip out onto the balcony, and Sam's voice floats up to greet me.

"You said this wasn't going to be a problem. You assured me, *assured* me this deal was squeaky clean."

So not about Ethan, then. Something else.

I start to go inside, but something in Sam's tone makes me step closer to the railing.

"Well, of course he does business with the city. Half my donors do in some form or another because they live here. They own businesses here. But that's not why they contribute. They contribute because they want their name listed on the back of the inaugural ball invitation, not because they're looking for kickbacks. And even if they are, I make things crystal clear before the first paper is signed."

This is only partly true. Sam may not grant his donors kickbacks when it comes to city business, but he has no problem bringing prospective ones into our social circles, then asking me to charm their pants off. I get them talking about their families, their hobbies, their favorite vacation spots. I laugh at their jokes and pretend to be impressed by their talk of sports cars and mountain homes and big-game hunting trophies. By the time Sam asks them to pull out their checkbooks, they've tacked on a few zeros. Hook, line, sinker. Go team.

Turns out I'm more like my father than I thought.

But exchanging money for favors? Sam is too prudent, too careful for that.

Although, he doesn't seem awfully worried about the neighbors, much less the reporters camped out at the gate. What if one of them has scaled the ten-foot fence? What if he's crouched behind the backyard bushes, listening to Sam's words now? Maybe I should call down for Sam to take this conversation inside.

"Hang on, hang on. Back up. *Who* was asking questions?" Whatever the answer, Sam doesn't like it. He swings around, his shoulders stiff and straight, twin blades jutting through his white cotton shirt. "Fuck. *Fuck.* You know what will happen if this gets out. We are six months out from the election. This is *not* the time for a scandal."

His words flash-freeze my skin, covering every inch of it in chill bumps, despite the morning's warmth. My mind rewinds to Josh's words just last night, his reluctant reveal that their office has sprung a leak, how whatever is going on at City Hall might be connected to Ethan's disappearance.

Sam pivots and heads for the door. "Give me a couple of hours to huddle with Josh. Marietta was his deal, and he's more intimate with the details than I am. I'll call you as soon as…" Sam's voice fades as he disappears into the house.

Marietta Street, home of the Bell Building and now, apparently, scandal.

I hurry inside and get dressed.

Sammy is up, his door open, the ubiquitous video game sounds bursting in fits and starts into the hall. I pause in his doorway, blinking into the darkness. The heavy curtains are drawn, blocking out the natural light and transforming his room into a cave. Intermittent flashes come from the flat screen on the wall.

"Yesssss," Sammy hisses, and that's when I spot him on the bed. He throws both hands into the air in victory. Neither is holding the controller.

My gaze scoots to his gaming chair, to the bare toe peeking out from behind it, the one with a chipped orange nail. "Mom, what are you doing?"

She swings her head around the side, grinning. "Sammy's showing me how to stick it to the locusts." She turns back to the TV, punching at the controller with both thumbs. "Now what, darling?"

Sammy springs up and runs to the TV, pointing to the left side of the screen. "Follow Dom. Him and the rest of Delta Team are looking for the locust source. Go up those stairs, but be careful because—look out!" He jumps up and down, right as the screen erupts in another spectacular explosion.

"What happened?" Mom says. "Where'd I go?"

Sammy turns to her, grinning underneath crooked glasses. "You got killed."

"What? Well, that's not fair. I wasn't nearly done."

He snatches the controller from her fingers, starts the game all over again and hands it back with her marching orders: find the locusts, kill them, don't get killed again.

"How about some breakfast?" I suggest, but by now Mom has blown another locust to smithereens, and neither seems eager to leave the game.

"Later," Sammy says, not taking his gaze from the screen.

"Later," Mom parrots.

I leave them to battle the beasts.

I spend the next hour or so in the kitchen, sipping coffee and scrolling through the ajc.com, channel surfing for news of

Ethan and listening for the sounds of Sam in his study. Multiple voices rise and fall through the double wooden doors—closed tight for privacy, which he hardly ever does. Another conference call, by the sounds of it.

I pause on the local NBC affiliate, where a solemn-faced woman stands at the entrance to what I recognize as Camp Crosby. She holds a microphone under overly glossed lips.

"The FBI is asking for information from the public in the disappearance of a second grade boy from Atlanta from the cabin where he was staying here, at Camp Crosby in Dahlonega. Police describe him as a four feet tall white male of approximately ninety pounds, with dark hair and hazel eyes. He was last seen wearing red plaid pajama pants and a black long-sleeved T-shirt with the words Don't Wake the Beast written across the front. Anyone with information is asked to call the tip line at the bottom of the screen."

The reporter moves on, something about a prayer vigil community organizers are planning in downtown Dahlonega for tonight, and by now I'm only half listening. I'm too busy thinking of Kat.

I picture her huddled in front of a television screen across town, watching the same reporter list off a bare-bones, generic description of her son and crying with frustration. Or standing at the edge of the woods in Dahlonega, screaming her son's name into the trees. I wonder if she spent the night pacing the floors while the clock ticked away at her sanity and the rest of us snored, oblivious to her midnight monsters. I wonder if Ethan is out there somewhere, frantic with fear and missing his mother, or if his body is rotting in a place nobody knows about. The last thought makes my heart race in fear, in sympathy.

A hand presses on my shoulder and squeezes, and I startle at the unexpected touch. "You okay?"

Sam, showered and shaved, in pressed khakis and a button-down shirt, dressed for work even though it's before eight on a Saturday. Sam likes to live his life as if there are always people watching. I give his hand a pat, and he moves away in a cloud of aftershave and starch.

"I'm fine. Just thinking about Ethan."

He rounds the island, pulls a cup from the cabinet and slides it under the coffee machine nozzle. "I noticed. I've been talking to you for at least a minute now. You didn't hear a word I said, did you?" He punches a button, and the machine comes to life, grinding the beans with a loud whir.

I wait for the noise to die down. "No. What did you say?"

"I asked if there was any word."

"Not on the TV." I awaken my cell on the counter next to me and check the screen, even though I know there's nothing. The ringer volume is turned on high, and the phone hasn't left my side. "Nothing from the kidnapper, either."

"Jesus, what a mess." Sam leans with both elbows on the countertop, the morning sun lighting him up from behind. People often refer to him as Atlanta's Golden Boy, and despite his Mediterranean coloring, they're not wrong. Even now, barreling toward the wrong end of forty, his beauty still dazzles me.

But his remark might just be the understatement of the century.

"There were more than two thousand comments on this morning's *AJC* article," I say, pushing off my stool to fetch a yogurt from the fridge. I offer him one, but he shakes his head. "You wouldn't believe the conspiracy theories. Someone suggested Ethan was abducted by aliens, or carted off to

Mexico by a gang of human traffickers. Most seemed to think it was a hoax, though. An elaborate and sneaky trick to garner attention."

"Attention for what?"

"To get you reelected, apparently. They think you've masterminded the kidnapping in order to drum up votes, and that when he's found safe and sound, you'll take all the credit. Voters do love a hero."

Sam pushes himself upright, digging a spoon from the drawer in front of him. "That's ridiculous. Tell those folks to check the polls. I'm up seven points. It's not like I need the publicity."

"Four and a half."

He holds out the spoon, but when I reach for it, he doesn't let go.

"The polls," I say. "The split is down to four and a half. Josh told me last night when he dropped by."

"Another ridiculous rumor." Sam releases the spoon, but his forehead doesn't uncrease. He pulls his cell from his pocket, his thumbs flying across the screen. "Shit," he murmurs, and I know Josh was right.

"He also told me about the leaks, and the possibility they might be connected somehow to Ethan."

Sam looks up from his cell. "Connected how?"

"I don't know. Didn't you and Josh talk about this last night?"

"I haven't seen Josh. He texted when he was on the way back from his sister's, but we've been crossing paths ever since. What else did y'all talk about?"

"The phone call, mostly. He said the Bell Building was part of the Marietta property."

Sam confirms it with a nod. "Smack in the middle, too. There's no other option than to raze it."

"The kidnapper said he'd kill Ethan if you did that."

"No, he said he'd kill Sammy. No telling what he'll do once he figures out he's got the wrong kid—that is, if he hasn't already."

I sink back onto my stool, the yogurt forgotten. "Does this have anything to do with this morning's phone call? I heard something about a scandal."

"You heard that, did you?" Sam inhales deeply, his chest puffing with a sigh that smells of coffee and toothpaste. "Long story, but a reporter is sniffing around, asking some pretty explosive questions about the Marietta deal. None of it's true, of course, but I need to get a handle on the situation before things blow out of control. I'm going to be tied up most of the day. What time is that detective coming again?"

The same detective I met at the camp, who gave me the side-eye while the sheriff delivered a barrage of questions in an accusatory tone. Who asked me about that phone call over and over, as if repetition might somehow carve out a new explanation for what was said in those six and a half minutes. And who called me late last night, demanding another round of questioning this afternoon.

"Not until two. Will you be here for that?"

Sam's cell buzzes in his palm, and he frowns at the screen. A text.

"Sam, did you hear me? I'd really like you to be there for the talk with the detective. I could use the support."

Nothing. His thumbs are tapping out a response.

"*Sam.*"

He glances up, his expression distracted, his body jittery in that way it gets after a third cup of coffee. "The police are going to find this guy, babe. They're not going to rest until whoever took Ethan is behind bars."

I try to believe him, really I do, but this isn't his campaign. Sam is not pledging to get tough on crime or patch up the city's potholes. We both know this is a promise he might not be able to keep.

"Okay, but that's not what I asked. Will you be here at two?"

"Huh? Oh, sure."

I'm pretty positive he doesn't have the first idea what question he just answered. I'd ask again, but he's already walking away.

My phone rings just after lunch, as I'm rinsing the shampoo from my hair in the shower. I swipe the soapy water from my eyes and lean my head out the glass door, trying not to drip directly on the screen. I want it to be the kidnapper. I don't want it to be the kidnapper. Relief surges when I see it's Emma, followed closely by irritation. *Now* she calls me, a full twenty-four hours after I crammed her voice-mail box with frantic messages.

I turn off the water, dry my hand on the bath mat and pick up, right before it goes to voice mail. "Hi, Emma."

"Omigod, Stef. I'm so glad I caught you. Please tell me you've got some good news."

I step out of the shower and wrap a towel around my body, wedging the phone between my wet shoulder and an even-wetter ear. "Unfortunately, no. I don't know any more than you do. There's still no word about Ethan."

"Oh Jesus. Oh God." Her voice spirals a good octave higher than normal. "Oh my God oh my God oh my God. I am just *sick* about this. Like, literally sick. I've been throwing up ever since I turned around and Ethan was gone."

The Emma I've come to know is even-keeled. Calm to the point of Zen, unruffled in the face of emergencies, like when Jamie Lawson's father dropped dead of an aneurysm during morning car pool. She had corralled the kids and was dialing 9-1-1 before his head hit the concrete. I've never once heard her raise her voice, much less wail and make herself sick.

Then again, Ethan disappeared on her watch. How could she not blame herself?

"I overheard one of the cops say something about a kidnapping. Is that what you heard?"

"No." I pad through the bedroom and slip out onto the balcony for some fresh air. It's a glorious day, neither too humid nor too hot, the kind of afternoon Atlantans spend outside, on terraces or in the park. Not cooped up in a house. I sink onto the couch under the eaves, curl my feet underneath me on the seat and lie my face off. "I haven't heard anything."

Emma makes a choking sound, and I realize she's crying. "I swear on a stack of Bibles, Stef. I only turned my back for two seconds. The fire was huge and the kids were screaming, and I was trying to keep everybody calm. You *know* how I am with those kids."

I start to hum, then stop myself, keeping silent instead. I do know how Emma is with them, but I also know this experience will put her out of a job. Whether it was her fault or not doesn't matter. The board will never keep her on after this.

"What's Kat going to *do*?" Emma is saying. "She doesn't have the money for ransom. She probably owes her divorce lawyer more than she earns in a year. I don't know how she manages to scrape together tuition, much less a ransom. What if the kidnapper wants millions of dollars? She doesn't have that kind of cash."

"I don't know." I sink back into the cushions, careful to keep my tone neutral. The police warned me to not speak to anyone but them or Sam about the phone call. No way I'm going to be the one to tell Emma that this isn't about money.

"And her husband sure as hell can't pay. In fact, for a while there I was positive he was the one behind it. I even told the sheriff that Andrew would be my first guess. I mean, he's not allowed to pick his son up from school except on his allotted Fridays, so she must have suspected he was capable of trying something awful. What if that kidnapping rumor is some sort of trick, to throw the police off? It's possible, you know."

She cries some more, and I shift uncomfortably on the couch. I don't like that she's spilled this little tidbit about Andrew's pickup limitations, about their messy divorce and Kat's finances. Emma and I aren't friends. If she's this loose-lipped with me about another mother, what else has she let slip, and to whom? If I had any questions before as to her discretion, she just answered them.

Mom's words come back to me suddenly: *Sammy knows more than what he's telling you.* If I'm totally honest, that's a big reason I picked up this call. "Emma, did anything happen on this trip? Something I need to know about?"

The problem is, there's always something. Ethan and Sammy can't be within a hundred yards of each other without name-calling or a shoving match or flying fists. When I suggested the school separate the two, put them in different classrooms on opposite ends of the building, they thought I was overreacting.

"Sammy and Ethan need to learn how to tolerate each other," Dr. Abernathy, the kind-eyed principal with wild salt-and-pepper frizz told me. "We wouldn't be doing either of them any good by separating them. Learning to coexist with people we don't particularly like is a life skill, and even if we did place them in different classrooms, different buildings even, they'd still run into each other on the playground, during lunchtime, at every school-wide event. It's better to put them in an environment where we can monitor their behavior and correct when necessary."

Which is all the freaking time.

Emma sighs, long and hard. "Oh, Stef, those two are like oil and water, you know that, but I talked to both the boys individually, and then we sat down together, the three of us, and talked everything out. I thought I had things under control. I was positive I did. They shook hands and told each other they were sorry. The argument was over. Buried."

For all her good intentions, Emma doesn't know my son at all. If she did, she'd know that Sammy doesn't bury any argument, at all, ever, unless he wins it, and her penal system would not be a deterrent but a spark, one that would only fuel his anger. Case in point? Sammy would sooner change the subject than admit he feels bad about Ethan. Whatever concessions he might have made that day for Miss Emma were only for show.

"But?"

"But then there was another argument at the camp. Pretty normal stuff for those two, a lot of shoving and finger-pointing. It's sometimes hard to tell who's tormenting whom."

"What was the argument about?"

"The stones they found at the mines, apparently. Sammy accused Ethan of stealing his. Ethan denied it, of course, but there was no way to prove who was right. I made them put all the stones in a pile and take turns choosing until they'd divvied everything up." The phone rustles as she blows her nose. "Anyway, will you call me as soon as you know anything?"

Hell, no. I will not be calling her, not after this conversation. Emma is mental if she thinks I'll be sharing confidences with her ever again.

"Of course," I lie.

"Thank you. And Stef?"

"Yes?"

"Please don't mention to anyone what I told you about Andrew. His pickup rules. I shouldn't have said anything, but I'm just so wrecked. I mean, I looked that woman in the face and told her I'd take care of her son, and then... She blames me, you know. She thinks this is all my fault."

Emma dissolves into a sobbing, blubbering mess, and I hold my tongue. I know she's waiting, expecting me to say something comforting, but I've got nothing. Maybe she did nothing wrong. Maybe none of this is her fault. But if I were in Kat's shoes right now, if the person who took Ethan had taken my son as planned, I'd sure as hell be looking for someone to blame.

And whether or not any of this is her fault, there's really only one obvious choice.

"Bye, Emma," I say, and hang up.

KAT

32 hours, 4 minutes missing

DUNWOODY STABLES IS A QUIET ENCLAVE OF million-dollar homes, separated from the bustle of Mount Vernon Road by a lazy creek, a thick fringe of evergreens and a heavy iron gate. The last is more for show than anything else, as it swings open all day long—for visitors, the UPS truck, the hordes of workers that descend every weekday to clean neighborhood pools and trim hedges. I stop in front of it now and press the button on my old remote, and after a couple of breathless seconds, the gate groans, then slides apart.

"We're in." I hand Lucas the remote, which he tosses onto the dash.

"Good thing Feckless didn't change the frequency."

"For the same reason he didn't bother changing the locks. Never in a million years would he think I'd actually dare to come here."

Neither did I. Neither did Lucas, for that matter, though he didn't argue when I told him what I was planning. He didn't bring up the restraining order or the fact that I could be arrested. He didn't tell me to let the police handle things or that

I had lost my mind. He just reached for his shoes and said no way he was letting me go alone.

Mac and his men have already searched the house and my son is not here. What the sheriff said at the camp was right: Andrew was nowhere near Dahlonega when Ethan disappeared. He was an ocean away, stretched out on the white sands of St. Martin. And yet here I am. Despite what Mac tells me, despite all the evidence that says otherwise, I can't seem to let go of my suspicions that Andrew was somehow involved.

We motor past my former neighbors, their McMansions looming like stone sculptures over half-acre lots, the yards pristine and untrampled by tiny feet. No abandoned bikes or scooters left on the sidewalks, no forgotten footballs or soccer goals tucked under a tree. The HOA requires all toys and sports equipment be stored out of sight in the garage or backyard.

"Where is everybody?" Lucas says, gesturing to the empty street ahead of us.

"The soccer field. The grocery store. Inside watching cartoons or playing video games. People generally keep to themselves."

"Well, what the hell kind of fun is that?" Lucas mumbles.

In Lucas's book, exactly none. Weekends at his house are a revolving door of neighbors and friends, stopping by to watch a game or shoot the shit because they know he keeps his pantry loaded with snacks and his fridge stocked with beer. If he spots a buddy on the road, he rolls down his window and stops to say hi.

But this is Dunwoody, and people here prefer their backyard lanais over the cushioned benches on the front porch. Neighborly interactions occur from the fancy womb of their air-conditioned cars, drivers waving to each other as they zoom past.

I pull to a stop at the curb and stare up at a monstrosity of brick and stone. The shingles have turned a darker shade of gray. The bushes on either side of the front door could use a trim. The attic shutter I was bitching about six months ago still sags on the left-hand side. I lean into the windshield, tipping my head to see all the way up to the peak. The place looks exactly the same, and yet it's like I'm seeing it for the first time.

"Those window boxes cost $750 apiece," I say, "and that's excluding the cost of the plants, which Andrew has replaced four times a year so the flowers are always in season. You can't see it from here, but there's a hose attached to the irrigation system so he never has to worry about watering them."

Lucas snorts. "That's the most ridiculous thing I've ever heard."

Exactly my point.

"Look at this place, everything about it is ridiculous. Its overplanted yard, all that tumbled river stone. But Lucas, I swear, the first time I walked through that door, it was like winning the lottery. I mean, how many people go from food stamps to a mansion in the suburbs? I felt so lucky, so blessed."

"You were never on food stamps."

I puff a sarcastic laugh. "No, but there were times I was close, and I wouldn't have said no to some free groceries. But I guess what I'm saying is, if I hadn't been so poor, would I have seen through Andrew's bluster? Because this house, his sports car and designer watches, the casually dropped comments about his big-number business deals. I can see now it was all for show—one I fell for like some lovesick sucker."

"Lots of people fell for Andrew's bluster. That's what a con man does. He cons people."

"But why was I so susceptible to it? I hate to think it was because of all the things he could give me, but maybe it was. You saw through him right away. Why didn't I?"

Lucas twists on the seat to face me, his gaze direct, unbothered. Confrontational as hell. Marines don't skirt around the difficult issues.

"One thing I learned growing up across the street from your mother is that people are put in our lives for a reason. Y'all moved in when I was lonely and in need of a friend and mentor, and Nicolette filled that void for me, just like I did for her when she was looking for someone to take care of you after she was gone. The way I see it, there's a reason Andrew came into your life when he did, and my advice to you would be to stop beating yourself up about it because you *are* blessed. You *did* win the lottery." He pauses, leaning in. "The prize was Ethan."

My tears are pretty much instant, because Lucas is right. Ethan is a prize. No, he's *the* prize—one my mother will never have the chance to know. A familiar grief swirls in my stomach. Graduations. My wedding. The birth of my only child. These are the moments when you long for your mother, but never in my life have I needed her more than now.

"Mom would have loved Ethan so much."

"Loves, Kitty Cat. Present tense." Lucas reaches for my hand, gives it a squeeze. "Wherever your mama is right now, she loves the heck out of that kid."

I press the doorbell, and a complicated melody starts up just inside. "I'll admit, that's a little weird."

Lucas bounces on his toes next to me, a soldier ready for battle. "What, the chorus of fancy church bells?"

"No. Ringing a doorbell that used to be mine."

Inside the house, the melody dies down into silence.

No voices, no footsteps, no nothing.

Lucas leans his upper body over the railing, presses his face to a side window. "Looks like Mac was right. Nobody's home."

"Are the sconces on either side of the hallway mirror on?"

So we don't have to put in the alarm code in the dark, Andrew always argued, turning them on as we were on our way out. I found it a colossal waste of energy and money. *We have sixty seconds to put in the code*, I'd argue back. *I think we can spare one second to flip a light switch.*

"Yeah," Lucas says, swinging his boots firmly back onto the porch. "They're on."

"Then nobody's home."

Just in case, he lifts a fist, bangs on the front door hard enough to rattle the stained glass.

Somewhere up the street, a dog barks, but inside the house, there's nothing but quiet.

"Now what?" he says.

I turn and head for the side yard. "Now we take a peek inside."

"What are we looking for?"

"I don't know. Maybe nothing."

Then again, maybe everything.

I lead us through the patch of monkey grass and onto the stepping-stones, following them around to the right side of the house. The pine straw is a wild and shaggy carpet, tickling at my ankles above my sneakers and I wish I'd worn boots like Lucas. His thick soles slap the dirt and stones right behind me.

We halt at the study window.

"What?" Lucas says, his voice eerily low, cautious.

"It's empty." I cup my palms on either side of my face and

squint into the glass. "The carved writing desk, the leather executive chair, the fringed Persian on the floor—he loved that stupid carpet. Is he moving or something?"

"There aren't any boxes, and look." Lucas taps a finger on the windowpane. "All his books are still there."

Lucas is right. The bookshelves are still packed.

"Maybe he's just redecorating," he says.

"But—"

A voice, pitchy with adolescence, stops my heart. "Hey, Mrs. Maddox."

I whirl around to face him—a teenager in bare feet and clothes that look slept in, clutching a dusty newspaper he must have just fetched from the street. The neighbor's kid. He's grown half a foot and sprouted a fuzzy mustache since I saw him last. Does he know I don't live here anymore? Does he know about the abuse, the divorce, the restraining order?

His name comes to me in a flash. "Hi, Brandon," I say, then stop, trying to think what to say next. The best I can come up with is, "You remember my friend, Lucas."

Brandon gives Lucas the side-eye. His size, his brawn, his ten-hut demeanor... Kids—especially boys—find Lucas either awe-inspiring or terrifying, and clearly, Brandon here falls in the second category. He takes a step backward. "So how was the camping trip?"

"I..." I shake my head. "I'm sorry?"

"Ethan. Wasn't he going on some trip up to the mines? He was pretty stoked about it. Him and Mr. Maddox were practicing putting up the tent all weekend. Did they ever figure out how to operate that thing? It looked pretty complicated."

I am completely speechless. Andrew's idea of "roughing it" is sleeping in a hotel with no room service. Now he has a tent? Since when?

But more important, why?

I turn to Lucas, whose eyes have turned a deep, stormy gray. They squint at me, and I know he's thinking the exact same thing: *camping*.

"Did Ethan say anything to you?" Lucas asks.

I shake my head, my head swirling with questions, with suspicion. Why didn't Ethan tell me he and his father were going camping. Why didn't Andrew?

Before I can think, before I can say the very first word, Lucas is pulling me toward the car.

STEF

35 hours, 30 minutes missing

AT A FEW MINUTES BEFORE TWO, I LET DETEC-
tive Macintosh through my front door. He's cleaned up since
the last time I saw him, when he was rain soaked and covered
in mud. He stands on my doorstep in a lightly starched shirt,
dark pants and black leather lace-ups, and I don't quite know
what to make of him, other than that he's not a fan. Not of me,
and not of my husband, who, officially speaking, is his boss.
A million bucks says he voted for the other guy.

He lowers his chin in greeting. "Mrs. Huntington. Sorry
to disturb you on the weekend. I know this is the last thing
you want to be doing on a Saturday afternoon."

Sam reaches around me to give him a hand. "Not a problem at all, Detective. Anything we can do to help."

He drapes his other hand over my shoulder. He's been holed
up in his study all morning, either on the phone or pounding
away at his keyboard, and I am beyond relieved he's put down
his laptop and phone to be here for me. I lean into his heat.

The detective's gaze grazes his surroundings while he gives
us a quick update—no leads, no sign of Ethan. The message

hangs in the air like a weighted balloon. Thirty-five hours. That's how long the police have been combing the North Georgia woods and my cell phone records, looking for clues. I think of Kat and I can barely breathe.

Sam motions us deeper into the house, through the sunken living room to the dining area, which I've set with crystal glasses and a tray of glass-bottled water. To our left, a wall of floor-to-ceiling windows overlook the patio and beyond, the pool shimmering in the springtime sun. The detective doesn't so much as glance that way, posing his first question before our butts have hit the padded leather seats. "If you don't mind, I'd like to start by going over the phone call."

I reach for the bottle of Pellegrino, twist it open with a hiss. "Of course. What would you like to know?"

Sam isn't that agreeable. He threads his fingers together on the table, his steel watch peeking out from his long-sleeved button-down. "Is this really necessary? Stefanie has been through it a million times already. She's already told you everything she can remember."

"I understand that, sir, but all due respect, a missing boy's life is at stake." He plants an elbow on the table and looks down at his notes, ticking off the specifics on his fingers. "You said the caller asked if he was speaking to Stef Huntington. You confirmed that he was. He told you he had Sammy. You screamed and begged. He said Sam was not to touch the Bell Building. He put Ethan on the phone, who said, Mommy, help. Did I miss anything?"

I shake my head, even though it's spinning. I don't think he forgot anything, but he rattled everything off so quickly, I can't be sure.

"I'm just trying to figure out how all of that fills six minutes and forty-three seconds of airtime when it just took me, what, ten?" The detective's hawk-like eyes latch onto me like a field mouse. "Seconds. Not minutes."

"I…" I swallow, darting a gaze to Sam. This is why I've been dreading this meeting. Why all day now, my skin has been crawling and my stomach has been in knots. The thing is, I don't remember all the things said in those six minutes. I promised him money, Sam's influence. To be the keeper of any intrigue, or to blow it all to pieces. I was babbling, trying to guess what he wanted from me, willing to trade anything to keep Sammy safe.

But six minutes is a long time. Too long. Logically, I know that.

I look across the table at the detective. "I already told you at the camp, it was early and the call was unexpected. His message didn't make sense. I wasn't thinking clearly. It took me a while to grasp what he was saying."

He scribbles something onto his notepad, and I try to read the messy handwriting upside down, but the only thing I can make out is *six minutes*. I picture him and all his colleagues seated around a conference table back at the station, listing all the ways my story doesn't add up on a whiteboard, and my palms go slick. I drop my hands onto my lap, wipe them dry on my jeans.

"I thought it was a joke. Some kind of sick, crazy prank. And then when I finally realized it wasn't, when that man's awful message sank in, I was too busy trying to figure out who would have done this to pay much attention to the clock."

"Stef," Sam says, draping a hand over mine under the table. "It's all right."

"No, it's not." I know my protest is making me sound guilty somehow, but I can't seem to stop myself. Ever since that phone call, a weight has been sitting on my chest, pressing down like a pile of bricks. The responsibility, the terror, the obvious suspicion from the detective sitting across from me… I can't take another second. "I was completely frantic. I don't know everything I said, only that nothing about the situation was making any sense. *You* try getting a call about your kidnapped son and see how you do."

The detective doesn't answer, but his expression goes hard, and I wonder if I misspoke. Maybe he's not a father, or maybe he wants to be. The bottles of water sit untouched in the middle of the table.

"And you're positive he hasn't called back." He doesn't phrase it as a question.

"Yes," I say, at the same time Sam says, "Your department is monitoring Stef's phone, so I'm pretty sure you know he hasn't." I can't decide if he says this because he's sticking up for me, because he's losing his patience with the detective or because he needs to get back to whatever has him holed up in the study. Maybe all of the above.

Detective Macintosh looks at Sam. "I thought maybe he called the house line, or your cell."

"He didn't."

"It would most likely be from another blocked number."

"There have been no more calls, Detective. We would have reported it." Sam's smile is friendly enough, but his message is clear: next question.

The detective returns his gaze to me. "Why do you think he called your cell and not Sam's?"

Another question I've spent hours pondering, and long enough to have a ready answer. "Maybe he knew Sam was in meetings. Maybe he knew that my cell was the only way he'd be able to reach either of us."

"I'd imagine as the wife of the mayor, your cell is unlisted."

I nod. "I don't go around advertising the number, but I'm also not stingy with it. I give it to stores, to Sammy's teachers, to my friends. It's listed in the school directory. It wouldn't have been all that hard for someone to track down."

The detective's next question is for Sam. "Let's talk about the Bell Building. Who wants to see that thing stand?"

"We've already had this conversation, too, Detective. Multiple times. For my answer, you can see my sworn statement. It still stands."

I suppose I shouldn't be surprised by Sam's answer, but I am. Sam spent most of yesterday at City Hall. He and I have barely spoken other than via text and hurried phone conversations. Of course the police would have already questioned him.

But sworn statement?

"It's just that it's highly unusual for a kidnapper to make contact, then go so completely silent without stipulating a deadline."

There's a question in there somewhere, but since he doesn't verbalize it, Sam doesn't answer.

My gaze darts between the two men. What is going on here? Why all the pushback, the barely concealed animosity? There's an unspoken tension between them I don't understand.

"It's only been a day," Sam reminds him, and with a shock, I realize he's right. The call hit my phone early yesterday morning. It feels like a million years ago.

"True, but Ethan has been gone for longer than that. In fact, by the time his teacher reported him missing, we'd already missed those most crucial first sixty minutes. His kidnapper already had plenty of time to drag him through the woods, shove him in the back of a car and take off before we had the first inkling he was gone. And the longer he's gone, the more sharply the chances of ever finding him diminish."

I know what he means to say. He means more than likely, Ethan is already dead.

"To be perfectly frank," the detective says, "we are growing more than a little concerned something scared the kidnapper off."

Sam all but rolls his eyes. "There are two armed men patrolling the yard and who knows how many journalists on the other side of the driveway gate watching them do it. If whoever's behind this is smart enough to use an untraceable number, they're smart enough to be keeping an eye on the house. On us." Sam bounces a finger between us. "Of course he's scared off."

His words skitter a chill down my spine because I'm terrified he's right. I think about poor Ethan, and a heavy weight clenches in my stomach.

"We're just covering all our bases, sir."

"Have you made any headway with the list of names my office gave you?" Sam says, moving the conversation along. It's one of the traits I've always admired about him, this ability to always be moving forward, to always be thinking ahead when the rest of us are still reeling from the news.

The detective gives him a look I can't interpret. "We're cross-checking them against property owners in the vicinity of Dahlonega and Murrayville, but so far, nothing."

"Why Murrayville?"

"We got a lead on an unidentified man and child stopping there for gas. A long shot, but unfortunately, it's all we've got. Security cameras are pretty sparse in that area, but we're hoping to catch a lucky break."

Another statistic I've learned: of the 800,000 children reported missing each year, only 115 are taken by strangers. The list of possible suspects Sam compiled for the police was shockingly long, encompassing everyone from city employees to household workers to neighbors and friends of friends. Surely one of those names will lead to Ethan.

"With your permission, sir, we'd like to put a tap on your phone lines."

"Which one?"

"Both. Home and cell."

Sam smiles, and the gesture feels so sincere that no one but me would know it's his politician's smile, the one he wears when shaking hands and kissing babies. "I'd love to help you out, Detective, but I'm afraid I can't do that. Those lines are used for official city business."

The detective doesn't look the least bit chastised. "I'm sure I don't need to remind you that a child is missing."

"No you don't, Detective, nor do I need to remind you that there are one hundred and eighty days left in this campaign. I won't have every conversation in my own home, with my own *wife*, being listened in on, analyzed and taken out of context. Just think what the media would do if they got a hold of it. How they'd twist my words and take them entirely out of context. Sorry, Detective, but if you want to tap our phones, you're going to need a court order."

"Which I'd probably be able to get."

But Sam has never liked being on the receiving end of an ultimatum. He leans back in his chair, and his body goes deceptively calm, his lips curving into another smile. "When you do, we'll have this conversation again."

Detective Macintosh puffs a sharp breath through his nose, slides his pen into his pocket and flips his notebook closed, and it's uncanny how, when he looks up, his smile is identical to Sam's.

And just like that, the meeting is adjourned. Everyone

stands, and Sam offers to walk the detective to the door. I'm gathering up the bottles and glasses, piling everything onto the tray to carry into the kitchen, when the detective stops.

"One more thing." He pauses, waiting for me to look up and meet his gaze, and something about his tone makes me brace. "Why do you think he called you Stef?"

I straighten. "Excuse me?"

"The caller. He asked if he was speaking to Stef Huntington. Not Stefanie." Detective Macintosh lifts his meaty shoulders high, then lets them fall. "I'm just wondering who would shorten your name to Stef."

He doesn't wait around for a response. It was a rhetorical question, and one everybody here knows the answer to: someone who's not a stranger.

Sam stands at the foyer window, watching the detective on the front drive. On the other side of the glass, the detective waves goodbye to the guards and drops into an unmarked car.

Sam sighs, turning away from the window. "That detective has a crappy attitude."

"So?" I would, too, if my job was to chase rapists and kidnappers and murderers all day long.

"So I don't like him. I don't like the way he keeps harping on that phone call. It makes it seem like you did something wrong."

Or you, I think. "He seems to think you know more about the Bell Building than you're saying."

"I already told him everything I know. I gave him the plans, the investor prospectus, the transcribed notes from the neighborhood meetings. That building is an eyesore and an environmental disaster, covered in mold and asbestos. Nobody wants it renovated, least of all the neighborhood."

"So who would want to keep it?"

He shrugs. "The only pushback we got on our plans for demolition were from a couple of loony tunes known for stirring up trouble. I gave Detective Macintosh their names, but I advised him to look at it from my viewpoint, as well. Keeping the Bell Building would flip the Marietta development upside down. It would destroy the budget and cause investors to bolt. So maybe it's not a preservationist but someone looking for revenge. If Marietta fails, so do I. So does my administration, or at the very least, my reelection campaign. Either way, until this guy is found, we have to keep Sammy inside. He's still in danger, and so are you."

I look up the empty stairwell, where video game thunder still floats down the wooden treads. My heart thuds at Sam's sinister words, as much for the warning as the fear Sammy might hear. This house is a fortress of steel and glass and concrete, but still. I don't want him to worry for his safety.

"The school has called a meeting tonight," I say. "For the parents of Sammy's class. Will you come?"

"Not sure." Sam checks his watch. "Josh said he'd drop by in half an hour, and then I have a couple of back-to-back calls. Think you can handle it on your own?"

I sigh. In a city like Atlanta, every day comes with a built-in crisis. Why should ours be any different? "I always do."

Sam drops a distracted kiss on my lips and takes off for the study, and I head up the stairs.

In the hallway, noise spills out opposite bedroom doors, a hair dryer from Mom's room competes against automatic gunfire from Sammy's. I stop in his open doorway and look inside, where it's gloomy and dark, the curtains drawn tight against the midafternoon sunshine. The only light comes from the giant flat screen, flickering images of a wartime scenario seen from behind night-vision goggles. It casts the room in an eerie green.

Sammy is slumped in the gaming chair before his unmade bed, surrounded by a rabbit's nest of toys and dirty clothes. By his bare feet, a half-eaten bag of popcorn has burped up its contents onto the hardwood floor, next to a collection of empty Gatorade bottles. The maid powered through here just days ago with a vacuum cleaner and a cleaning rag, and now it looks like she's never been.

"Hey, sweetie."

Sammy starts, and the game pauses in midshriek, plunging the room into silence. He peeks around the side of his chair, eyeing me suspiciously like he's been doing ever since yesterday, when I showed up muddy and still half-delirious with terror in Dahlonega.

"Yeah?" he says.

"Turn that off for a minute, will you? I want to talk to you."

"But I'm almost to the next level."

"Well, then save it. You can do the next level later."

"That's not how it works. If I stop before I kill all the juvies, then I have to start this level all over again."

I give him a look. "Either turn it off yourself, or I will."

With a sigh, Sammy turns back to the TV and punches a couple of buttons on the joystick. He tosses it onto a pile of clothes, then folds his arms across his chest, waiting.

I snap on the bedside lamp, straighten the comforter and drop onto the end of his bed. "Sweetheart, come here." When he still doesn't move, I pat the mattress.

He approaches the bed like it's a plank hanging over the side of a pirate ship, ready to drop him, blindfolded and bound by the wrists and ankles, into a churning ocean. When Sammy was little I couldn't keep him off my lap, but now there are no more unsolicited kisses, no more spontaneous cuddles on the couch. How did this happen? When did sitting beside me become something I have to force my son to do?

He sinks onto the mattress, careful to maintain a good six inches between our thighs, and this new and unwelcome lack of affection breaks my heart. I tell myself that this is only a phase, that it's only a matter of time before he clambers back onto my lap, but so far, the evidence proves otherwise.

"Why don't you come downstairs for a while? I'll make us something yummy, and we can watch a movie."

"I'm not really hungry."

"What? You're always hungry." I press my palm to his forehead. "Hmm, no fever. What about a headache? Let me see your tongue. I bet it's spotted."

"Mo-om," he says, but he's biting down on a smile.

"Seriously, baby. You can't stay up here all day and play video games. Your butt will become one with that stool, and then what? We'll have to call you Sammy The Gaming Chair."

"Well, you always said you wished I came with a volume knob."

"Ha-ha, very funny, smarty-pants."

The truth is, I love this about him—his cheeky sense of humor, his ability to make me laugh out loud even when I don't want to. I want more of it, more of this time.

But more than that, I want answers. Mom's right; there's something Sammy's not telling me, something he feels bad about, and I think I know what it is.

"Sammy, how come you were in Ethan's sleeping bag instead of your own?"

His head whips to mine, his chin jutting in defense. "I didn't want to trade. It was Jessica James's fault. She started it." His voice is sharper than it needs to be in the quiet room.

"Started what?"

"Well, Jessica took Naomi's sleeping bag, and then Naomi took Chloe's and Chloe took Valerie's, but then mine didn't fit where it was anymore, and I had the best spot in the whole cabin. Ethan's was shorter, so Jessica told us to switch bags."

"And what did Ethan think of this arrangement?"

Sammy bobs his shoulders. "Ethan's a crybaby."

And so, it seems, that we are back full circle.

"Miss Emma told me the two of you had an argument. What about?"

"He said I stole his rocks, but I didn't. He stole *mine*. Miss Emma made us put 'em in one big pile and take turns choosing, but it wasn't fair. He got my prettiest one."

"So was taking his sleeping bag some kind of payback?"

"No." His answer is too immediate and vehement. "I already told you, that was because of Jessica, not me."

"Still. You went along with it."

He slumps on the bed, slapping his arms across his middle with a huff, and I know that stance. That stance means he's done talking.

I sigh and nudge him off the bed. "Time for a shower, big guy."

Sammy sputters out a protest, but I herd him into his bathroom anyway. I flip on the water and stand guard until he strips and steps into the steam. Once his hair is good and lathered up, I head back into his bedroom.

A place that as far as I can tell hasn't seen sunshine for days.

I shove open the curtains, heavy strips of thick navy velvet that block out all but tiny strips of light. A bright afternoon sun pours through the glass, painting yellow streaks across the messy bedroom carpet. Unmade bed. Half-empty water bottles and wrappers everywhere. Dirty clothes strewn about in chaotic clumps—an impressive amount of them considering Sammy has been in the same T-shirt and shorts for two days. I fetch the laundry basket from his closet and start collecting.

I'm digging a pair of underwear from behind the curtains when the TV chirps. I straighten, see a flashing envelope on the corner of the screen, the universal icon for messages.

I frown and set the laundry basket on the bed.

I am not one of those out-of-touch mothers. I read the newspaper articles, watch the late-night news reports about freaks lurking behind computer screens in their mother's damp basement, luring young children into sketchy chat rooms or worse. I am neither naive nor complacent, and I'm sure as hell no Pollyanna. When I signed Sammy up for Xbox Live, I cranked every available parental control up to maximum security. The games Sammy plays have no bad language, and though he may obliterate a locust or two, no human blood is shed. I limited his interactions with other humans to three of his school friends: Ben, Liam and Noah. Nobody else is allowed in.

So who's GamerJoeATL?

I pluck the controller from the floor and fumble around with the buttons, trying to remember how to navigate the screen with the joystick. After a few tries, the message opens with a musical beep.

In the tomb hurry.

At least it's not some creepy predator sending a selfie of his private parts, I think, right before anger bites at my skin. My clever, sneaky son figured out a way through my firewall. The little shit hijacked my password.

I scroll through the names on the friends screen, twenty-four in all, most of them fairly generic handles like Joe's, all but three of them unfamiliar. By the time I get to the last one, I'm fuming.

I settle the controller on the dresser, unhook the console from the wall and march it into my closet, where I shove it onto the highest shelf. Even if Sammy dragged over a chair, even if he carted the stepladder up from the garage, he'd never be able to climb this high. Then again, I've already underestimated him once. I bury the thing under a pile of sweaters and push it all the way to the back of the shelf. I step back and study my handiwork, satisfied. Nobody but me will even know that it's there.

I return to Sammy's room, where he's still under the shower, a dark blur behind the fogged-up glass door. I lean against the counter, folding my arms across my chest. "Sammy, how come you're getting messages on your Xbox?"

Sammy's form freezes behind the glass. "I am?"

"Yes. Which I'm pretty sure you already know. What I'm trying to understand is why. I didn't approve anybody named GamerJoeATL, or for that matter, any of the other twenty-plus names I saw on your friends list. Would you like to explain to me how they got through?"

He clears a spot on the glass with a palm, blinking out at me with wide, guilty eyes. "What'd he say?"

"Something about a tomb and to hurry." Sammy slams off the water and throws open the door, yanking the towel from the bar. "But listen to me. You and I set things up so you could only play with the friends I approved of, remember?"

He throws the towel across his shoulders, superhero style, and skids across the tiles.

"Samuel Joseph Huntington, get your buns back here right now," I call out, but he's already disappeared around the corner.

I'm not going to get too worked up. I've already pulled the magician's trick, leaving nothing but a couple of wires dangling from the wall. I straighten the towels and follow behind, stepping into his room right as his voice slices the air.

"Mom!" He turns to me, stiff with animosity. "Where is it? Where's my Xbox?"

"I put it away."

"But you can't just take it. It's mine." Sammy's fists, his whole body is clenched. His face is burgundy with rage, his chest heaving like he just ran a marathon. His eyes, for once not hidden behind his glasses, shimmer with tears.

I sink onto the foot of his bed. "You knew I didn't want you communicating with people I didn't approve of online, and you did it anyway, so I took it away. Indefinitely."

"Mom, no. *Please*. I *need* it."

It's all I can do not to roll my eyes. "Nobody *needs* an Xbox, Sammy. In fact, if I had known a video game would elicit this type of behavior, I would have never given you one."

Sammy's protests start up all over again, his cries increasing in volume and pitch.

"I'm sorry, sweetie, but this is your punishment for being sneaky. For doing things behind your father's and my back. Online safety is that important."

Sammy's tears are flowing freely now, fat crocodile streams sliding unchecked down his cheeks, and they're as shocking for their intensity as for the way he doesn't bother to hide them. All these years, Ethan's greatest sin has always been that he's a crybaby, and now Sammy is stepping into his knockoff Nikes.

"It's important," he wails.

"Actions have consequences, Sammy, and yours could have put you in danger. You could have put this whole family in danger." I pause as a new question whispers through my mind:

What if one of those handles doesn't belong to a child? What if it belongs to a predator, one who listened in on Sammy and his school friends talking about going to Dahlonega? Someone who doesn't know the kids could easily mix up the two. "Did you tell any of your online friends you were going to the mines with your class?"

"No." He swipes the back of an arm across his mouth, but he doesn't quite meet my gaze when he says it.

I turn on the edge of his bed, putting us face-to-face. "Are you sure? Think about it. Did you tell anybody on the game that you and your class were going to Dahlonega?"

"They're all friends from school. They all knew. Half of them were there with me." Hope swells in his voice, as if offering up this answer might sway me somehow, might right some of his wrong. "Mom, please."

When I don't give in, Sammy loses it. He throws his head back, wraps both arms around his stomach and lets loose. His mouth opens in a clean note of grief that hurts my heart. This is not the sound of a child crying. This is something I've never heard before, a wailing, a keening eruption of soul-piercing sound.

"What is going on with you?"

Sammy *never* cries, and I don't understand where these tears are coming from now. This can't all be about a stupid video game.

"What happened to Ethan is not your fault. You know that, right?" When he doesn't respond, I rub a hand over his hair, tilt his head to look at me. He looks at me with my husband's dark eyes, heavily lashed and pleading. "What that bad man did to Ethan has nothing to do with you. This is not your fault."

My words only make him cry harder.

"Oh, sweetie, come here."

I tug him to me, and he doesn't struggle, but he doesn't give in, either. He just stands there between my legs and cries his little heart out. The anger that's been simmering in my chest for this ridiculous temper tantrum scatters like smoke, and my hear twists on the knife edge of a sword. I wrap the towel arou. 1 his still-damp body and hold on tight, then rock him back and forth until his sobs fade into hiccups.

Mom was right. There's something Sammy is not telling.

But there were sixteen other kids in that cabin, sixteen other sets of parents. Somebody must know something.

KAT

41 hours missing

"HOLY SHIT," LUCAS MUTTERS UNDER HIS breath. He takes in the thick carpeting, the oak-paneled walls, the underlit chandelier hanging in the foyer, swiped from some old French château. "This place is fancy."

I thought the same thing the first time I walked up the columned steps of Cambridge Classical Academy, a school Andrew was determined his son attend after reading they boasted the highest percentage of Ivy League graduates in all of Atlanta. The public school up the street was suddenly not good enough. Andrew wanted to pay more than twenty thousand dollars a year for his son to walk these hallowed halls next to the kids of CEOs and bankers, of socialites and trust fund babies. I balked at the thought of Ethan among the children of the one percent. He was already so different from the other kids. How would he ever fit in?

"Your network is your net worth," Andrew said when I voiced my objections, quoting from the title of a bestselling business book. "Fake it till you make it." Andrew was a big fan of one-liners.

"This way," I say, leading Lucas down the east-wing hallway to the largest of the conference rooms, the one they use to impress prospective parents. Polished cherry table that seats a crowd, Promethean board as big as the wall. Andrew had taken it all in with excited, eager eyes, but to me it had seemed excessive.

But tonight, Lucas and I aren't here to be impressed but "informed and supported." When I read the email for tonight's get-together to Lucas, he rolled his eyes.

"They're covering their asses," he said, and if I didn't believe him then, the security guard at the door, who shoved a confidentiality agreement in our hands with orders to sign here, told me Lucas was right.

At the end of the hall, a hum of excited voices spills out into the hallway. Both male and female tones, the words clattering on top of each other like football players in a pile, shoving the others aside to be heard. There are too many to make out more than just a word or two: *Police. Father. Ethan.* I stop on the carpet and take a deep breath, swallowing down my nerves.

"How many people are here again?" Lucas asks.

"Supposedly just the parents of Ethan's class, so what's that—thirty-five or so?"

But Lucas isn't wrong. The volume coming from that room makes it sound more like a mob, and I hesitate on the Oriental carpet. If Lucas's prediction is right, if tonight is one big charade so the school can cover their asses, I don't want to be part of it.

Then again, it's not like there's anything else I can be doing, other than pacing my floors and waiting for an update from Mac, who's parked himself at gate E34 at the airport, where Andrew's plane is scheduled to touch down any moment now. After Brandon's announcement that Andrew owns a tent, Mac and his men did another sweep of Andrew's home, where they found nothing. No tent. No camping equipment. Not even a muddy pair of shoes.

"There's no sign he's ever even thought about camping," Mac told me when they were done. "And we looked everywhere. In every closet. In the basement and attic. If Andrew owns a tent, he's not storing it at his house."

"His office, maybe?"

"We're working on the warrant right now. If it doesn't come through by the time he lands, we'll go straight from the airport to his office and persuade him to use his key."

"And you're sure he's on the plane?" DL919, landing at Hartsfield sixteen minutes late, at 7:43 p.m.

"Positive. I got both verbal and visual confirmation from the captain. My partner and I will be intercepting Andrew at the gate."

"What about the neighbor kid? Did he tell you anything else?"

"Nothing useful, though his mother had a lot to say about you, trespassing on private property."

The restraining order, coming back to bite me.

"We don't have to stay, you know," Lucas says, his hand warm and reassuring on my lower back. "We can go home and wait for Mac to call."

I shake my head. I don't want to go home and wait. I want to act, to search, to fight. I want to do anything other than continue to sit around, feeling helpless. "Let's do this."

We step into the doorway, and the voices fall away into a painful quiet. Fifty pairs of eyes, maybe more, stare up at us, their expressions a mix of pity and bald-faced curiosity. Fifty or more bodies crammed around the table, lined up in folding chairs against all four walls. Parents, of course, and by the look of the others' buttoned-up expressions, their attorneys. Of *course* they would bring their attorneys. I scan the faces for Sam and Stefanie, but neither of them are here. Miss Emma is noticeably absent, as well.

Dr. Abernathy, Cambridge's head of school, shoos two people I don't recognize from the chairs to her right—the school's lawyers?—and offers them to me and Lucas. In dead silence, we round the table and take a seat.

As soon as we're settled, Dr. Abernathy turns to me with an expectant smile. "Will your husband be joining us?"

"Ex-husband," Lucas says. "And no, not unless he wants to be arrested for violating the restraining order. Two hundred feet, minimum. More than half a football field."

Dr. Abernathy's eyes widen, just a hair, not so much at Lucas's revelation but at him putting my dirty laundry out there for all to see. At places like Cambridge, "restraining order" are words that should be whispered behind cupped palms, like "mistress" or "cancer." Polite folks don't just go around blurting them out. Lucas knows this, of course, but this is him, coming in guns slinging.

Dr. Abernathy swivels as much as she can in the crowded room, bumping up against my chair and the one behind her, nudging them out of the way until she's facing me. "First of all, I would just like to say on behalf of everybody here at Cambridge Classical Academy, we are *devastated* by your son's disappearance. Ethan Maddox is a valued and cherished student here at CCA, and we want him brought home and his abductor brought to justice as soon as humanly possible. Please know that we are bending over backward to cooperate with the authorities."

To my left, Lucas makes a sound I interpret as *I'll bet*. He hasn't encouraged me to sue the school for negligence yet—

too soon—but I know he's thought it, and honestly, so have I, though for completely different reasons. Lucas is thinking about the money, of padding my bank account so I'll never have to worry about money again, and I'm thinking only of revenge. I hate everything about this place, including the gray-eyed, frizzy-haired woman still waiting for my response.

"Thank you."

She plucks a remote from the table and punches a button, and across from us, the Promethean board flickers to life. Ethan's name appears in big block letters above a Cambridge slogan: "Embracing diversity, nourishing decency and fostering human dignity."

Her presentation is long and careful and rehearsed. She goes over Miss Emma's official police statement. A bulleted list of organizations participating in the search. An update from Detective Brent Macintosh of the Atlanta police. Each topic is accompanied by a graphic—a photograph, a logo, a colorful table. Leave it to Cambridge to express sympathy in charts and graphs. Nothing she says is news to me and Lucas; in fact, some of it is no longer current. The boot print the sheriff's team lifted from the forest belonged to an eighty-four-year-old neighbor, for example, not the abductor. But all around us, people are rapt.

She's finishing up when a flustered Stefanie steps into the room—a full fifteen minutes late. "Sorry," she mouths to Dr. Abernathy, who halts the presentation to find Stefanie a chair. Stefanie shakes her head and presses herself to a thin strip of wall by the door, her face blooming bright pink. "I didn't mean to interrupt. Please carry on."

She's accompanied by a man who is not Sam. Mop of mousy hair, slightly mushy jowls, ruddy cheeks squeezing a too-thin nose. He reaches over the table and gives Dr. Abernathy a hand. "Josh Murrill. Chief of staff for the mayor."

As he's pulling back, his gaze lands on mine for an instant, then darts off to take in the others in the room. I don't know this man, but I know his type. He's that guy who's always looking over your shoulder for a more interesting, more influential conversation partner. Judging by the waves of lifted hands and smiles, he knows half the people here.

After an eternity, Dr. Abernathy wraps up her presentation and opens the floor for questions.

My hand shoots up, my mouth blurting the question before she can even look my way. "How is it possible that nobody heard or saw anything?"

Dr. Abernathy wasn't expecting it, or the animosity that shot the words from my mouth. Her gaze seeks out the two men she shooed from our seats.

I don't give her long enough to craft an answer. "Because by now we know that the kidnapper set the fire in order to get everyone out of the cabin and to use as a distraction. We know Miss Emma and the kids were in the clearing while Avery ran for help. We know Ethan disappeared somewhere between the third and fourth head count. But *I* know my son wouldn't have left the group willingly, which means whoever took Ethan took him *against his will*. Maybe the kidnapper clapped a hand over Ethan's mouth, but surely he kicked and squirmed and tried to get away. There must have been a scuffle. How did nobody notice that?"

"I…" She shakes her head, a rapid back and forth that sends her earrings dancing. "The police have already questioned all the students. Are you suggesting one of them is lying?"

"I'm just having a hard time believing that everybody was looking the other way. There were nineteen people in that clearing and a kid just vanishes? I just don't see how that's possible. How is that possible?"

The attorneys sit straighter in their chairs, alert and ready to shoot down anyone who dares to answer. No one dares.

"And where's Miss Emma? Why isn't she here to tell us her version of what happened?"

One of the attorneys clears his throat. "Ms. Quinn is no longer speaking for Cambridge Classical Academy. She's on leave through the end of the summer."

Lucas and I share a look, one that says he called it. *That teacher is toast,* he told me up at the camp, and apparently, he was right. "You fired her." I try to drum up a scrap of sympathy for the woman, but I can't. She deserves to have lost her job. No, she deserves worse.

"It was a mutual decision between Ms. Quinn and the board," the attorney says, then says nothing more.

The parents look around nervously, and heat rises up from somewhere deep inside, gathering strength and threatening to explode in a full-blown fury. The grief. The terror. The frustration. It's all too much, the emotions too tangled up in each other, and I'm suddenly terrified I'm going to cry, which of course only makes me angrier. I suck in a long, slow breath, fighting back the flames, summoning the strength to pull myself together. The tears recede, but the anger remains.

"This is my son's life we are talking about here. If Miss Emma or any of your kids has information, if any of them saw or heard even the tiniest little peep, I am begging you." I slap both palms on the table and lean in. "It could be nothing or it could be everything, so please, *please* tell the police."

The silence is long and sharp and uncomfortable, stretching on for what feels like forever. Dr. Abernathy coughs into a fist. The woman across from her fidgets. I look at Lucas, and his expression is as dark as my thoughts. What a fucking waste of time. I'm reaching for my bag when Stefanie clears her throat.

"When I picked Sammy up, he was terrified. Just...completely shut down. I'm sure he was overwhelmed and confused, but the longer he's home, the more he processes everything that happened at the camp, the more he has to say. I don't know how much of it is relevant to the investigation, but I've been forwarding everything over to Detective Macintosh."

"Like what?" the man who walked in with her says. Sam's pompous chief of staff.

"Well, like some people Sammy noticed at the mines who stood out in his memory." She glances at me, then quickly away. "I also discovered he's been talking to some people online, most of whom I don't know and didn't give approval for. He claims they're kids from school, but you never know who's really on the other end of the internet. I've passed everything on to Detective Macintosh."

She holds my gaze, and her lips curve into the smallest of smiles. I smile back, even though I don't know why. What is it with these Huntingtons? What kind of strange, spooky power do they hold over me? One nice deed, and I find myself liking them—or in Stefanie's case, at the very least wondering if I've somehow misjudged her.

But all around us, people are dead silent.

Stefanie focuses her attention on a woman seated by the far wall. "Angela. Your little Brenna is so observant. At Sammy's birthday party she was the only one who noticed the flower arrangements matched the invitation. She must have seen something."

Stefanie's words raise a welt on my heart, because it's the party Ethan wasn't invited to.

Angela looks horrified to have been singled out. Her cheeks are two shiny cherries, and her gaze flicks all around the room, landing on no one. "Brenna said she didn't hear anything because of the fire. Apparently, the kids were a mess. A lot of them were crying. She said there was a lot going on."

Stefanie's smile drops, and so does my heart. It hits the bottom of my belly with an elevator-like thud.

"But then yesterday, she mentioned she might have seen somebody," Angela adds. "A person at the edge of the woods. At first she thought it was Avery, but then he came running up from the other direction. By the time Brenna turned back around, the person was gone."

Lucas reaches for the pad of paper in the center of the table. "Male or female? What color hair? How tall?"

Angela lifts both palms from her lap. "Brenna didn't say."

But Angela's confession unsticks something in the room, and one by one, the parents start talking. Harley's mother says her daughter might have heard a thump. James has been dreaming about a red truck. Rachel is suddenly terrified of men with mustaches. Lucas scribbles away while I sit here, clenching my teeth and trying not to scream. Mac said it's often one little lead, one seemingly random and unconnected clue, that breaks a case wide-open, and these parents waited forty-one hours—almost two whole days—to give up what they know.

I pull out my phone and find a text from Mac.

Plane just touched down. Waiting for it to roll up to gate.

My thumbs tap out a response.

We need another round of interviews with kids. Their parents say they're remembering things.

Two seconds later, his reply pings my phone.

Will start first thing AM.

I look up to find Stefanie watching me.

"What about a reward?" she blurts, and all heads in the room swing to her. "For information, I mean. What if we took up donations, set up a tip line and offered the cash as a reward to whoever calls in with the case-breaking clue?"

Dr. Abernathy's face is carefully blank. "Well, it could be worth a try, I suppose…"

"I think it would be great PR for the school. We're not just a school but a community. We take care of our own. I'm sure you'd do much better at crafting the appropriate message. Rod, you're on the marketing committee. What do you think?"

A man behind me clears his throat. "I can't make these kinds of decisions by myself. I need to talk to the other board members first."

Stefanie gives him a sweet smile. "I understand, and I didn't mean to put you on the spot. It's just that whatever amount the school puts in gives the rest of us parents an indication of what we should be putting in. I assume you'll be asking other parents for donations, no? I'm sure I'm not the only one here who's eager to contribute." She chews her lip and takes her gaze down the long line of faces, holding each one until heads bob in agreement.

"We'll have a little huddle after this meeting," Dr. Abernathy mumbles.

The conversation moves on to other topics, but I'm only half listening. My whole body is pulsing like a nerve ending. What the hell just happened here? Did Stefanie just accidentally talk the board into forking over reward money, or did she strong-arm them? Those parents who all nodded along, did

Stefanie work her voodoo magic on them, too? Either she's completely guileless, or she's fucking brilliant.

And then her gaze catches mine across the table, her eyes glinting with satisfaction and I have my answer.

STEF

54 hours, 9 minutes missing

ON SUNDAY, BY SOME MIRACLE, I SLEEP IN. THE chaos of the previous two days must have caught up with me, because I don't stir until almost nine, and then the first thing I do is check my phone. Forty-seven text messages and an email inbox in the thousands. Sam is always getting on me for not cleaning them out, but why bother? The texts are probably all from the mothers at school, nosy gossips looking for news of Ethan to pick apart in endless wine-fueled discussions, and it would take me days to clear my inbox from all the spam.

But the point is, no new calls.

I drag myself from the warmth of my bed and into the shower, my thoughts returning to last night. The nerve of Dr. Abernathy, calling us in for an hour-long infomercial under the guise of supporting Ethan. She wasn't there to "inform and support," but to cover her own damn ass. The *school's* ass. At least now she's doing it to the tune of ten thousand dollars— the reward money she pledged in an email last night. By the time I climbed into bed, the amount had tripled, thanks to the generosity of the other parents I called and put on the spot.

I turn off the water and dry myself off, pulling on yesterday's jeans and a fresh T-shirt. As I run a brush through my wet hair, I study my face in the mirror. Puffy cheeks. Bloodshot eyes. Sallow, saggy skin. I know Ethan's disappearance is not officially my tragedy, but it sure as hell feels personal. The kidnapper called *my* cell phone, meant to take *my* child. I flip off the light and head into the hall.

Sammy is exactly where I left him last night—sulking on his bed. An iPad is propped against his legs. SpongeBob, according to the voices floating up from the speaker.

"Good morning, sweetie. How'd you sleep?"

He presses his lips together and glares.

"Are you hungry? Did you eat?"

No response.

A dull throbbing starts up somewhere deep inside my head. Later Sammy and I will talk about managing anger without being rude, but for now I'm in no mood to go toe-to-toe with him, not before my first cup of coffee. I leave my moody son and head downstairs.

Familiar male voices worm their way through the wooden doors of Sam's study, and as I pass by on my way to the kitchen, I wonder if they even left. The attorneys were here last night when I got home, and they were here a couple hours later when I went to bed. I double back to the foyer windows and check their cars on the drive, a dark BMW and a boxy blue SUV, both parked in the exact same spots. Josh's car isn't there.

I spot Mom on the patio couch, her bare feet up on the coffee table, scrolling through something on my laptop. She looks up when I come out the door. "There's pancakes in the warming drawer and fresh-cut strawberries in the fridge. Sammy ate already—I don't know about Sam. He hasn't emerged from his study yet."

"Not even for coffee?"

"Nope. At least not that I've seen."

I sink onto the couch beside her, thinking this worries me more than a little. Are Sam's meetings about Ethan, or is the situation with Marietta really that dire? A scandal, Sam called it yesterday on the phone. Who was he talking to? And where the hell is Josh?

"Thanks for taking care of Sammy this morning. He's apparently still not speaking to me."

Mom closes the laptop. "Oh, he'll come around. He's a lot like you that way—stubborn."

"Me? I think you're confusing me with Amelia."

My younger sister was born with an attitude and an iron will. She talked back. She drew on walls. She cussed and clawed and scratched. She could have been the poster child for Ritalin until she grew into a remarkably laid-back adult. I was never the stubborn one.

Mom laughs. "I'm not the one who's confused, dear. You are. Oh, sure, you were the good sister. Whenever you did anything wrong, which wasn't all that often, all I ever had to say was that I was disappointed in you. That was always punishment enough."

A story I've heard a million times. I was the easy child, the practice baby for my naughty, defiant, whirlwind of a sibling. My parents didn't believe in spanking until Amelia popped out, and even that wasn't much of a deterrent. Mom always jokes that if she'd known Amelia was going to turn out so well, she wouldn't have worried so much.

I gesture to the laptop. "May I?" I passed on Sammy's offense and the Xbox log-in credentials to Detective Macintosh last night, but since I haven't heard back, I thought I would take another, better look at the names myself.

She hands the laptop to me. "Anyway, you'd cry and cry and cry, and I'd congratulate myself on being so much better at this motherhood thing than all those other women who came to see me. I couldn't understand why they were always so flustered and agitated and helpless, always reeking of spit-up and desperation." She smiles at me with a cocked brow. "And then your sister, Amelia, came along."

I fire up the laptop and type in the password: <3SamJosX2, which I use for everything. Another reason I can't be too angry at Sammy. I made it awfully easy for him to get past my flimsy firewall.

"So you're saying Sammy inherited this kind of behavior? Sorry, Mom, but I'm not buying it. His reaction earlier had nothing to do with his DNA. Honestly, I think he's just traumatized by what happened, and that it was supposed to be him." I open my internet browser, surf to xbox.com.

"I agree. That's where I was going with this story. Sammy takes after you. Your emotions always got the better of you, too, especially when you were ashamed. Sammy has all those same issues."

I look up from my computer screen, interested now. "I don't know if Sammy told you, but he was in Ethan's sleeping bag. That's why it took so long for the dogs to catch a scent. They were confused."

Mom frowns, thoughtful. "That would explain why his chakra's so blocked." She circles a hand above her head like a halo. "Completely stuck. I tried to clear him, but he wouldn't sit still long enough except to play that silly video game. These things work best when the subject is an active participant."

"Well, did you try talking to him? He believes in your energy healer mumbo jumbo, you know. If you tell him his chakra is blocked, he'll want you to unblock it."

"I tried that. He said he didn't have time."

I roll my eyes. "He's got loads of time now."

"I think part of what's blocking him is the energy in this house. No offense, but talk about energy demons. This place is swarming with them. They're sucking up all the good energy and throwing everything out of balance."

"So work your witchcraft. Chase the devils out."

"They're called demons, dear. And I can clear them, but what I'd really like to do is take Sammy up to my house for a while, just until this mess is all sorted out."

I'm shaking my head before she's reached the end of the sentence. "Whoever took Ethan is still out there. It's why there are a dozen cameras pointed at the house and two armed bodyguards patrolling the yard at all times. Those energy demons are nothing compared to the real threat of a stranger coming back to kidnap Sammy." Saying the words out loud gives me a full-body shiver.

"Why are you so sure it's a stranger?" Mom says.

Another memory pricks at me. The caller's voice on my cell, how he asked if he was speaking to Stef. I'm positive I didn't tell my mother any of this. "You're not?"

"I already told you, sweetie. Energy demons everywhere. These things are all interrelated." She swipes her feet from the table and pushes to a stand. "Anyway, I'm going to pop out for some sea salt and dried sage, if you don't need me here. I want to do something about the energetic imprints in this house, and maybe a protection spell or two while I'm at it."

The last time Mom saged this house, when we moved in six years ago, it smelled like a Grateful Dead concert, and Sam kept wondering why he was suddenly craving pizza. But in the grand scope of things, I figure what's the harm? At the very least, it'll keep her busy for a couple of hours.

"Knock yourself out," I say, returning to the laptop.

While Mom fetches her bag and car keys from upstairs, I sign in to my Xbox Live account. I type in my name and password, but when I hit Enter, bright red letters pop up on the screen.

Your account or password is incorrect.

I type the letters in again, <3SamJosX2, this time more slowly. I get the same message.

And then I get the bigger message, one that heats me from the inside out: not only did Sammy hijack my password, he switched it out for one of his own. That little brat locked me out.

I snap the laptop closed, slide it onto the table and march upstairs. I don't knock. I don't announce my presence from the hallway. I burst into the room without warning.

"Samuel Huntington, you are in such big tr—"

I stop on the thick, wool carpet, a curl of uneasiness cooling my chest. I turn in a full circle, suddenly recalling a sunny September afternoon when Sammy was two, when I'd left him for less than a minute. Just long enough to refill his sippy cup and cut up a banana from the fruit bowl. I had a clear view of him the entire time, sitting cross-legged on the living room floor, playing with his toy cars. But what all those parenting books say is true—all it takes is a second or two. In my case, to toss the milk container in the recycling bin by the garage door. When I came back around the corner, Sammy was gone. Vanished.

At first I thought it was a silly game of hide-and-seek, and I played along. I called out for him. I wondered aloud at where he'd gotten off to. I peered into the most obvious hiding places, figuring I'd find a beaming Sammy crouched under the dining table or giggling behind the curtains. But he wasn't in any of those places. I checked every room in the house, the yard, the sidewalk down by the street. By the time I got back to the house, I was frantic.

I called Sam at work on the house line and 9-1-1 from my cell. When the police banged on my door sixteen endless minutes later, I was hysterical, battling visions of Sammy toddling into morning traffic on Northside Drive or floating facedown in some neighbor's pool. I handed the police a recent picture, frame and all, and they scattered. Sam came screeching up the drive right as I found him, sound asleep and oblivious, bundled up in a basket of freshly laundered towels.

But this time is different.

This time I don't call out for him. I don't check where else he might be—my room, the basement, Mom's room across the hall. A blast of jasmine-scented heat hits me square in the face, and I know where he's gone.

Out the open window.

I lean my entire upper body out the window, limp with relief when Sammy isn't sprawled on the ground below. I eyeball the distance to the dirt—a good twenty feet or more—too far for an eight-year-old, especially one as small and scrawny as Sammy, to fall and survive.

"Sammy!" I shout it as loud as I can, and my voice echoes over the street. The reporters hear me. They rush the gate, their camera lenses winking in the sunshine. "Did any of you see my son, Sammy?"

My question is greeted by the metallic chatter of a dozen camera shutters.

I scan the yard, searching for any flashes of skin, any movement, but other than a couple of squirrels stirring the upper branches of a tree, there's nothing.

"Sammy!"

Gary comes jogging into view, his equipment bouncing at his belt. He stops under the giant magnolia, looking around for the source of my voice.

"Up here." I wave my arms until he spots me. "Have you seen Sammy?"

"He's not inside?"

"Check the yard, will you? I'm on my way down."

I shove off the sill and race out of the room, bumping into Mom in the hall. She's on her way out—car keys in her hand, purse slung over her shoulder, hair shoved off her face with a pair of ancient sunglasses. She takes in my frantic state, and her eyes go wide. "What's going on? What's the matter?"

"I think Sammy jumped out his window."

She gasps, pressing a hand to her chest. "What? But why?"

"Find Sam, and the two of you check the house just to be sure. I'm going out to talk to the guards."

I race down the stairs and burst out the door.

Like most houses on our street, ours is set on the back third of a generous lot, at the top of a gently sloping hill. Three-quarters of an acre, most of it sweeping lawn lined with a thick line of shrubs and trees and beyond, a ten-foot privacy fence of concrete columns connected by sleek iron rods. The barrier was built to keep people out, but it also keeps people in. The only way though is the driveway gate, now blocked by reporters.

But how did he get out the window?

My gaze lands on the massive magnolia hanging over the entire left front of the yard. It's one of the reasons Sam and I bought the lot, because of its dark, glossy leaves and the white blossoms that open up like velvety saucers every spring. We designed everything around the tree, positioning the house so the tree's thick branches reach toward the upstairs windows like giant fingers.

But I'm not studying the tree for its beauty. I'm following the canopy up and back toward the house, gauging the distance between the outermost branches and Sammy's window. Could he have grabbed on to one with a flying leap? Possibly, but no way those outermost branches would have supported his weight. Even if he did somehow manage to grab on, he would have swung like Tarzan straight into the hard Georgia clay.

"Mrs. Huntington," someone yells up from the gate, and I sprint down the hill on bare feet. People are lined up on the other side of the fence like cattle, a sea of bodies with cameras for faces, recording my every move.

"I'm looking for my son," I say, panting. I'm all too aware of the lenses pointed at my head, of the stuttering chatter of camera clicks capturing my frantic face in full-color, high-resolution images. "Did any of you see him? I think he came out of the upstairs window."

This prompts an explosion of conversation, every journalist hurling a response at the same time. I try to sort through the jumble of words, but it's impossible. There are too many of them speaking at once.

I point to one, a tall blonde in a blue-and-white wrap dress. "You. Did you see him?"

She shoves a microphone through the rods of the gate. "Mrs. Huntington, there are rumors that it was your son, Sam Junior, who disappeared from Camp Crosby in Dahlonega. Can you—"

"Did you see a little boy jumping out of that second-story window or not?"

The woman blinks at me, but she doesn't say a word.

Her colleagues launch a new barrage of questions, but I turn and run full speed up the hill to the house. I don't spot either of the guards, so I veer to the right and follow the path that leads to the backyard. The mulch is sticky under my feet but a million times softer than the ground underneath, sunbaked clay packed harder than concrete. I run as fast as I can in bare feet, dirt and twigs tearing at my soles.

The trail spits me out in the backyard, and I skirt around the pool, my gaze skimming the crystal clear water with my heart in my throat. I'm thinking of my Sammy, falling in and hitting his head. Of his body, bobbing around the bottom. But the only thing I find in the pool is the automatic cleaner.

I stop at the edge of the terrace. I search the yard for movement, scanning the shrubs that form a border with the neighbors for a fleeting-deer flash of scrawny limbs. Nothing.

"Sammmmmmy," I scream.

There are only so many places in this yard for a person to hide. Crouched down behind the built-in grill. Pressed between the outdoor fireplace and the stockpile of firewood. In one of the garbage cans lined up along the garage. High in the branches of the magnolia tree. I check everywhere I can think of.

I'm on the terrace when Gary trots around from behind the garage, his big chest huffing with effort. "Did you find him?"

"No. He's not here." I shove my hands in my hair and turn in a circle, my mind tripping over itself.

Gary swipes a sleeve across his forehead. "You're sure he's not still inside?"

A burst of commotion coming from the house sends my pulse spiking, and I whip around to see Sam running out the sliding glass door. His gaze lands on mine, and his naked fear sends ice shooting through my veins. "Where have you looked?" One question for the both of us.

"The yard's clear," Gary says.

My gut cramps. "The reporters down at the gate didn't see him, either."

"Check the camera feeds," Sam says, and thank God for the dozens of them perched in strategic positions around the house and yard, one of the many questionable perks of being mayor. Though I've always hated the thought of someone watching my every move, I'm awfully glad for them now. If Sammy went anywhere through the yard, it'll be captured on tape. We'll know which way he went, if he went alone or was being dragged.

Gary jogs for the house, dodging my mother, who's standing at the far end of the patio with her palm pressed to her mouth.

"Where's Diego?" Sam says.

I shake my head, indicating I haven't seen him. Fear kicks the air right out of me. "Oh my God, Sam. What if he—"

"He didn't."

I don't know which "he" Sam is referring to—our son or Diego or the kidnapper—but Sam sounds certain so I don't argue.

He slides his iPhone from his pocket, punches at the screen, then holds it to his ear. After a strangling silence, he says, "Darryl, I need your help. My son's missing."

And suddenly, I'm back at the camp, stumbling out of my car on that muddy field, wailing for my son. I only thought those two horrible hours were a false alarm—two days too early, a hundred miles too far removed. This time it's real, the moment reliving itself in stunning authenticity. You can't cheat tragedy twice in three days.

"How long has he been gone?"

Tears sting my eyes. When I left him sulking on his bed, it was before nine. Now it's nearing nine-thirty. Long enough to run into traffic on West Paces Ferry or busier Northside Drive. Long enough to be shoved in a trunk and carted halfway to the next state.

I lean over, bracing both hands on my knees, and try not to throw up.

"Stef. How long has Sammy been gone?"

Nausea shimmers in my stomach, and I glance up. "A half hour, maybe more."

Sam relays my answer to the chief of police, then starts doling out orders. "Send over every patrol car in a ten-mile radius. Get them to work in concentric loops starting at our house and working outward. Description is four feet tall, with dark curly hair and glasses, last seen wearing a white T-shirt and black basketball shorts. We think he's on foot but we can't be sure."

Sirens wail from somewhere far away, moving closer.

My heart pounds, the liquid churning in my ears as my mind beats out one thought.

He's gone. Sammy is gone.

KAT

55 hours, 23 minutes missing

I'M RUNNING THROUGH THE FOREST BEHIND the camp.

The woods are thicker than I remember, wild and uncontrolled. Tall trees pressed tight with monster shrubs, their limbs locked in a prickly embrace—I shove my way through. Thorns tear at me, snatching at my clothes, my hair, my skin, long, tenacious fingers grabbing at me like skeleton claws. I thrash my way through, then pick up the pace, weaving through the tangled trees. I am searching for something, but I don't know what.

I punch through the brush and emerge in a clearing. The forest is cooler here, deep and unfamiliar. I stand in the middle and turn in a full circle, filling my lungs with the sweet, drifting perfume. I'm trying to get my bearings, but it's impossible. I'm lost and yet entirely unafraid. I sink onto the carpet of lacy ferns and wait.

Somewhere above me, high in the canopy of trees, a bird sings.

"Hi, Mom."

I twist around, and there he is. My Ethan, standing under a
giant rhododendron. The branches are dripping with orange
flowers, the limbs arching around him like a vault. I take in his
curly hair, his crooked glasses, his thin frame and bony shoulders, and joy, light and unfettered, fills my chest like feathers.

"There you are," I say, laughing.

He smiles. "Here I am."

"I've been looking everywhere for you."

"I know." Ethan steps into the clearing. His feet are bare,
but his pajamas are pristine. Not a speck of mud on him anywhere. "I've been here the whole time."

I watch my son pick his way through the underbrush, and
there's something important I'm supposed to remember. Something essential I need to say. If only I could think what. I pinch
the skin of my underarm, trying to wake myself up, but I'm
locked in this dream.

"Where?"

Ethan cocks his head, stepping right up to me. His glasses
glint in a milky ray of sunlight. "Where what?"

"Where are you, sweetie?"

"Mom. I already told you. I'm right here." He touches a
finger to the center of my chest. "I'll always be right here."

I open my eyes and he's gone.

A knuckle raps against the passenger's window of my car.
Mac, watching me through the glass. I pop the locks, and he
slides in. He smells freshly showered, the soap and aftershave
mingling with the two Starbucks coffees he's got cupped in
a giant palm.

When I called requesting a face-to-face, Mac suggested a

Waffle House near the station, but I couldn't face a restaurant full of people laughing and shoving food in their faces like it's any other Sunday morning. I couldn't bear the station, either, a building full of cops who've seen and know too much. We settled on here, a lesser-traveled corner of a strip mall parking lot just off 285.

"You okay? I knocked like three times." With his free hand, he pulls the door shut with a soft click. For such a big guy, his movements are surprisingly gentle.

I shake off the last remnants of the dream. "I'm fine, just tired. I haven't been sleeping much."

I'm *not* fine. I've barely slept at all since Mac beat his fist against my door. Whenever I do manage to drift off, my dreams transport me back to camp, to searching for Ethan in endless, empty woods. I don't know what's worse, this constant state of exhaustion, or waking up to find I'm stuck in a nightmare.

Today is day three, and the logical part of me knows what that means. Three days missing means Ethan's body is lying in a ditch somewhere, or slithering around the bottom of a swamp in something's belly. Three days, and now I can think of nothing else. *He'sdeadhe'sdeadhe'sdead.*

Mac hands me one of the cups. "I didn't know what you wanted, so I got you a cappuccino. I hope that's okay."

The smell churns my stomach. "It's perfect. Thank you."

He rests his cup on a knee. "So the reason we didn't find the tent in Andrew's house is because it was returned. We checked with REI and they confirmed it. He got his money back almost two weeks ago."

I shake my head, not because I don't believe him, but because I don't want to. "But Andrew hates camping. He hates the outdoors. Why would he buy a tent if he wasn't planning something?"

"He claims your separation was making him feel alienated from his son. He was looking for an activity they could do together. Apparently, Ethan was unimpressed."

My eyes burn, but I'm too angry, too let down to cry. I've spent a lot of time and energy talking myself into believing Ethan was with Andrew. It was the least hideous of the possibilities, Andrew the least monstrous of the monsters. The slim chance that Ethan might be with his father is how I've survived these past three days, and I'm not ready to let it go.

I settle my cup in the console holder. "You don't know Andrew like I do. He's a planner, and that call to Stefanie, pretending to be the kidnapper? It's exactly something he would do to throw the police off his trail. He's sneaky that way."

"We questioned him all night, Kat. We've got a tail on him just in case, but I don't think he's our guy."

Frustration rises, pounding against me like hurricane waves against the shore.

"We're still sorting through the tips. Most of them are from crackpots or false leads, like that little boy in the backseat of a car in Murrayville. It was a boy and his grandfather on a fishing trip. But a woman called in a suspicious man sneaking through the woods behind her house in Gainesville. That's only twenty miles or so from Dahlonega and right around the corner from Murrayville." He pauses, and I brace. "We're taking a hard look at that area, and that includes the houses and cabins around Lake Lanier."

My heart trips at the thought of all that water, at the miles and miles of coastline. There must be thousands of houses on that lake, which means a door-to-door search will take forever. "What about the other students and their parents? Did you talk to them?"

"We're in the process of reinterviewing everyone, but it's going to take another day or two to get through them all, then more time to chase down whatever new leads come out of the interviews. I've requested more manpower to help us get through everything as quickly as possible, but even that takes time."

Time we don't have. It's been fifty-five hours since Ethan was taken, and every passing minute beats like a war drum in my head. How much more time does he have?

Suddenly, the smell of the coffee is too much. I hit the button for my window and breathe in the outside air—exhaust and fast food. "Last night at the school, Stefanie mentioned something about Sammy's online friends. She said she passed the information on to you."

Mac nods. "That's one of the items on my list for today, actually, but don't go pinning too many of your hopes on this one. If it's true what Sammy says, that the handles belong to kids from school, they'll likely lead us nowhere. Honestly, our best shot is that phone call to Mrs. Huntington, specifically, the statement about the Bell Building. That's where I'm concentrating most of my energy, on the mayor."

I can't hide my shock. I think about Sam's phone call at the camp, Stefanie's prompting of reward money just last night and I feel sick. "You think the mayor had something to do with this?"

"Not necessarily, but we know whoever took Ethan meant to take Sammy instead, in order to force Mayor Huntington's hand. That phone call is the best lead we've got."

"But you couldn't trace it. And he hasn't called back."

Mac concedes with a one-shouldered shrug. "Which is why I'm working on other ways to come at it."

I fall silent. Since the moment he showed up on my doorstep, Mac has not missed a call, ignored a text or skipped an update, which come at all hours of the day and night. That he's holding back now feels like a slap in the face.

"Come on, Kat, don't look at me like that. This is the mayor we're talking about. I'm not going to make any accusations I can't back up, not even to you. I will tell you as soon as I have something concrete to report, but for now, give me a little leeway here."

I stare across the console at Mac, wondering why on earth anybody would want a job like his. Especially in a city like Atlanta, where every day is a fresh barrage of evil and tragedy. How does he sit down at his desk and face yet another murder, yet another missing child? How does he stand it?

"Why?" It's a million questions in one. Why this job, why not tell me more about the mayor, why all this effort for a boy you've never met? I settle on the last one, for now the most pressing. "Why did you take this case? Why Ethan?"

"Because I took an oath to preserve, protect and defend, and I meant every word."

"Did that oath include carting me all the way to Dahlonega and trampling through the woods in your nice clothes? Did it include not eating or sleeping except at your desk? Because I've seen the time stamps on the texts and emails you send me. You're not sleeping any more than I am, and I want to know why. You don't know me, and you've never met Ethan."

"Honestly?" He gives me a sheepish shrug. "When I came to your house Friday night, you said you didn't have anyone to call, and that struck me as unequivocally unfair, especially after what you've been through with Andrew. And yes, I read your file before I knocked on your door. I saw the pictures from the assault. I know what he did to you." He shifts in his seat. "But mostly, I don't know why Ethan's disappearance keeps me up at night, and I also don't care. One of the things I've learned in this job is not to ask why. Some cases just grab on more than others. When that happens, you just grab on right back."

The cars coming and going in the lot, the low hum on the radio speakers, the swoosh of traffic on Lawrenceville Highway—it all disappears. Mac's words are not the answer I expected, and yet they are exactly what I needed to hear.

He twists to fully face me. "Look, in case you haven't figured it out already, this case is my number one priority. Scratch that. *Ethan* is my number one priority. And I promise you, Kat, if it's the last thing I ever do, I will find him. I am going to find him and put the monster who took him behind bars."

I have no reason to believe him, this man I barely know, and yet I do. I am certain he will live up to his promise to bring my son home, just as I am certain of the words he intentionally left out—*even if it's only his body*. The thought snags in my chest, and it occurs to me there's more to ask of him.

"Okay. But I need you to promise me something else, too."

He gives me a reluctant nod.

"When you find Ethan…" My voice cracks, then dries up completely.

"Kat." His voice is soft, kind, but I hold up a hand to stop him. I need to say this. I need to get it out of my head, out of my heart.

"When you find him, if he's not…okay…" I squeeze my eyes shut, squeeze out two hot streams. I'm crying, *again*, and

I wonder if my tears will ever stop. I open my eyes and focus on Mac's blurry face. "Whatever you do, please do not tell me that news over the phone. My heart couldn't take that. I need you to tell me to my face, and I need you to be gentle." I reach over, wrap my hand around his wrist, hard like stone. "Please, Mac. Promise me you'll be gentle."

"I promise," he says, and just in case, he says it again. "I promise you, Kat. You have my word."

STEF

55 hours, 34 minutes missing

"WHAT'S TAKING SO LONG?" I'M PACING THE kitchen, trembling not from the air-conditioning but from fear.

Mom is standing at the sink, filling a half-dozen glasses with filtered water. "Sammy's energy is strong."

"Is that what the spirits are telling you?"

It comes out mean and hopeful at the same time, neither of which I intend. For the first time since Mom traded in her psychologist's couch for tarot cards and crystals, I understand the appeal of her craft. Why people would plunk down their hard-earned savings for some self-proclaimed expert to prod their deepest, most private thoughts. Mom's words reach into my chest and squeeze my heart, because they're exactly the ones I want to hear. That wherever Sammy is, he's safe and unharmed.

And yet the rational part of me knows her sorcery is hokey.

"I'm sorry, it's just…I need a little more proof before I believe that."

"Proof is not always visible with the naked eye. Sometimes

it's here—" she pounds her chest "—a tingling that tells you things will work out in the end."

"How? Sammy disappeared out of a two-story window. I don't know where he is, who has him. If you want to make a believer out of me, I'm going to need something a little more tangible than a tingling, Mother."

The front door opens, saving us from this argument, and a jumble of heavy voices enters the house.

I run around the corner into the foyer, where Sam is trailed by two uniformed cops and a man I assume is a plainclothes detective, until Sam introduces him as a reporter from the *Atlanta Journal-Constitution*. He's tall and thin and overly eager, taking in the place with an almost-giddy grin. His gaze sticks to details like he's cataloging them for a piece he's already begun writing in his head.

"Mrs. Huntington, it's a real honor." The reporter almost trips over himself to offer me a hand, soft and slippery like rubber. "Truly. Though I'm awfully sorry to be meeting at a time like this one, of course."

"Did you see Sammy?" I don't have time for niceties.

"Yes, ma'am. He came out his bedroom window like these gentlemen said, like a little Cirque du Soleil acrobat, then took off around the side of the house. Almost missed him, though, because we were all talking about the truck."

"What truck?" I glance at my husband, flanked on either side by the two officers. The three men look interested but not all that surprised. This repeat is mostly for me.

"A souped-up F-150. Tinted windows. Oversize wheels. Like something out of a car show. It must have driven by a dozen times. We joked that if the driver was casing the joint, with all us journalists standing with cameras right there, he was the dumbest robber alive."

One of the officers takes over the questioning. "Sir, how do you know the driver was male?"

The reporter turns to face him, hiking a shoulder. "I don't. Like I said, tinted windows. But I've never seen a woman drive a truck like that one."

The cop grunts. "Did you catch the plates?"

The reporter shakes his head. "Only that it was a Georgia one."

My blood tingles with equal parts anger and disappointment. What kind of rinky-dink journalist is this guy?

"What about the county?" the cop says.

"No, Georgia as in UGA. The red-and-black ones with the bulldog on it. Pretty sure those don't list the county."

The questioning goes on for a little longer, but when it becomes apparent the reporter has nothing more to add, the policeman escorts him outside.

"The truck doesn't belong to a neighbor, that much is certain," Sam says to the second policeman, and he's right. Our neighbors drive foreign-made SUVs, not souped-up pickup trucks. There are plenty of yard and pool service trucks ambling up and down the leafy streets, but they don't all drive pickups, and the ones that do come with a logo splashed on the side. "Let's see if it shows up on one of the camera feeds."

"Gary's down there now," I say, referring to the small room at the back of the basement, the one we jokingly call Mission Control.

We hurry down the stairs and through the long hallway to the neat and functional space almost completely swallowed up by racks of hardware. Cable and internet, audiovisual, solar and geothermal controls, gray water irrigation system, the rooftop's photovoltaic panels—it's all run from these machines.

When Sam had everything installed, I asked him if he secretly worked for NASA.

We huddle behind Gary, seated at the desk against the wall, staring over his shoulder at four matching screens displaying feed from the security system. Each screen is divided into four sections, with views of every entrance, every bank of windows, the pool and terrace area, and several sections of the yard. Dozens of spying eyes recording our every movement.

"I started at the front," Gary says, glancing over his shoulder, "since Mrs. Huntington said Sammy left through his bedroom window, and started working back from 9:23 a.m., which is around the time she hollered out the window." He taps one of the screens, a partial still of the right front side of the house, then skips back until he finds what he wants. "I found him here, at 9:11."

I check my watch. Nine-eleven is almost an hour ago.

Gary pushes Play, and I hold my breath and watch a dark blur take shape behind Sammy's window. He flips the locks on either side of the glass, then moves in a rhythmic motion I recognize as his arm, cranking the lever. The glass peels away from the front of the house, and his determined face appears. He swings his head left and right, and then he unhooks the bar that keeps the window from blowing around in the wind.

"Oh my God." I want to reach through the computer screen and strangle him for being so reckless, because I know what I'm about to see. I know what he's going to do. "He's going to swing out onto the overhang."

The sloped roof just above the front door, providing shelter. A good six feet from Sammy's window. Too far for him to jump.

Gary nods like this is a test, and I just gave the right answer. "Watch this."

On the screen, Sammy climbs up on the windowsill, grabs onto the frame with both hands, shoves off with his feet, and swings out over the yard, his body dangling twenty feet above the ground like the world's most perilous jungle gym. Fear electrocutes every hair on my body, and I gasp and swat at Sam's arm. His biceps is tense like a slab of concrete.

Sammy undershoots the overhang on his first try, his scrawny legs cycling in the air so hard that his fingers almost lose their grip on the wood. The window swings him back toward the house with a clap, and he pushes off again with a toe, this time too hard. The window arcs him through the air for a second time and slams him into the siding. He lets go, falling a few feet, and lands on the overhang like an acrobat, arms wheeling around as he works to catch his balance. One foot skids out from under him, and he skates down the sloping surface, cedar shingles flying, and I clap a hand over my mouth so I don't scream. Sammy stops his downward slide just in time, by planting a foot in the gutter right before he pitches over the side.

For a long moment, all I see are his white-knuckled hands, clutching the copper gutter at the bottom of the frame. A second later, they're gone.

"Jesus fucking Christ," Sam mutters.

Gary reaches for the mouse. "I picked him up on the right side cameras."

I steady my nerves with the knowledge Sammy survived the fall. He made it to the ground without breaking his neck. I force myself to draw in air, to blow it out, to fight my building hysteria. He survived the fall. That's the good news.

Gary taps the left monitor. "Here he comes."

Sammy streaks across the same path along the side of the

house that I ran down, his sneakers kicking up the dirt and mulch, then disappears from the screen.

Gary points to the other monitor. "And then here."

The blur that races across the bottom of the screen is only the bottom half of Sammy. He's skirting the edge of the pool, sprinting toward the very back of the yard, and suddenly I know where he's going. To where just last week, in a fit of Spanish I understood less than half of, one of the yard guys coaxed me to the back right corner of the yard and showed me a gap in the fence. A gap just wide enough for an animal to squeeze through—or a tiny body.

I watch Sammy disappear into the trees, and my mouth goes dry. I check the time on the feed—9:16 a.m.

"Where the hell was he going?" Sam says from right behind me.

"I don't know," I say.

"A friend's house?"

I shake my head. "None of them live within walking distance, and even if they did, this isn't the 1950s. We don't just let Sammy stroll down the street unsupervised, especially with a kidnapper on the loose."

Gary pokes a finger at the place on the screen where we last saw our son. "That is one determined kid. He knew exactly where he was going."

"Yes, to a hole in the fence."

"And then where?" Sam's voice is impatient, and it sparks my temper.

"If only he'd thought to tell me before he jumped out of a twenty-foot-high window," I snap.

"What do you think was in his backpack?" Mom says, almost conversationally.

Sam and I exchange a look. He didn't notice it, either. Both of us were too busy watching our son dangle from a twenty-foot ledge to notice anything hanging from his back.

"Show me," Sam says.

Gary rewinds the first video and pushes Play, and there it is. Not really a backpack but the vinyl drawstring bag Sammy got from Kevin Macy's birthday party at the batting cages last summer. I recognize the Nike swoosh, remember thinking what a cute idea it was, a sports bag filled with Cracker Jack and Big League Chew and other sports-themed swag. Now Sammy has jerry-rigged it to hang from his shoulders, and there's not much in it, judging from the way it flops about when he runs.

"Can you get a view of street traffic?" Sam says to Gary, telling him about the souped-up truck. "The reporters out front thought it was odd that it kept driving by, but not odd enough anybody remembered the plate number."

While Gary fiddles with the feeds, Sam turns to me. "Start making calls. Start with whoever lives closest and go from there. The kid I saw climbing out the window had a destination in mind."

"That's just it. I'm telling you, there's no one. Liam is the closest, and Sammy would have to cross Paces Ferry to get to him. And I'm pretty sure he'd get lost. Argonne Forest is a maze of streets he's only ever seen from the backseat of a car."

"Call anyway."

My heart skips more than one beat, both at his dangerous tone and the idea of Sammy dodging traffic on the major Buckhead thoroughfare. Even on Sunday morning, West Paces Ferry is a madhouse, bumper-to-bumper cars whizzing by on their way to church. Nobody will be watching for a lone kid to dart across.

I scroll through my phone, looking for the number for Liam Lark's mother.

"There it is," Gary says suddenly, and my gaze darts to the screen.

I'm staring at a view of the front lawn and driveway, shot from high up by the roofline. The angle doesn't give us a clean view of the street, not with the reporters' cars and television vans standing in the way, but there's just enough slice of street that we see it, a black-windowed truck sliding by on the other side of the driveway gate. Gary presses Pause at just the right moment, then fiddles with the controls while Sam coaches him through the logistics of zooming in on the system. I take a deep breath, enough air to make my lungs ache, then blow it all out and wait.

"Looks like we've got a partial." Gary jots the numbers on a sticky note.

Everybody begins talking at once. There are so many voices, one leapfrogging over the other to be heard, we almost miss the most important one.

Diego's deep voice, coming down the hall. "Mr. Huntington. Mrs. Huntington!"

"In here," Sam shouts.

I twist around in my chair.

Diego appears in the doorway, his face dripping with sweat, his chest heaving like he just ran here from Alabama. He reaches back into the hall, gives something a good tug and there he is.

My recalcitrant, runaway son.

KAT

55 hours, 42 minutes missing

AFTER MAC LEAVES, I SIT IN MY CAR, WATCHING people pass by in the parking lot. Talking on the phone, pushing grocery carts loaded with food, searching for their keys, oblivious to Ethan's plight. And why shouldn't they be? They don't know him, don't know me. I watch them, these strangers going about their Sunday morning, and I'm torn between jealousy and spite.

I check the time on the dashboard—ten-twelve. The day stretches in front of me like a long, colorless road, endless and empty. Mac's smell still lingers in the air, soap and aftershave and coffee, and I think back on his words, specifically all the ones he refused to say. About the phone call, that downtown building, the demands made of the mayor. Mac said that's where he's concentrating his energy. Maybe, so should I.

I dig my cell from the middle console, type "Bell Building Atlanta" in the internet search bar, and wait for the results to load.

According to Google, the building has seen better days. What was once a telephone exchange in the 1920s is now abandoned, thanks to a summertime leak that flooded two upper floors. The tenants fled, the owner spent the insurance money on a fancy new house in Buckhead and the building deteriorated into a health hazard, every inch of it crawling in black mold. Nobody cried when the City of Atlanta condemned it, especially not the owner. They paid him good money for it last year as part of some flashy development on Marietta Street.

I scroll down to find a few ratty images. Three uninspired stories, featureless windows, dirty bricks under crumbling white paint. Why would anyone want to save it? Why is this building worth a little boy's life? I don't understand any of it.

I surf back to the top, to the search bar. Mac told me to stay away from the news and the internet, and Lucas backed him up. He said it was like asking WebMD how long you've got after a cancer diagnosis—the news will always be so much worse than you thought.

I push aside their warnings and type "Ethan Maddox missing" in the bar. My finger hovers over the enter key for only a second or two. I hit it and hold my breath.

The screen loads with news items, dozens of them, links to local and national articles, interviews with law enforcement and other "experts," clips from the morning news and CNN. I click on one from WXIA, the local NBC affiliate, but the article doesn't tell me anything I don't already know. Ethan disappeared from an overnight trip to Dahlonega, police suspect foul play, unsubstantiated whispers of a kidnapping, a rumor someone traced back to a cabdriver. No mention of Sammy or the Huntingtons, though it's only a matter of time before the whispers gain substance.

I scroll further, flip to the next page. Farther down on the screen, one of the results catches my eye, stopping my heart like an emergency break.

Child's remains found in Chattahoochee National Forest.

My body goes hot like a furnace, and my eyes sprout instant tears. Chattahoochee National Forest smothers the northeastern chunk of Georgia, dipping from Tennessee into a half-dozen counties, including Lumpkin, stopping right before Dahlonega.

With shaking hands, I press the link and a solemn-faced newswoman fills my screen.

"Hikers in North Georgia made a gruesome discovery earlier this morning, when they came across the body of a young boy. The tourists were trekking along the Dockery Lake Trail when they spotted the child's remains. State and local police have arrived at the scene, but so far, no formal identification has been made…"

Whatever she says next, I can't hear it over my own sobbing. Big, ugly, heaving sobs that burn in my chest and convulse my body like a seizure. A body. A *boy's* body. In the woods north of Dahlonega. How many missing boys can there be?

I call Mac, choking out the words in seizured spurts. *Hikers. Body. Boy.* My voice rising, spiraling into a steady wail Mac has to shout over.

"Kat, listen to me. It's not him. It's not Ethan."

I shut up for long enough to let his message worm its way into my brain, but it can't. The distance is too great. My body can't understand, either. The tears are still flowing, my hands are still shaking, and my lungs can't quite suck in enough air.

"Did you hear me? It's not him."

His words loosen the knot around my chest, but my breath still shudders and aches. "It's not? Are you sure?"

"Positive. This boy was older, and his body had been there for a while. A week, at least."

"Oh, thank God. ThankGodthankGodthankGod. I saw that news clip and I just…" I rest my forehead on the steering wheel and say it again. "Thank you, God."

He gives me a moment to pull myself together. "I thought you weren't going to watch the news." His voice is patient, even though his words are a reprimand. When he told me to stay off the internet, he said that included the news, as well.

"I know, I just feel so damn helpless. I want to do something, but there's nothing for me to do. All I can do is sit here and wait, and it's making me crazy."

"I know how hard it is for you to sit around and wait for news, believe me, I do, but go home. Get some rest. Take care of yourself. That's the best thing you can do, both for you and for Ethan."

I give him a shaky nod, even though he can't see. "Okay."

"I'll be in touch as soon as I've got something to report. I promise."

We hang up, and the raw emotions of the morning gather, swirling into a black hole of grief. Of fear and sorrow and missing my son. I give in to my tears again, allowing myself another good cry, and then I do what Mac suggested. I start my car and point it home.

STEF

55 hours, 51 minutes missing

I FALL TO MY KNEES WITH A HARD SMACK I feel all the way to my bones, snatch my son from the guard's hand and tug him to my chest. Sam steps up on the other side, draping his arms around both our shoulders in a full-family embrace. "A Sammy sammie," that's what the three of us always call it.

But after that first, singular moment of absolute relief comes anger. No, not anger. Fury. Fury sends me hurtling back to earth like a blazing asteroid, questions firing in my mind. Why did Sammy run away? Where was he going? What was so goddamn important he would dangle himself out a window, streak past the guards and the cameras, dodge traffic and who knows what else to do it?

"What were you thinking? You scared me to death." I pull back, clamp my hands onto his shoulders, and shake him until his teeth rattle, until his glasses fly off his face and clatter to the tile. "I thought he got you. Do you understand what I'm telling you? I thought the kidnapper came back for you."

A splinter in the back of my mind tells me I'm out of control, but I can't seem to stop myself.

Sammy's head bobbles around on his neck, but he doesn't cry out. His lips are pressed shut, but his eyes are peeled wide. I'm scaring him, that much is clear, and I'm suddenly glad for the burly guard standing right behind him. I've never, not once, raised a hand to my child, but I have to hold myself back now. I want to hug him, then throttle him, then hug him again while meanwhile my brain pounds out, *he's here, he's back, he's alive.*

"I found him on Pine Valley," Diego says, still panting in the doorway.

Pine Valley is more than a mile from here, across more than one busy street.

"You were going to Liam's?"

Sammy flinches, and I take that as a yes.

"Why?" When he doesn't respond, I shimmy the backpack off his shoulders and wrench the thing open. I see the device, I acknowledge it's there, cradled in the bottom of his backpack with crumbs and empty candy wrappers, but I don't understand any of it. "Your Xbox controller? You risked your life and gave your father and me a heart attack to play a fucking *video game?*"

The curse word plops out before I can snatch it back, not that I try to. I am consumed by rage. Eaten alive by it. My throat throbs with the strain of holding it in.

"Sammy, what were you thinking?" I give him another rough shake, and he bursts into tears.

Sam presses a hand between my shoulder blades. "Let's all just take a step back and regroup, okay? We're not going to get any answers like this."

His words slice through my furious haze, and I understand

what he's trying to say without actually saying it: *Settle down. Stop talking. You have an audience.* It's the Huntington curse—that we are always being watched, heard, judged. Even in the privacy of our own home.

I clamp my lips shut, but my hands are still sweaty and shaking.

Behind me, Sam begins doling out praise to the men in the room. He thanks them for their service. He apologizes for the trouble we've put them through. He shakes their hands and offers to walk them out like they're guests who dropped by for a glass of wine. Despite whatever emotions are brewing behind his mayoral facade, he's charming and cordial and polite. There will never be a more perfect politician.

But I am no public servant, and I no longer have the energy to pretend. I push to a shaky stand, take Sammy by the arm and drag him into the hall without a word. The men step aside so we can pass.

"Mommy," Sammy whimpers as I drag him up the stairs, and the word is like a vise to my heart. He hasn't called me Mommy in years, not even last fall when he woke up after having his tonsils taken out. I wait for whatever is coming next, an apology, maybe, or an explanation. He opens his mouth to haul air, his breath stuttering with the kind of sucked-in sob that comes from too much crying, but he doesn't say a word.

We step onto the foyer floor, and I stab a finger in the direction of the living room.

"Go sit your butt on the couch and do not move a muscle."

Sammy looks down at his upper arm, which my other hand still wraps around in a stranglehold, the tips of my fingers stark white against his T-shirt. I release my grip, and he ducks his head and scrambles off.

"What are you going to do?" Mom says from right behind me. I turn, and she hands me his glasses.

"I'm going to try really hard not to strangle my only child." My voice is shaking, not with the humor I meant to shove in my tone, but with fury.

"Compassion and anger can coexist, you know. Sit still. Listen closely to the messages of Sammy's heart and honor them. He doesn't always have the right words, but if you give him room to talk, he'll let you know why he did what he did."

I roll my eyes. "Mother, please."

Sammy is just where I ordered him to be, seated in the middle of the couch, his back pushed all the way into the cushion so that his legs dangle above the shaggy carpet. His sobbing has grown loud and messy, a mucousy gulping into his lap. I sink onto an armchair at the end, propping my foot on the coffee table, thinking about the little bottle of Xanax upstairs in the safe, left over from last year's brow lift. When all this is over, I'm going to poke a couple down my throat and sleep for a week.

Sammy's guilty gaze creeps from his lap to mine, then flits away.

We sit there for a long moment in silence, listening to Sam wrap up another round of thank-yous and let everyone out the front door. It shuts with an ominous click. Sammy flinches, then again with each one of Sam's footsteps coming our way. He sinks onto the arm of my chair.

"So, I've been thinking and I think I've figured it out." Sam's voice is surprisingly calm, his tone almost friendly despite the way his jaw clenches and his hands clasp on a thigh, his long fingers curling into a death grip. "You called an Uber, didn't you? A Yukon XL was on its way to take you to Six Flags."

This is one of Sam's more irritating techniques, to mask his anger under a steaming pile of smart-ass. Sammy looks up, his forehead wrinkled in confusion.

"No." The first word he's spoken since his choked-out *Mommy* on the stairs.

Sam tosses up his hands, lets them fall back to his lap. "What, then? Let's have it. Your mother and I are dying of suspense. What's your excuse? Where were you going?"

The silence that spins out lasts forever. It's the kind of silence that wraps around you like a shroud, the kind that turns the air thick and solid. Sammy presses his lips together and stares at his lap.

"Spit it out, Sammy. I figure no kid hangs out of a twenty-foot window for no good reason, so give it to us. What was so goddamn important you almost killed yourself to do it?"

Sammy's head pops up, and the look on his face is defiant. "It wasn't *that* hard."

It was the wrong thing to say. Sam loses it—his patience, his temper, every last shred of his politician's diplomacy. "You could have broken your neck. You could have *died*." Sam spews a volley of curses, his face turning an alarming shade of purple. "Now answer the question. Your mother and I deserve to know where you were going."

Sammy takes a couple of deep breaths, and I can't tell if he's scrambling for a lie or gathering up his courage. Tears drip from his chin onto his lap. His gaze locks onto mine, a silent cry for help. I reach over to a side table and toss him a box of Kleenex.

"I needed to get on Liam's Xbox for a minute," he says, ignoring the tissues.

I place my fingers at my temples and press in concentric circles.

"Are you shitting me?" Sam screams. "Are you seriously going to sit there and tell me that you risked your life and scared the living daylights out of your mother and me for a stupid video game? We called the police! We had I-don't-know-how-many people out there looking for you. And maybe you missed the memo but there's a kidnapper on the loose, and the kid he really meant to swipe from that cabin in Dahlonega is you. Not Ethan. *You*." Sam stops talking for a moment, breathing heavily as if trying to rein himself back in, but when he continues, his voice is still thick with emotion. "Do you have any idea how careless that makes you look? How selfish?"

By now Sammy's face is slick with tears. He flings his head into his arms and sobs onto his lap. "You don't understand," he says on the tail end of a wail. "It was important."

The same word he said to me in his room upstairs, right after I took his Xbox.

Sam hauls a breath to respond, but I press a hand to his knee, a not so subtle sign to give me a try. I scoot from the chair to the couch, wrapping an arm across Sammy's shoulders.

"Sammy," I begin, but it comes out angry. I smooth my tone into something more somber. "Sammy, look at me, please."

He peeks up from between his arms.

"Your father and I are trying really hard to understand you, but I need you to try to understand why we're so angry. When you left, when we couldn't find you anywhere, we thought the kidnapper came back for you. We thought he took you."

Sammy's face curls into itself again, and he swipes away fresh tears with the backs of both hands, first one, then the other. "Oh."

"Oh? Come on, Sammy. You can do better than that." I pluck a couple of tissues from the Kleenex box and start mopping up his face. Under the dirt and the snot, his cheeks are covered in angry, red scratches. "I need you to tell us why you tried to run away. What was so important?"

"I don't want to tell you."

"Why not?"

His lip wobbles and there they are again, the relentless tears. "Because."

"Because why?"

"Because."

"I've got nowhere to go, Sammy. We can do this all day. Because why?"

"Because I thought you would be mad. I thought you'd hate me."

My chest tightens, and I cup a hand under his chin, tilting his face to mine. I wait for his watery gaze to find mine. "I am your mother, and I will always love you no matter what. Do you understand?"

Sammy nods and squeezes his eyes shut.

"So help me understand. Tell me what you were trying to do."

"I wanted to apologize." His expression is sad and eager at the same time. "I wanted to tell him I was sorry."

My son has so many transgressions to apologize for. Hijacking my password, jumping out a second-story window, running away, lying. But it's clear this apology is not for me. "Apologize to whom?"

"To Ethan."

"What do you need to apologize to Ethan for?"

Sammy wipes away his tears with the backs of his hands, then dries them on his T-shirt. "For making him trade sleeping bags, even though I knew his was brand-new. For making him cry. Lots of stuff."

"But why? Why would you take his sleeping bag?"

"I don't know. His mummy bag was so much nicer than mine, and he was acting like it was the greatest thing in the world. I don't know why that made me so mad, but it did."

"So what you told me yesterday, about Jessica and those other girls telling you to switch, that was a lie?"

It takes a full five seconds for Sammy to nod.

"Oh, Sammy."

My son is a bully. It's the first time I've allowed the words in my brain, the first time I've let myself fully acknowledge the possibility, even though if I'm being totally honest, I've tried hard *not* to think it plenty of times. I've seen the way he acts around Ethan, heard the way Miss Emma dances around the point without ever saying the word and this confirms it. Sammy is a bully, and it's up to me and Sam to fix him.

Sammy's voice grows defensive. "Dad does it. He said he'd get more trains for the city even though there wasn't any money. He lies all the time."

"That's different," Sam says. "Those are campaign promises. They're things I *want* to do, not things I guarantee *to* do."

"Then why are they called promises?" Sammy says, and Sam doesn't answer. He looks at me, and I don't answer, either. Technically, Sammy's right. Empty promises aren't promises, but lies.

"Anyway, Nana says my energy won't clear until I say I'm sorry, and I want to but I couldn't get up on the roof. I tried to tell him a whole bunch of times on the stairs, but he kept running off and now my energy's all messed up."

"What the hell is he talking about?" Sam pops off the chair and begins pacing the edge of the carpet.

I shush him with a wave of my hand. A little tickle has started up at the back of my mind. Last night, Sammy told Mom to follow some locusts up the stairs.

"You tried to tell who?"

"Ethan. But I kept getting killed on the stairs."

My heart kicks like Sammy used to in my belly, hard and swift. "The stairs on the video game?"

Sammy nods. "He was there. He ran right past me on his way to the rooftop."

Could it be true? Could Ethan really be sitting in a room somewhere, battling the locusts on a television screen while the police search the North Georgia woods? I try to summon up the handles on the list of Sammy's friends, try to recall if one of them might have belonged to Ethan, but can't. They were all so obscure.

"When? When did you see him?"

"Yesterday. And Joe said he saw him in the tomb. Remember? You told me."

GamerJoeATL's message whispers through my mind. *In the tomb hurry.*

"Liam was gonna help me find the hammer of dawn so I can kill all the locusts and get to the next level. It's hidden in the grass by the steps, but there's a troika right there so I can't get to it. Liam was gonna show me how."

"Somebody want to tell me what the hell he's talking about?"

I hush Sam, thinking not about Sammy's words, the tomb or the locusts or the troikas, but the greater picture. That my son might have just found Ethan.

"Can you show us?"

KAT

55 hours, 53 minutes missing

I GET HOME AND GO STRAIGHT TO BED. ETHAN'S bed. I pull his tattered dinosaur sheets over my face and breathe in a lungful of my son. How long until the fabric stops smelling of him?

The Xanax I took when I came upstairs is doing its work, dulling my senses and clouding up my thoughts like a pea soup fog, but I take another just in case. The pill dissolves into a bitter mush I swallow with a grimace, waiting for a second rush of calm to hit my bloodstream. I haven't told Lucas I'm taking them, raiding the leftover bottle the ER doctor pushed in my hand after Andrew's assault, though part of me suspects Lucas already knows. I see the way he watches me when he thinks I'm not looking, like he used to watch Andrew in the last few years of our marriage. Lucas is keeping tabs, cataloging the clues, watching for warning signs I might do something dangerous. If Ethan doesn't come home soon, I just might.

There's a knock at the door, and Lucas sticks his head in. "Hey, you up?"

"No. Go away."

The door creaks as he steps inside, his socks swishing across the bedroom carpet. I peek around the sheet, and there he is, looming above me. "I made breakfast."

"I'm not hungry."

His gaze lands on the prescription bottle on Ethan's bedside table. "You have to keep up your strength."

"Why?" It comes out dull and lifeless instead of angry and confrontational the way I intended. What do I need my strength for? So that when Mac comes to give me the bad news, I will have enough left for a proper breakdown? To be honest, I'd rather that be the final blow, the last little tragedy that tips me over the edge.

"You're right. Better to just waste away in your bed. And why not? Andrew can take care of Ethan just as well as you can."

As long as I've known Lucas, he's been brilliant at this, at hurling passive-aggressive snark to manipulate me into seeing things his way. He said something similar the summer I turned sixteen, when my mother was dying of ovarian cancer and I wanted to die with her. Lucas glued himself to my side, carting me to the hospital, the hospice, the funeral home, the graveside. "Now's your chance," he whispered as they were lowering her into the ground. "I'll push you in if you want me to."

It got him an elbow to the ribs, but it also got him what he was looking for: a smile.

Now his words punch through my Xanax haze, and I sigh and sit up in bed. "You're an asshole, you know that?"

Lucas grins. "I love you, too." He reaches for my hand and heaves me out of bed.

Downstairs, Lucas shoos me to the table and prepares the plates. He piles them high with more food than I could ever eat in one sitting, eggs and bacon and pancakes, which he tops with thick tabs of butter and too much syrup. I watch him move around the tiny space, bumping up against the counter like a giant trapped in a dollhouse, and my eyes prick with tears. If Ethan doesn't come home, if I have to live the rest of my life in this house without him, I want Lucas to never leave.

He's pouring the last of the milk when my phone rings.

Not bad news, I tell myself. Mac promised.

Still.

I stare at the screen and a vibration starts up somewhere deep inside my body, spreading across my skin like a tuning fork. My brain fills with equal parts hope and terror.

And then a name fills the screen: *Andrew Maddox.*

An instant sense of relief, pickled with dread. Andrew is not supposed to be calling, and he wouldn't risk defying the restraining order unless he had something important to say. I swipe a shaky thumb across the screen.

"Tell Captain Douchebag I'm calling the cops," Lucas says, settling my plate onto the table with a clunk. "The restraining order applies to phone calls, too, asshole."

I shush him with a palm. "Andrew? What's wrong?"

Whatever Andrew says is lost in Lucas's booming voice. He cups his hands around his mouth and points his face toward the phone. "The cops are on their way, dickweed."

"Lucas, stop. I can't deal with this on top of everything else, okay? Just stop." I push past him for the stairs, taking them by twos and racing to my room. "Andrew, where are you? What's wrong?"

"I see Lucas hasn't changed."

I bristle at his abrasive words, the way his tone is filled with accusation and blame. "Is this why you called, to complain about Lucas?"

"No, but you can tell him not to bother calling the cops.

I spent all night at the station, and one of them has been following me ever since, and he hasn't been the least bit subtle about it. By now that guy knows everything about me, all the way down to my preferred gas station and the label on the back of my jeans."

I sink onto my bed. "Where were you?" I know where he was; I just want to hear him say it.

"On vacation. Out of the country. When I heard about Ethan, I came back."

His answer is typical Andrew. No apologies, no explanations. Andrew has never apologized for what he did. Not for the name-calling, not for the abuse, not for anything. Nothing is *ever* his fault.

"Why are you calling me?"

"Because the police won't tell me anything, and I didn't know what else to do. I'm going crazy out here, Kat. Seriously losing my mind."

I blink around the messy room, taking in the crooked lampshade, the stack of books on my nightstand that has toppled over onto the floor, the dark stain on the rug from where Ethan knocked over my glass of red wine. I remember being so angry at the time, fuming at yet another chore for me to tackle when I already had more than I could handle. I close my eyes and wish I could go back; there's so much I would do differently, starting with that moment.

"Please, Kat." A desperate note has crept into Andrew's voice, as sincere as I've ever heard it. "Whatever you think of me, whatever mess we've made of us, I'm still Ethan's father."

But one thing I would never change is the night Andrew and I made Ethan. Regardless of everything that came after, all the screams and the fights and the tears, Andrew is right about one thing: he's still Ethan's father.

"They're searching a lake, Andrew. A *lake*. Mac said something about the cabins and houses, but all I could think is all the water they surround. Ethan can barely make it across a swimming pool, much less a giant body of water known for sucking dozens of kids down every summer. Every time I close my eyes, I see him bobbing with all those other bodies around the bottom."

It's almost a relief to say the words out loud. The worry has been ricocheting around my head, growing faster and louder and more insistent with each passing second, and Lucas wouldn't want to hear it. Andrew is the only person I talk to who will understand, who as soon as I said the word *lake* will be thinking the exact same thing.

But Andrew is still hung up on another word. "Who's Mac?"

I wince. "Detective Macintosh. He's the one who showed up at my door when Ethan went missing. He's giving me regular updates."

I brace for the barrage that always used to come whenever a male name that was not Ethan's or Andrew's crossed my lips. All those years we were married, Andrew accused every man who looked my way of wanting me, and me of drawing their attention on purpose. Projection is the worst kind of head-fuckery, this sneaky practice of accusing me of the very thing he was doing himself, and in a way that made me think *I* was the problem, not his ridiculous jealousy. Six months away from Andrew and my skills are already rusty. Even though Andrew lost any claim the minute he raised his hand to me, even though Mac has shown me nothing but professionalism and kindness, I still feel like I did something wrong. I still feel guilty for even mentioning another man's name.

But Andrew surprises me by mowing right over my answer. "Jesus, a lake?" He blows out a long, shaky breath. "Why didn't anybody tell me?"

There are so many things I could say here. Because your default stance is combative. Because you're a *suspect*. I press my lips together and say nothing at all.

"But they're searching *around* the lake, right? Not in it. I mean, they don't have any reason to think…" His words fade into that high-pitched squeak men's voices sometimes get when they're trying to pinch back tears. He pauses to get a hold of himself, then exhales into the phone, a long and loaded sigh. "Listen, I have something for you. Something Ethan made the last time he was at my house. With him…missing, I thought it would be nice for you to have. Will Lucas tackle me if I leave it on your front doorstep?"

"Are you outside?"

"Only if Lucas isn't listening," he jokes, but it falls flat. We both know if Andrew walked up my front walkway, Lucas *would* tackle him. He's already got half the DeKalb police force on speed dial, and his shouted threats through the phone were not empty ones. Andrew can't come near the house, but whatever he has for me, I want it desperately.

A car motor starts on the other end of the line, followed by a rustling like he's putting it in gear.

I push off the bed, looking around the room for my shoes. "Can you put it in the mailbox?"

"I just did. Bye, Kat. Talk to you soon."

STEF

56 hours, 31 minutes missing

I REATTACH THE XBOX TO THE DANGLING WIRES under Sammy's TV, fire it up and pass Sammy the controller.

"First I gotta find the hammer of dawn and kill all the troikas." He delivers his message with solemnity, a remarkable recovery since his crying jag downstairs. He settles onto his gaming chair and readies for battle, facing the screen with eyes that are red and puffy, but with shoulders that have perked up from the attention. "It'll take me a minute to get there."

Sam sits beside me on the bed, his leg bouncing like a jackhammer, jiggling my body on the mattress. Behind us, Mom hovers by the door.

"Get where?" Sam's voice is testy, his expression telling me he's still not sure this isn't some ploy of Sammy's to get himself out of trouble, and honestly, neither am I. What are the chances the gamertag Sammy is trying to make contact with is actually Ethan?

"To the tomb," Sammy says.

"That's where Joe said he saw Ethan," I explain.

"Isn't there a way to see if he's online before you start playing?" Sam asks, ever the pragmatic politician. Why waste time and effort if there's a faster, easier way? Especially now, when every second counts.

The Xbox Live logo pops up on the screen, and Sammy logs in. "I guess I could check my friends list."

"I thought you and Ethan weren't friends," I say.

"Not all Xbox friends are really friends. They're just people you play games with." Sammy navigates to a screen with a long list of handles.

Mom moves closer, coming to a stand right behind Ethan. Her eyes are closed, both hands facing outward and her lips move in silent prayer. Energy healing from afar, and for once, it doesn't fire up my last nerve. If she can make some kind of subconscious contact with Ethan, if she can ease some of his fear and channel him some of her strength, then by all means, go for it.

"He's online!" Sammy pops out of his chair and rushes the screen, jumping up to point at a handle toward the top. MadIQ158.

My heart gives an excited kick, and I swat a hand in Sam's direction. "Call the police."

But Sam is one step ahead of me, his cell already pressed to an ear, the chief of police already on speed dial.

The screen changes to dozens of heavily armed figures moving through a postapocalyptic landscape. "Which one is Ethan?"

"He's gonna be up on the roof. I just gotta find the hammer and kill all these locusts before I can get there. Hang on."

I grip the edge of the mattress and watch my son dodge strange, hostile creatures through a dark and dystopian world while Sam relays our discovery to Chief Phillips. The sound of the special effects and Sam's voice are muffled by the roaring of blood in my ears.

"Ethan's force is strong," Mom says, her eyes still closed, and I don't swallow down the swell of hope I feel at her words. After all, she was right about Sammy; maybe she's right about Ethan, too. "I'm getting lots of conflicting emotions but no physical pain."

Sammy's soldier locates the weapon in the grass, which looks more like a futuristic laser and which vaporizes everything in his path. Once he clears the way, he lumbers up a stone staircase to emerge in a labyrinth of dark, confined rooms.

"We're at the rooftop," he says, his voice high and excited. "Start looking for MadIQ158."

The rooftop is more like a dungeon, a web of low-slung spaces connected by a central corridor and expanse of open sky. There are creatures, both human and not-so-human everywhere. Sammy stays one step ahead of them, swinging left then right then left again, killing them with massive explosions. The television speakers erupt in a chorus of screeches and gunfire.

I lean in and hold my breath. There's too much to look at—people and aliens and exploding body parts. It's like my brain came down with ADD. I can't concentrate on just one.

Suddenly, Sammy leaps out of his chair. "There he is! I told you. He's right there. Look." He points to a heavily armed man crouching at the lower edge of the screen, currently engaged in a firefight with an otherworldly enemy. Tiny letters float above his head: MadIQ158.

"How do you know it's him?" Mom says from beside me, "and not somebody who happens to have the same nickname?"

"Two people can't have the same gamertag." Sammy's answer has an unmistakable undertone of *duh*. "If somebody's already taken it, you gotta choose another."

"Can you talk to him?" I say, referring to Ethan. "Ask him where he is, if he's okay?"

"Sure. I can send him a message."

"Do it," Sam says, and I grip his arm, skin and muscle tight with strain. If this is true, if this is really Ethan on the screen, then surely the police can track him. Surely an Xbox has a specific online address, just like a computer. Surely there must be some way.

Sammy navigates to a different screen and presses the button for a new message. "What should I say?"

"Ask him where he is," Sam says. "Who he's with. Tell him to give us as many details as possible so we can find him."

Sammy gets started on a message, but there's no keyboard and progress is slow. Sam loses patience before the second word, lunges off the bed and snatches the controller from his son's hands.

Sam isn't much faster than his son in the messaging department. Without a keyboard, he has to navigate the alphabet with only a couple of buttons, scrolling up and down and side to side to enter the necessary letters. He's been going at it for more than a minute, but so far, all he's got is Where r u? U ok? He hits Enter, then immediately begins on the next message, his thumbs punching at the joystick.

"He's gone," Sammy shouts.

My gaze whips back to the television screen. Next to MadIQ158's name is a message: Offline. Last seen 2 seconds ago. "Where'd he go?"

Sammy shrugs. "I don't know. He didn't die. He just stopped playing."

Still, Sam's thumbs don't stop moving on the controller.

I settle back onto the bed, hold my breath and watch as his message takes shape. Who took u? Help on way.

A low rumbling from just outside alerts us to a car, coming up the driveway. Sam's head and shoulders rise in tandem, like a puppet on a string, his head pulled to the window as if by magnetic force. I look, too, and it's Josh.

Sam hands the controller to Sammy. "Keep searching for Ethan. Let me know the second he's back online."

"Sam, no." I hop off the bed and slide a few feet to the left, stepping between Sam and the hall. "We're in the middle of a family crisis here."

"Ethan's is not the only crisis I'm dealing with at the moment." He rests his hand on my shoulder—a show of support, a plea—then pushes past me for the door.

I turn to argue, but he's already gone.

KAT

56 hours, 58 minutes missing

I COME DOWNSTAIRS TO FIND A NOTE, TAPED to the inside of the front door. *Gone to the store, back asap. —L.* I shove my feet into some sneakers, unlock the door and step outside.

Outside on the stoop, the street is quiet, the whole neighborhood locked up tight. My neighbors are still sleeping off last night's mischief, and most won't emerge from their beds until much later this afternoon. Then their noise will carry until deep in the night, but for now, there are only birds and the low hum of the highway, miles away.

Sometime in the past hour, clouds have rolled in, low and bottom-heavy, ushering in air thick with humidity. It clings to my skin and sticks in my lungs and turns everything in the mailbox damp and tacky. I thumb through the soggy papers— bills, a stack of coupon flyers, a box of checks from the bank. I flip through everything a second time, bend down and peer inside the mailbox. Empty. There's nothing here but mail.

"Kat."

The voice comes from right behind me, lurching my heart

into my throat. I whirl around and there he is, standing in the middle of the empty street. My tall, familiar-looking almost-ex with his fancy clothes and familiar smile, his thick brown hair swept off his forehead by a generous cowlick.

The last time we stood this close, he punched me in the face.

I press my free hand to my pounding chest. "Andrew. You scared me."

He's scaring me now. Andrew knows full well he's not supposed to be here, and I'm pretty positive he chose this moment, after Lucas motored off to the store, to emerge from whatever bush he was hiding behind. I glance up and down the road, scanning for cars or a neighbor smoking a cigarette on their front porch, but there's nothing. A woman peeks out from the house behind him, a curious face in the grubby gray sheets stretched across an upstairs window. Just as quickly, she's gone.

He cocks his head to the side, watching me with a slight frown. "You're frightened of me?"

I nod.

He holds up both hands as if to prove that they're empty, then shoves them in his front jeans pockets. *See?* his expression seems to say. *Innocent.*

He's lost weight since I saw him last, and not in a good way. His cheeks are sunken, his body too trim to be healthy.

"The sheriff told me you were on St. Martin."

"That's right."

I study his face, his arms, the tops of his hands. "How come you're not tan?"

Andrew scowls, and his eyes skit away like Ethan's do, whenever I ask him if he had fun at his father's. "I used sunscreen."

"Where's the gift from Ethan?" I shake the papers in my hand. "You said you put it in the mailbox, but it wasn't in there." I see his expression, a combination of pride and defiance, and the realization sinks: "You tricked me?"

Andrew doesn't deny it. "You wouldn't have seen me otherwise."

Even for him, the level of deceit is evil. "Our child is missing and you've lured me outside under false pretenses. What kind of asshole does that?" The first flame of anger licks at my insides.

"I needed to know whose side you're on."

"What are you talking about?" I shake my head, frown. "Whose side of what?"

"Whose side are you on, mine, or the police's? Because those dickheads still think I had something to do with Ethan's disappearance, and I want to know if you, my wife and mother of my child, think the same. Even though I was an ocean away when he disappeared. Even though you're the one who let him go on that stupid school trip in the first place. I told you an eight-year-old didn't have any business spending a night away from home, and as usual, you didn't listen. So pick a side, Kat. Which one is it?"

For the longest moment, I don't respond. Andrew wants me to say, out loud and to his face, that I don't suspect him of snatching Ethan, but of *course* I do. I told him as much when I left that voice mail from the camp, begging him to bring Ethan back. I meant what I said to Mac: he doesn't know Andrew like I do. After hearing the police are still watching him, still trailing him to gas stations and coffee shops, my suspicions have only grown. I press my lips together and say nothing.

Andrew shakes his head like he's scolding a naughty child. "That's what I thought."

"Oh, come on, Andrew. What am I supposed to say? I couldn't reach you, and now you pull this stupid stunt? Of course I suspect you. You broke my bones. You broke my heart." My voice cracks on the last word, surprising both of us.

He shakes his head. "You broke mine when you filed for divorce."

"So you attacked me? You thought you'd make me pay?"

Andrew's forehead creases in a frown. "That's not what I meant and you know it. When I followed you to that CVS, I swear I had no intention of hurting you. I don't even remember doing what I did."

"You ran. You left me bleeding in that parking lot and you ran."

"I didn't mean to. I was just so angry, like something inside of me was on fire. I didn't think, I just reacted. I didn't want to lose you. And just so you know, I've stopped drinking. I haven't had a drop in four months."

It's the apology I've been waiting for, and yet it's not. He didn't say he's sorry. He didn't express regret for what he did. Just *I didn't mean to* and *I stopped drinking*. The nonapology rubs across my nerves like acid.

"So now what? You come here to make me pay for suspecting, even for a split second, that you took Ethan? To use me as a punching bag for all your little self-centered frustrations again?"

"What? No. Stop blaming me for something I didn't do." And just like that, he's pissy again, his voice sharp with accusation.

"Okay, so maybe you wanted to remind me if I hadn't let Ethan go on this school trip, he'd be upstairs in his bedroom right now and this whole weekend wouldn't have happened? To rub in my face that I'm a bad mother?" I say the words, and another flash of anger sparks in my belly. I'm suddenly glad he's here. I'm glad we're talking. I've held these words in for so long, it feels good to let them out.

Andrew shakes his head. "That's not what I said at all. Yet again, you're putting words into my mouth."

"Then what? Is it to check out my crappy house and dollar-store dye job so you can tell all your friends at Dunwoody Country Club how far I've fallen? Because you know what? I don't care about your fancy cars and vacations. I don't want a house in the suburbs if it means I have to live there with you. I only want Ethan back. *Give me back my son.*"

"Jesus, you're just as bad as the police. Did you know they searched my house, my computers, they even sicced dogs on my car. Cadaver dogs, Kat. They think because of what I did to you, I would do something worse to my own son. It's all bullshit. I was on a beach a thousand miles away. I want him back just as much as you do."

Maybe it's the Xanax pumping through my bloodstream and making me impervious to danger. Maybe it's the hardships of these past six months, and the way conquering them has given me back my spine. Maybe it's because without Ethan here, I've got nothing left to lose. Whatever the reason, I don't hold back. I fling the mail to the ground, plant my hands in the center of his chest and shove. Andrew stumbles backward across the asphalt.

"Tell me what you did to him." The words echo around the neighborhood.

"Would you just calm down? Jesus." His tone is patronizing and all too familiar.

"Where is he, in the trunk of your car? Tied up in your basement? Tell me you didn't hurt him."

Andrew holds both hands in the air. "Kat, I'm not going to talk to you if you can't be reasonable."

His reprimand ignites static in my ears, a sharp hissing like my head is spouting steam. I know that tone. It's the same tone he once used, right before hauling back his arm for a backhand. *Conditioning*, I think somewhere in the back of my mind, but this time I'm the aggressor. I shove him again, this time with all my might.

"You monster! Give me back my son!"

I go to push him again, but he snatches my arms out of the air, his fingers clamping down on the bones of my wrists like a vise. I struggle to wrench free, but he's too strong, his grip too solid. I do the only thing I can think of; I start kicking. The first couple of swings catch air and the empty hem of his pants, but then my foot connects with bone and he curses. "Ow. Stop it, Kat. Just stop."

A police siren whoops farther up the road, a warning sound, and we freeze. Andrew, because he's just been caught with his hands on the woman he's not supposed to be within two hundred feet of, and me because I'm thinking of Mac. Of his promise to deliver bad news in person. Of my cell phone, silent and still in my back pocket. I think this and I start trembling, my skin and blood and lungs turned to ice. Because if that's Mac with his finger on the siren, I know what his appearance here means.

Andrew releases me like I'm a hot poker, scrambling backward on the street, putting some much-needed space between us. His hands are up, palms flat in the air like a man caught red-handed.

I look over, and my heart stops.

It's Mac. Coming to blow my whole world apart.

STEF

I OPEN THE DOOR, AND NEVER HAVE I BEEN SO happy to see three policemen standing on my front stoop.

Not cops. Federal agents. I know it from their clothes, well-tailored suits in varying shades of black and navy. From their matching mirrored sunglasses on grim but clean-shaven faces. And when they pull out their wallets, from the laminated cards they flash in front of my nose, and the three letters written across them in bold, blue ink.

FBI.

I scan their names, and nerves chase them from my memory almost instantly.

"Come in. The Xbox is upstairs." I close the door and point to the ceiling, to the steady rumbling of video game thunder above our heads. "I told Sammy to keep playing in case Ethan came back online."

The men exchange confused glances.

"That's why you're here, isn't it? Because my son saw Ethan Maddox on a video game."

The name falls into the foyer and sticks to the silence. For a good couple of seconds, no one speaks. The middle agent flips off his shades and hooks them by an arm in his suit pocket. His voice is low and gravelly like a smoker's. "Did you notify the authorities?"

"Well, of course we did. My husband called Darryl Phillips at least ten minutes ago. I thought…"

The words die in my mouth, because that's when it hits me: these men are not here about the Xbox. Chief Phillips would have sent a patrol car, not the FBI. These agents didn't come to collect the machine or trace the IP address back to Ethan. They're here for something else entirely.

My body goes hot like an oven.

Sam steps up behind me, reaching around to give them a hand. "Gentlemen. What can I do for you?"

The tall agent pulls an envelope from his pocket, offers it to Sam like a gift. "Mayor Huntington, we have a warrant to search the premises."

My nerves, already wired from the weekend's events, explode in a ball of fiery static. I struggle to come up with an innocuous explanation, but then I realize there isn't one. A warrant means the authorities suspect Sam of something criminal. A warrant means they have convinced a judge there's good cause to search through his things for evidence. I picture the agents driving through the dozens of reporters down at the gate, their cameras capturing everything in full-color, high-definition, and my skin prickles. A warrant means scandal.

Sam's body is concrete against my shoulder blades. "A warrant. For what?"

The agent jiggles the paper in the air. "Take it, sir, and then step aside."

After forever, Sam takes the paper.

The men head straight for the study, filing past Josh at the edge of the foyer. I stare across the space at him, wondering why everything about him exudes calm. His pleasantly bland expression, the relaxed slope of his shoulders, the way he's slumped against the wall, one hand casually tucked into his pants pocket. And then I see his other hand, curled around a crystal glass of amber liquid, and my heart revs at the sight. Whatever is going on here, it calls for a good three fingers of Sam's best bourbon.

I look back to Sam. "Sam, what—"

"Not now." His face is a furious mask, and I have to remind myself his rage is not directed at me. Sam glares across the foyer in a way that makes it seem like all this—the agents, the warrant—is somehow Josh's fault.

There's more commotion at the door, a uniformed Atlanta police officer coming to collect the Xbox.

I shoo Sam and Josh to the living room. "Let me deal with this. I'll get rid of him as soon as I can."

Once they've disappeared around the corner, I open the door and let the officer inside. If he's surprised to see a slew of federal agents here, carting armloads of office supplies out the door, he doesn't say a word.

"The console is upstairs," I tell him. "Wait here. I'll just be a minute."

He gives me a polite nod. "Thank you, ma'am."

I turn, taking the stairs by twos. Video game thunder greets me in the upstairs hallway, Sammy still battling the troikas. I can tell from Mom's face there's been no further sign of Ethan.

"He's not here, Mom." Sammy's voice is distraught, his gaze steady on the screen. His thumbs punch at the buttons on the controller. "I've looked everywhere, but he's still not back online."

I ruffle his hair. "It's okay, bud. Thanks for trying, but the police are here to pick up the console."

This time, Sammy doesn't put up a fight. He powers everything down, unhooks the machine from the wall and hands it to me himself. "The password is supersammy123. Sorry."

I give him a we'll-talk-about-this-later smile, then turn to Mom. "Keep him up here for a while, will you? I'll come get you when you can come out."

She agrees, but just in case, I say it again. "I mean it, Mom. Don't open that door until I say."

Downstairs, I pass the console and the password to the cop. He thanks me, tucks the Xbox under an arm and falls in line behind two FBI agents carting cardboard boxes out the door. The backseat of one of their cars is already full, as are both trunks. The cop falls behind his wheel without giving them a second glance, as if federal agents at the mayor's house happens every day.

At the bottom of the hill, Gary punches the code to crank open the gate, and the reporters swarm. They stand shoulder to jostling shoulder in the opening, a human wall to the street and beyond, their zoom lenses pointed up the broad expanse of lawn. I leap away from the glass, hiding behind the open wooden door.

The entire search-and-seizure process takes a half hour at best, which is terrifying on all sorts of levels. It means they knew what they were looking for and where to look for it. Sam watches from a spot by the plate glass window in the living room, cataloging every box they cart out the door. All his files and binders, his collection of Moleskine notepads, his laptop. By the time the last box is loaded up, his skin is pink and shiny.

One of the agents pauses on his way out the door. "Sir, I need to collect your cell phone."

To the point and matter-of-fact. Not an order, but not a request, either. Said with neither remorse nor apology.

After a long, painful pause, Sam digs the device from his pocket and slaps it in the man's palm.

The agent leaves, the door closing behind him with a soft click, and I wait for someone to speak. I stare at Sam, Sam stares at Josh, and Josh stares at his glass, clutched in a fist so white-knuckled I'm afraid he might shatter the glass. I don't know what's more terrifying, a warrant or the silence.

Sam's voice, when it comes, is low and deadly. "Somebody want to tell me what the actual *fuck* just happened here?"

Blood thrums in my ears at the alarm in his tone. Sam is never nervous, about anything, ever, not even when Sammy almost choked on a grape when he was two. The fact that he is now—and not hiding it— dries my throat.

But as for Sam's question, he needn't have asked it. Sam saw the three federal agents waltz out of here with his laptop, his cell phone and all his bank records, too. It's painfully clear what just happened here.

"Shit. *Shit.*" He plows a hand into his hair and gives it a good tug, his whole body wound tight. "No way we're going to get in front of this one now, not with all those reporters down at the gate."

"Want me to call Brit?" Josh suggests. "She might have an idea or two."

His question hits an obvious nerve with Sam. "If you had answered any one of my million phone calls, you'd know she's in Macon. Her mother had a stroke or something." Sam scowls. "Why didn't you answer my phone calls, by the way? Where the hell have you been all weekend?"

"Wait, you two haven't talked to each other since Josh got back?" My gaze whips between Sam and Josh, reading their expressions, then sticks to Josh. "But you were on the way to City Hall Friday night, to find Sam. You couldn't stay because he was waiting for you. And then yesterday, when you met me at the school, you said Sam sent you in his place. You made it sound like he told you to come."

Josh looks at me—looks straight into my eyes—and lies. "No, I didn't."

"Oh, yes you did. You said, and I quote, 'Sam told me to tell you he's sorry but he can't make it.'" I look up at Sam, but his gaze is laser-locked on Josh. "He said that, Sam. I swear."

But Josh seems unaffected. He leans a shoulder against the wall and shakes his head. "You must be confused, Stef. I said Sam was in a meeting, and that I was volunteering to go instead. And anyway, I don't see why it matters so mu—"

"How'd you know I was in a meeting?"

Josh's head whips up, and something changes on his face. Something small and barely noticeable, a tightening around his eyes. He sips from his glass, his gaze fishing away like Sammy's does when I ask why there's an empty box of cookies in the pantry. A silent alarm starts up in my head. "I have access to your schedule, remember?"

Sam's eyes go squinty with suspicion. "That meeting wasn't on my schedule."

Lying, again.

Josh sighs, now, for the first time, becoming agitated. He pushes off the wall and moves farther into the house, the fingers of his free hand turning fidgety. "Why are we splitting hairs about this? I knew you couldn't make it to the school meeting and I figured Stef could use some moral support. And as for where I've been all weekend, I've been putting out fires all over town. Tomorrow's *AJC* is not going to be kind, Sam, and not just about what happened here today. Someone's been talking to them about the Marietta deal. I hate to break it to you, but I'm pretty sure we have a leak."

Okay, now I *know* I'm not crazy. When Josh stopped by here Friday night, he asked if Sam had told me about the leaks. We talked about Nick, the four-and-a-half-point split, how he and Sam have had conversations about who it might be. And now Josh is acting like he's telling Sam for the first time? Nothing about this makes any sense.

"Interesting," Sam murmurs, shaking his head at Josh.

Josh frowns. "What is?"

"That you chose this weekend to go MIA. That you disappear off the face of the earth the same weekend Stef receives a phone call about the Bell Building and some reporter starts asking questions about Marietta." Sam takes two steps in Josh's direction. "*Your* deal."

Josh's brows dip into a V. "It's not *my* deal. You're the mayor."

"But you're the one who convinced me to make it the centerpiece of the campaign. You're the one who convinced me the benefits outweighed the risks."

"Not if you keep the Bell Building, they don't."

"Would you shut up about the Bell Building? I'm more concerned about who talked to the reporter. Who talked to Nick."

"That's what I'm trying to figure out."

"Swear to God, Josh, if you had something to do with this—"

"I didn't."

"If you even *looked* at that reporter funny—"

"Jesus Christ, Sam. I *didn't*." Josh's back goes straight with indignation. He stalks to the center of the foyer. "And I'd advise you to be very careful. I don't like what you're implying."

Sam stands his ground, lifting a nonchalant shoulder. "I mean sure, I suppose it's possible you can't make ends meet on a quarter-million-dollar salary, though I can't imagine why not. You're single. You don't have kids. Where does all that money go?"

Josh glares across the foyer, but his voice is eerily calm. "Of course you think this is all about money. You're a Huntington."

"So are you."

"No. I'm a Murrill. There's a big fucking difference of seven or eight extra zeros in the bank, last time I looked. And if I didn't already know my place in our family tree, your daddy sure as hell reminded me every chance he got. Do you remember what he said when I asked him for a college loan?" Josh pauses, but at Sam's blank expression he grimaces. "He said no, and that one day I'd thank him. He said I'd appreciate having pulled myself up by the bootstraps. Newsflash, he was wrong. I only ended up hating him more."

Sam tosses his hands into the air. "So my father could be a tightwad and an asshole. Lots of people hated him. Hell, I did, too, most of the time."

"My mother had to work two jobs, scrubbing toilets and making beds, just to make ends meet."

"You just said this wasn't about money."

I wince, not because Sam is wrong but at Josh's expression. He gives Sam such a look of abject hatred, I wonder if I should call Gary and Diego in here to pat Josh down for weapons.

"Not all of us were born with a trust fund, Sam."

And there it is, this tiny fissure that's been quaking between them since before either of them were born. Even though

Josh has never said the words out loud, it must suck to be the hard-up cousin, the loser relegated to coach while Sam is living it up in first class.

"I'm not going to argue about something that happened long before you and I were born. I had nothing to do with what my grandfather did or didn't do, and whatever is going on here, whatever the feds find, it has nothing to do with me. My hands are clean." Behind him, the sun punches through a cloud and lights up the yard, blinding me with its brilliance. It glows around Sam, creating a spiky halo around his head—the golden boy. He stabs a finger in Josh's direction. "Whatever those agents found here today, *you* are taking the fall, not me."

"How's that gonna work? This is your house the FBI just raided. This'll be tomorrow's headline on every newspaper in the nation."

Sam's expression turns rabid, but he doesn't deny it because it's true. It will be. The reporters down at the gate are probably filing their reports this minute.

"Do not fucking move." Sam storms to the front door and yanks it open, hollering out into the yard. "Gary. Diego. Somebody give me a goddamn cell."

It's the last thing I hear before he slams the door hard enough to shake the foundation.

KAT

57 hours, 1 minute missing

THEY HAVE TO PEEL ME OFF THE ASPHALT. Andrew on one side of me, Mac on the other, both of them heaving me up by my armpits. I am sobbing, the grief washing over me in great, full-body convulsions. I can't look at Mac, can't stop howling long enough to hear the awful words he's come to say. I was wrong before, when I made him promise to be gentle. There's no gentle way to slice open a mother's heart.

"Kat, listen to me," he says, and I howl harder. His lips are moving, but the words are not pushing through the noise. The kindness in his expression only makes me sob harder.

He presses his hands on either side of my face, tips it up to look into his. "It's not what you think. That's not why I'm here. This isn't about Ethan."

I haul a stuttering breath. "It's not?"

He releases me, shaking his head. "Well, it is, but it's not what you think. Didn't you get my text?"

My fingers flutter to my back pocket, feeling for the shape of my cell. If it beeped, I didn't hear it. Probably because I was shoving my ex across the asphalt.

"I should have followed it up with a phone call," Mac says, keeping his eyes on mine but shifting to keep one on Andrew, as well. "The last thing I wanted was to scare you like that. I'm sorry."

I nod because I know just how sorry.

Mac's gaze wanders to Andrew, just for a second or two, and I can't believe I ever had trouble reading this man's thoughts. His is not a poker face. It's a neon sign, projecting his every deliberation with twitchy lips, squinty eyes, an intentionally cocked brow. *So this is the ex*, it says now. *Standing less than three feet away.* And when his gaze lands on mine, *You okay?*

I give him a slow nod.

"I didn't touch her," Andrew says, his tone defiant. "She pushed me, but I didn't touch her."

Mac flicks him a dismissive glance. "We might have a line on Ethan, but I need some more information to be sure."

My heart gives a hard kick. "You found him?"

"We haven't found anything yet. We don't even know for sure that it's him. But I need to know if Ethan owns an Xbox."

"No," I say, at the same time Andrew says, "Yes."

I turn, frowning at him. "Since when?"

"Since Christmas. Didn't he tell you?"

I shake my head, trying not to let the hurt show on my face. I keep telling myself it's not about things, keep trying not to measure my salary to Andrew's, but Ethan is old enough to notice the difference. It's hard not to feel like Andrew's winning.

I shove the insecurities aside, concentrate on the more important matter. "Why are you asking about an Xbox?"

"Because a boy from his class, Sammy Huntington, thinks he may have seen Ethan online—"

"What?" Andrew and I say in unison.

My heart starts to pound, tripping over itself with excitement, with hope. "When?"

"Earlier this morning. A couple of times yesterday. By the time Sammy alerted his parents, Ethan was already offline. But since the Xbox wasn't on the list of electronics you provided us, I thought I'd double-check."

I stand there for a long moment, listening to my blood pound in my ears and trying to process what I just heard. Sammy saw Ethan on an Xbox game. I hold my breath and pray this means what I think it does—that all this time, while cops were out searching seven hundred miles of shoreline, he has been sitting in some room somewhere, playing a video game. Could it be true? I press a hand to my chest, the possibility making me breathless.

Mac directs his next question to Andrew. "Can you confirm your son's Xbox handle?"

"He set it up himself," Andrew says. "I don't ever go on the thing."

Meaning, Andrew doesn't know.

"Where's the device now?" Mac says.

"At my house. In Dunwoody."

Mac reaches for his cell. "Is there somebody there to let one of my guys in?"

Andrew shakes his head, right as a throaty rumble blooms down the street, the unmistakable sound of a big bike moving closer. Lucas leans into the curve like it's a racetrack, careening toward us at twice the legal speed. He squeals to a stop by Mac's car, kills the engine and whips off his helmet, and under all that dark stubble, his cheeks are pale.

"A kid from school thought he saw Ethan on the Xbox," I tell Lucas, "and we're trying to figure out if it's really him."

Air rushes out of Lucas in a big whoosh, and he punches the kickstand with a heel. "Seriously?"

"We're trying to confirm his handle," Mac says.

"MadIQ158." He swings a leg over the bike and climbs off. "Ethan and I play together when he's at Daddy Dickweed's."

"I'm standing right here," Andrew mutters. "Jesus."

Mac swipes a thumb across his cell, punches at the screen and presses it to his ear. "I've got confirmation on the handle from the uncle. What's the status on the trace?"

While Mac stares at the pavement and we wait breathlessly for whatever the person on the other end of the line has to say, Lucas worms himself between Andrew and me, a physical roadblock with a puffed-up chest and don't-even-try-it scowl. Not even Andrew would be that stupid.

Mac lifts his head, looking at Lucas. "They want to know your handle."

"TNTomcat."

Mac repeats the handle into the phone, then listens without interrupting for what feels like an eternity. "Text me the coordinates," he says, already moving to his car. "Tell them we're on the way."

STEF

57 hours, 29 minutes missing

I STAND AT THE FOYER WINDOW, WATCHING Sam pace the driveway, one of the guards' phones pressed to an ear. He seems oblivious to the reporters down at the gate, watching his every move, and I wonder who he's talking to. The attorneys, probably. Isn't that the first thing you're supposed to do when the FBI shows up with a warrant, call your attorneys to swoop in and save the day?

Only, how can this day be saved? I imagine tomorrow's headlines, the news alerts about to pop up on cell phones all across town. The FBI doesn't just show up unless they're certain they're going to find something, and Sam wouldn't point a finger at Josh—a cousin, his blood family, a trusted member of his staff—unless he was pretty darn sure Josh was guilty of something. I push away from the window and return to the living room, thinking he doesn't look guilty. No darting eyes, no jittery muscles. He lounges on the leather chair, looking relaxed and unruffled.

He also looks a little drunk. His movements are sluggish and syrupy, and the corners of his mouth droop in a way that makes me think that glass of bourbon in his fist isn't his first of the day.

"Josh, how's your sister really?"

"Huh?" He looks over, seeming genuinely surprised at the question. "Oh, she's fine. She says to give y'all her love."

"Want to tell me what's going on here, then?"

His gaze creeps past me, and I look over my shoulder at Sammy and Mom, standing at the edge of the room. I wonder how long they've been standing there, stiff with shock, how much of the drama they've witnessed. I frown at my mother, who's never been keen on following directions from anyone but the great beyond.

Sammy waves. "Hi, Uncle Josh."

"Hey, buddy." He makes the shape of a gun with his free hand, pretends to shoot.

Mom wraps an arm around Sammy's shoulders, a protective stance. "Darling, when you get a minute, Sammy and I would like to talk to you." She's speaking to me, but her gaze is on Josh. "In private."

"Mother, I'm kind of in the middle of a crisis here."

"I understand that, dear, but Sammy has something he'd like to say. Something he needs to get off his chest."

I know my mother means well, and later I will thank her for keeping my son entertained while I dealt with disaster downstairs, but now a burst of irritation heats me from the inside out. We are in crisis mode, and Mom wants to navigate a kumbaya moment. I'm thinking her energy healing mumbo jumbo can wait.

"I'll be up as soon as I can."

"But—"

"Mother, please."

Disappointment slides up her face, but she turns and drags Sammy back up the stairs.

Josh waits until a door closes in the upstairs hallway before speaking again. "I've always liked your mom, but she's a bit of a kook."

Tell me about it. I place the focus back on him. "Please talk to me. Sam might be angry right now, but I know him. You're family. He'll want to help, you know."

Josh doesn't answer, but his snort comes across loud and clear.

"What is going on here?" I am unsure where this sudden hostility is coming from. "Why are you acting like you're angry at me?"

Without a word, Josh heaves himself to his feet. Something black and boxy falls out of his pants pocket, bouncing off the leather and onto the carpet under the lounger. His wallet, I think, until I look again. It's a phone, an old-school model I haven't seen for ten years, maybe more. I open my mouth to tell him he dropped it, but Josh beats me to the punch.

"You thought you could talk him out of it, didn't you?" he says, shuffling off for the bar.

I shake my head, confused. "Talk who out of what?"

For the longest time, the only sounds in the room are the hollow glugging of liquid, the clinking of glass on glass, a squeaking as he recorks the bottle. He turns for the living room with a full glass, then rethinks and returns for the bottle. He carries both back to the lounger and falls into it with a groan, plunking the bottle onto the carpet.

"Sam, of course. You thought you could talk him out of this life, even though I could have saved you the trouble. If you'd have asked me at the time, I would have told you he was bred for this." He arcs a hand through the air, gesturing to the room and the house and beyond, and whiskey swells over the side of his glass onto the custom cashmere and silk carpet. "Atlanta's Golden Boy Mayor and his pretty Barbie-doll wife."

I rear back, stung. Josh has known me almost as long as Sam has, and he's never treated me like the mayor's arm candy. His words now are intended to cause pain, and I chalk them up to the alcohol. I swallow down my pride, keep the focus on the problem at hand.

"Maybe you missed the memo, Josh, but the FBI just came by with a warrant. A *warrant*. Even if they find nothing, there are fifty reporters down at the gate uploading the pictures to the internet as we speak. Sam's sheen is already tarnished. He'll never live it down."

"Oh, please. Stop playing the part of the martyr. We all know if he loses this election, you're not gonna be heartbroken." He swings his feet up onto the leather and leans back, wriggling around like he's settling in for a nap. "You know what I can't figure out? Is how Nick Clemmons got his hands on our polling. How did he get the results of our market research or our list of donors?"

Nick Clemmons. Sam's opponent. The one breathing down his neck with a four-point split. The one who came out of nowhere.

"Because your office has sprung a leak. You told me that, remember?"

Josh pokes a finger at the ceiling. "Exactly. That's how he knew about Roy Perkins, too."

"No, he knew about Roy Perkins because Roy Perkins is a sanctimonious ass."

He's also former chair of the Atlanta Faith Alliance and one of Sam's loudest advocates. A self-proclaimed family man, vehement Bible beater and outspoken backer of traditional family values—or he was until he was photographed dirty dancing with a very young, very shirtless man. Sam got wind of the scandal and started working to distance himself from Roy, but Nick broke the story before Sam put enough space between them. Even now, months later, the connection follows Sam around like a bad smell.

But whatever accusations Josh is fishing around, I have to give him at least a little credit. I *did* try to talk Sam out of this life, starting on our second date, at a little dessert place in Virginia-Highland. I told him I couldn't see myself living in Atlanta forever, couldn't imagine being the first lady of anything. I didn't want it for me, and I didn't want it for my future children. Sam laughed because that's what you do when a girl talks about your future together on a second date—you laugh. Either that, or you run.

And Josh is right about another thing. Sam *was* born for this life. His looks and his smile and his name and his charm, everything about him is built for the camera and the campaign trail. I knew it the first time I met him, when he reached over my shoulder at that Falcons game and took my hand into his. *This man is a first-class politician*, I thought in that very first moment, and then I went and fell in love with him anyway.

"Tell the truth," Josh says. "Those feds running through here is what you've been waiting for all this time. Finally something that'll extinguish that damn spotlight and bring Sam home. You won't have to share him with me or the people of Atlanta any longer. Though, how long do you really think that'll last? I'm sure Sam's got a run for Senate in him at some point. Governor, too."

I struggle to keep my face neutral. Yet again, Josh is right.

My gaze drops to Josh's glass, already half-empty. "I think there's half a loaf of Mom's bread still in the cabinet. You should probably use it to sop up some of that bourbon before any more of it gets in your bloodstream."

"Or how 'bout we just cut to the chase. I know you're the mole." He says it slow and flat, almost as if he were bored.

"Now you're just being ridiculous."

"Am I?"

"Yes, you are. I'm the mole?" I laugh, light and sincere. "You can't be serious."

"Prove it."

"Prove it how? Do you want to see my phone records? Do you want to search my laptop?"

"What do you think Sam'll say when he finds out?"

I throw up my hands because this conversation is no longer entertaining. "I'm not the mole, Josh. And it would be a far better use of your time and energy to figure out why Sam seems to think it's you. That's what he meant when he brought up the money, you know. He was accusing you of selling information to that reporter."

"He's wrong."

"Maybe. But you might want to get yourself a lawyer anyway. If the FBI were here, you better believe they'll be banging on your door next."

"They won't find anything."

I open my mouth to respond, but it's Sam's voice that slices through the air.

"The cops might not, but I'm pretty sure I just did."

KAT

57 hours, 44 minutes missing

MAC PUNCHES THROUGH THE STREETS OF MY neighborhood and hurls us into a thick soup of traffic lumbering down all six lanes of 285. We're stuffed in Mac's unmarked sedan—Lucas and Andrew on the backseat, their big bodies taking up all the space, me on the passenger's seat next to Mac.

"What's going on?" I say. "Where are we going?"

Mac swerves onto the shoulder and flips on the siren, whizzing past the sea of cars at dizzying speed. "An Xbox uses the same technology to get online as a computer, with the exact same protocols. In order to communicate with other devices on the network, every machine has an IP address, which is good because an IP address can be traced." He glances over, one brow raised. "So far so good?"

I nod. "My company verifies the IP addresses of any claims that are filed remotely, just to make sure the person filing is who and where they say they are when they file the claims. It's part of our fraud prevention department."

Mac dips his chin. "Right. Only problem is, these IP addresses aren't exact geographical locations, and this one will likely lead us to the office of the internet service provider rather than to the device using the IP address. Also, a savvy criminal will know how to mask the IP. They'll use anonymizers, spoof another IP or hide behind a proxy. Things like that."

"Can't you call the ISP for the IP address?" Lucas says from right behind me. "They should be able to give you an exact address, no?"

"We did. They are. But we need a warrant, and it's Sunday." Mac dodges an abandoned tire, then guns the gas. "Unfortunately, these things take time."

Time we don't have. As we were piling into the car, Mac told us the last message was sent at just after eleven, which means Ethan—or whoever has logged in with his credentials—has been offline for over an hour now. By the time the police haul some judge from the golf course and get his signature on the warrant, Ethan could be long gone or worse.

Lucas is thinking the same thing. "Surely a city like Atlanta has a judge on call. There's got to be a way to get around the red tape."

"There is, and we're doing it. Someone is hand-delivering the warrant as we speak. As soon as they trace it back to an address, I'll know."

I glance onto the backseat, where Andrew has gone silent. He punches at his cell phone with both thumbs, texting when he should be paying attention. It makes my skin go itchy with new suspicion. "Who are you texting?"

He glances up. "Nobody you know. It's business."

"Then why do you look so funny?"

He jerks his head at the back of Mac's. "Because this guy is driving like a maniac."

I make eye contact with Lucas, and I can tell he's thinking the same thing. What kind of father handles a business email while racing to rescue his missing son?

Lucas plucks the phone from Andrew's fingers. "Dear Mr. Blanchard, while I appreciate your willingness to negotiate my debt, I can only settle with those creditors who are willing to meet my terms. At this time, I do not have sufficient funds to pay blah blah blah." He tosses the phone back onto Andrew's lap. "Sucks for you."

Which explains Andrew's fierce opposition to paying a dime more than the judge ordered him to. His cheeks bloom red with both anger and embarrassment.

"If you don't have the right address," I say, turning back to Mac, "then where are we going? And how do we even know for sure it's him?"

"Because Ethan left us a trail of crumbs."

I think about the trail Lucas found in the Dahlonega forest, gemstones and hairs and candy wrappers that all led to nowhere. By the time he and the dogs tracked it to the road, Ethan was long gone.

Lucas scoots forward on the seat, leaning his head between us. "What kind of crumbs?"

"About half a dozen Xbox messages he sent to you over the course of yesterday and this morning, with a decent description of who took him, the car he drove away in, the direction they were going, how long they drove before getting there. And get this, Ethan even remembered the license plate number."

"Ethan has a photographic memory," Andrew says.

I roll my eyes out the window. If Ethan were here, he'd argue that memory is a learned skill, one that can be honed by the right technique. Techniques like visualizing the letters and numbers around his bedroom, for example, imagining them painted on his wall, lined up across his desk or strung in blinking strobe lights from his ceiling. Anyone can have photographic memory, he'd say. All you need is a good system.

But at least now we know for sure it's him.

Chatter comes from the police radio in fits and starts.

That they got a hit on the license plate.

That the warrant resulted in an address.

That the local police are arriving now.

Mac plugs the address into his GPS and the system points us to an exit just south of the airport, twenty minutes away. Plenty of time for Ethan's captor to find him online, to fly into a rage, to force him to log off in a hurry—or worse. I lean into the dash and try not to scream. What good are crumbs if we're twenty minutes too late?

The highway loops us south of the city, and the road before us clears like magic, the trucks fading into shiny shapes in the rearview mirror. The GPS dumps us onto a winding two-lane road that looks oddly similar to the one Mac and I drove down the first time I sat on his passenger's seat. There's a lone police sedan parked at a turnoff by the road like the one to the camp, the back bumper pushed into thick brush. Two uniformed passengers stand in the sunshine, leaning against the side. Behind them, a steep driveway, more pothole than dirt, disappears into a sea of brown and green.

We pull onto the grass, and Mac hits the button for the window. "What's going on?"

One of the cops shakes his head. "False alarm. Nothing up there."

False alarm. The words are like a fist to the neck, and I want to howl with frustration. After all this time, all this worry, for a false alarm. I can't believe it. I *won't* believe it. I reach for the door handle, ready to tumble from the car and take off running if Mac doesn't hit the gas this second.

"Mind if we look for ourselves?" He doesn't give the cop a chance to answer, just punches the car up the dirt drive.

STEF

57 hours, 59 minutes missing

JOSH TWISTS ON THE LOUNGER, TURNING TO where Sam stands at the entrance to the living room wearing his mayor's mask. If I didn't know him so well, if I didn't see the hard set of his chin or the ticking vein low on his neck, I'd be hard-pressed to detect any sign of distress without a blood pressure cuff.

"So I've been on the phone with the attorneys—"

Josh stops him with a finger. "Before you go any further, I'm not sure we should be discussing this in front of your wife. I hate to tell you this, Sam, but Stef's the mole."

Sam's gaze lands on mine with an almost audible thud.

I roll my eyes. "He's drunk. Don't listen to him."

He just poured himself a third glass, and his eyes have gone glassy.

Josh's tone is adamant, his slur getting sucked up by enthusiastic insistence. "She has both access and motive. One hell of a motive. If you lose this election to Nick, she'll be the second-happiest person in town. You know how much she wants you here at home with her and Sammy, instead of working for a bunch of people you've never met and who probably don't appreciate you. Ever thought about that?"

Sam's frown doesn't clear. I don't like his expression, the way his eyes have narrowed into a squint.

"Sam," I begin, but he gives me a look. *Not now.*

He sinks onto a chair at the far end of the couch, settling in and crossing his legs like this is any Sunday afternoon get-together. "As I was saying, the attorneys and I have a hunch. They thought there was something fishy going on with that election day voting-security operation you keep pushing us to donate more money to, but I told them they're wrong. That initiative is legit."

"Damn skippy, it is." Josh slurps from his glass.

I'm only half listening. The way Sam just scowled at me, the way he's studiously avoiding my gaze now...it's almost as if he believes Josh. Does he really think I would do such a thing? Run to his opponent and betray him that way?

"Which is why I told them to take another look at the Marietta deal," he says.

I force myself to focus. Marietta, the LEED-certified mixed-use development downtown. The details of which someone leaked to a reporter.

"The thing is, last night I started thinking. What is it with Josh and Marietta? Why does he love that deal so much? You're a Republican, for God's sake. You think recycling is for hippies and liberals. What fucks do you give for sustainable, carbon-neutral living?"

"Zero. But I give plenty for how people are looking at Marietta as the flagship development for the South. This project is going to change the way people live. It's going to define your tenure as mayor for years to come, long after you've passed on the baton. You're going to be the most talked-about man in town."

"Right. Me and Marty Seabrook."

Seabrook. The name hits me like a tuning fork, and I rack my brain but come up empty. Sam and I don't talk about the details of city business. He usually only introduces me to a partner after a deal is done, nine times out of ten at the groundbreaking ceremony. Now that I think about it, maybe Josh had a point when he called me Sam's pretty Barbie doll. As much as I rail against the label in private, I've never really made much of an effort to show people there's more than what they see, that I'm not just a pretty face.

Sam looks over, explaining like we're the only two people in the room. "Marty Seabrook is a developer out of Charlotte. He was an early donor to my reelection campaign, but when he submitted a bid for the Marietta project, I ordered Josh to refund every penny he gave us. I can't have even the slightest whiff of misconduct when it comes to who's awarded city contracts, or why. The city's procurement process can't be compromised."

This makes sense, and giving back the money sounds like something Sam would do. I nod.

But Seabrook. I watch the back and forth, trying to pinpoint where I've heard that name before.

Josh's eyes narrow into tiny slits. "What are you getting at here? We checked Marty's background. He's squeaky-clean." His tone is almost petulant.

"Maybe you're too drunk on my hundred-dollar bourbon to understand what's going on here. The FBI just raided City Hall and my home while dozens of reporters down at the gate filmed their every move. They don't do that unless they're pretty damn sure they're going to find something. What are they going to find?"

"How should I know?"

"Because you're the one who brought Marty to the table. And you're right. Marty looks great on paper. His references all check out. Everybody who's ever worked with him has only positive things to say."

"But?"

"But then I started calling around, and I found that the reason everybody loves Marty is because he's so generous. He's known for greasing palms with promises of a stake on the back end."

Greasing palms. The very definition of a kickback.

And that's when it hits me. "Wait. Is his company Seabrook Investments?"

Sam nods, and the conversation replays in my head. Me, blathering on about how I didn't understand. The caller's distorted voice, telling me to shut up and listen, repeating himself over and over, eating up the minutes. The memory crystallizes into a moment of perfect clarity.

"The caller mentioned them. He said Seabrook Investments would push back against the Bell Building but not to listen. He said it's all for show, that they can't walk away from this deal any more than Sam can."

"They can walk away," Sam says, "but they won't. They think they have me in their pocket because Josh didn't give back the donation."

Josh's face hardens, and I catch a flash of alarm in his eyes. "Yes, I did. Check the bank records. I gave it back to Marty weeks ago."

"No. You didn't. The forensic accountant I hired found—"

Josh swings his feet onto the floor, swiveling on the lounger to face Sam. "Forensic accountant? Since when?"

"Since last month. I hired him the end of April."

Josh's eyes go wide in slow motion. "And you're just now telling me? Why?"

Sam doesn't move. Not a twitch or a breath, and I read the answer in his silence: because he suspects Josh of something.

"Unbelievable." Josh plunks down his glass on the carpet, next to the bottle and the cell phone, and pushes to a shaky stand. "You...are you really accusing me of stealing that money? After everything we've been through? I thought we were a team." His doughy chest puffs in indignation.

Sam lurches to a stand, his cheeks pink with fury. "I'm not accusing you of stealing it. I'm accusing you of hiding it in the discretionary funds. That's where the forensic accountant found it, by the way, but only after the *AJC* called yesterday, asking why we were spending Marty's donation on campaign posters."

"Why the hell would I hide Marty's money in the discretionary funds?"

"That's what I'm trying to figure out."

Josh looks away, shaking his head in disgust. "You Huntingtons are all the same, you know that? Accusing us of the very thing you're doing yourself. Family means nothing."

"Jesus, this again?" Sam throws up his hands. "My grandfather paid Ned good money for his shares."

"Back then, maybe. But what are those properties worth now?"

"That's what real estate does, Josh. It increases in value over time. If your grandpa had been thinking with his brain instead of his dick, he would have invested all that cash in some real estate of his own. That's *your* problem. That you can't see it was his own stupid fault."

The argument only goes downhill from there. Josh calls Sam spoiled and entitled and likens his side of the family to Atlanta's version of the mob. Sam says Josh has always been bitter, and that it's just like a Murrill to be looking for a hand-out. They go at each other at the far end of the couch, hurling insults and accusations in shouts loud enough to break the windows. My gaze starts scanning the room for breakables, my mind prioritizing which ones to gather up first, because it's only a matter of time before one of them starts shoving.

For reasons I don't entirely understand, my gaze settles on the phone, peeking out from under the lounger. It's still on the carpet where it fell out of Josh's pocket, half-hidden behind the bourbon bottle and Josh's empty glass. I think about the *AJC* reporter sniffing around the Marietta deal, the surprise visit from the FBI with a warrant and all those boxes. Josh just accused me of being the mole, and yet he's the one with the mysterious-looking cell phone.

I glance to my left, to the two red-faced men still holding a pissing contest about some Huntington scandal that happened long before either of them was born. They're consumed with their stupid argument, neither of them looking my way. I fetch the phone from under the lounger and carry it into the kitchen.

I lean a hip on the island and try to remember how to navigate a phone so rudimentary. No retina HD display. No touch screen with a million apps. Just a tiny black-and-white screen, an up/down button and a numerical keyboard. I push the down button with a thumb, and a menu appears on the screen. Contacts, none. Voice mails, empty. Calls logged, a couple dozen at best. Most are to a 478 area code number, which I'm pretty certain is the same one for Josh's sister, or to a 770 number I'd bet my every last penny leads to the reporter.

I'm about to call it when my gaze lands on a third number. It leaps out from the list like it's strung up with strobe lights.

It's the number for my cell.

I receive calls from numbers I don't recognize all the time. Telemarketers, salespeople from the stores I visit, an occasional wrong number. I almost never pick up. Maybe this call was one of those times I hit Ignore and went on with my day, but why would Josh do that? Why wouldn't he call me from his fancy, government-issued iPhone?

I scroll to my number and hit Call. Two seconds later, my cell phone buzzes in my other hand. One word pops onto my screen.

Unknown.

Goose bumps break out on my arms. "Sam?"

Sam doesn't hear me over the argument, still raging in full force in the next room. Something crashes to the floor, smashing into pieces with a loud thud, and I don't even flinch. With shaking hands, I hit Ignore on my phone and drop it onto the marble. On Josh's phone, I scroll back to the call log and check the time on the original call. May 21, 10:02 a.m. Duration: six minutes and forty-three seconds.

The realization is like static, like something pressing down on me and singeing my skin with heat. Josh is the caller. The person behind the almost kidnapping of our son, the one who took Ethan instead.

"Oh my God. Sam. *Sam.*"

I don't know if it's my volume or the panic swirling in my screech, but I whirl around and there he is. Shiny-faced, his chest puffing with fury, his concerned gaze on me. "What's wrong?"

As usual, Josh is right behind him, lurking in his shadow. I stare across the kitchen at him, trying to reconcile the man who held a sleeping Sammy in the hospital with the monster capable of kidnapping an eight-year-old child, but I can't. He still looks like Josh.

"What?" Josh says, taking in my expression, his phone in my hand.

And then he lunges.

KAT

58 hours, 27 minutes missing

THE ONE-LANE DIRT ROAD ENDS IN A CLEARING just big enough for the house at its edge, a wonky, wooden structure pressed up against a forest thick as a storm cloud. The windows are filthy, the roof is sagging, and the yard is littered with junk—bald tires, broken lawn chairs, discarded Coke cans and beer bottles. What was once the front door, a simple slab of wood, is now in splinters. One good chunk of it still hangs from an upper hinge.

"Holy shit," Lucas says, leaning his head between Mac and me. "What are the feds doing here?"

They're everywhere, dozens of them in jeans and matching navy jackets, hoisting shovels and what looks to be a metal detector. They trample around the clearing like an army of worker ants, traipsing in and out of the open front door.

"Feds, GBI…and those guys are APD airport zone." Mac points to a cluster of uniformed officers dressed like all the others, four men and two women with dark guns and darker expressions. He swings the car to the right, aiming it at an empty spot at the edge of the yard.

"Is that standard protocol, to send in the airport zone for something like this?" Lucas says.

"No. They're here for a reason. I just don't know what." Mac shoves the gear in Park and kills the engine. "Don't say anything. I'll do the talking."

We scramble out of the car, right as a jet lumbers by overhead, piercing my eardrums and sucking up all the sound. I look up, watching as the belly of the plane slides by, low and slow, its wheels locked for landing. Is this why airport zone is here, because they were the closest unit?

"Who's in charge here?" Mac flashes his badge at the cop closest to us, an older man with hair white as snow.

"Last I heard, they were still duking it out." The cop pokes a finger across the yard at another man in uniform, currently getting an earful from a plainclothes woman who looks both annoyed by the intrusion and excited to be at the center of it. I'm guessing she's the owner. "You might want to talk to Major Coombs. He's from—"

"Thanks," Mac says, cutting the man off midword.

We turn and hurry across the dirt.

"…can't just bust into a house like that," the woman is saying, pointing a nail slathered in bright orange paint at his face. She's wearing an Atlanta Braves T-shirt that fit her forty pounds ago. "Y'all 'bout gave me a heart attack. Do you understand what I'm telling you? I could've dropped dead right there on the floor, and who's paying for that door? Not me, that's for goddamn sure. You break it, you buy it." She spits out the last sentence like a threat.

Major Coombs looks over, relieved at the interruption. He shakes Mac's hand like they're old friends. "Hey, Mac. Been wondering when you'd get here."

"Hey, Kurt, what's the update?"

Major Coombs—Kurt—looks over with a polite nod. "This is where the ISP pointed us, but there's no sign of him. House was empty other than Miss Mona Webster here. No Xbox, either. Only an ancient laptop too slow to be doing any game streaming. Dispatch is double-checking with the ISP, but looks like a false alarm."

There's that term again. It hits me just as hard, harder maybe, than the first time.

Mona takes me in with a side-eye. "I'm sorry about your son, lady, but he ain't here. No offense, but I don't even like kids all that much."

Mac ignores her, directing his question at Major Coombs. "So where's the car?"

"What car?"

"The vehicle Ethan was transported in. A black Ford Explorer with a dented fender and Alabama plate." When Major Coombs doesn't answer, Mac adds, "Ethan sent an Xbox message with the description and license plate number. I was under the impression the vehicle led to this address."

But Major Coombs is still frowning. "No, the ISP led to this address, not the vehicle. Who'd you say it belonged to again?"

"Charlie." Mona says it like she's announcing the weather or an item from her grocery list, lackadaisical and without emotion. Our gazes whip to hers, and her spine straightens from the attention. "She's a neighbor. Not a very neighborly one, by the way. A real a-hole, if you know what I mean, always blaring her TV at all hours and dumping her trash everywhere. She lives that way." She points a finger across the yard, but all I see is trees.

"How far?" Mac says.

"Not far enough." She hesitates, waiting for us to laugh at her joke.

"How far?"

Mona's face falls. "Just on the other side of the creek."

What happens next, happens in a blur. Mac shoves me in Lucas's arms and orders him to keep me out of the way. He shouts out some names, gathering a hasty team and holds a quick huddle at the other end of the yard. Another plane slides by overhead, the engines drowning out his voice and the birds and my heart pounding in my ears.

"Watch out for Charlie's dog," Mona calls out once the scream of the engines has faded. "That thing is one mean son of a bitch."

Without even a glance in my direction, Mac leads his men into the woods.

STEF

58 hours, 29 minutes missing

FOR A MAN WITH HALF A BOTTLE OF BOURBON in his system, Josh is surprisingly fast. He lunges for the phone in my palm before Sam can stop him, snatching it with one hand and shoving me aside with the other. I skid along the island and stumble backward, falling to the floor with a thud that resonates deep inside a hip. My cell phone hits the ground next, pinwheeling away across the polished wood floor.

Sam hauls Josh back by the scruff of his shirt and swings him back around. "What the hell are you doing? Get your hands off my wife."

"Sam, it's him." I scramble to a shaky stand, the words bursting out of me before I can bite down on them. "Josh is the one who called me. He's the kidnapper."

Hurling blame before I've warned Sam or called for Diego and Gary as backup is reckless. Any man who would steal a child from a cabin would be capable of doing much worse to me, but I am consumed with fury, with hatred for this man.

Sam freezes. He stares at Josh, then at me. "Stef, what are you talking about?"

I want to fly across the room, to slap and claw and bite, to kick him in the balls and wrap my hands around his throat until his eyes bug. I want to kill him. "He's the one who called me, and with that phone. I saw it on the call log. The date and time matches. When I called my phone with it, my screen said 'Unknown.' Sam, it was him."

It doesn't take Sam long to catch up, and when he does, he doesn't look sad or incredulous or even surprised. He doesn't ask why. He just steps around the island and plucks the cordless from the charger, and I know what he's doing—calling the chief of police, a number he knows by heart.

"Put it down," Josh says.

Sam ignores him, punching at the screen with a thumb.

"Sam." Josh's voice is louder now, more persistent. He pulls the cell from his pocket and flips it open. "Put the goddamn phone down or I will give the kill order. That boy will be dead before you can say the first word."

"You're bluffing."

Josh hits a button on the phone, and it gives an electronic beep. "Try me."

Sam stares at his cousin across the kitchen, and I can't breathe. Can't move or think straight. So Ethan's alive? Is Josh lying or just completely out of his mind? And who's he calling? Which number on that phone? The 770 number I didn't recognize, or the one for his sister, Charlie? I used to think I knew this man, but now I can't tell.

A tinny voice sounds through the cordless speaker.

Sam debates for less than a split second. "False alarm," he says, then hits End and settles it onto the island, facedown.

He braces both palms on the counter. "So walk me through how this is supposed to go, now that Stef and I know. Because two armed guards are standing right outside, and when you walk out of here covered in our blood, I'm pretty sure they're smart enough to put two and two together."

The cell is still in Josh's hand, his thumb still hovering above the button. "Shut up, I'm thinking."

Sam lifts his hands, conceding. "Okay, but you should probably also take into consideration what I told you before—the accountant will find whatever land mines you planted in the city's business. The way I see it, your only leverage here is Ethan. What do you want in order to make the trade? To take the fall for your crimes? Ethan's life for mine? Tell me what you want here."

Josh doesn't answer. He doesn't move. If it weren't for his face, red and waxy like an apple, I'd wonder if his heart was still beating.

"Seems to me you've painted yourself into the proverbial corner," Sam says. "You'll spend the rest of your life in jail, and what about Charlie? Who's going to pay her way when—"

"Shut up."

"If you're lucky, you won't get the death penalty though Georgia doesn't look too kindly on people who bring harm to innocent children—"

"Shutupshutupshut*up*."

"Typical Murrill behavior, really, not thinking this through. You should have spent more time on your Plan B, should have learned from your grandpa Ned's mistakes. But y'all always were a bunch of losers."

At that last word—*loser*—Josh lets out a primal scream and tackles Sam from the side. Sam wasn't expecting it, and he doesn't have time to brace. The move lifts him off his feet and lurches his body across the kitchen, Josh clinging to his middle like a monkey. They hit the hardwood, their bodies writhing like snakes, and the phone skids across the floor and disappears under the stove. Their legs connect with the bar stools and they scatter, toppling over and clacking against the wooden floor.

I race to my cell, shoving aside chair legs to pluck it off the carpet under the table. I flip it over and the screen is shattered, the apps underneath indecipherable. *Shit.* I hold down the home button with my thumb. "Siri, call 9-1-1."

Her familiar voice answers. "Calling Emergency Services in five seconds."

I wait for the call to connect, debating my next move. My first instinct is to run upstairs, to Mom and Sammy and safety, or maybe call for one of the guards, oblivious to the commotion thanks to Eco Villa's shell of concrete and double glass.

The men tussle across the floor, trading blows like a couple of kids on a playground, but this fight is unfair. Sam is much stronger, and Josh's movements soupy. It's only a matter of time before Sam gets a good punch in, right to the center of Josh's nose. His face explodes blood, splashing up Sam's white sleeve.

"Mother*fucker.*" Josh plants a heel into the floor, flips them and hauls back an arm. At the very last second, Sam jerks out of the way, and Josh's fist slams into the floor. He screams, the sound feral and frightening.

"What the fuck is wrong with you?" Sam shouts. By now he's bleeding, too, a bright red stain at the corner of an eye, and the right side of his bottom lip is swollen. He shoves Josh off and springs to a stand. "This isn't about you and me. This is about a little boy. An innocent, impartial child. What kind of monster are you?"

Josh grabs on to the counter and drags himself upright. He spits on the floor, swipes a sleeve across his mouth, but none of it helps. His nose is still streaming blood, coating everything below it in a shiny red, including his teeth.

Sam shakes his head, the gesture both of disbelief and disappointment. "This is over, Josh. You're done. Hear those sirens? The police are on the way."

I listen, and Sam is right. Sirens wail in the distance. Relief hits me like a wave at the swirling sound, almost pushing me off balance. I pray Josh wasn't lying before, that Ethan really is still alive. I pray it's not too late.

Josh hears the sirens, too, and he responds the same way he did before, with furious desperation. He balls his hands into fists and sucks a breath, gearing up for another full-body tackle.

Only, instead of charging, Josh surprises both of us. He reaches across the island, whips a knife from the block and aims it at Sam's face. Josh smiles, an oily, self-satisfied smile.

I freeze, but Sam seems the opposite of intimidated. "You've got to be shitting me." He's always been a natural athlete, his body strong from decades of football and weight lifting and track, while Josh is the type who prefers to drink beer from the bleachers.

Josh waves the blade closer. Twelve more inches—one more lunge—and he'll draw blood. "Does this look like a joke?"

Sam snorts. "No, but you do. You look like Hannibal Lecter after he took a bite out of that liver. Put the knife down."

"I know you think you're the king of Atlanta and all, but for now," Josh jabs with the knife, and he would have stabbed Sam in the ribs if he hadn't jumped back at the very last second, "I'm gonna need you to call Sammy down."

KAT

58 hours, 37 minutes missing

"WHERE THE HELL IS HE?" I SAY, PACING AT THE edge of Mona's sorry excuse for a yard. I check my watch for what must be the thousandth time. Mac and his men disappeared into the woods more than seven minutes ago. "What's taking them so long?"

I point an ear to the woods, listening for a struggle, a grunt, a scream. My muscles are twitchy, ready to snap.

Lucas and Andrew are planted by a giant pine tree, arms folded across their chests. I know Lucas, and I know if given a choice, he would be out there with Mac and the others, storming through the woods, busting down Charlie's door, sweeping the place room by room in search of Ethan. His body is tense and jittery, his muscles coiled up tight like a runner in the starting blocks.

Not far enough, Mona said of Charlie's house, *just on the other side of the creek.* But how far is the creek? And how long can it take to run across it, grab Ethan and run back? Not seven minutes, not unless something went wrong and Charlie put up a fight. I lean into the trees, straining to pick out any sounds of struggle from the birds and swaying trees, but then another plane slides by overhead and all I hear are the engines.

Without warning, Lucas slaps the phone out of Andrew's hand.

"What the hell was that for?"

Lucas ignores him, fishing the phone from a clump of ferns. He picks it up and starts punching at the screen.

"Hey, asshole, what do you think you're doing? Give it back." Andrew's smart enough to not go after it himself. Lucas would put Andrew in a headlock before he knew what was happening.

"Just making sure you weren't warning Charlie we were on the way."

"Jesus, what is up with you people? Do you want me to take a lie detector test? Write *I didn't do it* across the sky with my blood? What?"

Lucas rolls his eyes. "I'm checking your emails, too. And don't even *try* to make a run for it. Me and all these cops'll take you down in two seconds flat."

Andrew looks at me for backup, for vindication, but I have none to give. I want Lucas to look through his phone, but I also want him to do it without me. The only thing that matters right now is what's happening on the other side of these woods. I move farther down the clearing, away from their escalating argument.

By now the other cops have gotten wind of the situation. The stragglers who didn't follow Mac into the woods are gathered in clumps, talking in low voices and casting grim glances at their watches. Sometime in the last couple of minutes, an ambulance has emerged in the clearing, swung itself around and pointed its nose down the drive, positioning itself for a speedy exit. Two medics stand by the open back doors, awaiting a patient. Mona is the only one here who seems to be enjoying herself. She's parked her ass on a lawn chair she dragged over from Lord knows where and lit up a cigarette, watching the spectacle in her yard like her own personal episode of *Cops*.

I slide my cell from my back pocket, look at the time. Nine minutes and counting. Surely it can't be much longer.

A dog barks in the not-so-far distance, the deep, animated chuffs of a very large, very angry animal. Mona's words play on repeat through my mind—*watch out for that dog, he's a mean son of a bitch*—and my heart twists into a painful knot.

And then, from deeper in the woods come shouts. A call for help. A series of sharp orders. First one voice, then another and another, building into a chorus, the notes tripping over themselves with urgency. I lunge in their direction, and Lucas pulls me back by the wrist.

"Wait," he tells me, his voice firm in my ear. His grip is like a vise on my arm. "Wait until it's safe."

I hold my breath and wait.

The shouts move closer.

My gaze sweeps the murky woods for movement, for the jumble of messy curls or the familiar curve of a cheek. It comes in the shape of a man. Mac, emerging from the brush with a child-sized lump in his arms. His gaze finds mine like a heat-seeking missile, and my heart lurches into my throat and stops. He's not smiling. The lump is not moving.

The pair of medics tears past me and toward him, big bags of equipment bouncing in each hand, and before I know it I'm tearing after them. I'm not a runner, have never been the kind of person who can dart around a track without my lungs exploding or a stitch stabbing me like a knife in the ribs, but now I am flying through the woods, churning up dirt and leaves with the thin soles of my sneakers. My breathing mixes with deeper sounds coming from right behind me, big male bodies in my wake.

"Ethan!" I scream. "Is he okay? Is he breathing?"

By now the medics have reached Mac, and I can't see anything but their backs. They cluster around Ethan, a wall of skin and bones between me and my son. I hear their words—*You're going to be okay, buddy. We've got you*—and I cling to them like a lifeline. *Please, God. Please let my son be okay. I'll do anything.*

And then I hear it. A small voice, soft and scratchy and as familiar as my own heartbeat, the most beautiful sound in the world.

"You found me."

STEF

SAM STANDS VERY STILL, HIS HANDS LOOSE BY his hips, his legs fluid and ready to leap. He keeps his gaze trained on Josh's bloody face, not the butcher knife in his hand, its silver blade glinting in the recessed ceiling lights.

Josh points it at Sam's chest and repeats his horrible demand. "Call Sammy down."

Panic buzzes like hornets in my chest, but I don't move. I barely breathe.

"First tell me what's with all that Bell Building nonsense," Sam says. "I thought you hated that building."

After almost getting stabbed in the ribs, he's taking things a lot more seriously. He's no longer antagonizing his cousin, no longer trying to rile him up with insults and threats. Distracting Josh with the Bell Building question is part of Sam's defense, as is the way he steps in front of me, a human wall between me and the tip of the blade. Unfortunately, he's also blocking the fastest way to the stairs, where Sammy is—*please, God*—still in his room.

I squeeze my eyes shut and pray my mother's gifts are not a

scam. *Mom, if you can hear me, lock the door and shove some furniture in front of it. Don't come out until I tell you it's safe.*

"That's where you're wrong," Josh says. "I *love* that building, because it's getting everybody to take a closer look at the Marietta deal. The police, the media, your beloved half-wit voters." He lets out a hateful laugh. "I promise you, when the Cult of Sam finds out what you've done, they're going to finally turn their backs on you."

"Because you didn't give back Marty's money." Sam gives a slow, impressed nod. "You made it look like the campaign was using it, like it was dirty. You made me look guilty of taking a bribe."

Josh grins, and he looks almost proud.

"You were thorough, I'll give you that. The accountant almost missed it," Sam concedes with a good-natured shrug. "But you know me, know how I feel about this job. You had to know I would deny the accusations. You know I'm not just going to sit back and let people smear my good name."

"Come on, Sam. You're smarter than that."

Sam thinks for a moment, while I stand, paralyzed, waiting for something to happen. For Sam to wrestle Josh to the floor, for Josh to slide his knife into Sam's belly. My gaze is superglued to the blade, only inches away from his skin.

When Sam speaks again, his voice sounds almost reverential. "Because by then, you'd have Sammy. *That's* why you tried to take him. You were planning to use my son as leverage. If you had Sammy, you knew I'd do anything you told me to."

Josh's bloody mouth parts in a hideous smile. "Bingo."

"What I can't figure out is how you took the wrong kid. You know Sammy too well to confuse him with somebody else. Or was taking Ethan part of the plan?"

Josh's smile disappears, and he waves the blade in Sam's face.

"Hell, no, Ethan wasn't the plan. What kind of moron takes the wrong fucking kid? Charlie *knows* Sammy. How could she not see it wasn't him? I mean, sure it was dark and all, but still. And now she's too chickenshit to kill him, which means that yet again, I'm gonna have to go down there and clean up her mess. As usual."

Charlie, Josh's deadbeat sister, the one languishing in a trailer in South Georgia. So she's guilty, too.

My gaze flicks, just for an instant, to the camera in the corner by the curtains, then to another on the far wall, nestled between a pair of antique candlesticks on the bookshelves. Essentially, Josh just made a confession for both of them, in high-definition and Dolby sound. I press my lips together and say nothing.

Josh sniffs, a wet, mucousy sound. "Do you remember when we were kids and your daddy taught us how to skin a hog?"

Talk about a question coming out of nowhere.

Sam shakes his head, but not because he doesn't remember. "We were in high school, and it was a squirrel."

"That's not the point. The point is, your father loaded us up in his Cadillac, drove us down to his hunting estate, and then as soon as we walk through the door, gets called back to work. Some break in the Dilane case, that crazy baseball player who had his pregnant wife gunned down on Ponce. Do you remember that?"

"Why are you bringing this up?"

The sirens are closer now, insistent. I'm guessing somewhere in the neighborhood, but I can't gauge from which direction. The streets are a tangled mess of hilly curves, not easy to navigate at top speeds. Even if they're close, it could take them five or six minutes to get here, plus another for Gary or Diego to open up the gate.

Josh acts like he doesn't even hear them. "If you'd shut up long enough for me to get there, I'm about to tell you. Anyway, your daddy sent his assistant, some sucker barely out of college, down to babysit us. Do you remember what we did to that poor kid? Pushed him in the creek, parked him on a mound of fire ants, tied him to a tree and pelted him with rotten tomatoes. I thought your daddy was going to kill us when he came back, but he didn't, did he? He just made that poor boy stand there, covered in welts and stink, while he showed us how to skin that beast on the lawn. I think he thought it was funny."

"So? I already told you my father was an asshole."

Josh's brows jerk into a frown. "He's more than an asshole, Sam, and without being too obvious here, the apple doesn't fall far from the tree. You've always treated me like you treated that poor boy you pummeled with rancid vegetables—like we're put on this earth to serve your every whim. That's the whole problem, you know. You Huntingtons have always been so goddamn entitled."

"That's bullshit, and you know it. Yes, I once tortured that 'boy,' but I was young and stupid and I've since apologized profusely, and seeing as that 'boy' now runs the Office of Intergovernmental Affairs for the city, I'm thinking he accepted my apology. And I'm sure I don't have to remind you of this, but I gave you a job, too. One with power and prestige and my absolute, unguarded trust, all of which you proved you didn't come close to deserving. Seems to me the only crime I'm guilty of here is bad judgment."

"I never thought you'd actually win."

"Welcome to the club. Nobody thought I'd win, including myself, and yet here we are."

"You don't deserve this life!" Josh roars.

And there it is. The real reason for the FBI, the kidnapping, the knifepoint aimed at Sam's heart. Because Josh's jealousy has festered into a living, breathing thing. I stare at Josh now and I see it. The fury. The hatred. All for something that happened ages ago.

His face screws up in disgust. "I thought for sure when you ran that first time, people would see through you like I do. I thought they'd see past your money and your name and that shiny, save-the-planet bullshit, but you fooled everybody, didn't you? That damn Huntington glow."

"So your revenge is to sabotage my career? To kidnap my son?" Sam's voice is incredulous, sharp with hurt. "Sammy is your family. Your blood."

"He's not my family. He's yours. Your priceless, precious heir. The end of the Huntington line. Without Sammy, there'll be no number six. That godawful name will die out."

Josh's words flash-freeze my skin. He meant to kill Sammy. He wanted him dead.

And then I think of other words he said to me just days ago, his promise to take Sammy white-water rafting so Sam and I could have a couple of days to ourselves, and the room spins. If I hadn't picked up that phone, I never would have known Josh was plotting his revenge, that he was waiting for his chance. I would have handed him my child and thanked him for giving Sam and me a break.

"Stef?" Josh says, plucking me from my thoughts in a voice sweet as pie. "I'm gonna need you to call Sammy down."

I shake my head, a rapid back and forth. I'm already judging the distance to the stairs. The clearest path—the only one without Josh blocking it—is through the living room, but Josh is closer. Even with the bourbon slowing him down, he'd easily get there first. Sam would have to tackle him from behind—a dangerous undertaking with the knife clutched in Josh's hand.

He waves it at Sam's face, but his words are directed at me. "Call him down."

"No." I grab on to Sam's shirt with both hands, balling it in my fists at his back. My legs are weak with fear, but I am desperate enough to outrun Josh. Desperate enough to snatch that knife out of his hands and use it to kill him myself if I have to. "Sammy has nothing to do with this. He's an innocent bystander. He's a *child*."

The sirens are so loud now they're almost deafening. It sounds like they're spinning in circles around the house. Where the hell are the police? Where are Gary and Diego? Why isn't somebody busting down the door?

Sam has to shout to be heard. "Josh. My brother. Let me help you. I promise you—no, I swear to you, if you put down the knife, I will personally see to it you and Charlie are protected. I will pay for your lawyers and see that you're both taken care of. I won't let them hurt you."

I can't believe he's making this promise, and I can. Sam is loyal to the point of stubborn, the kind of man you want in your corner, the brilliant politician able to say just what a person wants to hear, and in exactly the tone they want to hear it. Is he speaking out of loyalty, or is this a politician's promise, the kind that's made with two fingers crossed behind your back? I can't tell.

And just like that, the sirens stop. I listen for footsteps, the chink of a key in the lock, breaking glass. Anything. All I hear is silence.

"It's over." Sam's voice is lower now, and undeniably sad. "You have to know this is over. Put down the knife before the police see it in your hand."

"This isn't the way it was supposed to go," Josh says, and in a tone that's meant more for himself than anyone else. His gaze bounces around the room, and I know what he's doing—hedging his bets, thinking through his options, even though anyone can see he has none. The net is closing in all around him. "This isn't the way we planned it."

"If the cops see you with that knife, they'll shoot to kill." Sam steps closer, and I cover my mouth with both hands to keep from screaming. "Put it down, Josh. Let me help you."

There's commotion in the foyer, multiple footsteps and the soft swish of fabric moving our way, and Josh's resolve wavers. His hand shakes so hard, I'm surprised he's still holding on to the knife.

And then all of a sudden, he isn't.

I blink, and the knife is in Sam's hand. Josh's hang empty at his sides.

Police swarm from all sides—the foyer, the living room, from behind me and Sam. They aim their guns at Josh's head, shouting at me and Sam to step back, get down, move out of the way. The whole time, Josh just stands there, smiling that same close-lipped smile I've seen him aim at Sam all these years. I always thought it was a sign of approval, of satisfaction at a job well done, but I see it now for what it is. Bitter. Hateful. Ugly.

"Tell them, Sam," Josh says. "Tell them what you just told me."

Sam turns to the nearest cop, dropping the knife in the sink with a clatter. "If he tries anything, put a bullet in him."

KAT

"LUCAS FOUND ME," ETHAN SAYS, TRYING TO push to a sit in the ambulance. "He found the messages I sent him on the Xbox and he found me."

The medics nudge him back onto the gurney with murmured warnings of wires and machines, but their reprimands can't stop Ethan from wriggling with excitement, or me from pressing myself flush with his side. There's not enough room in here for all of us, but after three torturous days without him, without knowing where he was or if he was breathing, no way were they going to separate me from my child.

"Lucas didn't see the messages, sweetheart. He's been with me the whole time."

I can't tear my eyes off him, off his messy, confused curls, his lopsided glasses, his cheeks rosy with life. With *life*. I can't stop running my hands up and down his body, feeling for warmth, for holes, even though the medics have assured me there are none. A slight case of dehydration seems to be the worst of it, nothing a couple bags of saline won't cure.

"Then who was it?" Ethan's eyes are bright but dry, his voice high and fast like when I let him eat too much sugar.

"The police. Mac. Mac's the one who carried you out of there. He's been looking for you nonstop. He's driving right behind us with Lucas and your dad. We'll see them at the hospital."

"Oh." Ethan sounds almost disappointed somehow.

I thrust my nose into his curls and breathe him in, dirt and sweat and the faintest scent of pine. "Thank God you're okay. You are okay, right? Did she hurt you in any way?" I lean back, cupping his head with both hands, tipping his head up to mine. "Please tell me you're okay."

"Yes. Not really. I'm okay."

Despite everything, his answer is so classic Ethan that I laugh, and so do the medics.

"She kept calling me Sammy. Charlie didn't mean to take me. She meant to take Sammy."

"I know. Mrs. Huntington got a phone call saying somebody had kidnapped Sammy."

He thinks for a bit, frowning as the puzzle pieces slide around in his brain. "I still don't understand. If Lucas didn't see my messages, how did you know to look for me at Charlie's?"

"Mac found the messages you sent to Lucas on the Xbox, but only because Sammy reported seeing you on a video game. The police traced the signal, but it led us to the wrong house. To Charlie's neighbor's house, a woman named Mona. But Mac had also put a trace on the license plate you told Lucas about, and that's what led us to Charlie."

"So basically, Sammy is the reason Mac found me?"

"Pretty much."

Ethan frowns. "I really would have preferred Lucas."

I'm not surprised. All those times Ethan has come home

from school crying, about how Sammy put slime in his backpack or shoved him on the stairs, aren't so easily forgotten.
Sammy is both Ethan's tyrant and his savior. The reason he
was carted through the woods, and the one who pointed the
police the right way. None of it would have happened without Sammy.

"You don't have to be friends with a person to appreciate their actions, or for that matter to thank them for doing
something really awesome." I brush a cowlick down with a
palm, and a dark curl slides through my fingers then settles
right back where it was, spiraling around to point straight at
the sky. "Because no matter what else Sammy has done in the
past, he's still a hero in my book."

Ethan's mouth screws up all over again. "I'm going to have
to think about that one."

I smile and run a hand over his head, feeling the soft curls
slip between my fingers. "You take all the time you need."

If there's one thing we have now, it's time.

It's only at the hospital that Ethan fills in the missing pieces.

About how the fire drove everyone outside and into a panic,
including Miss Emma, who was so busy helping Avery put out
the fire that she didn't notice when somebody clapped a hand
over Ethan's mouth, pressed a blade to his ribs and dragged
him into the woods.

About how Charlie forced him, gagged and barefoot and
at knifepoint, through the forest and into a car, a black Ford
Explorer with tinted windows and a dented fender and an Alabama license plate that read *40A62K3*, all descriptors Ethan
cataloged in his multiple messages to Lucas.

About her trailer and the pile of expensive toys, including
an Xbox fresh out of the box, all meant to indulge an overin-

dulged child while she waited for Sammy's parents to respond to her demands. About Charlie's dog, a vicious Rottweiler mix named Rufus that prowled around the double-wide, barking and snapping his teeth whenever Ethan would press his face to the window. About how Charlie kept calling Ethan Sammy, and how Ethan let her.

"Why did you do that?" I say. We are gathered around Ethan's bed—Andrew and Lucas and Mac and me, a circle of admirers hanging on his every word.

Ethan shrugs. "Because by then we were already in the car, and I didn't know what she'd do to me. I figured it was better to play along, see if I could get her to like me some."

"And your backpack? Why did you have it with you?"

"Because I didn't want the compass to burn up in the fire." He looks at me, and his lip quivers, but his eyes stay dry, his body too parched to produce tears. "I don't have it. It must have fallen out of my backpack somehow."

Three days ago, his words would have crushed me. Today I feel a pang, then nothing.

"I'll go back up to the camp," Lucas says. The offer is both for me and for Ethan, a balm over his guilt. "The compass must be somewhere near where I found the pouch. I'll find it."

"It's fine." I mean it, too. I drape a hand over Ethan's thigh. I can live without the compass.

"Can you tell us about Charlie?" Mac says, eager to move things along. His notebook is balanced on a thigh along with his cell, set to Record. "Whatever you can remember is fine."

Ethan gives him a look, one that means *I remember everything.* "Brown hair, hazel eyes, five foot six, a hundred and sixty pounds. Really strong Southern accent. Born February 20, 1962."

"She told you her birth date?" Mac says.

"No, I saw her driver's license. It said a hundred and forty pounds but she was lying. Georgia number 0377564948."

Andrew looks ready to burst with pride.

"She wasn't very nice," Ethan says, "and neither was her dog. She said if I stepped one foot out the front door, Rufus would eat me."

Mac's voice is slow and careful. "Will you be okay if I show you a picture? We need an ID, but we don't have to do this now if you don't want. We can wait for whenever you're ready."

He's being overly cautious, and he's not the only one. As much as the doctors have assured us Ethan is fine, not every wound is physical. So far he hasn't said a word about the terror he felt when Charlie held a knife to his throat, the deep and silent sorrow at being held against his will, any residual resentment that it took us three days—fifty-nine eternal hours—to find him. Maybe these are all things that bubble up later, like a coffeemaker on a delay setting, but for now, with all of us hovering around him, Ethan seems the opposite of distressed.

Ethan looks at me, then back to Mac. "I'm ready now."

The picture Mac pulls up on his phone is of a woman, that much I know, but for the life of me, I couldn't tell you the color of her hair, the shape of her lips, if she was thin or had three chins. The only thing I see are her eyes, mean marbles pushed into a doughy face.

"That's her." Ethan's body creeps deeper into the pillows. "That's Charlie. What's going to happen to her?"

Mac slips his phone into a pocket. "She's going to jail for a very long time. Her brother, too. We arrested him, as well."

"What about Rufus?"

"Rufus will go to a shelter, where they'll feed him and monitor him to see if he's mean or just underfed. Dogs are like people that way. Bad behavior is typically the result of circumstance, not genetics. If Rufus can be rehabbed, the trainers at the shelter will know how to do it."

"He was okay to Charlie, so I guess he can't be all *that* bad."

A nurse bustles over with a tray of food. American cheese on spongy white bread, mushy apple wedges that have gone slightly brown, the ubiquitous hospital Jell-O jiggling in a plastic cup. Food Ethan would normally turn his nose up at, but now he picks up a triangle of sandwich and stuffs the entire thing in his mouth.

"I still don't understand how you got online," Lucas says. "Mac said the trailer didn't have a working internet connection."

Ethan's eyes go wide with excitement, and he speeds up the chewing, swallowing with an audible gulp. "Okay, so whenever Charlie went outside to take care of Rufus, I'd look through her stuff."

Mac holds up a palm. "If she left you alone, why didn't you try to escape?"

"Because she locked me inside and let Rufus off his chain. If I got out, he would have eaten me for sure."

"Okay, go on."

"Anyway, whenever Charlie was outside, I would look through her stuff. I knew she had a satellite on the roof, so when I found an old Yagi antenna and USB cord, I made them into a Wi-Fi antenna. I had to wait until she was out front with Rufus to climb out the back window and switch out the LNB for the antenna. Rufus came around the corner and he almost saw, but then he got distracted by a groundhog. He went after it and Charlie went after Rufus, and I quickly pointed the antenna all around until I found a signal."

There's a long, stunned silence as everyone takes in the idea of an eight-year old jerry-rigging a nonexistent internet connection with a pile of old junk.

Mac clears his throat. "Let me get this straight. You Mac-Gyvered a Wi-Fi satellite and hijacked Mona's signal?"

"Duuude." Lucas holds out a fist. Ethan grins and bumps it with his.

"Somebody should tell her to secure her internet connection," he says. "A WPA2 will give her the least amount of vulnerabilities."

"Which is why the ISP sent us there, busting down Mona's door instead of Charlie's." Mac shakes his head, incredulous. "My colleagues at airport zone were there, too, accusing Mona of hacking into air traffic control. They thought she was a terrorist."

"I only pinged them a couple of times. I didn't threaten to do anything bad. But I heard the planes so I knew we were close. I figured they'd get there the fastest."

"But just in case, you also hacked the 9-1-1 system and three fire stations."

"Four," Ethan corrects him. "I was working on the police station next but then I got tired. When I woke up, you were there."

And thank God for that.

Andrew must be thinking the same, because he reaches for Ethan and so do I, my hand moving as if by magnetic force. I wait for the spark of hostility, for the begrudging jealousy to bruise my skin, but the only thing I feel is gratitude and a bone-deep exhaustion. I'm tired of being angry all the time. Of lugging all my old resentments around like a backpack full of lead. Andrew and I made this creature—this beautiful, brave, brilliant creature—and yet we keep tugging at him like a wishbone at Thanksgiving dinner, never stopping to consider that the only way to win is to break the bone in two.

I wonder: what would happen if I stopped? Would Andrew win, or would we simply stop tugging?

Mac packs up and leaves, and so does Lucas, heading down to the cafeteria to fetch some food for both of us. Andrew is called away, too, by a nurse with a stack of papers three inches thick—paperwork and forms in need of a signature. After they're gone, Ethan watches cartoons on the television on the far wall while I watch him—his short delicate fingers, his ribs rising and falling with breath. Was he always this bony, this thin?

"Knock, knock." I recognize the voice, look over as Stefanie Huntington pokes her head in the door. She gives me a shy smile. "Can we come in? I promise we won't stay long."

I flip the TV to Mute and wave her inside.

A reluctant Sammy trails her, dragging a cloud of balloons the size of a small car. He shoves his glasses higher on his nose with the back of a hand, taking in the room with wide eyes. They graze over the metal hospital bed, the row of medical equipment along the wall, the IV bag with a slow drip into one of Ethan's left-hand veins. Sammy stops at the foot of the bed, the balloons bobbing against the paneled ceiling.

"Sam sends his regards," Stefanie says. "He would be here, but he's at the police station, giving a statement. It was his chief of staff, Josh Murrill, who was behind Ethan's kidnapping. He's the one who called me Friday morning."

Josh, the man who accompanied her to the meeting at school.

Ethan straightens against his pillow. "Murrill. That was Charlie's last name."

"Charlie is Josh's sister. The Huntington history is...complicated. An ancient family feud that festered into much more than it should have. I don't know how we didn't see it earlier." Stefanie drapes a hand over Ethan's ankle, a skinny lump under the thin polyester blanket. "I'm sorry you got caught up in our family's drama, sweetie, but I'm so happy you're okay."

Ethan gives her a faint smile. He's smart enough to know that's not what she came here to say.

"Okay, buddy." Stefanie reaches behind her for her son. "You're up."

Sammy comes lurching forward, the balloons dancing above his head. His gaze sticks to the coil of tubes running from the IV into Ethan's arm, the slow drips of clear liquid. "Is that medicine?"

"It's saline." Ethan's words are careful, watching Sammy like he's waiting for him to pull a Super Soaker from behind his back or try to short sheet the hospital bed. "I was dehydrated when they found me, but I'm better now."

"Oh. That's good, I guess." Sammy shifts on his feet, thrusting the balloons at Ethan. "These are for you. I'm sorry that I took your sleeping bag. After we leave here, Mom's taking me to the store, and she's making me buy you a new one with my own money, so..." He shrugs.

As apologies go, Sammy's is pretty pathetic, and I'm not the only one who thinks so. Ethan doesn't move, doesn't respond. Sammy stares at the floor.

Stefanie stabs a knuckle between his shoulder blades, and he sighs, digging around in his pants pocket. That's when I notice the lump jutting out from his upper leg, the way the weight of it pulls at his pants. He pulls the object out, and I know what it is before the glass catches the light.

The compass.

Behind his glasses, Sammy's eyes bloom with tears. He settles the compass carefully on the blanket, his voice going halting and croaky. "I was never going to keep it, I swear. I only wanted to hide it from you, to make you think you'd lost it for a while. I was going to put it back, but then the fire happened and you disappeared and..."

His face screws up, and his cheeks sprout splotchy pink spots. He looks so much like Ethan when he cries that I get why in the dark woods, Charlie might confuse the two.

"I'm sorry!" Sammy wails. "I don't *know* why I'm always so mean to you. Why you always make me so *angry*. I'm not that way with anybody else, and I don't like being that way with you, but you're just so smart. You know *everything*, and it makes me feel stupid."

Ethan blinks at him in surprise. "I don't know everything."

"You *do*. You always know the answer, way before anybody else does. That's why Miss Emma always sits with you at lunchtime. That's why she likes you so much."

"No, she doesn't. She sits with me because nobody else will. She doesn't want me to eat alone."

Ethan's words reach into my chest and squeeze my fragile heart. I think about the mummy bag in the middle of the cabin floor surrounded by all the others, the lone black bag at the far wall, all those times I was called in to the principal's office, fuming at Sammy when I should have been fuming at the school. At Miss Emma and the other teachers. For not protecting my son, for not shielding him from his bullies. I think of Dr. Abernathy's long litany of slides, her proud recitation of the Cambridge motto of diversity and decency and dignity, none of which they've offered my son. I should have known a little boy—mine, Stefanie's—could not be the entire problem.

I know something else, too, with sudden white-light clarity: Ethan will never go back there. He will not step one more toe on Cambridge Academy property, will not sit alone in the cafeteria or on an outside bench while all the other kids play. I think this, and the cord of muscle between my shoulder blades loosens, my breath coming light and easy for the first time in months. There's a school out there for Ethan, but it's for damn sure not Cambridge. I won't put him through that again.

I can barely put him through it now. He glares at Sammy, seething and defiant, clearly not ready to forgive. Honestly, neither am I.

"He's been such a mess, carrying this around for days." Stefanie pulls Sammy against her, and he buries his face in her middle. "And I don't mean the compass, but the guilt. It was his idea to come here today, you know. He really is sorry."

I nod, because I believe her. What I don't know, what I can't yet decide, is if sorry is enough.

And yet he apologized, which is more than I can say of Andrew.

All these months I've been waiting for words of regret for what he did, but then what? Will I be unable to forgive him, just like I don't want to forgive Sammy now? And if so, what good is an apology?

"Thank you, Sammy," I say, trying not to choke on the words. "It couldn't have been easy for you to come here and say all that you did, so thank you for being brave."

Sammy sucks a hitching breath, swiping at his cheeks with the back of a hand. "You're not mad?"

I look at him, and I don't know what I'm expecting. A revelation? Absolution for all his past sins? He's the same kid I've been looking at for the past two years, as much of a brat to me as ever. He may be a hero now, but he's a terrible one.

The bully and the liberator, a horrid little hellion in shining armor. I hate him and I love him for what he did.

Ethan will be okay. He'll bounce back from this, I'll see to it. But it's up to me to point him the way.

"Oh, I'm still mad. But if you hadn't told somebody about the Xbox game, Ethan would still be with Charlie, and we'd still be searching. In the end, the good you did outweighs the bad. I'm going to do my best to remember that."

Stefanie gives me a grateful smile, but the weight of Ethan's silence becomes too much for Sammy. He screws up his face and cries his heart out, the tears streaming down his cheeks, past his chin, rolling over his neck and into his shirt collar. His sobbing is loud and intense, overwhelming his little body with convulsive gasps. He's like one of those red-faced kids you see at Walmart, having a meltdown in the middle of the aisle—all wails and tears and snot. Ethan cups his elbows and taps his skin—the tic that means he has something to say but no plans to say it—watching Sammy's tantrum with wide, dry eyes.

There's commotion at the door, Andrew coming into the room. I watch his long legs, his thick hair with that cowlick he hates so much, the familiar bump in his step, and my mother's words rise in my mind, powerful and clear, the day she placed her grandfather's compass in my palm. *This thing can help you find your way, but first you have to know where you are. Don't ever forget where you are, sweetness. Don't ever lose sight of your true north.*

For the longest time, I thought it was him. Andrew was my true north. Maybe that's why it felt so unforgivable to me when he tumbled from his pedestal, because it left me feeling lost. Rudderless.

And now that I think about it, maybe that's why when Ethan disappeared, I was so quick to blame. Why I pointed my finger at Andrew and allowed myself to assume the worst. All those resentments I'd been holding on to so tightly these past six months, they seeped into my opinion of Andrew as a person, as a father, and I let them. I'm not the only one here who deserves an apology.

Somewhere deep inside, where I've been clutching my anger in a hot, tight fist, I feel something releasing, relaxing its hold.

"Okay, well, we're going to go," Stefanie says, jerking me out of my thoughts. She gathers a still-sobbing Sammy against her side, holding him close and leans over to give Ethan's leg a squeeze. "So relieved you're safe, sweetie. Take care of yourself, all right?"

Andrew steps back to let them pass, but he doesn't smooth his scowl. He knows who Sammy is, too, knows he's been terrorizing Ethan.

"He came to apologize." I gesture to the compass, still nestled in the blanket folds by Ethan's leg. "And to return the compass. He took it from Ethan's backpack."

Andrew's chest puffs with indignation. Not for me, for the piece of my mother I almost lost, but that someone would dare steal something from his son. I feel his anger in the air, his eagerness to chase them down the hall. Andrew has never been the type to walk away from a fight. "What'd you say?"

"I said thank you."

"What for?" he says, frowning, not the answer he was expecting. And why wouldn't he? I've fought him on everything else.

"Because Sammy apologized. Because he came here and confessed what he did."

"So?"

So, indeed.

The thing is, I may never understand why Andrew did what he did. Why he snapped, the faulty reasoning that propelled his fist into my face, just like I may never understand Sammy—and maybe that's okay. Maybe the goal here shouldn't be to understand but to let go. Of all my old resentments, of my residual anger, of the bitterness and endless questioning why. The compass. The bullying. The fists and the fury. Just let it all go.

Stop tugging.

"So Ethan is home," I say. "And that's all that matters."

ETHAN

IF I'M AS SMART AS EVERYBODY SAYS, THEN how come there are some things I'll never understand? Like how a knife against your neck can feel cold and hot at the same time. Like how somebody can be so nice to a dog but so ugly and mean to a person, a kid. Like why, of all the people in the world, it had to be Sammy who saved me. As long as I live, I don't think I'll ever understand that one.

Mom doesn't know half of what he's done to me. The names and the shoving and the torture. All those times he spit in my food or cornered me in the bathroom. There are some things I'll never say. Some things I'd rather forget.

Like his face when Charlie dragged me into the woods. He saw her knife in my side and her hand on my mouth, and he just stood there. He squeezed his eyes shut and pretended not to see. I knew Sammy hated me, but I didn't know he hated me *that* much.

All those clues I left in the woods? They weren't for Lucas to find, hours and hours later. They were for Miss Emma and Mr. Fischer and the police, who I thought would be right behind me. Behind *us*. I kept waiting for someone to catch up, but nobody ever did.

And then he comes to the hospital with his lame apologies and excuses. The compass and those dumb balloons. Sammy says I make him feel stupid, but maybe I'm the stupid one. He came here looking for forgiveness, and I let Mom give it to him. Even though I could tell she didn't want to. Even though anybody could see he didn't deserve it.

Especially Sammy. He knew what he did. That's why he cried so hard. Buckets and buckets of tears. They were real, and they were *awesome*.

Who's the crybaby now?

★ ★ ★ ★ ★

Acknowledgments

AS ALWAYS, I MUST START WITH MY LITERARY agent, Nikki Terpilowski. Sometimes a story comes out in something close to its final form, and sometimes it needs more work. Nikki put in endless hours reading countless drafts, and she never lost sight of the tale I was trying to tell. Thank you for all your hard work and, whenever I couldn't see the forest for the trees, for pointing me the way. This book is better because of you.

At Park Row, a village. To Liz Stein, my editor, who showed me how to take a good story and make it even better. To Natalie Hallak, who stepped in in the ninth inning and hit it out of the park. To Emer Flounders, my publicist, and to all the talented folks working behind the scenes at Park Row Books. I'm honored by your faith in me and thrilled to be part of the Park Row family. *Thank you* will never be enough.

To Laura Drake, critique partner extraordinaire, and my parents, Bob and Diane Maleski. Thanks for suffering through early drafts and still finding encouraging words to keep me going. To my writing BFFs Marina Adair and Joan Swan for all the encouragement, plotting sessions, cocktails and laughs. Where are we going next? To Diana Orgain, who suggested Ethan's *MacGyver* trick and helped me figure out what that might look like. Writing is a lonely endeavor, but you guys help keep me sane.

To Gabriela Maleski, my niece and real-life child genius who inspired Ethan's smarts. Your love of books makes me happier than you will ever know.

To Nicolien Eckelboom, who paid good money for the dubious honor of having her name in one of my books, and to de Molenwiek, the Dutch school in Atlanta on the receiving end of Nicolien's generous contribution. De Molenwiek's teachers and board members are some of the hardest working, most dedicated folks I've ever met, and I can't think of a better beneficiary.

Every girl needs a girl squad, and I am beyond grateful for mine. Elizabeth Baxendale, Christy Brown, Lisa Camp and Raquel Souza, thanks for all the dinners and the trips and the laughs. Y'all complete me. Nancy Davis, Marquette Dreesch, Angelique Kilkelly, Jen Robinson, Amanda Sapra and Tracy Willoughby, thanks for being good listeners, steady shoulders to cry on and the very best cheerleaders a girl could ask for. Our get-togethers are my favorite day of the month.

And my forever thanks to Ewoud, Evan and Isabella. *Jullie hebben mijn hart.*

Questions for Discussion

1. Kat and Stef come from very different walks of life, made even more apparent when their paths cross in a shocking way. Did you sympathize with one mother more than the other? How did those feelings change as the story progressed? Do you think they could be friends under other circumstances?

2. As a single parent, Kat struggles to balance her personal and professional lives, and feels like she's failing her son. Are her feelings grounded, considering what she's been through? Are there ways she could better balance work and home? Do you think many single parents feel this way?

3. In contrast, Stef seems to have the perfect life: money, prominence in the community, a popular son and a loving husband. Do you think she's really happy? Are there parts of her life that don't seem genuine to you? What do you think the future holds for Kat and Stef?

4. The final straw for Kat's marriage was the very public attack in a CVS parking lot. How do you think this changed Kat's view of divorce, and of herself as a victim of domestic

abuse? Why did she choose to stay with him until that point? How does her story impact your view of domestic abuse?

5. Kat has a hard time finding forgiveness for Andrew, especially because he's never asked for it. Does he deserve her forgiveness, and does a person have to apologize in order to be forgiven? What are some ways you've been able to let go of anger toward someone who has not expressed regret?

6. When Sammy is caught in a lie, he points to his father's campaign promises, saying, "Dad does it. He said he'd get more trains for the city even though there wasn't any money. He lies all the time." Even unintentionally, was Sam teaching his son to lie? What kinds of parenting mistakes do you think Sam and Stef made, and how should they go about correcting them?

7. After the attack, Kat takes out a restraining order against her husband, but she struggles with coparenting when physical and phone contact is forbidden. Is coparenting with an abusive ex possible? What would you do if you were in Kat's shoes?

8. Besides Sammy, who were the bullies in this story? What do you think will become of them? What kinds of people do you think Sammy and Ethan will grow up to be?

9. A compass plays a recurring role in this story. Discuss its significance and why you think the author decided to use it as a motif. Were you surprised when it reappeared at the end?

10. Speaking of the ending, did you anticipate this one? Knowing who the kidnapper is now, discuss the clues that the author left for the reader along the way. Was Ethan right to keep his secret? Did keeping silent give him the revenge he was looking for?

A Conversation with
KIMBERLY BELLE

Three Days Missing tells the story of a child who is kidnapped during a school camping trip and the two mothers who must race against the clock in a desperate search for the truth. What was your inspiration for the story? Did the novel end up the way you first imagined it or did it evolve along the way?

I was working on another story when the idea for *Three Days Missing* began whispering in my ear. I have no idea where it came from—sometimes inspiration appears when you least expect it—but I've learned that when a story won't let you go, it's one that needs to be written. I ended up shelving the other story and began writing *Three Days Missing*. Like most of my stories, this one changed and evolved as I was writing it, but ultimately it ended up the way I originally imagined it: two very different women are thrust into a shared circumstance that gives them new understanding of each other as well as of themselves.

You bring the reader deeply into the minds of two very different women: Kat and Stef. How did you go about

developing their characters? Was there a perspective you enjoyed writing more than the other?

When I began writing *Three Days Missing*, I think I underestimated how difficult it would be to write a novel from two very different perspectives. This one was essentially two separate stories that crossed paths throughout the book and then converged at the very end, and though I love reading those kinds of books, I had never tried my hand at it. It took me almost twice as long as my other books to write, mostly because I took a lot of wrong turns along the way. Most of those wrong turns had to do with plot, but a lot of them had to do with Stef, too. She went through multiple transformations before I got her the way I wanted her—affluent but not arrogant, celebrated but not conceited. I wanted her to come across as very different than the image she projects to the outside world. She didn't loosen up for me until the last few drafts, and then I ended up really rooting for her.

What was your toughest challenge writing *Three Days Missing*? Your greatest pleasure?

Merging the two stories in a way that made sense was definitely the toughest challenge. There were so many hurdles I didn't consider when I started writing them. Two very different voices. Cramming two tales into the same amount of words I usually use for one. A main character (Ethan) who appeared only in the first and last chapters, but who insisted on the last word. I ended up writing one story at a time, then threading them together at the end. You have to really know your story to do this, and know where it's going. It was way harder than I thought it would be…which, strangely enough, was also my greatest pleasure. There is no better feeling than that light bulb moment when you figure out the best way to tell your story.

Can you describe your writing process? Do you write scenes consecutively or jump around? Do you have a schedule or routine? A lucky charm?

I am very structured when it comes to writing, and I treat it like the full-time job it is. I have a lovely office where I never, ever sit, preferring to move around the house with my laptop instead. I choose a writing spot depending on my mood and the weather—outside on the back porch is where I usually end up. I usually aim for a thousand or so words a day, which isn't a huge amount, though typically most of those words are keepers. I tend to lose steam around three or four o'clock, and then I spend the rest of the day catching up on emails and social media. Two things are a constant in my writing day: scented candles or air diffusers, and yoga. If I'm ever stuck in a scene, I wring my body into a pretzel or stand on my head for a while, and voila! The plot knots unravel.

Do you read other fiction while working on a book or do you find it distracting? Is there a book or author that inspires you the most?

I read almost as much as I write, usually plowing through two to three books a month. My favorite genre is suspense, but I try to stay away from it when I'm writing so another story doesn't sneak into my plot. I read a lot of women's fiction and historical and romance instead, and I usually have more than one book going at the same time. As for favorite authors, there are so many! Harlan Coben's stories always amaze me, as do

Karin Slaughter's and Tana French's. I will read anything Jonathan Tropper writes; his stories are laugh-out-loud funny. I could go on and on; you can find more of my favorite books and authors on my Goodreads page.

What would you like readers to take away from the story?

Clearly, I had something to say about domestic violence, especially the way outsiders view it. There's always a tinge of schadenfreude in the way people talk about the victims, in whispers and with wide eyes. But I think the bigger point I was trying to make is that you never know what's going on in another person's life. What happens in their home, behind their closed doors. From the outside, Stef seems like she has it all—money, power, prestige, a stable and loving family—but just because she doesn't air her dirty laundry doesn't mean she has none. Which woman had it better, really? That's the question I hope readers asked themselves at the end.